INAUSPICIOUS

A NOVEL

R. L. K. EASTABROOKS

Printed in the United States of America

ISBN: 978-1-7349647-0-7

First Printing, 2021

Cover Art: Susan Szabo
Author photo: CME

This book is dedicated to Roop Kanwar
Whose life and death shook me
And took me
To India and beyond.

sati (su te′, sut′e), n. 1. a Hindu practice whereby a widow immolates herself on the funeral pyre of her husband: now abolished by law.

BEAUTY DENIES THE WHEEL

The gruesome day.
Her day of sati:
Angry men shouting.
Wailing women chanting.
Moaning conflagration ghosts,
stench of flesh and corpse aflame,
her crumbling widow's pyre.

Then Durga Maa's weeping -
The sudden monsoon deliverance!

Shrouded by violet haze,
singed hair trailing,
charred feet flying -
she runs!

The innocent child bride
breaks the rough bonds
of ancient cruel sorority -
she runs!

Runs through tangled forest,
the whipping sands of Thar.
Runs toward the promise
of a life of little mercies.

All exquisite ones
must run.

ONE

Central Rajasthan, India
Summer 2000
Midnight

HER LEGS BEGIN to fail her, yet she pushes on. Slashing through the scrub forest's underbrush, the terrain torturing her burnt feet, the girl slows just enough for a whiff of her seared flesh to catapult her back to the horror: pinned beneath a crushing weight; white-blue flames erupting all around; his head lolling on her thighs; her own screams as the wooden platform collapses and she plummets, flailing beneath the roaring blaze.

Adrenaline jolts the girl back into her body, into the running. Her overnight sprint exacts a cruel toll. Every breath she draws now is a stab to her lungs. Her heart pounds within her rain-soaked chest, rattling her ribs with every beat. Dehydration forces her to pause frequently to lick raindrops from her arms; the salt and ash bitter on her tongue. She tries to hug herself, but the agony in her palms stops her. Moaning, she uses her unscathed forearms to assesses her body: face, throat, breasts, hips, legs, nearly the whole of her is charred. The angry wounds on her feet and hands throb with rage.

"Still here…"

The girl longs to cry out for help, but who would hear her? Even if the winds did not swallow her plea, who would come?

"Not them!" Panic clamps shut her throat mid cry.

Despair tempts her to surrender, but she will not submit. Nothing would stop her escape. From the angle of her tread and the speed she gains, she realizes that she is descending out of the low-sloping Aravali foothills. The girl plods on, shivering in silence toward a faint, distant light hovering just at the edge of the great Thar Desert.

The last of the thunderstorms passes by her, leaving an eerily quiet night. The girl shakes her head in a vain effort to clear it as a light wind tosses her long black hair, singed and stuck through with twigs and leaves. She is feral now, crouching low as she scrabbles down the mountain. Her eyes flicker side-to-side, alert to the slightest quivers of branches' silhouettes.

A gravelly bark suddenly breaks the heavy silence. She drops to the ground, believing her own voice a predator's.

Petrified, she waits until the rockslide beneath her ruined feet caroms its last echoes off the hillside before rising to run again. Slipping into shock, she fights the urge to close her eyes.

"No… must stay awake."

Stars twinkle out from beyond the distant band of monsoon clouds that saved her life and sail high on the northeast winds toward Delhi. The air sweetens. Dawn is coming. Something inside her knows that should she fail to cross the last fifty meters of stones and sand, the unforgiving Rajasthan sun will claim her spent body where she drops.

"Must…keep…moving."

In the waning darkness the girl stumbles badly, landing hard on her knees. Acacia thorns have shredded the blackened remains of her arches and sliced her ankles into red ribbons. Leaning on her forehead and elbows, she manages to stand again. She bites her swollen bottom lip. Swallowing her warm blood reawakens a terrible thirst. A quick clamp of her jaw and she opens three more bidi-sized holes in her mouth.

Her salvation glows before her. From the window of a spare, wooden structure wedged between two rock crags shines the beacon that has guided her flight. She wills her legs to run, but they buckle and she crumples again to the ground. Stunned, she sits awkwardly, tilting her head at the light. Her vision blurs into a golden kaleidoscope. Minutes are born, only to fade away.

Beyond language, past thought, she forces her blistered fingers onward across the rocks, dragging her wasted body behind her. Reaching the back door of the shack, the girl collapses against its rough boards and slumps face down in the cool, wet sand. Her eyes close and she is still; a slight mound of tattered red and gold silk.

T W O

T his will not take long.

In seconds, the young wheat farmer was lost in his dark reverie: eyes closed, chin down, jaw tight; his narrow pelvis thrusting. Mala knew his eagerness would betray him, as it always did. She pulled casual strands of her black hair from her face as her breasts jounced with his rhythm against her pink choli.

All she wanted was to finish him quickly.

She drifted, smiling at the memories of her married days and her husband's deliberate touch, when sex was a joy. How she had ridden him long into the chill of the desert nights, and all the urgent ways he had taken her to the brink and back. Those mornings when she had lingered in happy exhaustion on his broad, hairy chest…

Mala stopped her mind's wanderings cold.

The past was past.

For Mala, there was scarcely time for reminiscing. With a knock on her front door every hour most days, she had barely enough time to wash her body before the next client arrived. Of course, there were some memories too valuable for her to forget. Ten years old; the uncle's secret assaults on her body; the remorseless thief ravaging her out behind the deodar tree, forcing her to master the skills that were now the tools of her survival. Rupees meant dal. And flour. With every paper bill she folded into her black moneybag, Mala insured that for at least one more week, she would survive.

Still, she thought, if only it was three years ago…the smooth beauty of her married-woman self…the safety of her marital bed…the strength of her husband's arms…his guttural murmurs against her throat.

Three years.

Yesterday is dead, she thought. For now, sex meant money.

She had rules.

All of her patrons knew Mala's rules. If the braided yellow rope hung on her front door, she was unavailable. No rope? Knock twice and enter quickly. Once inside her spare single-room cabin, customers were to make their requests and deposit the negotiated fee on an earthenware plate before the small Lakshmi statue at the foot of her silk-covered bed. Then they had to rinse their hands and genitals in the bowl beneath the cabin's lone rear window. Kissing her mouth was forbidden. Everything else was negotiable. Additional services during the sessions had to be compensated afterward without quarrel, or the patron was permanently banned. Once relieved, the men had to dress and leave immediately. Mala's rules were rarely questioned. She was the only vaishya for several miles. The village men needed their whore so they paid, and played, Mala's way.

Not all of Mala's customers compensated her with rupees. Some were traveling merchants who brought her embroidered slippers, cartons of colored nail polish, and bolts of satins trimmed with gold and silver gota. But most of these fineries were not for her use. Just months after her arranged wedding, Mala suffered a common misery of Indian women: widowhood. As a child she had seen the devastation suffered by village women who had the misfortune of surviving their husbands. She grew up knowing the Hindu tradition that when a woman's husband dies, so too must she. Widows were expected to suffer a kind of living death. She knew that widows must wear plain clothing and eat dull foods. She recalled feeling deep pity for the widows in her home neighborhood. From the moment of her husband's death, she knew that having failed to protect her husband from ultimate harm, she was considered unlucky. She, like all widows, was banned from social gatherings. Remarriage, especially in rural sectors, is frowned upon most severely. She recalled feeling deep pity for the widows in her home neighborhood. Then, overnight, Mala became a living blight on her dead husband's family and the entire village. From the very moment of her husband's death, she was shunned. Denied the right to self-adornment, Mala had no other choice but to sell most of the luxurious items she earned in her bed at the local bazaar.

On Saturday mornings, Mala walked the two dusty miles into town carrying a large cloth satchel of goods slung across her proud back. Once there, she arranged her items on a cloth in front of a sweets shop on the main road alongside dozens of other merchants. The village square was crowded all day. Throngs of shoppers on foot vied for passage amidst oxen carts, camels, and bicycle rickshaws. Invariably, Mala's items drew attention. Some weeks she showed intricately embroidered cholis and shiny arm bangles to tempt the village women and the occasional European tourist. Other times she displayed rare silks in lavender and crimson, or gold-tipped saris for discerning local brides and their wedding parties. On her best days she was sold out by mid-morning, which left her time before the desert sun soared too high to putter amongst the other vendors' stands. She spent her money on sangari vegetables and fresh chaat pulses, and would regularly visit her favorite attar wallah's stall where she selected perfumed body oils of cassie and pink pepper. On such good days, she took delight in the scruffy donkeys pulling creaky carts of red bricks past the rangwallah shop with its rainbow display of gulal powders, and the lazy-lidded cows, draped ears-to-tails with bright marigold garlands, lounging before a makeshift altar to the monkey god, Hanuman, on the side of the town's dusty main road.

Even among the local crowds that swelled before the produce stalls and sundries storefronts, Mala could not move about anonymously. Many of the townspeople had known her husband, a well-respected silver craftsman with a modest jewelry shop in the center of the village's merchant rows. His sudden heart attack on the morning of his sixtieth birthday shook Mala to her soul. Never had she imagined that she would witness him tumble down the front steps of his store and fade to alabaster right before her eyes. Nor could she have foreseen that merely three weeks after his funeral rites on the ghats at Lake Pushkar, his father and two adult sons would liquidate his husband's business and move their families southeast to Jaipur without her. In the eyes of his family, she was to blame for his death. When Mala refused to die on her husband's funeral pyre with him. Although illegal, her brothers-in-law suggested sati as something for her to consider, and when she refused the honor of burning to death alive on her husband's corpse, they promptly stripped her of all her jewelry and abandoned her in a vacant shack on the outskirts of the village. As a final indignity, her father-in-law even took the meager cash savings her parents had saved for years to provide her in case of emergency. She could not go home to her family as both her parents had died from tainted water only one year after her marriage. At nineteen years old, newly-wedded and newly-widowed Mala was alone, illiterate, and penniless—and everyone in her village knew it.

Mala did possess one valuable asset—voluptuous youth. Even in her white widow's sari and devoid of makeup, her sensual allure was undeniable. When the first grinning goatherd scratched on her shack's front door that desolate winter night, Mala knew exactly what he wanted. Instantly, she understood that her survival depended on selling it to him, and to all other comers.

Once the word spread of her availability, every manner of men and teen boys solicited her services. Some traveled from as far as three villages west: men whose wives were pregnant and unavailable for sex or older men with wives too sickly to accommodate their desires. There were the inebriated bridegrooms whose sheltered, teenage brides staunchly refused to give their husbands the hardcore sex they had masturbated to while watching grainy, bootlegged copies of American porn films. Mala's workdays were long. To attend to her clientele, she often had men in her bed from noon until dawn.

Mala often mused that the women of the neighboring villages should be grateful to her. After all, she provided a valuable service to them in alleviating their husbands' desires for lascivious, extra-wifely duties. When she first began selling her skills, she was genial in public, chancing a timid wave to former acquaintances on the street. Not surprisingly, no women offered Mala friendship after her husband's death. Soon the judgmental stares and hisses became embarrassingly obvious. For the most part, she managed to ignore them. She just had to accept that every time she made her way down the teeming, winding streets of her desert village, her notoriety walked with her. She thought it pathetic that the townswomen had no qualms about spending money on her table items each week, but when she moved among them, they looked away. Whenever she stopped to pay for spices, clutches of chattering schoolgirls in their pleated skirts and blue blouses abruptly fell silent, their dark eyes searching for something, anything, at their feet. The truth, should it ever be known, was that on any given night, in dozens of village beds, married women muttered prayers to their kuldevis that Mala would continue plying her rude trade. For as long as she did so, they might continue to enjoy their occasional, unmolested slumbers.

Enough. This must be done.

Her evening's last chore had become tedious. Now she rushed the finale, arching her fine, smooth back and bucking hard against the wheat farmer, all the while tallying the day's earnings in her head. Soon she would hang the braided yellow rope from her front door. She would turn her lamps low, wipe off the black eye kohl and ruby lipstick, and stare into her looking glass, longing for a glimpse of the young girl who had once beamed with life on her joyful wedding day—that day of dancing and laughter and sticky-sweet ladoos. Soon she would surrender to the brief mercy of sleep.

Only once had Mala considered leaving her shack life; the day a tax collector knocked on her door demanding money or services rendered. Before she could protest, he beat her so badly that her eyes were swollen shut for a week. That day she begged the stars for guidance, but they were mute to her. With no heavenly answers, Mala resolved to work and save all that she could. She never dared dream of a new life, though. To do so would mean she had options.

As far as she could see, her karmic path was clear: to count handfuls of moist rupees and wipe between her thighs.

ENOUGH.

The farmer, whose young wife had just delivered his second son, convulsed and sank back on the mattress with a muffled grunt. Mala quickly stood, turned her back on the farmer, and wrapped her sari about her waist. Glancing over her shoulder, she shook her head as he inverted his pyjama pockets to shake free a few extra paisas onto her silver dhurrie rug. Without a word, he cinched up his pants and left. She would scrounge later for his tip, as usual.

Mala hung the yellow rope on her front door and prepared for sleep. She methodically toweled clean her vulva and armpits and slipped into a long, cotton kurta. Mala rubbed ghee in small circles across her cheekbones, thinking how sleep would refresh her reddened eyes. She gathered the day's soiled bed sheets and went to set them outside, but when she tried to open her shack's rear door, she could not budge it. She tried again, shoving hard with all her weight, but the door would not yield. Bewildered, she scooped up a half-melted candle and stepped out her front door. Holding the small torch before her in the predawn darkness, she tiptoed to the rear of her cabin. There, the candle's flame revealed a pile of shiny cloth. Bending down, Mala saw what appeared to be a body.

She leaned in closer.

At her feet was a slender, young woman in a traditional Rajasthani bridal poshak—or what was left of one. Mala shrank from the odor of burnt hair and flesh and fought the urge to vomit. She reached down and touched the girl's face. *So cold.* Then she checked her breathing. There was little life in the girl. Carefully, Mala slid the young bride away from the back door, opened it fully, and then dragged her into the cabin. She managed to heft the girl up onto her unmade mattress and then rushed to secure the doors and window. She lit more candles. And not once did her eyes leave the bride.

With incredible gentleness, Mala removed what remained of the bride's clothing. Her hands shook as she cut away piece after piece of burnt cloth from the girl's wraithlike frame. One by one, she placed each sad, scorched patch on the stone shelf beside her bed.

"You're barely a woman," said Mala.

When she touched a damp cloth to the girl's lips, the bride did not stir. Worried, Mala filled her tin pot with fresh water and a fistful of dried neem leaves then brought the powerful, analgesic broth to a boil over her cooking fire. The pungent smell filled the cabin. Once the liquid cooled, she set to washing down the girl's singed flesh in long, tender strokes. With each rinse, Mala stared into a terrible consommé of mud and blood and soot.

When she stepped out her back door to toss the swill, Mala startled at the brightening sky above the hills.

Daybreak.

Mala tended the unconscious girl for hours. She shuddered as she examined the girl's scorched hands and feet. Never had she seen such horrible burns. Intent on her task, she clipped away the ragged strips of dead, blackened skin that hung from the girl's fingers, knees, and heels. Eventually, the young stranger began to shiver. Mala worked late into the morning, carefully dressing the girl's wounds with a paste of crushed neem seeds to prevent infection and speed healing, just as her mother had taught her. With great effort, she managed to wrap the bride in her warmest blankets. Once she had settled the girl into her bed, Mala tried again to get her to drink. This time the girl stirred long enough to sip the water, only to fall unconscious again. Patiently, Mala sat beside her and worked through the brutal tangles in the girl's hair with her laq comb, pulling out handfuls of thorns and leaves. She trimmed away the scorched, matted sections. Then she smoothed the bride's long, ragged lengths with sesame oil and twisted them over her slight shoulder.

Mala double-checked the yellow rope on her front door. She would leave it there that night and all the next day. Word would spread quickly, as it always did, that her menstruation had begun. The men would stay away for one week.

One week.

Mala knew that she would need every minute of that time if she were to save the girl.

But how? What if the girl should perish? Worse, what if she survives?

Mala's terrible thoughts raced down the shadowy tunnels in her mind. She felt powerless to control her surging panic as the nightmarish images swirled, collided, then raced off again, pulling her deeper into the darkness of sickeningly-familiar fears. If only she could stop them. Or at least slow them down.

Just for a little while.

She closed her eyes and placed her hands on her belly. Her pulse thudded strong but way too fast beneath her palms.

Breathe.

Soon the weighted silence of the desert morning settled over her like a great, certain blanket. Aching for sleep, she blew out the candles and crawled under her bedcovers. Just a few minutes rest, she thought.

She fell asleep staring at the beautiful bride beside her.

No time

So jaa

So jaa raajkumaari so jaa

So jaa mainbalihaari so jaa…

Go to sleep

Go to sleep, princess, go to sleep

Go to sleep, my precious one, go to sleep.

"Ma…"

Yes, darling, my *beti*…

"I love that song. Please sing it to me again."

Hanji. So jaa…

"Ma, tell me again how you chose our names. What was it like when we came? Were you happy?"

So many questions you have, my little one…

"Yes, Ma… Hanji."

Oh, my beti… On that day, I was the happiest I've ever been. You could not wait to come—bursting from me with such power, such purpose. You did not cry out, but cooed so that I would know you were there. They put you on my chest and I saw your face; angelic, so fair…your hair, soft and black, and then you opened your eyes and in them I saw the entire universe. It was a moment I would never forget, so I named you Triti—A Moment in Time.

"And Dilip, Ma…what of Dilip?"

Your brother waited to make his entrance. Seems he wanted to make sure that you were first safely in my arms. When he finally came, the women kept him from me for what seemed like a long time. Once he was placed on my other breast, gray and sleepy, he wriggled to get close to you. That is why your father named him Dilip—Protector; for he knew that no matter what happened in your lives, your brother would always watch over you—your Champion.

"Ma, why you are crying? Are you sad? Why did I have to leave you?"

Shhhh, beti. You need your rest. There now… Close your eyes and let the sleep come.

So jaa…

T H R E E

A golden dawn poured down Snake Mountain's western slope illuminating Mala's patch of wilderness, but it did nothing to brighten her. Two days of worry had hollowed dark crescents beneath her eyes. She paced a narrow track in the shack's hard dirt floor, stopping intermittently to stare out her window at another desert sunrise. A grey francolin flitted amongst the spiky, silver branches of a nearby acacia tree. Mala whispered a prayer to Durga Maa as she sipped a cup of masala tea. Its familiar, spicy fragrance somewhat soothed her jangled nerves.

The crunch of gravel on the path to her cabin cut short her prayer.

The yellow rope is out. They'll see it and leave.

Mala stood and looked down at the sleeping girl. Tucked under the blankets, she had barely stirred in two days. The neem paste seemed to be drying her blisters and she had no fever; but on the few occasions when the girl woke, she refused everything but water. To Mala's mind, this was not a good sign. Her anxiousness grew.

Noises out on the stoop drew Mala to the front door latch. She slid the lock bolt and cracked open the door to see the dairy wallah, Avram, pouring the last few drops of fresh milk from his pot into her empty, waiting urn.

He has never come this early.

The old widower had taken pity on her when her husband died. They were neighbors of a sort, his small haveli two miles due north of her shack where he lived alone, tending seven dairy cows and selling the raw milk to sweets merchants in town. Once a week, just before noon while on his way into the village, Avram delivered milk to her. He usually found reasons to linger for a few minutes, offering snippets of the latest local news: weddings and births, squabbles and deaths. The only man to come to her shack without sex on his mind, Avram was eager to share a laugh or a funny story with Mala, never failing to remark on how much she resembled his long-married daughter in Jaisalmer. Mala looked forward to his mid-morning deliveries for they provided breezy respites from the sweaty drudgery of her working day.

Mala watched as Avram hastily capped her urn and shambled off the stoop toward his wooden cart, a strange urgency in his bearing.

Rupees. She had forgotten to place money beneath her urn in payment for his milk.

"Avram!"

Mala reached beneath her choli to her moneybag and slipped all the way out of the door and pulled it shut behind her.

"Here. I'm sorry…I didn't expect you now."

She stepped to the edge of her crumbling stone porch and held three paper bills in the air.

He smiled at her as he clambered up onto his cart's plank bench.

"No problem," he said, his wizened face bright. "I'm in a hurry, you see! I'm heading over the mountain."

"That's half a day's journey."

"No matter. To receive a sati's blessing, I would go twice as far! Even the crowds won't deter me."

Mala's stomach tightened and she inched back to her door.

"Sati, you say?"

"Yes, yes! Everyone is talking… A devoted bride has made her family very proud. Such a sacrifice! Tragic, of course, for the young husband, but a triumph for his village! I must go buy coconuts, and garlands. For a perfect offering, perhaps the Sati Mata will bless me with a wife. One can only hope."

Avram clicked his tongue and brought his mule's head around in the direction of town. The cart jerked into motion and quickly disappeared down the path; the dust from the wheels and hooves rising like grey clouds into the air.

Mala trembled as she stared up at the face of Snake Mountain.

An hour later Mala sat at her small table, turning possible calamities over in her mind as she ground cumin seeds in her stone pestle.

Across the room, her guest's eyes fluttered open.

"Mujhe…peaas…loghi…hai."

The words emerged from the bride's mouth like butterflies reluctant to leave the safety of their cocoon.

"Panni? Of course, you must be thirsty," said Mala, moving to fetch fresh water from her terracotta matka. The girl coughed hoarsely and then drained two full cups.

"You need *more* than drink."

Mala reached behind the curtain of her plastic cupboard for the bowl of dough she had prepared the night before.

"I'll have this done soon."

She knelt in the corner besides the cooking fire and her treasured collection of broad pans.

"The coals are just hot."

In the tradition of her mother and grandmother, Mala prepared the roti with ease. She took care to sprinkle loose flour on her hands and her wooden chopping block. Cupping the ball of dough between her palms, she broke off a small piece and formed it into a circle. She pressed the mound flat and placed the raw patty on the hot skillet and waited. A minute later the cabin filled with the delicious smell of baking bread. As the edges of the roti began to crisp up, Mala flipped it once, revealing a perfectly browned side. Then, with a pair of wooden tongs, she placed it on a small wire rack directly above the hot coals. In seconds, the round flat puffed into a warm, air-filled ball. Mala set the steaming bread in the center of her finest plate - a treasured gift from an appreciative Udaipur merchant. Moments later, the roti deflated and she drizzled a circle of warm ghee over her creation.

Kneeling beside the bed, Mala broke off a bite-sized bit and put it to the girl's mouth. The bride chewed slowly at first, swallowed, and then gobbled the entire piece.

"Another," Mala said, quietly.

As she pressed her knuckles into a second circle of dough, Mala ventured aloud the question that had loomed in her mind since the night the shattered girl crawled into her life.

"Aap kanaam kya hai?"

Mala watched as the girl's eyes clouded over. Mala thought she might lapse into asleep again, but then the girl croaked out a reply—haltingly, as if dreading her own words.

"My name is Triti."

Triti? Triti! He called his new bride Triti…the boy groom… six nights ago…too drunk to become a man that night. Rakesh— left on my doorstep by his brothers, with his pitiful tale of unwanted virginity…so afraid his bride would have cause to leave him…Yes, he called her Triti…Rakesh—such a handsome boy, smooth-skinned, ropey…That one wouldn't listen… Come back another day, sober, ready to learn, but no. Of course, he

failed again…nothing I could do… His 100 rupees a fine fortune for never parting my legs. That boy—here beside me one moment, and then gone the next, stumbling off into the darkness.

The girl stirred on the bed. Mala moved closer to sit beside her. Trembling, she cupped the girl's face in her hands.

"Were you…Rakesh's bride?"

The girl shut her eyes and turned her head away, her tears falling in dark droplets onto the pillow. Mala slumped to the floor and raised her hands to the sky.

"Oh, Durga Maa, please help us!"

What happened to your husband, little sister?

After fleeing Mala's cabin in shame, Rakesh had headed back to the village, intent upon finding his brothers and drinking his sorrows away. Drunk and incoherent, he rambled off the main road into a shallow ravine near the edge of town where, in a fateful miscalculation on a moonless night, he stumbled down a sandy ledge— twisting his ankle badly and surprising a Russell's viper on its midnight rodent hunt.

Half a kilometer from the nearest farm, Rakesh had cried out as the five-foot long male snake sank its fangs into his calf, but not a soul had heard his screams. He knew, as everyone in the region knew from childhood, that he had a narrow window of time to receive anti-venom. Sadly, the quantity of alcohol in Rakesh's bloodstream served to accelerate the venom's effects. Wildly, he felt along the rocky ground trying to find his way back to the road, but the poison raced through his body and his eyesight faded rapidly. He managed to stand and shuffle a dozen yards before nausea forced him down into the brush. Searing pain and swelling spread from the wound site up his thighs to his torso, inflating his abdomen until it bulged like a fat, russet grape. His pulse rate doubled. He wheezed uncontrollably. The advancing venom set off violent seizures, throwing his largest muscles into full spasm as he twisted and writhed in the sand. Deadly neurotoxins sped to his oxygen-depleted brain, and in less than an hour, he slipped into a coma.

Sometime before that dawn, Rakesh died.

Late the next morning his worried brothers found his body only yards from the edge of the road. They rushed him back to the town's barbershop makeshift medical clinic, but it was far too late to save him. Townspeople huddled nearby, looking on in uneasy silence. Mothers stared and little ones covered their ears as the brothers wailed in their grief. After an hour of sobs and tears, they placed Rakesh in the bed of their rusty flatbed truck and made the heartbreaking journey across the mountain back to their farm.

Two days after Rakesh's death, whispered conversations in Mala's village began and ended with talk of his devoted bride becoming a sati. For a beautiful young woman to make such an offering was a rare and precious event—one that could inspire all who heard the story.

Everyone but Mala.

She remembered the breath-taking horror after her husband died when his family took her aside to suggest that she go to the pyre with him. Defiant, she had wept in protest, arguing that she did not want to break any laws, that she wanted to live. She had loved her husband with all of her young girl heart, but she could not imagine going willingly into the flames. Her father-in-law had railed that modern laws would not deter truly devout women from joining their husbands in death. Did she not want to become a goddess in her own right while bringing great honor to her ancestral lineage? Or would she rather live forever unwanted and unlucky, bringing shame and misfortune to all who knew her? Mala rarely regretted her decision.

She could not help wondering if the teenage bride in her bed had been given such a choice.

When she heard Avram's cart rolling up her path the next morning, Mala threw a worried glance at Triti and went out to meet him. The startling news he brought of his journey over the mountain confirmed her worst fears.

"All praise to the great Sati Mata Triti!" Avram chanted again and again, his old eyes sparkling anew. "Her blessing was worth every mile. I am sure of it."

For the next half hour, he regaled Mala with the account of his trip: how he and the faithful multitudes waited in mile-long lines to pray at the sati sthall, how many had brought their sick relatives and even animals, hoping for miracle cures. He seemed unfazed that every pilgrim had to pay four hundred rupees to the groom's family just to enter the sati site.

"I only wish I'd had *more* money to spend…the family had photos for sale—wedding pictures of the couple. She was *so* beautiful. The perfect daughter."

Avram kept talking as he filled Mala's urn with milk.

"And you should have seen the coconuts! Mountains, I tell you! So many people…they were coming from five towns away, and even further. The crowd was bigger than Deorala, if I recall. Was that twelve years ago already? Thirteen? Didn't make it to the others— Jodhpur, Jhunjunu…"

He stood up to adjust his yellow turban.

"The many thirsty souls… Had I brought my tins full, I would have made a fortune."

Carefully, he wiped the mouth of her urn with a rag and then sat on the stone step to rest.

"I could never have afforded the tariff the family is charging vendors to put up their tables."

Mala listened with growing horror.

Rakesh's family had quickly realized the economic boon from a having a Sati Mata to claim as their own. Yet there had been no talk of a missing goddess.

How could that be? Surely only one set of bones was discovered in the ashes. Someone must know that Triti was missing.

Mala's thoughts darkened. Perhaps they did not want to find her, that way she would always remain their Sati.

What if the truth came out? What if someone recognized Triti one day?

Mala's mind raced.

They might be searching, right now!

Just how far would Rakesh's family go to find their bride? Every horrific "what-if" ended the same way. The killers would realize that Triti had fled the fire and survived, and they would do anything to find her and complete the ritual. Surely death awaited Triti if she stayed in Rajasthan.

That night, unable to sleep, Mala paced and agonized over her dilemma. She could not avoid sex work to hide Triti much longer. In three days, her menstrual excuse would end and she would have to remove the yellow rope from her door or risk raising suspicions.

Mala stood at the foot of her bed and watched Triti sleep.

Beautiful, pitiful thing.

The burns on the bride's hands and feet had finally crusted over, but there would be scars.

With such markings and with such a past, what man would ever want her?

Triti had not spoken a word since revealing her name, although her appetite and energy had improved. Mala was relieved that the girl was able to sit up to take food and hobble to the toilet bucket. She might be well enough to travel in a day or so.

She would have to be.

No Time

So jaa raajkumaari…
"Papa-ji?"
Go to sleep, Triti.
"Father, I cannot."
Shhhh…
"Why did you choose Rakesh for me?"
Such a perfect match, my daughter! He will soon be in medical school. You, a doctor's wife! Such blessings. And the hectares of land his family owns! Your lovely eyes may search, but they will never glimpse the boundaries of their farm.

"Yes, Papa, but I'm afraid. I know little of purdah."

Respect your husband and your in-laws. Keep your head and face covered with your odhni.

"I want to go to university…"

Quiet your urges now. Obey, and one day it will be your turn.

"I'm lonely. I miss my home."

You have a new home now.
"But what if I fail?"
Don't worry, my daughter. Failure is not your fate.
So jaa…

FOUR

Mala's first customer of the day loved to tell the ferenghis he met during his travels as a successful rug merchant from Bikaner that his birthplace was the "home city to the largest wool market in all of Asia."

A proud Rajasthani Bania, Rattan Mewar was an immaculate bear of a man, blessed with soft eyes and such a gracious way of speaking as to make him a perfect foil to his boorish, local competitors. His female patrons adored his genteel manners. Their husbands appreciated his reportage on national and world events. With scores of customers from Jodhpur to New Delhi, his trade took him the width and breadth of Rajasthan, often keeping him on the road for weeks at a time. He was as familiar with the rutted back roads of the rural villages as the chaotic super highways of the urban centers. One Saturday morning nearly a year earlier, heading to Ajmer to close the sale of four hundred rugs to a Heritage hotel, he spied Mala selling her wares on the street. One look at her face and he was smitten.

Rattan's travel schedule permitted him little time to appreciate the luxuries his hard work afforded. Yet he much preferred life on the road to the emptiness of his marriage. In moments of reflection which he often conducted as a matter of personal accounting, he wondered whether his frequent absences had precipitated the demise of his marriage, or if their matched union suffered from a fatal lack of sexual chemistry. Plain and childless, his wife became a woman of fine tastes who favored the pursuit of material acquisition to conjugal connection. Without children to dote on, she devoted her days to making the Mewar home a monument to sumptuous living. Every resplendent detail came at the behest of the lady of the mansion; not a Moroccan tile laid or Italian drape installed without her say so. She had her priorities, and seducing her husband was not among them.

Like many of the matched couples in their social circle, their marriage had devolved over time into a cleverly-crafted pretense. Rarely together but for public events, they lived in polite obligation. At temple holidays they made pleasant banter, and when surrounded by houseguests their unspoken agreement to appear warm and generous toward each other held sway. An observer might notice a touch on the elbow, or perhaps a shared smile, but the real secret was that they each retreated to their separate living quarters after the performances were over. The doors to the connecting passageway between their bedroom suites had been unopened for more than a decade.

Rattan's wife campaign to rebuff his overtures began soon after their arranged marriage. It long pained him that she would deny her own pleasure as well as his. He was a skilled and confident lover, and believed that his enthusiasm would eventually warm her, but reluctantly, and with much private sorrow, he had come to accept that they would never enjoy romantic adventures together. As it was in many households, they cultivated separate pastimes: she made exorbitant purchases and hosted grand parties to suit her moods, and he made blissful love to Mala for half a day, twice a month, every month.

Rattan arrived at Mala's door as he always did—beaming behind an armful of elaborately-wrapped gifts.

This day she wore every piece of jewelry he had ever given her. Her arms jangled with a dozen bracelets in silver and gold. She had scented her hair with lotus flower oil, his favorite fragrance. A new purple sari clung tightly to her curves, a marked contrast to the shapeless, off-white saris she put on whenever she left her shack. She welcomed him warmly, kissing his cheeks, but she could not mask the dark note behind her hello. Stepping through her door, Rattan discovered the source of her anxiety. Perched on the edge of her bed was a young woman dressed in a rust brown kurta, her face well-hidden beneath a matching scarf.

Mala shut and bolted the door and motioned for Rattan to sit down at her table. Her hands shook as she poured mint tea from her finest clay surahi. As she spoke, Rattan turned to face the young woman on the bed. He listened intently as Mala related the story of the past seven days. Treading circles around her small table, she left no detail untold. Meanwhile, Triti sat rigidly beneath her veil, memorizing the cracked cow dung and lime walls. She trained her eyes on a thin, vertical crease in the coarse plaster, wondering in fear if the man at the table would save or betray her.

Thirty minutes later, Mala squeezed Rattan's warm, broad hand.

"...And then you arrived this morning. Tan, I don't want to die...and if she is found out, they could come for me...for me!"

With the secret finally released, Mala could no longer choke back her tears.

Rattan sat silently, looking first at Triti, then Mala. Then he closed his eyes. Mala did her best to stifle her sobs. The women waited. Finally, he cocked his head back and cleared his throat.

"Mala, don't you have cousins in Bikaner?"

Rattan asked the question then reached out to stroke Mala's trembling shoulders. She daubed her nose with the rolled edge of her sari.

"Yes," she said, hesitantly. "My mother's youngest sisters and their families are there."

"Well, why can't this girl be a distant cousin needing a ride to Delhi to meet her fiancé and his family?" Rattan nodded toward Triti.

Mala scrunched her face, puzzled at first. She leaned closer to Rattan.

"I'm not sure that I…"

"Delhi is my *next* stop."

Mala's eyes widened with realization.

"Yes, I see! A distant cousin. But what shall we call her?"

Rattan shook his head.

"It doesn't really matter, I suppose."

"Yes, it *does*."

Unused for nearly a week, Triti's voice broke saying the words. Rattan and Mala turned in unison to stare at her.

"I wish to be Minu." Her great, great grandmother's name had always been special to her.

"She *does* speak," said Mala, in surprise.

"Very good," said Rattan, nodding. "So, Miss Minu, what else can you tell us about yourself?"

Triti had always hated lying. It made her feel weak. But she knew that her life and the lives of other people would literally hang on the ingenuity of her deception. She had eavesdropped during Mala's talks with Avram. She knew *they* would be coming for her.

The cruel ones.

She must get away, fast and far. Since awakening in Mala's cabin, all she had been able to think of was her family. She ached for her mother's comfort, but she knew she would never go home again. She could not bring danger to her family. If the cruel ones were to hurt any of them, she would never forgive herself.

She would be Minu—a girl who loved movies, sweets, and books. Her mind scrambled to piece together her new identity.

"I'm… looking forward to meeting my fiancé and his family in Delhi. He is a bookseller, with his own shop. My uncle's cousin met him during Pushkar Mela five years ago while on vacation with his family. He seeks to marry a simple Rajasthani girl. Our match has long been set."

Behind her thin veil, Triti held her breath.

"Very good," said Rattan, smiling appreciatively. "You say that your fiancé is a bookseller? How fortunate that I am acquainted with a bookseller in Karol Bagh, with his own shop, no less. Pity he already has a witch of a wife. The man owes me a sizeable favor. Perhaps he can make use of an industrious shop girl. Do you like books, Minu?"

"Yes, Sir. I can read and write in both Hindi and English. I passed the tenth standard with 92 percent."

"Is that so? Well, I hope you'll be ready to travel in a few hours, Miss Minu. We shall be driving straight through to Delhi. Wear the veil."

Mala threw her arms around Rattan's neck.

"Tan, will you really do this for me? For us? Saach?"

"Yes, really. This is not a difficult request to grant."

Rattan winked at Triti and patted Mala on her hip.

"I am simply giving a ride to a cousin's cousin. Is that not so?"

Triti felt light-headed with hope.

Suddenly Mala's smile vanished.

"But, Rattan, what shall become of her once she arrives in that city? Delhi? My God! Such a place. What will she do? How will she live?"

Mala wrung her hands again. She checked the position of the sun in the sky beyond her window and realized that she had but a short time before her customers would come and their conspiracy could be discovered.

Rattan took another sip of his tea.

"Mala, the girl is from Jaipur, remember. Two million people. Not exactly a simple village. Of course, it is *no* Delhi."

"In Jaipur, my girlfriends and I went where we wanted; the cinema, shops…and the like," said Triti, with a hint of pride.

"Well then, there is no problem," said Rattan. "Except, of course, that I need your marvelous hands on my back, Mala. All the driving has left me sore. And a bit stiff."

Rattan grinned at Mala and then looked down at his bulging crotch.

Mala swept across the room and whispered in Triti's ear.

"I'll prepare a bag for you with some clothes, the rest of the ointment, and some money. Rattan will keep his promises. He always has. I must take care of him now, if you understand. Go out to his car and keep your face covered. I'll call for you when we are through. Oh, Durga Maa has blessed us! A special puja to her this night! Go now! Jao! Let me seal this deal properly!"

Mala came as close to feeling love for a man that day as any day since her husband passed away. Were it not for their fraught circumstances, she would have kept Rattan in her bed all day long. When he stopped at the door before leaving, Mala rose up on her tiptoes and kissed him deeply, willingly breaking her own rule.

"Soon, yes?"

He smiled at Mala and walked to his car. Once inside he turned the air conditioner on high against the day's rising heat.

Mala called out to Triti to come back in the cabin. Once inside she turned the girl's hands over gently to check her bandages. Then she pulled six gold bangles from a red drawstring bag. Triti winced as Mala slipped them one at a time over her wrists. The metal sparkled brightly, flashing slivers of light about the room with her slightest movements.

"Every bride needs a proper dowry," said Mala, with a sigh.

Overcome, Triti fell speechless once again.

Mala forced a smile, hoping to assure the girl that she would be safe, and that her future would not be as brutal as her past had clearly been.

A few minutes later, Rattan's car pulled away from Mala's shack. Triti waved shyly from her rear passenger window, a ghost behind a veil. She felt as if she were leaving a sister behind: a wise, loving sister of whom she had often dreamed. She vowed that somehow, one day, she would repay her debt to Mala.

Mala felt a twinge of guilt for the relief coursing through her. The threat was gone. Mala raised her hand one last time in goodbye. Beyond the tips of her red fingernails, she saw her next customer trudging toward her up the road.

Yellow braid or not, she would turn them all away.

FIVE

Karol Bagh
Delhi, India
July 2000

Triti could see her destination long before she reached it.

Suspended above the vast, metro region of India's capital, a suffocating quilt of ashy smog that insured travelers a three-day bout of Delhi-lung blanketed the brick-and-mortar skyline for more than five hundred square miles. Although Triti had no idea that Delhi was still two hours away, the increasingly dark skies created in her a sense of impending gloom. Throughout their day-long drive from Rajasthan, Rattan jockeyed from lane to lane on the notorious NH 48, weaving past the innumerable accidents and vehicle stalls. Overheated oil trucks, fuel-parched rickshaws, and the occasional obdurate camel all tried with limited success to avoid the congestion that daily clogged the main traffic arteries leading into the city often called the 'Heart of India'.

For Triti, the trip was sheer torture. She sat silently, her body sprung tight with fear as the same questions rounded back in stark echoes in her mind.

How will I live?

Where will I go?

What if someone recognizes me?

She wanted to trust that the gods and goddesses she had worshipped since childhood had let her live for a reason. She wanted to believe that Lakshmi was watching over her. Were Krishna and Durga using their powers to keep her safe? She needed to believe that her destiny was stronger than her terrors. Somewhere along the highway, her brain, at last, grew weary. Eventually, the droning of the engine and the faint sitar music from the car radio took her under and she drowsed off to sleep.

When the pain of her wounds stirred Triti from slumber, Rattan suggested they stop at a roadside stand outside the city for breakfast. She found it difficult to eat the crispy samosas and sip chai with the veil over her face. Still, she was careful to stay completely covered. Between bites and sips, she answered Rattan's polite questions about her favorite movies and songs. With his clever coaxing, she related the time when she and her girlfriend, Lokhi, had taken a bicycle rickshaw to her grandfather's fabric shop near Chaupar

Bazar in Jaipur to convince him to give them all of his day's turban scraps. They spent the rest of that day sewing raj and rani dolls for their elaborate, homemade puppet show.

"My doll had pointy feet," said Triti, quietly remembering. "I made red slippers for her. It took many stitches to keep the stuffing from falling out. Lokhi made a patchwork kurta of gold for her raj."

"I'll bet your king and queen looked very royal," said Rattan.

"A bit raggedy, but beautiful," said Triti. "I don't know where they are now."

Talking with Rattan temporarily distracted her from her anxiety, but when they reached the traffic-choked streets at the center of the city, Triti grew quiet and cowered in her seat. Delhi was nothing like her precious Pink City with its wide, regular roads and peony-washed buildings, and familiar marketplaces where fruit vendors who always saved their ripest mangoes for her. Delhi seemed ugly and foreign, with gangs of grime-covered children who swarmed any stationary vehicle, pounding on car windshields for money. She flinched when a trio of small, filthy faces pressed against the window glass at her left shoulder, their eyes murderous with hunger.

"Don't open the window, Miss Minu!" begged Rattan, as he inched the car through yet another stagnant red light. "They'll be on us in an instant."

Triti and Rattan arrived in the district of Karol Bagh in northwest Delhi in a late day swelter.

Rattan pulled his car up in front of a row of well-kept shops. He told Triti to stay in the car and disappeared up a set of neat, brick steps leading into the bookseller's store. Ensconced between a glittery, two-story fabric shop and a fine jewelry boutique, the store's front window featured local and national authors' books as well as international bestsellers, all arranged against an azure blue background. To her eyes, the shop was a visual oasis in a sea of red and yellow doors.

Triti looked out at her strange new world, trying to assess its similarities to her far-away home. The people's faces looked generally the same, but their dress and manners seemed far more confident and sophisticated. Women swept by in modern saris and salwars boasting bold, geometric patterns, while school-aged girls and boys hurried past in Western skirts and long trousers. Some men wore crisp white short sleeved shirts, their faces smooth and clean-shaven. Several women wore their hair cut to the top of their shoulders. She felt decidedly old-fashioned in Mala's borrowed clothes and her waist-length hair covered with a veil.

The white-faced clock in the bookstore window showed twenty minutes had passed, and Triti grew impatient for Rattan to return to the car. She tried rolling down her passenger window halfway, but the stifling heat overwhelmed her in seconds. She could hear two men arguing loudly inside the bookstore. After a few minutes the voices grew quiet. All she could hear was the traffic in the street and Indian hip-hop music blasting from a men's shoe store a half block away.

Rattan returned to the car, visibly sweating. He pointed to her door handle. She opened the door, but stayed in her seat.

"It is all arranged," Rattan said quickly just as another man hurried down the bookstore stairs toward the car. "Mr. Ajit Gupta, this is Miss Minu…"

"Vanik," said Triti, appropriating the surname Vanik from Rattan's road atlas' author on the seat beside her.

"Hello," Ajit said, shifting nervously in place.

"Mr. Gupta's agreed to have you work here for two weeks."

"Two weeks?" said Ajit, his voice rising. "I told you, Rattan, I just can't…"

"You will start today," said Rattan, looking from Ajit to Triti.

"Two weeks, Rattan. That's *all* I can do," said Ajit, clearly in dismay.

Triti took in Ajit Gupta with his soulful eyes, wispy moustache, and pit-stained shirt. She could tell he did not want her there.

Ajit turned and trudged back up to the top of the bookstore stairs where he stopped and waited, his thin arms tightly crossed against his chest.

Rattan motioned for Triti to get out of the car. Clutching her cloth parcel, Triti stepped cautiously into the midst of the bustling street. Traffic flowed about her in every direction: bicycles, rickshaws, cars, and mopeds were all moving too quickly. She froze on the spot.

"Don't be afraid," whispered Rattan. "I have known this man for a long time. He is mostly honest. When I pass through Delhi again in two weeks, I'll stop by to check on you."

Triti's feet in Mala's borrowed leather saindalas felt stuck to the paving bricks beneath them. She longed for the relative safety of Rattan's car.

"It shall work out, you'll see. Take off your veil, if you'd like. You won't need it here. With 12 million people in Delhi, no one will even notice."

Rattan pointed to the door of the shop, five short steps up from the sidewalk.

"Bahut dhanyabad, Mr. Mewar," said Triti as she slid the veil from her face. She avoided his eyes, worried that he might see her fear.

Rattan joined his hands beneath his chin as their eyes met for the first time. Dumbstruck by her beauty, he struggled for words.

"You have… no need to thank me, Miss. I've only done the right thing."

Embarrassed by his stare, Triti shifted her gaze to the storefront. Rattan fumbled in his back pocket and removed a roll of rupees. He tucked the money into a crease in her parcel.

"I'll see you soon, Minu. And don't worry."

He climbed back into his car and pulled hastily out into the street, nearly colliding with a motor scooter. The bearded driver yelled and spat at him. Seconds later, Rattan's car disappeared behind a delivery van.

He's gone.

Triti felt as if she had just fallen from the sky.

Over the city's din, she heard her new name being called.

"Miss Vanik! May I please show you my establishment?"

Ajit motioned to her and with a nervous sigh she followed him up into the store. Even though the air conditioning was substandard and the plastic table fan clattered, Triti breathed with relief. Ajit led her through the maze of tight aisles and book displays. Each shelf was stacked half way to the loft ceiling with books.

"I'll clear the upper storage room for you. It'll be a quiet space to sleep. The bathroom is to your left at the top of the stairs. I have no cooking facilities, and I apologize for that. However, just down the street there are restaurants that open early and close quite late."

Triti watched Ajit's mouth moving, but she barely heard his words. Surrounding her were hundreds of books stacked high on wooden shelves: volumes of every size, color, and description. Their titles blurred, came into focus, and then blurred again. She shook her head and felt dizzy.

"What type of books do you enjoy, Miss Minu?"

Caught off guard, she answered honestly.

"Poetry."

"Really?" His response was tinged with surprise. "Do you have a favorite poet, Minu?"

"Naidu. Even though her poetry makes me sad."

Triti thought of Sarojini Naidu's poems about family and instantly she was floating up from the bookstore aisle out the shop door, up through the grey city clouds to soar across the hundred desert miles back to her Rajasthan home. She squinted her eyes tightly and the faces of her parents and her brother appeared.

"You'll want to freshen up," said Ajit, and he rushed off, disappearing down the aisle.

She opened her eyes and was back in the bookstore.

"Thank you," she said softly to his back. "I'll be right down."

"Oh, no, Miss. Please take your time," Ajit insisted from his usual stool perch behind the front counter.

Triti carried her satchel up a short flight of metal stairs, wincing from her tender feet with every step. At the top of the landing, she turned left and pushed opened a flimsy plywood door. A beam of sunlight hit her face. The bathroom was small but cheerful: the walls freshly painted in a wash of lemon, square white floor tiles, a Western toilet, and a clean, serviceable tub.

More than ample space to do laundry.

She set to the task of bathing. The wounds on her hands made it difficult to even grasp the washcloth, so she crouched in the small tub and splashed her body clean. She wished for the sureness of her mother's hands on her back… always such gentleness in her touch. She thought of the night before her wedding, in the final hours with her mother. Although both women knew that the daughter was old enough to bathe alone, the melancholy ritual took them back to a time of innocence.

In the wall mirror above the tiny pedestal sink, Triti caught herself smiling. She felt it odd to work the muscles in her face that way again, and slightly painful. She could not recall the last time she had smiled. She could barely remember much of anything that happened after her wedding. *Maybe it was best not to remember.* Sitting on the hard, Western toilet seat she tended her sore feet, spreading Mala's seed paste into her burns and rewrapping them carefully before slipping into her beige punjabis. Her hands were healing, but she still rubbed sesame oil on them. Then, despite the summer heat, she pulled down the lengths of her sleeves to cover all but the tips of her fingers.

When Triti descended to the shop floor, Ajit was speaking with an elderly woman at the register. She felt restless so she walked the tight aisles of the shop, studying the spines of the books on the shelves. They were arranged in alphabetical order by author, just as the books in the library in Jaipur had been.

I can do that.

The bell on the shop's front door jingled and Ajit found her in the mystery novel section.

"Mrs. Pandit…you'll see her here often," he said. "She's one of our regular customers. Her husband is a ministry official."

Ajit chatted in the same cheery tone he had used with Mrs. Pandit, somewhat soothing Triti's nerves.

"She wanted a certain picture book of Agra for her niece from Britain who will be visiting the Taj next week. I have only one copy of the latest edition, and she's asked me to have it delivered to their bungalow in Rashtrapati Bhavan. Could you wrap it for me while I finish the fiction inventory?"

Thus, began Triti's new life.

She fell into her routine quickly, rising before dawn each morning, grateful for her small room with its hard cot and plain-woven rug soft under her tender feet. Squatting carefully so as not to press against her wounds, she chanted before a makeshift altar on the floor beneath the iron-barred window in her room. She lit a small black candle and sprinkled white sweets before a blue plaster figure of Krishna, his plump, cherubic cheeks shiny in the early light.

"Lord, you see everything. Do you see me?"

She did not regret spending the few paise on a sprig of fresh miniature roses at the flower wallah stand two streets away. As she rolled the fuchsia blooms between her fingers, their sweet smell lifted her spirits. Once bathed and dressed, she left out the shop's back door. As the rest of the neighborhood awakened, she made her way down the narrow alley and into the city.

Her weekly salary of 400 rupees was more than enough to afford daily breakfasts of aloo paratha and chai at a popular food concession two blocks from Ajit's shop.

Often, she waited on a long line and had to eat her meal standing outside the café. She rushed back to meet Ajit curbside as he and his merchant neighbors hoisted their storefronts' heavy gates in earsplitting unison; the clanging of the galvanized steel stockades rolling up and out of sight serving as the defacto start of the retail workday.

Once inside the shop, Ajit moved about in his well-rehearsed routine, cranking open the twin front French windows, turning on the shop lights, and listening to messages on the store's answering machine. Without prompting, Triti swept the slatted, wooden floor with an old straw jharoo, just as her mother had taught her when she was a mite and the brooms were bigger than she was. She wiped clean the front counter and register blackened from a thin layer of grime that settled nightly on every possible surface throughout Delhi. Then she walked the aisles with champa incense to freshen the stale air. Ajit moved two folding stands of local and national newspapers and popular periodicals out onto the sidewalk, while Triti organized the candy displays next to the register. She would spend the rest of the morning opening shipping boxes of color postcards and arranging them in their vertical holders on the shop's north wall. She could not help but stop to gaze at the pictures of the far away places she had only heard of: Bangalore, Sri Lanka, Paris, New York. How many times had she shocked her brother with her childhood proclamations that one day she would go to Amreeka and see the great sights of the West? He had always laughed at the notion. No one in their family had been on a plane, he reminded her.

Perhaps our people were never meant to fly.

"Dilip, my Dilip…what are you doing right now, my brother? Are you in school, fiddling with your pen as you do? Do you look out your window and wonder about me?"

By eight o'clock a.m., the shop was set for a full day of selling. Ajit taught her how to use the four-line telephone, and by the end of her first day she had memorized the script he had taped below the counter. He seemed relieved not to have to take business calls in addition to attending customers' questions, ringing up sales, and finessing the accounting books. For her part, Triti tried to anticipate his needs, keeping one eye on the front door and the other on the phone bank while she unloaded new shipments and re-shelved errant volumes. Ajit's initial abruptness mellowed and he became increasingly patient with her. With every new chore she mastered, her confidence grew and her fear of him diminished.

Every afternoon at two o'clock, Ajit insisted that she take a break for lunch. She walked around the corner to Saleem's Restaurant where she savored dal, tandoori rotis, and shahi paneer sitting on a plastic chair at one of a dozen, wobbly tables. The crush of afternoon patrons helped her feel less conspicuous, but she kept her eyes on whatever book she had picked up on her way out of the shop, careful to hide her face. At first, she worried constantly that someone might recognize her, even though she knew that the chances of anyone knowing her were literally twelve million to one. As the days passed, her worries of being discovered began to subside. She hid her face less often, instead wearing the end of her dupatta in a soft drape over her right shoulder.

In her private moments when her thoughts swirled back to her life in Jaipur, her tears came. She yearned to call her parents, to tell them she was alive, to beg them not to worry. By now they must have known of her disappearance. They would be frantic with fear not knowing what had happened to her. At least a dozen times each day, her fingers trembled above the store's phone keypad. How she longed to hear her mother tell her that everything would be okay; to hear her father's voice telling her that he loved her. But in her mind, the danger in contacting her family was too great. Their lives would be at risk if they were to learn that she was alive.

They must never know.

Triti wondered if she would ever find a way to live with the anguish in her heart. When her sadness felt beyond measure, instead of eating lunch, she would venture out into the neighborhood, discovering where the finest bangles were sold and which music shops played her favorite movie songs. As she walked, she felt the despair fade, and by the time she returned to the bookstore, her mood was somewhat brighter. She turned her attention to her duties until seven p.m., when Ajit closed and locked up the shop with her inside it.

"I'm sorry, Miss Minu. I hope you understand. If I gave you a key and someone else got a hold of it…well."

The chains and locks on the main gate kept the storefront well secured, and the solid metal back door locked automatically when it shut. She was bound to remain inside the store until Ajit arrived the next morning, or risk being locked out. That was fine with her. Instead of feeling frustrated about her situation, she actually looked forward to curling up on her cot and drifting off safely to sleep each night.

Five more days went by and Triti did not once feel the need to walk her worries away. Her hands had nearly stopped shaking. But when she returned to the bookstore after a pleasant lunch at Saleem's to see Ajit slam the telephone onto its cradle, her serenity vanished. She hesitated just inside the shop door, her pulse quickening, and looked at him. Ajit stood abruptly behind his desk and straightened his shirt with a two-handed tug.

"Minu, I have to close up early today," he said brusquely, without so much as a glance her way. "I won't be back until tomorrow morning. I hope you had a sufficient meal."

Without waiting for her response, Ajit shoved an armful of paper folders into his leather briefcase. In a rush to empty the register's cash into a bank bag, he dropped his store keys and banged his head on a packing crate beneath the counter. Cursing, he cranked shut and bolted the front windows and locked the front door. Triti watched in disbelief as Ajit brought down the front gate with a single, violent yank and hurriedly clapped the padlocks in place.

With her ear to the front door's glass panel, she heard him hail a taxi and shout to the driver, "The airport! Jildi!"

Stunned, she tried to make sense of what had just happened. Her heart thumped as she sorted a handful of postcards into their slots on the display wheel; something to distract her mind. Two hours went by. She restacked the street maps on the front counter, and dusted all of the bookshelves. Her stomach felt queasy and she went up to her cot where she lay staring at Krishna on his puja.

"Help me."

The blue boy did not respond.

Somehow, she fell asleep. When she awoke, her room was dark.

She turned on the small reading light beside her cot and checked the alarm clock. It was just after ten p.m. She flicked on the light at the top of the stairs and went down into the shop.

Hungry, Triti scanned the front counter for anything edible. The candies by the register would not sustain her. True, she and her cousin Lalita had survived an entire sleep over with only a bag of elaichi roll toffees between them. But she was not fourteen. She eyed the back exit. If she could brace something in the door, just prop it open slightly, she could rush to Saleem's and back with a cup of rice palak, and tuck into a good book.

A book!

Down the aisle, she pulled a slim paperback copy of the Bhagavad Gita from a shelf. She riffed through the pages and checked its width.

This should work.

She slowly opened the back door and stepped out into the dark alley. Carefully, she wedged the volume between the door and the lock.

Simple.

As she turned to step away, she watched helplessly as the book slid to the ground and tumbled back inside the store. She lunged to grab the edge of the door, but it closed just beyond her fingertips with a heavy click.

"Oh, my God! No!"

She yanked and tugged on the smooth steel handle for a futile minute, but the door did not budge.

"No, no, NO!!"

This cannot be happening.

"Idiot girl!"

Disoriented, Triti stumbled down the dark alley bumping into overflowing garbage bins and stacks of empty cardboard boxes before making it out to the sidewalk. The bustling neighborhood seemed unfamiliar and affronting, as on her first day in Karol Bagh. Colors flashed too vividly; passersby brushed too closely. Car horns blared. Overflowing gutters reeked. Her senses overloaded and she walked until her wounded feet demanded respite. She entered the nearest restaurant and sat alone near the entrance. A radio on the wall announced that the time was eleven p.m. Eight more hours before Ajit returned. She ordered malai kofta and ate the soft dumplings slowly, making sure to sop up every bit of the thick, tomato gravy. When she finished her meal, she ordered chai, letting the steaming tea cool before taking a taste. A strategy emerged. She would pay her bill and then search for the next place to sit. From one eatery to the next, she ordered a single cup of chai and sat and sipped as slowly as she could. Her eyes skimmed the newspaper she carried, but the words on the pages did not register in any orderly way. She found herself staring at the second hands on black-and-white clocks hanging above steaming rice pots; the uncaring black arms sweeping in their slow circles, unwilling to accelerate their pace despite her silent pleas. She squinted beneath harsh fluorescent lights as her restless fingers fashioned paper napkin creations on her lap, hidden from strangers' eyes just below the table. A mangled swan, a lopsided lotus. When the kitchen help began to stare at her—a solitary girl sitting too long at a table—she paid her bill and moved on to the next place.

The last restaurant closed its doors at two a.m., and wearily she headed back to the bookstore and down the dark alley. She squatted just outside the shop's rear door on the edge of its concrete stoop. Late night sounds of the city closed in around her. Stray dogs howled. Colicky babies wailed.

Desperate for comfort, her thoughts flew to Dilip.

"Oh, my dear, brother…if *only* you were here."

When she opened the day's newspaper to sit on it, the moonlight spilled across the masthead.

July 25, 2000.

It was their eighteenth birthday.

Triti pulled her dupatta tighter around her shoulders and retreated into the memory of their birth story when, as her mother had recounted a thousand times at her wide-eyed insistence, she came first: strong and pink and loud and large. Dilip, who should have preceded her out of her mother's womb to fulfill age-old cultural dictates, came last; weak and pale and still and small. She had found her mother's breast instantly, effortlessly pulling the flat, brown nipple into her mouth, while her brother struggled to stay latched on long enough to gain nourishment. She met every childhood milestone first and best: rolling over, talking, crawling, and even walking before nine months of age. Dilip lagged behind on all counts, but he watched his sister with keen interest, emulating her as best he could at every chance.

The twins were a burden for their young parents, and her paternal grandparents pressured them to give Triti away and focus on raising Dilip. "She will cost you," they warned. Even well-meaning neighbors echoed the heartless but common sentiment, pointing out that Dilip was after all, the boy—the future patriarch and best hope for the family's financial enrichment. Their father's salary from driving produce trucks between Jaipur and Pushkar was constantly stretched thin. They often made do with little more than chapattis and dal for the evening meal; yet their parents never considered the twins to be burdens. To them, Triti and Dilip were blessings from the gods. Give their daughter away? They would not hear of it. Her parents devoted themselves to raising sister and brother together, with equal measures of love and attention. In spite of the twins' vastly different temperaments and personalities— Dilip with his dreamy, sentimental nature, and she with her lucid, pragmatic seriousness—brother and sister became inseparable.

"My Dilip, on this our special day, my dear brother, am I dead to you?"

She cried herself into a fitful half-sleep. Later, something shook her awake, and she bit a raw knuckle to stifle a scream as a pack of large rats scurried past her feet into the shadows, their silver backs flashing as they ran.

The next morning, when Triti met Ajit outside the shop's front gates after breakfast as usual, she wondered if he noticed that she wore the same clothing as the day before. If he did, he said nothing. Once inside the shop, she fled upstairs to the bathroom to bathe and re-bandage her sore feet. She took her time and put on her only other clean outfit—a dark crimson salwar kameez set from Mala. She would have to do her hand laundry that evening before bed. She swore to herself that she would never try to prop open the back door again.

Just after nine o'clock a.m., as she sorted through a box of paperback mysteries at the rear of the store, Triti overheard an argument begin near the register. She peaked above the shelf and watched as Ajit and a well-dressed woman exchanged heated words.

"I was in Kerala for only one month! My GOD!" yelled the woman. "My sister has a damned telephone! A decision such as this, and you didn't think to call me?"

"Rani, you know that I have been needing help for months since Deepak left. And the girl has been of good service thus far. She's bright and she listens. Look, I've even been able to catch up on the monthly statements." Ajit gestured toward his clean desk, free of paperwork.

Rani was unmoved.

"Where is this girl? I will meet her at once." Her angry eyes flashed about the store.

"Of course, as I had hoped you would, dear. Rani, please don't be upset. She's really quite harmless—a young Rajput girl. She's a widow," he whispered. "She had nowhere else to go."

"A widow? And she's living here? The two of you, alone all day?"

"We're hardly alone, Rani," said Ajit, as two young couples walked into the store and headed to the bestseller's aisle, chatting about their university course selections for the next semester, oblivious to the tension around them.

"She belongs in Vrindavan with the rest of them!" Rani sniped.

"Lower your voice," demanded Ajit.

Triti's face reddened as Ajit revealed her secret truth. Vrindavan? She knew of that place. Everyone did. The City of Widows—where women, young and old, rich and poor, went to suffer for no other crime than outliving their husbands. It was rumored to be a place of deprivation. She watched as Rani adjusted her lavish green sari and leaned into Ajit's ear. Triti could no longer hear their conversation, but she could tell the woman was furious.

Ajit found Triti at the back of the store, crouched over a half-emptied carton of books. Rani came close on his heels. Triti stood at the sound of their footsteps.

"Minu, this is my wife, Mrs. Gupta. She's been away on holiday and has just returned. I was telling her how helpful your assistance has been."

Ajit's normally sad eyes opened wide in alarm. He struggled to keep his voice measured.

"Nice to meet you," Triti said to Rani, her eyes lowered. "I'm very grateful for this position."

With one look at Triti's beautiful face and slender figure, Rani spun on her heels and stormed from the shop. For a brief moment, neither Triti nor Ajit could move. Then Ajit raced out the door, pushing past a group of tourists whose tour bus idled noisily in front of the bookstore.

The front door's bell rang again, and Triti lunged down the aisle and slid behind the cash register. The tourists, a dozen retirees from Quebec in khaki pants and plaid shirts, surged into the shop, their words and dress completely strange to her. One by one, they presented their purchases and she wrapped their merchandise, wrote receipts, and counted exact change. Twenty minutes later the rush ended, and she rested on the swivel stool behind her. Satisfied, she picked a peppermint ball from a clear jar on the counter, untwisted the pink, plastic wrapper, and popped the sweet in her mouth. From her money purse she retrieved a single paisa and dropped it in the register's coin box. Then she checked the count total on the receipts: she had sold 4,200 rupees worth of books.

When Ajit returned soon after, Triti could not wait to tell him of her fledgling sales coup. She was breathless to think that she had mastered the basics of running the shop. But before she could share her news, he apologized for what he was about to say.

"Miss Minu, I regret that I must do this, but there is no other way."

He could not bear to look at her. He stared at his shoes; now scuffed toe to heel.

"What is it?" Triti asked, worriedly.

"My wife, she…well, it's not going to work out. You can't stay here any longer." He could hardly say the words.

"I…I can find another place … a room to rent, somewhere not too far. I can look in the papers…"

She grabbed the nearest daily off the stand and flipped it open.

"No. That won't work. Rani doesn't believe I need an assistant."

"You don't agree with her, do you?"

Ajit slumped against the wall, defeated.

"No, I don't. But it doesn't matter. She wants you *out*. And it's her bloody store!"

Triti struggled to keep from crying.

"But Rattan…He'll be here in a few days. He'll know what to do," she pleaded.

"Please, get your things."

Stunned, Triti turned and darted up to her room and quickly gathered her belongings. Her heart pounded as she tried to focus on what her tender hands were doing.

"No, no!" Her new beginning was over.

She would have to run again.

In the bathroom one last time, she forced out the last drop of urine, knowing that it might be hours before she found a place to relieve herself. She descended the narrow stairs a final time. With her satchel over her shoulder, she walked to the front door where Ajit waited stoically for her. He had already hung the "CLOSED" sign in the window.

Once she reached the sidewalk, Ajit pulled down the front gates and secured the chains. Then he stepped to the curb and flagged down a tuktuk.

"I have nowhere to go," she said to him.

"There is a place," he said.

He motioned for her to get in the back seat of the auto rickshaw and then climbed in beside her.

"Hazrat Station," he hollered to the turbaned driver who nodded and revved the motor.

Instantly they were part of the mobile masses. En route, Ajit did not speak. He handed Triti a thick, hardcover book, wrapped hastily in his finest paper. At first, she waved him off, but he shoved the package toward her again, and she relented, tucking the gift deep into her bag.

"Thank you," she murmured.

When they reached the hectic train station, Ajit instructed the driver to wait for him, and then plunged into the tide of departing passengers flooding out of the front entrance. Triti ran to follow him, barely managing to keep him in her sights. They scurried past scores of the station's wretched denizens: dirt-smudged toddlers riding their mothers' starved hips; elderly sadhus puffing on chillam pipes; entire families begging with their hands outstretched. She dodged a pair of cows that stood, immovable, in the center of the mall chewing on marigold petals. A street peddler hawking samosas and chapattis from his steaming cart tossed stale bits of food to a trio of mangy dogs, while a dozen bahoots in red shirts and metallic armbands ducked and swirled amidst the chaos—ragged suitcases stacked three and four-high on their heads—while their traveling owners struggled to stay within eyesight of their lofted belongings.

Triti caught up to Ajit, and he pointed up at the blinking departure boards.

"Taj Express!" he shouted. "Track 7! You've less than five minutes!"

Triti's feet stung as they raced up two flights of staircases, across three steel transverses, and down more stairwells to reach the outbound train platform. There, the #2180 to the city of Agra sat chugging its engine and spouting white steam clouds into Delhi's rancid air. Ajit dashed alongside the train, searching for the women's passenger compartment. He approached a uniformed conductor taking tickets, and once the pile of rupees in the man's hand reached a height to his liking, he waved Triti toward the steps of the car's sliding door.

"You have to get off at Mathura," said Ajit. "It's the closest stop to Vrindavan."

"What am I going to do?" asked Triti, her voice breaking.

"God, Minu, this is not how I wanted…"

"Tell me!"

The train's engine roared and heaved the car southward.

"Get on!" Ajit screamed above the grinding of the iron wheels.

Triti stumbled up the grimy train steps, clutching her satchel. The train lurched forward again and she fell hard against the handrail. Ajit shuffled lamely alongside the train, his eyes wide as he tried to find something to say to her. The locomotive gradually picked up speed and he broke first into a slow jog, then a run. Triti lunged to the bottom of the stairs and clung to the handrail watching his image shrink until he disappeared into Delhi's morning smog.

SIX

With seven women and three infants jammed hip to thigh on the compartment's worn, wooden bench, Triti's two-and-a-half-hour train ride from New Delhi to Mathura seemed to last forever.

Half an hour into the trip, she noticed that she was the only person awake in her car. The rocking rhythms of the train chugging at speed had had their somnambulistic effects on everyone but her. Babies lolled open-mouthed and drooling in their mothers' laps while older women snuggled into each other, snoring. Squished up against one of the railcar's grubby windows, Triti rested her temple against the warm, green glass and watched as ninety miles of impoverished villages flashed by. A silent witness to the countless images of poverty just beyond the tracks, she saw a singular portrait of want. Yet she found it impossible to sympathize with the hollow-cheeked mothers and naked toddlers scrounging for food along the edge of the tracks. Her personal crisis demanded her complete attention. She flashed back to the times as a little girl, whenever she scraped an elbow or lost a toy in the street, her father had been there to soothe her. In her earnest days of chasing clouds, when the occasional squall rattled her world, she would climb like a tree squirrel up his solid frame and nestle her head beneath his chin. She felt that old urge surge again; to climb up, high, anywhere above, and rest her mind, slow it down, and be still. But she could not slow down now. Nor could she sleep. She was back into the running.

Triti's bladder throbbed with every wobble of the train car, and when finally she disembarked in Mathura, pissing was all she had in mind. She elbowed her way through the swarming crowds on the open-air platform and moaned in agony at the predictably long line for the women's restroom. Tears streaked her face when at last she took her turn squatting above the foul, open pit. She screamed as she finally let go her urine stream, trying not to splash on her oozing, bandaged feet.

Her mind clearing, she shifted her attention to transport. She followed the ebbing crowds into the parking lot and drop-off stand where car taxis and bicycle rickshaws jockeyed for fares.

"Do you go to Vrindavan?" she shouted at one of the many tuk-tuk drivers idling noisily at the curb.

"Yes, of course," he said, picking his rotted teeth with his hair comb. "Two hundred rupees, no less."

"Nahi! Bahut jyaada paiesa. Don't pay more than seventy-five rupees, Miss."

A fair-haired European man interrupted in passable Hindi as he dragged three overstuffed travel bags up to the taxi curb. His young blond wife followed close behind with a chubby infant asleep in a sling across her chest.

"Hare Krishna," she said, smiling at Triti, bringing her palms together beneath her chin and bowing slightly at the waist.

"One hundred and fifty rupees, Miss," countered the driver, motioning to Triti to step up into his rickshaw cart.

"We're heading to the Sacred Krishna ashram," the European man told Triti as the driver started up his engine. "Where are you going?"

"I don't… I'm not sure."

"Are you alone?" asked the wife in a caring tone.

"One hundred and twenty-five rupees, not less," insisted the driver, growing impatient.

Triti nodded, and the wife and the husband exchanged glances.

"Well, Miss?" barked the driver.

With a yowl, the baby awoke from his nap.

"You'll take us all for one hundred rupees," said the European man as he piled their luggage into the rickshaw's back passenger seat.

"Lana, make room, dear."

The man motioned to Triti to sit beside his wife and slid in beside the driver on the short front seat.

Triti had barely time to sit when the tuk-tuk swung out into the congested streets of Mathura. As they bounced along the rutted roads leading out of town, Triti learned that the couple, from Malta, was making their fourth trip to Vrindavan, this time for the blessing ceremony of their newborn son. Although she had often seen foreign tourists in her hometown of Jaipur, snapping pictures of each other in front of the red-and-white Hawa Mahal Palace and haggling with roadside jewelers for the best prices on cut emeralds—she had never actually spoken with any foreigners. To her relief, the couple was very friendly and respectful, asking her nothing about her reasons for traveling to Vrindavan, or her marital status. Instead, they took turns describing their initiation into Krishna Consciousness and their previous trips to India.

Triti found herself staring at the couple's pale hair and skin. Despite their authentic Indian clothing and sandalwood face tilakas typical of Krishna devotees, the little family stood out starkly amidst the rest of the brown-skinned populace. They seemed completely at ease with their surroundings, in spite of this. They explained that their pilgrimage to the childhood home of the blue god and worldwide center of Krishna Consciousness was a crucial rite of passage—an integral part of the journey toward their spiritual destinies. Never mind the stifling heat, spine-splitting roads, and one very cranky baby.

The late afternoon sun refused to take pity on Vrindavan, blistering the city's paved streets and dusty footpaths. Scabby dogs lay panting in the gray dirt, their yelps lost to the summer heat. Hordes of sooty pigs commandeered every dark hovel, rankling cows and humans attempting to shelter within the few precious swaths of public shade. Camels stood by unfazed, fanning their long, black lashes while their two-legged masters slurped icy bottles of soda and complained about the sorry state of India's cricket teams. When the rickshaw finally came to a stop in front of a lush, gated property near the outer edge of town, Triti offered the Maltese money, but they refused to accept it.

"Thank you," she said as she stepped out of the rickshaw and peered between the iron rails at the ashram's dense, green garden.

"You can find a room here," said Lana. "Talk to Rupa Jaya. He's usually in the main office."

Just then a young female devotee ran through the gates and greeted the couple. Her plump face was decorated with a cream-colored clay tilaka. She took the baby from Lana and began cooing to him.

"Umi, this is Minu," said Lana, gesturing to Triti. "We met in Mathura."

Umi smiled sweetly at Triti, then spun around in a circle, causing squeals of delight from the baby.

One of the male guards stepped away from his post to help carry the couple's luggage into the compound.

"See you at the temple later!" said Lana, as she followed her husband and Umi into the garden.

Exhausted beyond her nerves, Triti covered her head with her scarf and approached one of the other uniform guards patrolling the main entrance to the ashram.

"Pardon me. May I please speak to Rupa Jaya?"

"Did you just arrive with the Bondins," he asked.

"Well, yes. Lana, er, Mrs. Bondin suggested that I see him."

The man smoothed his black mustache and shifted the brown rifle on his narrow shoulder. He stepped inside the guard booth and talked briefly on a walkie-talkie.

"Wait here," he said.

Triti peered through the iron gates and saw a winding path bursting with orange tulips and banana trees. She wondered if she would ever get to stroll in the garden. Too tired to stand and too sore to sit, she squatted off to the side of the guard booth as dozens of devotees came and went.

They seem so happy.

Twenty minutes later, a jaunty man dressed all in white came through the main gates to the booth.

"I am sorry to keep you waiting, Miss. So, you're a friend to the Bondin's. Do you wish a room here?"

His perfect English surprised Triti. His clipped pronunciations were distinct.

"I, well, how much is..."

"The tariff? 100 rupees a day," he said.

Triti could not recall precisely how much money she had left, but she was certain that she had at least enough for one night. The man turned and strode through the main gate toward a grand three-story building.

"Come, Miss," he called back to her.

She hesitated, watching as he disappeared through a doorway. She needed some sign that the ashram was the place she must stay. This could be her chance to stop running, to be still, but she needed a sign. She closed her eyes and caught the scent of wood smoke in the air as families across Vrindavan built their cooking fires. She knew this smell. She opened her eyes and saw the haze rising above the city and she remembered the evenings of her youth in Jaipur, when fire meant food, and family, and sleep.

The man in white poked his head out of the door down the path and waved her on.

"This way!"

She followed his voice into the reception room of the ashram's main dormitory. Behind the tall front desk, her escort spoke quietly to a male clerk who finished making change for a devotee.

"This girl—she came with the Bondin's. She can take 324. I'll be back to show her up."

The clerk took 100 rupees from Triti, and she signed her new name to the dormitory register.

"Miss…Vanik," he read aloud. "I'll have to send someone for your room key."

Triti sat on a padded bench and waited, newly aware of an ache in her belly and stiffness in her lower back. Her swollen hands and feet throbbed. As dusk descended outside the office window, she felt sure that bad luck was about to take a seat beside her again.

But why?

She had done everything her mother had taught her to guarantee a good marriage and a good life. She had prayed to Lucama for blessings. She had decorated the entrance to their home with the peacock Rañgoli design. She had kept the vrat for three whole days, eating not one morsel of food throughout her fast. Still, the wedding mehndi on her hands and feet would not take. "It is unfortunate," her paternal aunt had remarked just as the wedding procession began. "The deeper the stain on the palms, the more the bride will be loved by her husband. No stain, no love."

Parched dry as she had ever been, Triti assessed the cruel fact before her. She was without a future.

Devotees shuffled into the office to check their charge accounts and to use the telephone room. Each one greeted her the same way.

Hare Krishna.

Triti brought her clasped hands to her forehead and replied in kind.

A door at the back of the office opened to reveal a burly man in a yellow dhoti and white kurta. His head was completely shaved but for a braided topknot. His bushy eyebrows— lively red caterpillars—danced as he spoke.

"Hare Krishna. I'm Rupa Jaya, the general manager of the ashram," he said, walking over to greet Triti.

"I'm…Minu."

"Welcome. How long are you with us?"

"I've paid for tonight."

"Only one night?" he replied, quizzically.

"Tomorrow I need to find employment."

"What type of work can you do?" he asked.

"Well, I've worked in a bookstore. In Delhi. I can read and write in Hindi and English. And I can sew."

Rupa Jaya nodded and smiled politely.

"I regret that we have no jobs available now. Had you come in the winter perhaps, but even then, those positions are rarely open, and we generally offer them to our devotees from the West."

Triti dropped her chin to her chest.

"Mr. Virmani will show you to your room now. Take dinner upstairs in our cafeteria and then get some rest. Perhaps things will seem better in the morning."

"Dhanyavād," said Triti, gloomily.

"Praise Krishna."

Triti awoke in her spare dormitory room as fine rays of morning sun lit the pale blue ceiling. Above her bed, dust of the city floated in the light. Slowly, she moved her legs and arms, reuniting her mind and body in a languorous stretch. She felt rested. For the first time in weeks, she had slept straight through until daybreak.

She recalled her first night in Vrindavan as a sequence of sensations…cool tiles beneath her feet, warm water falling on her face, a firm mattress catching her body. Dreamless hours. Late in her nocturnal sojourn came city sounds: the predawn clanging of temple bells; the chanting of priests, the lowing of cows in the streets. These sounds and more blended into a harmonic hum that lulled her out of a restful sleep.

The gods must be happy here.

Even though she could barely stand to look at her wounds, Triti tended her feet and hands with meticulous care. Mala's paste was healing the burns, and there was far less pain when she touched the blisters. Yet she found herself hurrying to rewrap them and put them out of sight. She worried that the clerk had seen her hands when she had signed in. She resolved to be much more careful.

Before dressing for the day, she sat on the bed, opened her bag, and spread out her meager fortune. Carefully, she counted every paper and coin. The grand total: 212 rupees and 11 paise.

There had to be more.

"What is this?"

Ajit's gift. She had completely forgotten about it. She retrieved his package from the bottom of her satchel and tore open the gold wrapping paper. Surprise pulled a faint smile across her cheeks. The biography of Sarojini Naidu lay in her lap. She ran her hands across the book's red-and-blue front cover and prayed that The Village Song was somewhere within its pages.

"Honey, child, honey, child, wither are you going?" she recited from memory as she opened the book. Pressed tightly against the book's inner spine was a slim stack of rupees. Her severance. The new skin on her fingers stretched painfully as she counted the bills.

500 rupees.

Opening the double doors of her room, Triti stepped out onto the marble veranda and into the bright sun. Three floors below her, the magnificent garden abounded with orange bougainvillea, magenta frangipani, and head-high sprays of green ferns.

Have I gone to heaven?

"Be careful, Miss! Mind the bandars!"

A stooped, pale man stood a few yards away on the veranda in front of his room and pointed to a troop of gray monkeys lounging on the clay-shingled roof across the breezeway.

"They'll tear right into your room, Miss. Snatch whatever's not tied down!"

Triti glanced at the creatures then turned her attention to the steel lock on her door. On her fourth failed attempt to secure the bolt, she grunted in frustration.

"Need a little help?"

The man shuffled toward her, and with a practiced click secured the device.

"Seems we're neighbors," he said, indicating his room next to hers. "I'm Darius."

"Thank you for that," she said, eying him warily.

"Not at all…everyone has difficulty the first time. You arrived last night?"

"Yes," she said, noticing that the man could not stand upright. Unconsciously, she bent slightly when she answered him.

"So, you've met our manager?" he asked.

"You mean Rupa Jaya?"

"R.J. Nice enough mate. Has this place running like a clock. Of all the managers in the past 20 years, he's had the steadiest hand. Scotsman, you know. They have a way with efficiency."

"Well, I must go…"

"Oh, no need to fret about time here, Miss. The ISKON temple is open day and night. It's the cafeteria's schedule you'll want to learn, 'cause when they close up, that's it for refreshments. Unless you're willing to go into town, of course. I'm afraid the trek is too much of a production for me anymore."

Triti set her satchel down at her feet to adjust her kurta which was still damp from her hasty hand wash the night before.

"Oh, and mind your bag, Miss!" he warned. "Two of the monsters pushed open my screen door and made off with my rucksack last year. I bribed them with bananas. Pretty lucky in that trade. Watch the dominant male. He's known to filch hats right off people's heads!"

Darius pointed to the largest monkey who promptly scampered off the peak of the roof and indulged himself with the pink hindquarters of a young female.

"Thank you, Minu. And if they don't have coconut water, almond milk will do."

Darius' list of needed sundries was longer than usual, but Triti did not mind. He had been very helpful to her during her first few days at the ashram, giving her advice about which items to order on the cafeteria menu, and how to adjust the water pressure in her shower. He told her which guards would hail a tuk-tuk without rancor, and when the best time was to use the telephone, should she ever have the need. He had lived at the ashram on and off for more than twenty-five years, abandoned by his wife in Australia after a car crash that left him handicapped and her unscathed.

"She felt guilty every time she looked at me," he told Triti, his voice shaking as though the revelation had just come to him. Triti felt sorry for Darius: his life lived bent in half, forever in physical pain; always looking up at people and being looked down upon. Despite his misfortunes, she never heard Darius complain. He was uncommonly gracious, and Triti began to let down her guard with him. When she confided that she desperately needed a job and would knock on every door in Vrindavan to find one, he asked her if she would be willing to do some shopping for him.

"Nikkos used to get things I needed; razors, toothpaste, lemon drops. I paid him a few rupees twice a week. Nice enough mate."

"Is he still here?" she asked.

"Sadly, no. Malaria got him on a jaunt to Orissa. He went home to Mykonos nothing but bones, poor fellow. He was a real help to me, until he got sick. If you're planning on going to town soon..."

She would need to stop at several markets that day. Down the congested side streets, she threaded her way among the deep wheel ruts and abandoned tires to reach the main bazaar thoroughfare. Like honey bees buzzing en masse from blossom to blossom, housewives, servants, laborers, tourists, and devotees swirled and bargained their way through the vast maze of vending stalls. Sari fabrics, car repair parts, bicycle chains, silver jewelry, candies, fresh-picked fruits and vegetables, grains, spices, cooking pots and utensils…all the selections presented in abundance were arranged to entice. There, in the midst of the swarm, Triti felt free. She was anonymous: just one of thousands of beings floating on the currents of commerce. Her confidence surged as she moved about the market. She tasted an offered bit of sweet melon and sniffed sticks of Patchouli-Amber. Less than a week into her stay at the ashram and she had already found the shops that offered the finest savories for the best price, and the sweetest gulab jamun dripping with butter.

Her shopping tasks nearly complete, Triti entered an electronic store that also sold bidis, plastic toys, and an impressive selection of chilled sodas. She found the batteries Darius needed and paid the clerk, who slouched behind the cashier's counter smoking and playing both sides on a miniature chess set. Her attention was drawn to the back of the store where several people sorted papers atop humming copy machines. A middle-aged American man groaned at the clerk and took his cigar stub out of his mouth.

"You don't speak English? Well, then you certainly can't read it, can you? Honestly, if I can manage a bit of Hindi, surely…but no, eh?"

The man dismissed the clerk with a wave of his pudgy hand and held a sheet of paper at the furthest extension of his arm. He shook his head and put the paper on the dusty floor, squinting at it again. He rolled his eyes, picked up the paper, and looked around.

"English? Anyone? Miss, do you read English? Yes?"

He gestured to Triti. The expression on his face reminded her of her father's grimace whenever he struggled against the rare challenge too difficult for him.

"I do," she answered modestly.

"Brilliant. My eyes are no good and my damned glasses are back at the homestay." He pointed to the paper in his hand.

"This fax from California—I need to know how to respond. Would you read it aloud to me? Of course, I am happy to pay you."

Triti shook off her shyness and took the sheet from him. She read the two-paragraph message aloud, careful to enunciate every word clearly. Something about a delay in flights and a second party arriving the next evening from Bangalore.

Another man who had stopped to purchase the day's Indian papers and a bottle of pear juice tuned his ear to Triti's voice. A tall man, he opened one of his papers and pretended to read it. From the corner of his eye, he watched as Triti accepted the reward of rupees from the

American and left the store, noticeably flushed from her experience.

The tall man followed her, staying a dozen paces back as Triti walked the stone paths through the green gardens of the ashram's sister property just beyond the site of Vrindavan's largest Krishna temple. He was within a few feet of her as she re-entered the paved road that fronted the Sacred Krishna ashram. When she stopped to admire a ruby bracelet at a jewelry concession, the man made his move.

"Red *becomes* you."

His bass voice at her left shoulder startled Triti. She turned to see a handsome Indian man, impeccably dressed in a dark suit and fine leather shoes. His gold watch glinted in the sun, blinding her for a moment. The man's hands appeared strong and smooth; his skin was creamy almond, his face close-shaven. She took all of him in with a single look—a survivor's skill.

"Thank you," she said, reflexively ready to walk on— though she did not take a step.

He bowed his head slightly, his eyes never leaving hers.

"I didn't mean to frighten you. Please forgive me."

She met his coal black eyes without a flinch.

"I'm not afraid."

Behind his broad, square shoulders, she could see the ashram gate and the guards playing cards in the shade of a banyan tree. The sight of their rifles slung high on their olive khaki uniforms gave her comfort.

"You were so helpful to the man in the fax store. Your English is quite lovely," said the man.

Triti felt the heat rise again in her face. She considered looking at the ground, but the temptation of the bangles was too great and she lifted her eyes to them. Rapture. Cut, jeweled, varnished, striped, mirrored—the colorful bracelets enthralled her. Shelf upon shelf, rack after sparkling rack of shiny, beautiful bangles. She sensed the man beside her. Did he hear their tinkling voices as she did? She longed to slide the bracelets, eight at a time, over her tender hands to her wrists; to stack them up her forearms past her elbows to her armpits, just as she had as a little girl. Greens, turquoise, reds, yellows, laq, and pinks—they all dazzled.

The tall man took a step closer to Triti. She reflexively tugged at the long sleeves of her blouse. Her pulse rocketed. She suddenly felt thirsty.

"Please pardon me," said the man. "I am rarely this forward, but I've need for someone who can assist me in translating Hindi and English correspondence. I'm in Vrindavan to attend a sale of real estate. I don't know many people here, you see."

In his refined speech Triti heard the sound of a foreign education and a privileged childhood, similar to the voices of the wealthy tourists who found her beloved Jaipur enchanting. She wondered how much of the world he had already seen. Had he been to Paris? America? Other places on the bookstore postcards?

She did not move away.

Sensing an opening, the tall man continued.

"Of course, someone as proficient as yourself, I'm sure you already have an excellent position. However, if you would consider working for me, my employer would compensate you well."

Before she could respond, he reached into the inner breast pocket of his suit and produced a lavender linen business card. She took it from him and ran her fingers over the raised silver inscriptions. She looked up at him once again, in his white tailored shirt and tie clip with its gleaming mother-of-pearl inlays.

"My name is Samir Desai, as you can see. Thank you for your time. I hope to hear from you."

He smiled at Triti and turned to leave.

"Kya aapako joota chamakaana hai?"

A barefoot young boy planted himself on the curb in front of Samir. In one hand he held a stained cloth. He flipped open a chipped, plastic box and rattled through his collection of shoe polish tins.

"How much?" asked Samir.

"Ten rupees," chirped the boy, scratching at the dirt caked on his throat.

Samir looked at the boy and with a nod agreed to the service. The boy's cohorts dodged and weaved behind him on the street, slapping each other's backs and laughing uproariously.

Triti used the distraction to leave, turning once to see Samir in a lively conversation with the boy who stooped to his work, buffing and polishing Samir's shoes with vigor. She was stunned by Samir's kindness to the urchin, who others would have ignored. She grasped the business card in her hand and hurried the last few steps to the ashram gates.

Late that night, Triti looked out from her room's rear window across the barbed wire fence that separated the ashram from the shanty slums, riveted by the evening customs of the lowest castes. Amidst the squalor of the tin and plastic bag shacks, women swathed in brilliant cloths with infants slung low on their backs stoked smoky, cow-dung fires. She watched as they boiled rice, patted chapattis, and bathed their children with water from rusted buckets.

Will that be my fate?

There were only 120 rupees left in her bag.

She knew by the sweet smell in the air and the aching in her hands and feet that big rains were gathering to the southeast. With Krishna's blessings, they would come and wash the dust and soot to the ground, making all of Vrindavan clean for a brief, blessed moment.

Triti placed Samir Desai's business card in front of her miniature Krishna statue and made a special puja with sandalwood incense and a handful of sweets. She sang chants as her mother had, all the while swaying in place until memories of her family brought tears fat enough to douse the candle's flame. She was alone, yet again, in the darkness of midnight's belly.

Early the next morning, Triti leaned against the balcony railing outside her room and watched as the sun seared the olivine mist that shrouded Krishna's city. Wan from a sleepless night, she lingered, letting the warming rays bathe her face. It felt good not to wear her veil. Nearby sounds of ruffling feathers alerted her to the presence of an enormous male vulture perched atop the ashram's television antennae. Barely thirty feet away, the great bird stood over three feet tall; its gleaming, yellow beak curved upwards on its black face in a mocking grin. The vulture dipped its head nonchalantly to groom its chest feathers, then casually unfolded all ten feet of its wingspan. Triti waited, hoping for flight. Suddenly, with a turn of its majestic head, the bird flapped its white-tipped wings and was instantly aloft. The creature hovered, weightless in its pause, just above the garden. Then, it turned and soared up and over the golden spires of the nearby temple toward the sun.

Triti followed the spiral stone stairway down to the ashram's office, closed the telephone cubicle's door behind her, and dialed the number on Samir Desai's card.

SEVEN

"**M**inu, have you given any more thought to the idea we discussed last week?"

Samir deposited an armful of mail in the holding tray on Triti's desk. Floor-length sheers fluttered through the open terrace windows beside her. The estate's central garden hummed with the sounds of day workers tending the jacaranda and mango trees. Triti looked up from her paperwork and feigned an expression of ignorance.

"What was that, Sir?"

"Sir? It's been more than three weeks since you came to work for me and still you do not call me Samir? Please, Minu, it would make me happy."

"Yes...Samir."

He broke into a wide smile.

"The *idea* that you leave the ashram and move into one of the bedroom suites here. Why not save the money you pay for your accommodations there? Besides, it would free my staff from having to collect and return you every day."

"But I would be another burden for Sadhna…"

"Nonsense. She has absolutely nothing to do but dust empty bedrooms all day. She complains how the tedium is driving her mad. And the poor cook! He prepares meals for me alone. Please be generous, Minu. Move onto the estate. Give the staff someone to care for."

Clever of him, Triti thought, using his employees' grumbles to convince her to come to him. He had made the same request every day for a week, each time using a different rationale: the monsoon's morning puddles would soil her clothing getting in and out of the car or the road to the ashram was scheduled to be dug up for a new water line soon. Then there was the newest revelation that his new driver was terrified of the ashram's head guard who insisted upon seeing the man's driver's license the moment he arrived at the gates for her each morning. Although it was becoming clear to her that Samir would continue to craft contrivances until she agreed to move onto the estate, given the fright she had had the previous morning, accepting his offer might be her only recourse.

She had been walking her usual route from the market to the ashram on her day off when she was stunned to see a neighbor from Jaipur—Mr. Hajid. A childhood acquaintance of her father, Mr. Hajid was a tire salesman, known for his sharp tongue. He appeared immersed in a noisy harangue with two Sikh taxi drivers. He had not seen her.

Or had he?

She had dropped her bag of oranges and toothpaste, rushing down the side streets back to the ashram, where for hours she lay trembling beneath her bedcovers. The fruitless promise of a safe life of anonymity in Vrindavan was gone, replaced by the familiar impulse to bolt. Even completely veiled, she would never feel safe to walk Krishna's city streets again. She would have to run again.

Unless…

"It's a gracious invitation, Sir…"

His playful frown nearly made her smile.

"For Sadhna's sake, you say?"

"I would be…less lonely as well," he said, and left the room.

For the rest of the afternoon, Triti was filled with both curiosity and fear. Part of her wanted to flee Vrindavan, yet she could not imagine leaving. *Not now.* From the very first time she had seen Samir, she realized that her teenage flirtations had not prepared her for the sensations she was feeling. This man made her nervous, yet when she was with him, she felt safe.

The next morning, Samir's voice rose near to a song as he and Sadhna escorted Triti toward the back of the main house.

"We're so grateful that you've decided to stay here, Minu," he said. "Aren't we, Sadhna?" The white-haired servant nodded obediently, but did not reply.

"I know you'll be comfortable here," he said, directing Triti into an opulent bedroom suite. Sadhna scurried past them to deposit fresh towels on the stately, four-poster bed. She pulled back the ceiling-high chintz drapes and lit scented candles on a mirrored dressing table beside the empty walk-in closet.

"Should you require anything…anything at all, Sadhna will see to it for you." Samir tilted his head toward Sadhna and she bustled from the room.

"Thank you again for letting me stay," said Triti, awed by the luxury surrounding her.

Careful not to step beyond the suite's threshold, Samir pointed as he spoke.

"The bath is to the right beyond those book cases. And through those double doors is a private garden. It's a pleasant place to sit…"

Just then a crash of thunder shook the room.

"…unless the rains chase you back inside!"

Samir and Triti laughed simultaneously and then laughed at that as well.

"Well, what do you think?" he asked.

Triti stepped further into the suite and was immediately struck by a life-size portrait of an Indian woman above a long, glass-topped vanity. Though she could not place her, Triti felt certain she had seen the woman's face before. Her expression in the painting was somber, and Triti thought she looked like an old soul confined in a young beauty.

"She's…lovely," said Triti, still trying to place the face.

"Yes, isn't she? I miss her," said Samir.

A knot of sickness seized Triti's stomach. Her thoughts flew unchecked. She felt faint. Was she but a jealous child? *Who was this woman?* She had to know.

"Is that your wife?"

"Married? Me? To Guru Mari?" Samir chuckled. "No, my dear…She is my guru. And my *boss*." He chuckled some more but stopped when he saw the seriousness in Triti's face. "Alas, there is no wife. Yet."

Triti felt the color return to her face.

"You see, I've been Guru Mari's assistant for nearly ten years, although I've known her for most of her life. She's quite famous—especially in Northern India, Europe, and America. I often accompany her on her speaking tours, though less frequently now that I work at her primary residence in New York. These were her living quarters whenever she visited Vrindavan. As you know from the correspondence you've read for me, this estate is one of her Foundation's properties. I'm very close to selling it."

He wasn't married after all.

Triti blushed and turned away from Samir.

"Well then, I shall leave you to unpack," he said, matter-of-factly. He hesitated then left, closing the suite door behind him.

In the stately white bathroom, Triti splashed cool water on her forehead. She let the newness of the moment settle over her, surprised at the measure of relief she felt. *Sadhna was pleasant enough.* There were locks on her doors. Most importantly, she felt safe with Samir. Still, she felt the need to distract herself. Fear could not get a foothold in her mind if she kept busy, she reasoned. She explored the grand suite, peering into every empty closet shelf and cupboard. She imagined what it would have been like to spend her childhood in such a place. She opened the garden doors to see that the rain had tapered to a light mist. The sweet smell of frangipani floated into the suite. When she turned and looked at Guru Mari's portrait again, she realized that she knew the face of the woman who stared back at her. Instantly she was filled with appreciation for the tile floors beneath her feet.

The guru had walked upon them.

Triti remembered hearing of Guru Mari while she was in grade school in Jaipur. The guru's accomplishments were spoken of with hushed reverence. The stories were told that as a girl barely ten years of age, Guru Mari had memorized all of the Vedic texts in Sanskrit, and could elaborate on profoundly sophisticated aspects of Hindu philosophy. It was widely reported that in her adolescence she had spent months in and out of yogic trances, frequently emerging from an altered consciousness with prophetic visions. She was best known for the simple elegance of her speeches, with her signature closing to her public talks for every person to remember that 'God is All in All.' Triti remembered wishing that she could one day meet her. How lucky was Samir, she thought, to spend his life in service to a living guru.

At the start of her fourth week living at the estate, Triti noticed that the daily volume of documents she opened and sorted had measurably declined.

Alone for hours, she dallied through her nominal administrative tasks, longing for more time with Samir. Only when he was near her did she feel uplifted. Early on in her stay, they had taken every meal together. They enjoyed mornings talking over chai and long evenings walking in the estate's gardens. She had listened intently as he related stories of his many travels, of his love for Renaissance art, and his penchant for exotic mustards. His deep, soothing voice always put her at ease. Although she was beginning to trust Samir, she was careful not to reveal anything about her true past. Instead, she conjured up vignettes of the make-believe Minu: winning a childhood game she had never played, finding a lost ring she had never owned. When he began taking all-day meetings in town with realtors and bankers, she rarely saw him for more than a few moments. To appease her, he often brought her misri rotis and silver bangles. But as her loneliness grew, her appetite declined. She began to worry about what she would do once the estate sale became final.

One morning, Samir came into the office dressed in one of his finest dress suits.

"I'll be in Delhi for several days, Miss Minu. My usual contact numbers are on my desk, should you need them. There are a few more letters for you to file...nothing too pressing, really. Please go through the library and select the South Asian and American classics for shipment to the U.S."

Before Triti could respond, the room shook violently. The lights blinked off, then on, then off again for good. Lightning lit the darkened garden in great flashes as the deafening downpour deluged beyond the windows.

The heavens are crying with me.

She didn't want him to leave.

Not now.

Samir shouted to be heard above the torrent.

"Tomorrow Sadhna will accompany you to the bazaar! Select the finest fabrics and have five saris made for Guru Mari. Let the tailor measure you for the blouses. You're nearly the same size as her."

He pulled a small camera from his travel bag and motioned for her to stand against the bare white wall.

"I want a couple pictures of you, Minu," he said, and snapped the shutter several times. "If they come out well, I'll have one framed in Delhi. As a keepsake."

Then he ducked under an umbrella and hurried out through the security gate to his waiting car and driver.

The three days without Samir seemed an eternity for Triti.

She missed the way he smiled at her, and the ease with which they talked together. She could listen to him for hours. Whenever he spoke to her of his native Srinagar, she could actually see the cerulean skies and endless fields of scarlet poppies. Mostly, she missed the feeling of calm he brought to her. When he was there, doting on her, her mind could be quiet. Now, she was virtually alone all day. Sadhna rarely came by the office, and then only to deliver what little mail there was and to bring her a pitcher of fresh water or chai. All day she heard the older woman's footsteps echoing loudly up and down the barren halls. Nearly all of the estate's rooms had been emptied, their contents wrapped and stowed into large shipping containers at the rear of the property. Triti consoled herself by focusing on the few projects that Samir had asked her to complete, but once she had sorted the library books and seen to it that the saris for Guru Mari had been tailored, she sat at her empty desk and worried about her future. What would she do once her work for Samir was finished? When he said he would frame one of her photos for a keepsake, she knew what that meant. Her time at the estate was ending. She had saved a bit of money, but where would she go? The prospect of having to start over again was overwhelming, so she shut her mind to it. All she would think about was Samir's return. He would come back and her world would make sense again.

On the second morning without Samir, Sadhna met her in the office and told her she would be out for the day. She had errands to run in town for Samir, but the cook would prepare her meals as usual. Triti listened as the putter of the tuk-tuk faded into the distance. For the first time, she felt completely alone on the estate. Thoughts of her family raked her heart. The more she tried to push them aside, the stronger they became. The ache soon became unbearable.

"Ma, Papaji, I miss you. Dilip, my brother…"

She gazed at the telephone on her desk.

If I could only hear their voices, just once more…

Hesitantly, she picked up the receiver. The dial tone was strong and clear. She tried to convince herself that it would be simple. Dial the number, wait until they answered, then hang up. It was just after breakfast. They would all be there together. If she was lucky, she might hear the others in the background. She would listen carefully. She would say nothing. She had practiced the exercise in her mind a thousand times before. Just to hear their voices once more.

Her fingers trembled as she hit the keys. *141264341.* She hesitated on the last digit.

She took a deep breath and pressed the number 1.

Click. Ring…ring…

A recorded male voice. "The number is no longer in service."

"That can't be!"

Her parents had had their landline since she and Dilip were two years old, the year her paternal grandfather passed away and they moved to their own apartment near Bani Park. It was the first number series she had ever memorized. She must have dialed incorrectly.

141264341. She would do it again, and this time she would not pause. She would dial straight through.

The recorded voice again.

141264341. Again.

"The number is no longer..."

NO!

She put the phone back in its charger and wept.

Predawn on the morning of Samir's return, Triti was asleep in her bed when a faint rap on her door awakened her.

"Yes, Sadhna?" she said in the dark.

The nightstand clock showed just before five a.m. The rapping continued. She pulled a dupatta around her sleeping tunic and went to the door.

Before her stood a breathless Samir, beaming. She smiled and stepped into the light of the hall lamps.

"Please Minu, forgive the intrusion, but I've just returned from Delhi and I have much to tell you."

"Actually, I was having difficulty sleeping," she said, trying to mask the joy in her voice. "The rain is SO loud; it's as if I'm lying beneath enormous drums."

"I've signed the papers! The estate is sold! The new owners arrive in two days," said Samir, excitedly.

Triti's smile faded.

"Minu, what is it?" he asked.

She blinked and shook her head; her thoughts scrambled as she tried to make sense of them.

"That's good news, indeed, Sir."

"Minu..."

She began mumbling to herself. "I'll move back to the ashram…wash out my clothes and dry them…look for a new job tomorrow…"

Samir reached out and held her shoulder.

"Minu, listen to me," he said, his voice deep and clear. "I took the liberty of calling Guru Mari to tell her how helpful you've been to me here. She confided that she needs someone well versed in English and Hindi to assist with the cataloguing of her speeches. The position is in her main library at the New York ashram where I work. She's authorized me to offer you the post."

"Work for Guru Mari?"

"Yes, if you want to."

"Me?"

Could it be true?

She wanted to cry, to laugh. She felt as if she had just been ushered into the grandest sweetshop in the world.

"Yes, Minu. Would you like to go to America?"

She saw it then, just as she had always envisioned: she was in the taxi, her carry bag at her feet, her sari tightly wrapped, her hair shining with oil, her kohl well-drawn, her English dictionary in her hand. She would be on her way, past the factories and fields to the airport, where people from all corners of India went with their dreams to chase; the magical place where she would glide through the hatch of a mighty, silver bird and fly toward her destiny. It was so incredibly, wonderfully perfect...

Reality snatched the dream from her mind.

"I'm sorry, Samir. I …cannot accept the offer," she said, her voice flattening.

"Why not, Minu? Why not?" His jubilance collapsed beneath the agony in her voice.

"I've no passport—no papers of any kind."

Too devastated to look at him, she hung her head and stepped back into her room.

"But Minu, wait…"

"I have nothing! I'm so sorry."

She muffled a sob with the back of her hand, and before he could say a word, she disappeared behind the suite's door.

Triti walked into the near-empty office two hours later, her face puffy from crying. A stack of large clothing boxes sat on her desk. A card with her name written by hand lay beside them. She guessed what the words would say. After all, she had received a dismissal before. She thought to reach for the card, but her arms hung lifelessly at her sides. The wounds on her hands and feet itched. In the garden, a steady drizzle of rain fell.

Samir entered the office, his shoes clicking loudly as he strode in with Sadhna at his heels. Triti turned and looked up at him, tight with sadness.

"Good morning, Minu," he said, positively buoyant.

Samir took one look at the desk and turned to his servant.

"No, Sadhna! Those don't belong here. Collect them and follow me."

The servant blanched, gathered up the boxes, and skittered out the door down the hall.

Samir turned to Triti.

"Minu, would you come with me, please?" he asked, his tone, though pleasant, not open to disagreement.

She followed him, growing more puzzled by the second. The piney scent of his aftershave wafted over her as the three of them wound their way through the estate's passages toward her suite. Once there, Samir opened her door and for the first time since her arrival, he stepped inside her suite. He took notice of her few belongings folded in a pile on the bed next to her traveling bag. Sadhna placed the stack of boxes on the mirrored vanity and left quickly.

"Save room for this, Minu," said Samir as he removed the top from the first box and lifted up a stunning turquoise sari sparkling with mirrored inlays.

"Samir? Guru Mari's clothes?"

"Yours. And these."

He opened the other four boxes of new saris.

"How much more packing time do you require?"

"Well, I...but..." Triti looked in disbelief from the clothes to Samir. "You said that the new estate owners arrive here in two days, and I'll be..."

"On a jet plane to the U. S.," he proclaimed, with a satisfied grin.

Samir held up a one-way ticket and a green passport folder. He handed them both to her.

Incredulous, Triti took the ticket and studied the words. *Depart: Delhi. Arrive: New York.*

Her hands began shaking. Then, she opened the passport. There was one of the snapshots Samir had taken of her before his car trip to Delhi. She read the name to the right of her picture—now official in bold typeface.

VANIK MINU.

"Finish packing later!" shouted Samir. "I'm famished, and we have some celebrating to do!"

Luggage-laden travelers mobbed the entrance to Delhi's Indira Gandhi Airport, pushing to join the snarled lines that stretched the length of the teeming terminal complex. Samir held Triti's right elbow and escorted her to the correct queue, savoring his last few minutes with her. Bawling babies and sharp crackles from the loud speakers greeted them as he negotiated the maze of queue partitions.

"I'm not permitted to go any further, I'm sorry. But I shall see you in a few days. Someone will pick you up at JFK. Look for a sign with your name. It will be fine, you'll see. I'll be there soon."

Then he kissed the top of her head and was gone.

"Samir?" She scanned the crowd, without luck.

"Miss?"

A squat security officer waved her toward one of half a dozen Customs checkpoint vestibules.

A sign with my name. She opened her passport and re-read the two words aloud.

"Minu Vanik. Minu Vanik…"

It became her mantra.

The female customs clerk held Triti's passport in her gloved hands and looked back and forth from Triti's face to the documents.

"You're aware that this Temporary Religious Worker Visa is valid for only six months?" asked the woman, a slight scolding in her voice.

"Hanji. Yes, Ma'am," said Triti, her nervousness clearly evident on her face.

The woman's demeanor softened. "First flight?"

Triti nodded.

The woman nodded back sympathetically and wielded a metal ink stamp on her passport with two heavy thumps.

"Follow the blue arrows to the gates. Good luck, dear."

Triti watched from her window seat as the jet accelerated down the runway and lifted off the ground. Her pulse raced and she grabbed the end of her armrest. The earthly lights of her beloved home and once-terrifying hell quickly dimmed into specks of nothing.

Somewhere, far below, were her parents.

And Dilip.

A spray of stars glittered off to left, the only witnesses to her tears.

EIGHT

Queens County
New York, U.S.
September 5, 2000

Triti remembered little of the flight to America. After changing planes in Paris, exhaustion claimed her and she slept nearly the rest of the trip, waking only to use the lavatory and nibble at the meal of rice and green peas. When her plane landed at JFK, she was in a sleep fog, but managed to collect all of her belongings and shuffle down the gangway. Her grogginess lifted as a Customs agent riffled through her bags and motioned her toward a pair of sliding glass doors.

She hesitated at the top of the escalator that led to the International Arrivals bay.

Durga Maa, what have I done?

Impatient fellow passengers streamed by her. She watched their heads disappear down the escalator and out of sight.

"Did you forget something, Miss?" asked a flight attendant as she rolled her travel case past her and onto the moving stairs. She looked up at Triti with an expression of polite concern.

Forget? Yes, she must.

At the periphery of the crowded baggage claim lobby, she saw a bearded young man holding a cardboard panel with the name VANIK printed in black marker. He stood amidst the dozens of other commercial drivers awaiting their passengers.

"Me! Me, I'm Vanik!" shouted Triti, waving for his attention as she dodged a convoy of luggage carts to reach him.

"Please follow me," said the man. "The car is parked across from the terminal."

The man reached for her new red suitcase—a last-minute gift from Samir.

"Ma'am… I'll take that for you."

The driver did not speak another word to her during the two-and-a-half-hour drive north to the Hudson Valley. Just as well, thought Triti. Still loopy with jetlag, she was grateful not to have to formulate coherent English responses. She traced the tips of her fingers over the wounds on her hands, feeling their unmistakable ridges and bumps. Hard scars were forming where open sores once were. Mala's neem paste had done its job. In a rush of sadness, she realized she could no longer remember what her hands looked like before the horrible time. Seeing that their overall redness was beginning to fade brought her some solace. She slid her long sleeve up and dug her thumbnail deep into the smooth flesh of her forearm.

A pinch of pain as she made another crescent-shaped dent in her healthy skin meant that she was not dreaming. She was awake, in the back of a town car. Beyond the smoked glass of the car windows, her new world was rushing by: narrow, traffic-choked arteries leading to endless concrete tunnels; trucks and cars barreling past towering granite buildings, and green, overhanging street signs. Triti kept watching as the new land of America whizzed by. Sometime later, the increasingly suburban tableau gave way to miles of emerald pastures that rolled out like velvet on either side of the road. Spotted horses frisked beneath willow trees. Black and white cows emerged from their red barns.

She tried to take it all in.

When at last they arrived at the ashram's imposing iron gates, the surrounding Catskills' hills shown ginger-gold in the late afternoon sun. Triti lowered her car window and drew in fresh breaths of country air. The sticky summer heat was on the wane, hinting at a cool evening to come.

America. Beautiful.

The driver handed a stack of paperwork to a uniformed security guard and the massive gates swung slowly open.

They drove along a single lane road that cut through a dense forest and turned a half-mile later into a large, circular driveway. Triti could see four separate buildings of differing sizes. The two largest—with facias of gray and white stones—were three stories tall and set back from the drive. The footpaths leading to them were lined with beds of white and baby pink flowers. The car stopped in front of a brick bungalow and the driver instructed her to leave her suitcase and go inside. Triti scooped up her satchel, thanked him, and got out of the car.

She felt strange to be standing on the ground again.

Am I still moving?

When she walked through the building's open door, she stopped short. On every wall were large framed photographs of Guru Mari: in a turtleneck and beret, in a sari, walking in a garden, even sitting on a golden throne. The guru's serene expression was identical in every photograph. Triti wondered how she managed to be so calm all the time.

A young Japanese woman stood behind a counter talking on a telephone. She held up her hand for Triti to wait.

"Name?" the woman asked dryly.

"I'm Minu…Vanik." Triti's voice cracked, and she cleared her throat.

"Passport?"

Triti flinched. She turned away slightly and reached beneath her sari blouse for her moneybag with her passport and handed it to the woman.

"I'm not sure what I'm supposed to do," said Triti, watching as the woman scribbled something on a guest roster beside the telephone and rummaged through a clear plastic bowl filled with keys.

"English? You have English." said the woman.

"Well, yes, I…"

"Follow," said the woman as she led Triti out of the bungalow's back door and down a short gravel path to a two-story dormitory.

"Women only," said the woman as she slipped her own key into the lock on the glass front door. Once inside the foyer, she handed Triti a set of two keys on a metal ring.

"Don't lose."

The dormitory's main hall was brightly lit and completely quiet. Triti wondered where the other women were. More pictures of Guru Mari hung on the walls, including replicas of her portrait in Vrindavan.

Vrindavan.

Her time there seemed so far in the past, even though it had only been two days since she left the estate to climb aboard the plane for America. Triti followed the Japanese woman who padded past a series of numbered doors to the end of the hallway.

"A14," said the woman as she unlocked the heavy door. "Bath across hall. Dinner start 6:15. You late, best to hurry."

With that, the woman turned and left.

Triti pushed open the room door and rolled her suitcase into the center of a small, stuffy cubicle. She crossed the beige tile floor in three steps, knelt on the sheet-less twin bed, and pushed open the double windows. Warm breezes floated in. She clamped her hand over her mouth to stifle a yawn and smelled wood smoke and curried sweat on her sleeve.

She ventured across the narrow hall to the communal shower, and beneath the spray of hot water, her tears finally came. Too tired to eat, she returned to her room where she found a set of fresh sheets. Drowsily, she made her bed and collapsed into a dreamless sleep.

The next morning, immaculate in a new green sari, Triti ate alone at one of the commissary's dining tables beneath an enormous portrait painting of Guru Mari. Conversations flowed around her, but they seemed muted, as if happening on the other side of a wall. The only familiar sound was the clang of her gold bangles each time she took a spoonful of oatmeal.

"Miss Vanik, this is for you."

Triti looked up to see her airport driver standing just behind her. He handed her a folded note.

"Oh? Thank you," she said, turning to him, but he was already walking in the direction of the kitchen.

She opened the note.

Welcome to Ankara Ashram. Your seva assignment, Library Assistant, will commence on September 8. Your supervisor, Samir Desai, will meet with you to discuss your schedule and duties. In Peace, A.A. Management.

Samir was coming in two days!

Triti gulped down the rest of her cereal and slipped out of the building to reread the letter just as an enthusiastic group of ashram visitors disembarked from a van near her. She followed the well-dressed men and women into the bookstore. Inside she was stunned to see rows and racks of souvenirs: tee shirts, lockets, magnets, candleholders—

all bearing Guru Mari's beneficent face. The store's walls were covered with her pictures. Paperback books of her writings and speeches crammed the shelves. Everywhere Triti looked, the guru's eyes stared back at her. Suddenly, she was overcome with gratitude to Samir, to Guru Mari, and to Krishna.

For the rest of the day, Triti wandered the ashram grounds. She passed clusters of devotees, but not one person acknowledged her. Men looked right through her. Women avoided her gaze. At dinner she summoned her courage and walked to a table where three Indian women chatted in Hindi. Just hearing the sound of her mother tongue gave some comfort. But the moment she sat, the women picked up their trays and moved to another table.

What have I done?

Humiliation staunched her hunger and she retreated to her room where she lay puzzling on her bed. She felt numb and groundless. She reminded herself that Samir would arrive soon, but when she tried to conjure his face in her mind, his image was blurry. She thought of her mother and father, and realized to her alarm that she could not recall their faces clearly, either. Even her brother Dilip's face seemed hazy.

The next morning, Triti took the top sheet from her bed and two apples from the commissary, stowed them in her satchel, and set out walking. She needed to find a private place away from the sounds of flushing toilets and showers. The gravel path she followed into the woods ended abruptly and she continued up a hilly rise through a grove of maple trees. The dark forest floor was dappled with sunlight that streamed through the leafy canopy. She slowed her stride to saunter from shady spot to shady spot. How much cooler it feels beneath the trees, she thought. Emerging from the forest, she looked out at a vast pasture of tall grass. Without hesitation, she sprinted to the middle of the field, spread out her sheet, and laid on her back with her face to the sun—just as she had done as a girl on visits to her uncle's mustard farm in Bilara.

Well-hidden amidst the grass, she let the warm rays consol her.

At least I have the sky.

Was this one bluer than her Jaipur sky?

She could not remember.

When Samir knocked on her dormitory door later that evening, Triti's melancholy evaporated.

He insisted that she join him for a proper tour of the grounds, and as they strolled together down the manicured paths, she felt surge upon surge of happiness. He asked how her stay at the ashram had been so far.

"Bahut acha," she said, shading the truth. All had not been 'very good'.

But now that he was with her, she felt generally relieved.

For his part, Samir could not stop grinning.

He walked Triti back to the women's dormitory entrance at the end of their visit. He told her she would begin her seva the next morning.

"So, get a proper rest tonight, my dear. I shall meet you in the library at the west end of the campus at 8:00 a.m."

"Thank you, Samir. I can't wait to begin."

"And there is much for you to do. Filing copies of speeches, collating conference handouts, and the like."

"Filing? But I hoped I would be..."

"A professional in California transcribes Guru Mari's most recent events. It's exacting work, and requires a great deal of experience, you see. But your work is very important, and I know you will do a wonderful job."

Triti tried to hide her disappointment with a thin smile. She knew that she should be grateful for any chance to serve the guru. She would work hard and do her very best.

"What is it, Minu?"

"Nothing, Samir. Really."

"Do you have any questions for me about the ashram?"

"I don't understand why people visit here while the guru is away."

"Well, they come for lots of reasons...to take seminars, to make offerings. Many who've heard her speak come to connect with her powerful essence. It's everywhere here."

"Will I get to meet her?" she asked.

"When she returns from her European tour later this month, perhaps," he said. "The celebrations go on for several days before she enters into silent retreat, so her private time will be very short," said Samir. "I cannot promise."

Every morning after breakfast, Triti walked alone from the commissary to the library. The new, two-level structure was only five minutes from the main campus, but with construction not yet completed, few visitors or residents made use of the facilities. The two resident devotees who performed their seva in the library's lending and periodicals section had yet to return her friendly hello.

She felt invisible.

In a windowless office at the rear of the silent library, she toiled straight through the hours of the sun, sorting and stapling copies of the guru's speeches and interviews that stood in meter-high stacks along the walls. Initially, the dullness of her routine had been a comfort. Knowing where she would be and what she would be doing allowed a portion of her mind to rest. But after the first few days, she found herself becoming restless. Her concentration continually drifted to the scars on her hands and feet that ached with the pain of deep healing. By the dinner hour, her eyes and neck were so tired that all she wanted to do was eat, shower, and crawl into bed.

Yet, her nightly rests were not to be.

Each night at precisely 11:15 p.m., a knock came on her dormitory door and she found Samir standing before her—handsome in his pressed shirt and tie—ready to escort her on a walk. Sometimes they strolled for more than an hour. Other times, he would ask her to join him amidst the asters and hydrangeas on the granite benches in the Vision

Garden, his favorite place at the ashram. In the flickering lights of tiki torches, and with only the marble likenesses of Lakshmi and Parvati in attendance, he talked to her about the world.

"Of course, there's been nothing to compare to my time at Cambridge," he said, as late summer moths swarmed the lantern on top of a nearby post. "Back then, I felt as if each day was a year long and I had a century of adventure to jam into it."

Listening to Samir speak about his education reminded Triti of the promise Rakesh's parents had made to her father upon their matching: after Rakesh finished medical school, it would be her turn to attend university. She had wanted to study literature and art. She had even fantasized about one day teaching.

Such long ago dreams.

"Was university difficult for you?" she asked. She had come to know that Samir would gladly elaborate about the numerous rigors of advanced academic study. And the more she could keep him talking, the less she had to lie about her past.

On the fifth consecutive night that Samir knocked on Triti's door, she opened it a crack and peered out into the hall.

"Samir," she said, barely able to keep her eyes open. "Aren't you tired?"

"It's a spectacular night, Minu. Come, let's walk down to the stream."

He saw that she was already in her sleeping clothes.

"I'll wait near the fountains while you change."

He turned and hurried down the hall and out into the night.

"Yes, Samir," she said, begrudgingly.

Annoyed, she tugged on her blouse and hastily wrapped her sari. The more she tried to convince herself to refuse Samir, she felt her resistance fade and give way to a mixture of attraction tinged with uncertainty. His desire for her was plain. She saw it in his eyes, and heard it in his voice. And yet, he had not even touched her hand.

She found him next to a concrete statue of Hanuman.

"You look beautiful, Minu."

"I look tired, Samir," correcting him.

"Nonsense," he said. "Come, let's see how high the water is running since yesterday's rains."

He led her down the eastern path toward a footbridge lit with hanging paper lanterns. When they reached the edge of the stream, Samir held out a small box to her.

"This is for you, dear Minu."

"What is it?" she asked, trying not to let her exhaustion color her words.

"Let's see," said Samir, moving closer to her.

Triti lifted the lid of the turquoise blue box and pulled aside a layer of cotton. Inside was a silver chain.

"I'll help you," he said, and he took the necklace from the box, stood behind her and placed it about her neck.

She touched the silver knot that hung at the center of the necklace and was about to speak when Samir placed his hands on her shoulders. Her words of thanks caught in her throat.

"Minu, you are very precious to me," he said. She could feel his breath on the back of her hair as he spoke.

"I know I haven't been very attentive since you arrived, and when Guru Mari returns next week, you'll see even less of me. But I promise you that once she leaves, you and I will have time together. Alone. You want that, don't you?"

Triti slid her fingers back and forth over the necklace. She wasn't sure what to do. She wanted to turn around and kiss Samir, but at the same time she felt she had to run away. Sensing her hesitation, he wrapped his arms around her and pulled her back against his chest. She felt lightheaded. She was about to speak again when voices came through the forest toward them. Security patrol lights flashed along the ground on the path.

"Go back to your room, Minu," he whispered.

The next morning, Triti awoke exhausted.

Despite her aborted night visit with Samir, thoughts of him kept her awake until dawn. In the bathroom mirror, she stared at the silver chain around her neck and wondered what she would do the next time Samir came for her. She took a shower, hoping that the water would refresh her, but her fatigue held on. She slumped on one of the bathroom's benches to dry herself. She struggled to slide on her cotton knee socks and long-sleeved blouse. Her stomach growled, and she hoped that she could stay awake long enough to eat. Just then, a middle-aged woman entered the bathroom. Triti had seen her several times in the hallway and at meals, but the woman always seemed to avoid her. She must be American, she thought, with her perfectly trimmed short hair and fancy wristwatch. As she had done before, the woman took one look at Triti and reversed her course. This time, Triti had had enough.

"Have I offended you?" Triti asked her sharply.

The woman stopped and turned back to look at Triti. She looked surprised.

"Listen, you seem like a nice person, but…"

"But what?" asked Triti. "Why won't you talk to me? Why won't *anyone* here talk to me?"

The woman shrugged her shoulders and shook her head.

"You really don't know why, do you?"

"Tell me."

The woman shook her head sadly.

"You belong to Samir."

"What?"

Triti's face reddened with embarrassment.

"I belong to no one. No one!" Triti rose to her feet and faced the woman.

The older woman stepped closer to her and dramatically lowered her voice to a whisper.

"That's what his other girls said, too."

"*What* are you talking about?" Triti demanded, angrily.

"Listen, it's none of my business. I've been here for eight years on and off, that's all I'm saying. Be careful."

The woman went into a toilet stall and closed the door behind her.

Dumbfounded, Triti grabbed her belongings and ran to her room. Her hands shook as she finished dressing. Wide awake and her appetite ruined, she went directly to the library. She removed Samir's necklace and dropped it into the empty pencil shelf of her desk drawer. With the faint clinking of the chain against the drawer's metal tray, the nausea in her stomach backed off, ever so slightly.

She left work early and went straight to her room.

That night, when Samir came to her door, she did not answer. After ten minutes of knocking and calling her name, he left.

The next day, the ashram's bucolic atmosphere exploded into near pandemonium at Guru Mari's return.

From dawn until midnight, the faithful arrived in raucous caravans of buses and cars from all over the country. Dormitories and guest residences filled to capacity. Empty fields doubled as parking areas. Sounds of group chanting and guitars echoed across the main campus. Resident ashram workers and guests alike endured long lines for food and toilets, but beneath the palpable tension was a shared excitement—the joyful expectation that the guru would soon be with them.

Triti could not share in the mass elation. She was haunted by what the old woman in the bathroom had said.

What if it was true that Samir has brought other girls to the ashram?

She wished she hadn't turned him away the night before. She needed to talk to him. She needed to hear from him that the rumor was false. When she finally got up the nerve to call his office from her work desk phone, a secretary stated that he was in a meeting. All day Triti waited, but Samir did not call back. That evening when she headed back to her room from the library, she passed by hundreds of people gathering for purification classes. They seemed so content. She looked on wistfully, wanting so much to be swept up with them.

That night Samir did not come to her door.

The next afternoon, Triti watched from the black-tarred roof of the library as devotees swarmed Guru Mari's motorcade with the fanatic adulation shown to rock stars. Multitudes lined the long driveway leading to the ashram's reception hall, cheering and waving white silk scarves, and screaming out her name.

What is her power?

Triti stood on the roof watching until her feet ached. Reluctantly, she made her way out of the library and through the crowds to go back to her room. She could barely hear herself think for the chanting and blasting of car horns. Afraid to make eye contact, she edged her way through the sweating, swarming crowds. Their unchecked jubilance frightened her. There was something about their zeal that felt almost sinister. She lay awake on her bed all night as the music, dancing, and fireworks raged until dawn.

Triti awoke before seven a.m. to an eerie silence. Looking out her window, she was astonished to see a single, silent trail of people inching down the main path toward the central garden. Every head was uniformly bowed, every mouth closed.

How strange.

She dressed quickly and stole along the unpaved foot trails to reach the rear of the central garden's grand dais. Hidden within a hedgerow of thick evergreens, Triti witnessed the spectacle of the guru's darshan reception. From her vantage point, she could make out only the back of the guru's head and the broad swag of her golden tunic. What she could clearly see were the ecstatic faces of the worshippers, coming one at a time to pranam before their living goddess. Each ten-second audience culminated in a touch or a word of blessing from the guru and seemed to be the fulfillment of every supplicant's greatest desire. Triti watched the procession for hours, utterly transfixed by the spectacle.

She wondered to herself what the guru would have said to her.

Guru Mari's return demanded Samir's round-the-clock service, and five nights passed without a visit to Triti. She had seen him hurrying into buildings—a glimpse here, a nod there—always with a stern look on his face. His nods of acknowledgment were enough for Triti, though. In truth, she was glad for the reprieve from his attentions. She stuffed cotton balls in her ears to dull the sounds of ashram activities outside her windows and rested in the relative luxury of consecutive nights of sleep.

That evening however, another force seemed to be at work. Visions of the guru played over in Triti's mind; her black hair shifting in waves against her shoulders, the kindness in her gestures. Eventually, she surrendered to her wakefulness, dressed with care, and stole alone from the quiet dormitory. The hot summer air had cooled. The fragrance of wild roses mingled with the tang of freshly-cut grass. Across the lawn and down the eastern terraced steps, she made her way to her favorite bench. She sat for several minutes, appreciating the chirping chorus of crickets. Eventually, she yawned. It was a good sign. She would go back to her room and give sleep another chance.

As Triti stood to leave, a figure appeared in front of her on the path. She recognized the guru instantly. Younger looking in person than in her photographs, Guru Mari was petite, almost fragile, her eyes enormous, black pearls. Not kind exactly, more life weary. Triti dropped to her knees to touch the guru's feet, a show of elder respect ingrained in her from childhood. Guru Mari reached down and guided her back to standing. Her expression was open and warm, not the practiced mask of official beneficence she commonly wore. She spoke softly to Triti.

"Namaskar, Minu. You *are* quite lovely. No wonder Samir's been hiding you."

"Dhanyavaad," said Triti, her cheeks burning.

"Stay focused on your tasks and you shall be rewarded."

Then the guru disappeared down the path as suddenly as she had come, her ocean blue dupatta floating on the night air behind her.

Triti rushed back to her room where she lay awake until morning, replaying the encounter over again and again in her mind.

Triti drifted through the next day. The ashram complex was still teeming with seminar participants, but the library was closed to the public and she was able to work without interruption. She was sleepy, and by midday she caught herself stapling all four corners of a two-page handout. She put her head down on her desk and closed her eyes to the pile of transcripts before her.

Just a few minutes were all she needed.

A slight rap on her office door eventually stirred her. She squinted at the clock on the wall.

2:45 p.m.? It couldn't be.

To her shock, she had slept for more than two hours.

When the soft knocking came once again, she moved quickly to the door and opened it.

"Hello, Minu."

Guru Mari stood before her, resplendent in a saffron sari and jeweled sandals.

"Mujhe afsos hai," said Triti as she bent low to touch Guru Mari's feet. The guru stopped her with a pat on her shoulder.

"Please, there is no need to apologize. I've come to see your progress."

Triti's heart pounded as she sprang to show Guru Mari the stacks of handouts, and the file drawers she had filled with copies of her past speeches. The guru nodded her approval.

"I'm grateful for your efforts, Minu. Please accept my thanks. Are you being well-treated here?"

"Yes, Ma'am," said Triti. "All is fine."

"Well, if not, let my private secretary know, directly. No need to trouble Samir, eh?"

Guru Mari reached into the large bag she carried and pulled out a package. She presented it to Triti.

"This color seems made for you. Open it."

Triti pulled apart the wrapping tissue and opened the box to find a cherry red sari lavishly embellished with sterling silver thread.

"I… don't know…"

The guru cupped Triti's chin in her hand.

"You'll wear it for me, Minu. I want to see the whole effect."

Guru Mari opened the door and stepped out into the hallway.

"I'm expected at darshan now. We will see each other again."

NINE

The visitor was persistent. Triti's only waking thought was to silence the knocking and return to her sleep. She yanked open her door, startled to see Samir looming above her, his fist cocked to bang again.

"Samir! It's *so* late, I was…"

"Yes, I see." He looked over her to her disheveled bed. His voice was stony, unapologetic.

"I really can't go walking now. I mean…I'm sorry, it's been a long day and I have to get up early for work in the morning. What time is it, anyway?"

The hall clock's nightglow hands showed 12:45 a.m.

"Can we not arrange a time tomorrow?" she pleaded. "Before dinner?"

"I have news that requires more privacy than we're afforded here."

His reply chilled her in spite of the night's mugginess. He gestured down the corridor to the exit door.

"Meet me outside in five minutes. And wear the new red sari."

What news could it be? And how did he know of my new red sari?

As she dressed hurriedly, she considered, yet again, everything that Samir had done for her. Walking with her rescuer was not too unreasonable a request to honor. Importantly, it would give her a chance to ask him about the rumors. With a tug, she pulled the long sleeves of her cotton blouse down to her knuckles. She blinked away her weariness and checked her reflection in her small hand mirror. The guru was right, she thought. The color *was* beautiful.

Outside the dormitory's main doors, Samir waited. He swept his eyes over her as she slipped from the building's side entrance and then briskly strode away, his movements stiff and unnatural.

She wanted him to slow down, but he pushed the pace and she struggled to keep up with him.

Who is this stranger?

"Samir?" she said, finally catching up to him. "What *is* it?"

She was out of breath.

He slowed his walk to a stop and stood with his back to her.

"The guru has granted you a private audience."

Triti's face brightened. Instantly, she was fully awake.

"Really? But *that's* wonderful! When will it happen?"

"Now."

Triti stopped walking.

"Now?"

"This way."

Anxious and unsure, Triti followed Samir beyond the pasture where she had taken refuge in during her early days at the ashram. They walked toward the stream that bisected the old growth forest at the center of the property. They crossed a narrow footbridge and followed a flagstone path that led to a sprawling mansion. A bright porch light illuminated the nearest entrance.

As they approached, two security guards sauntered by, staring at them.

"Get back to your post," snapped Samir, and the men instantly retreated to a guardhouse near the home's circular driveway. When he and Triti reached the heavy gabled door, he rapped the brass knocker twice, waited, and rapped once again. Then he turned and walked away without saying a word.

"Samir, wait. Please!"

He stopped and turned to look at her.

"Why are you angry with me?"

His shoulders sagged and he shook his head.

"Minu, you give me only joy."

His voice softened when he spoke her name.

"What have I done?"

He cleared his throat. "It's what I have done, Minu. What I *regret* doing."

"But I don't understand…"

"Just know that I care for you, Minu. I always will." He wrenched his eyes from her and walked slowly across the lawn.

She could not understand why Samir was so upset. The guru had asked to see her.

Why wasn't he happy for me?

She wanted to call out to him, but his knocks had summoned a male servant to the door. As she stepped into a candlelit foyer, she turned back to see Samir vanish into the dark woods. Her questions to him hung unanswered in the thick night air.

Inside the mansion, Triti trailed the servant down a labyrinth of corridors; from opulent antechambers to towering great rooms, the home was opulently decorated with furniture and art from around the world. Paintings, wall hangings, sculptures, and glassworks filled every hall and alcove. Triti was in awe. At last, the man pushed open a set of black double doors and directed her inside a cozy library. Gilded portraits of long-dead gurus hung on the paneled walls between bookshelves filled with leather-bound volumes in Hindi and Urdu and English. Two stained-glass lamps cast a carnival of sparkles on the ceiling. She sat for a moment on a plush velvet couch, but her nerves forced her to rise. As she pulled a yellowed copy of the Laws of Manu from the nearest shelf, she thought she heard a sound.

"That tome hasn't been touched in decades. To my mind, it's just as well."

Guru Mari stood within a hidden doorway on the far side of the room, an apparition in gold. She gestured to the velvet couch and Triti resumed her seat. Then her mind went blank.

What should I say?

Stunned by the significance of the moment, all she could think to do was to try to remember everything she was about to experience.

"I'm pleased you could join me," said the guru. Her elegant sari swished gently as she moved toward the sterling teacart beside the sofa.

Guru Mari handed Triti a cup of warm Darjeeling and set a plate of buttery lidos on the table before her. She took a seat next to Triti and sipped her own tea.

"Dhanyavaad," said Triti, trying her best to relax.

"Do you enjoy sweets?" asked Guru Mari, breaking a pastry in half. "I do."

"Za ruur. Yes, of course."

The two women sat quietly for several minutes, sipping their teas. A look of satisfaction crossed the guru's face. She was pleased to see the girl was wearing her gift.

"Time like this for me is rare," she said, sinking back into the cushions.

"Do you mean time away from all the people?" asked Triti.

"Yes, the people…"

Guru Mari looked directly at Triti over the rim of her cup. She saw the wonderment in the girl's eyes.

"It's ironic, really. With all the speaking I'm required to do, there is rarely the chance to just…talk."

"But surely, you and your friends…"

"Friends? The people closest to me are here because it is their seva to serve me. It has been this way as far back as I can recall. For my followers, I must always be the guru, the wise one. I must listen to the moanings of those living free lives."

Guru Mari sighed and continued to speak.

Triti listened.

How lonely she is, thought Triti. She suddenly was filled with compassion for the famous woman beside her. To her surprise, it seemed that they shared something in common after all: loneliness. The beautiful, vibrant young woman was choking on the taut reins of her goddess head. She presided over multitudes of adherents, who, sanctioned by her prolific teachings, experienced love and personal fulfillment that she herself had apparently never known.

"You help *so* many people," offered Triti.

"Help them? How?"

"Your words… Since I arrived, I've overheard many people talk of their epiphanies after darshan with you. Your teachings and advice have changed their lives."

"My dear Minu, each person must make her own decisions. As to offering good counsel, I have no right to advise anyone about life's mysteries. Love, especially. I've never come close to knowing that pure power. Have you?"

As Guru Mari leaned closer for an answer, Triti caught the scent of jasmine in her hair.

"Life has tested me," said Triti. "But I'm here now, and I am so grateful for your kindness…"

"Have you ever loved anyone?" the guru interrupted, carefully.

Triti was embarrassed to tell the truth. She could feel herself blushing.

"I'm…not sure. As a girl, I believed that love could be like romance in the movies. I don't know—tender, silly. I suppose I expected to be swept away…"

"Yes, go on, Minu."

"Well, it all became very confusing. I wasn't thinking seriously about boys, marriage, and the like, as so many of my friends were. I studied well in school, and passed all my exams at the top of my class. I wanted to attend university, find a good position, and help my parents. We're brought up as Indian women to believe that we must relinquish our worldly aspirations and worship our husbands. Yet my mother encouraged me to think for myself…"

"And to love whom you want to?"

"No. When the time came, *that* choice was made for me…"

Guru Mari frowned.

"Am I making you sad?" asked Triti.

"No, Minu, not sad. Decisions were made for me, too. And yet somehow, here we are."

Guru Mari stood and looked down at Triti.

"Do you still long to be swept away?"

Without waiting for a reply, the guru walked back to the secret door, turned, and beckoned to Triti.

"Come."

Entranced, Triti followed the guru into a grand bedroom with a vaulted timber ceiling and shining, black marble floors. Sprays of fresh gardenias bloomed atop mirrored bureaus. Sitar music played from modern speakers. Frankincense sap smoldered in elephant-shaped bowls. At the center of the room beneath a violet canopy stood a massive bed mounded with tasseled pillows.

Fit for a maharani.

"Welcome to my *oasis.*"

"It's…just as in a fairy tale," said Triti, stunned.

"I want you to see something," said Guru Mari as she walked toward a leather-bound steamer trunk at the foot of the bed.

"Open it," she said to Triti as she knelt on the edge of the bed.

Triti bent over and pulled the trunk's heavy lid up by its brass latch. She gasped at the sight of a dozen boxes of crystal perfume bottles twinkling in the candlelight.

"Pick any one you like," said Guru Mari.

Triti stared in wonder at the intricate carvings and jeweled embellishments on the diamond and pear-shaped bottles. There were vial stoppers shaped like dragonflies and Egyptian cats, and butterflies and pouncing tigers. Some of the bottles were tinier than her thumb, while others were as large as melons. They were frosted and stenciled, colored and clear. Carefully, Triti picked up several different bottles and held each one in front of the nearest candle, mesmerized by the refractions of light that glittered about the room.

"What's your favorite fragrance, Minu?"

"I'm not sure I have one. Roses are lovely," she said.

Guru Mari shook her head.

"No, you're far too young to wear rose scent. You need something fresh and exotic; like white ginger."

Triti could not decide between an emerald crane and a frosted lotus bottle. When she picked the lotus bottle, Guru Mari smiled.

"Perfect choice," said the guru. "I'll have it filled for you. That way whenever you smell your scent, you'll remember this time. Please…you may."

She patted the bed beside her.

Triti sat lightly on the edge of the mattress, barely touching the purple satin. She had only ever seen such beautiful fabric before in the guru's quarters in Vrindavan. Shyly, she nestled her stocking feet into the white flokati rug beneath them and turned the perfume bottle over in her hands.

"Thank you so much," said Triti. "It's magnificent."

"Like you, my dear," said Guru Mari.

The lights of a dozen candles flickered about the room. The guru ran her hand down the length of Triti's hair.

"You are *so* very special." She encircled her arms around Triti and pulled her close in an embrace.

Triti closed her eyes. The guru's cheek against hers felt as soft as velvet. Soft on soft. The sitars, the jasmine…it was all like a beautiful dream. How kind the guru was, she thought. She felt safe and cared for, and she wanted the moment to go on and on…

The guru's kiss on her neck sent a shiver down Triti's back. She caught her breath as the woman traced her fingers across her lips and smoothed her hands down her throat and along her collarbone. Triti's eyes widened as the guru cupped her breasts in her hands. Though her body trembled at the pleasure of the touch—so much of her wanting to know more of such things—in a millisecond Triti realized her predicament. The spark of desire that might have surged with a man's caress sputtered and died. But before she could protest, Guru Mari clasped Triti's head in her hands and kissed her fully on the mouth, her tongue dancing and prying to meet Triti's.

"No!" cried Triti as she pulled away from the guru's embrace.

Guru Mari clasped her wrist, but Triti twisted free and rose to her feet. She dropped the lotus bottle on the rug and fled through the hidden door.

The candles hissed in their metal cages.

The sitars droned on.

With the rare taste of rejection bitter on her lips, the guru crawled to the center of her great bed and stared up at the purple canopy.

Back in the dormitory, Triti packed her belongings and waited for a knock on her door.

TEN

"I *must* speak with Samir. Now!"

Triti stood in the center of her dorm room with her arms folded, immoveable. She glared at Guru Mari's day assistant, Rohit. Judging by his scowl, Triti guessed that he was deeply annoyed at his predawn assignment. She didn't care. She wanted answers.

"As I've already told you four times, Miss, Mr. Desai is not available. He's asked me to convey his good wishes to you."

Rohit grimaced at his wristwatch. "The bus is leaving in fifteen minutes. You must be on it. Guru Mari insists…"

"I'm not going *anywhere* until I speak with Samir," said Triti, raising her voice. She was filled with confusion; but each time she defied Rohit's command to pick up her suitcase, her defiance grew.

"Miss, you're going."

"Going where?" cried Triti. "I've only just arrived…"

Two men came to her door. One glimpse of their black jackets and earpieces and Triti recognized them as part of the ashram's security detail.

"Finally," said Rohit, gruffly.

The larger man spoke. "There a problem here?"

"She needs some *assistance* getting on the bus," said Rohit as he slid between the two men to get out of the room.

"Really?" said the larger man sarcastically. He grabbed Triti's suitcase and tossed it to the other guard, who disappeared with it down the hall. "Believe me, it'll be easier if you walk."

Triti gasped, realizing that the man meant to bodily remove her.

Why weren't they letting me talk to Samir? Does he even know what is happening to me?

She had to find out somehow.

"Fine, I'll go," she said.

She stormed out her door and down the hall with Rohit and the guard several paces behind her. Some of her hall mates had cracked open their doors to see what the riot was all about, but she kept her eyes on the exit. It was just after dawn, and beyond the door's glass window she could see people streaming toward the central garden for the morning chant. When she reached the exit door, she pushed it open and broke for the guest cottage near the stream where Samir stayed. She ran until she reached its front door. Lights were on in the cottage's living room.

"Samir! Samir!" Triti yelled, and banged her fist on the door.

Behind her came the sound of heavy footfalls. Triti turned and saw the guards hurrying toward the cottage. The woods behind the cottage were still dark. She could hide there until the guards left. She was about to run again when the door opened and Samir stood before her. He was dressed in a suit and had a travel bag on his shoulder.

"Is it true?" she blurted. "Are you sending me away?"

Just then the two guards rounded the back of the cottage and approached, but Samir waved them off.

"I'll handle this. Get my car," he growled. "Radio and tell them to hold the bus."

The men disappeared around the side of the cottage.

"Well? Tell me!" said Triti, still catching her breath from her sprint.

Samir stepped out of the cottage and closed the door behind him. Then he descended the porch stairs and turned to look back up at Triti.

"I'm not sending you away, Minu. The guru has decided it's time for you to leave the ashram."

"But what have I done to be punished this way?"

"This is not a punishment. The guru's command is extremely auspicious."

"I have nowhere to go! Samir, please!"

He walked quickly toward the road. Triti ran down the steps and overtook him. She held onto his arm, but he kept walking.

"Samir, what am I to do?" Triti scurried beside him, fighting to hold back her tears.

He heaved a heavy sigh and looked down at his feet.

"You'll find your way."

A black car with its lights on slowed to a stop in the middle of the road near them. Samir opened the back door and got in. He motioned for Triti to sit beside him.

"Come. I'll drop you at the bus," he said. His voice was emotionless. Triti looked at his face and knew that her pleas were in vain.

"No," she said, resignedly. "You *won't*."

She stepped up to the car and slammed his door shut. Then she gathered her sari drape and reset it over her shoulder.

"I'll walk."

ELEVEN

"The mystery of autumn," mused the thin man sitting alone at the back of the crowded charter bus.

He had boarded the Ankara Ashram express to Manhattan with uncharacteristic anxiousness. His intention: to put serious miles between himself and the guru. It would be fine to ride without a seatmate, he decided. He could use some quiet time to process what the hell had just happened to him. Most of the others leaving Ankara were wealthy, white devotees—urbanites with existential angst and disposable income—who would take full advantage of the two-hour road trip to recoup the considerable sleep they had lost as participants in the ashram's pricey weekend programs like "Higher Self Awareness" and "Meeting the Guru Within," followed by hours of standing on cattle-lines for the chance to kneel before the exalted Guru Mari.

He'd never bowed to anyone in all his thirty-nine years. Why start now?

He had gone to the ashram on the recommendation of a "friend", but given how badly the weekend turned out, he thought he might have to redefine that word. It was supposed to have been his chance to get out of the city, enjoy simple food, and breathe fresh air. As he climbed on the ashram bus in Manhattan for the free ride to the Hudson Valley, he thought he sniffed the stink of cult but stayed on board anyway, hoping that his radar was off. When, only a few miles north of Manhattan island, a promotional video of the guru's life and teachings began blasting from the bus's four, wide-screen televisions, he realized too late that he was indeed in for a two-day indoctrination party. The promised yoga sessions, meditation seminars, and afternoon nature walks were all geared to convince participants to sign up for the more advanced, two-week courses in Guru Mari-style spiritual awakening.

As soon as he had arrived at the ashram, he made several attempts to steal away from his assigned group. He just wanted to be alone to enjoy the shade of a maple tree, but the twenty-something woman designated as his "guide" managed to be always at his side. When he grilled her about the ashram's exorbitant class fees, she assured him that any questions he had would be answered once he received the guru's darshan. Perfect, he had thought. He would go right to the source. After waiting on line for three hours, his turn before the guru finally came. With steely contempt in her eyes, she ignored his questions and his hand shake, and turned her attention instead to the next worshipper. Just as he had thought. A scam.

His refusal to genuflect before the guru's bejeweled feet had set off silent alarms all over the ashram, and just after midnight two men in black uniforms entered his shared guest room to inform him that he was to pack immediately and wait by the security building for the city-bound morning shuttle. He had gladly complied, grateful to be heading back to civilization. Of course, he declined his free CD copy of "Guru-Guru: Take Home the Love." Fortunately for him, the only sounds on the bus that early were muffled middle-aged snores and the humming of an anorexic, teenage girl who clearly had memorized one of the worship chants.

Govinda jaya jaya…

At the front of the bus, unable to stand another minute of her seatmate's seismic flatulence, Triti rocketed to her feet at her seat directly behind the driver. She felt trapped in an endless nightmare. As the bus inched down the southbound highway in heavy Sunday traffic, she surveyed the sleeping passengers and spied the only other available seat in the rear.

"Ma'am, you need to sit down."

The driver shot her a condescending glance in his wide rearview mirror. She was about to resume her place when suddenly the stranger beside her let loose a loud explosion of gas so foul that the passengers seated behind him jolted awake and covered their noses.

Convinced, Triti hurtled down the aisle.

"May I take that place?" she asked the man with long legs in the back row.

"As you like," he said. He stood and let her sit next to the window.

"Thank you," she said, wearily.

The man extended his slender hand to her.

"My name's Brown…Jeremy Brown. But everyone calls me Jitter."

In the two hours it took them to return to New York City, Jitter Brown regaled Triti Sharma with hilarious stories of his youth in the Deep South—what he liked to call the 'anti-urban jungle.' At times, she could not stop laughing.

There is something special about this man.

"My people, as far back as we know, come from Kingstree, South Carolina," he said in his slight Southern accent drawl. "Black River swamp country. Mosquitoes there so big they've been known to carry off small dogs."

Triti's eyes widened at the thought.

"Backwoods, see. But not 'backwards'. Don't you go thinkin' that we Southern folks can't hold up our part in intellectual conversation, now. No, Ma'am. We *do* know how to read. Some of us. Hell, I made it through Ulysses three times. I openly admit to pausing on the 16th of June like all devoted Leopold Bloom fans. Point of fact, my high school English teacher pitched a fit when I wrote in my final essay that the novel's true hero was actually the reader. He just didn't appreciate Joyce, I reckon."

Jitter paused to look out the window and pointed at the deciduous trees lining the highway.

"In a few more weeks, those will all be Fruit Loops."

"I'm sorry?"

"The leaves…" he said. "In the fall…like the rainbow-colored cereal?"

Triti did not follow. She shook her head.

"Well," he said, "anyway…"

"What does this mean—Jitter?"

He smiled patiently and held his right hand flat out in front of him, palm down. Despite the ruts on the highway, his hand remained absolutely level.

"You see? Nothing shakes me. The name came from kids thinkin' that since I'm so steady, a handle like Jitter would balance me out. It always made people laugh—the folks who knew me anyway 'cause I never get the jitters. Ever. When I was eight, I had my official baptism in the Black River. Pastor Clarence dunked me good that day, with my whole family watching. When he finally pulled me back up to the surface, the first thing I saw was a brand-new brood of cottonmouth babies and their mama swimming by. Didn't even faze me. I wasn't bothering them. Why should they fuss with me?"

"Cottonmouth?" she asked.

"Snakes. Some people are sorely afraid of them."

Jitter looked out the window and then bent his head closer to Triti.

"I don't know about you, but I'm really glad to be away from the Ankara ashram."

"Why?" asked Triti. The moment the question left her mouth she realized she felt the very same way.

"Well, it seems that the 'lady in charge' expects certain protocols to be followed. And when I didn't, they wanted me out in a hurry."

"You met Guru Mari?"

"Yes, but let's just say I didn't make a great first impression. Are you bolting the brainwashing seminar early too?"

Triti's mouth went dry.

"I...used to work there."

"Wow, no kidding," said Jitter. "What happened? If you don't mind me asking?"

Triti closed her eyes and pulled her long sleeves down over her fingers. She was back in Guru Mari's bedroom with the candles, and the flowers, and the music...

"She told me to leave," said Triti.

"Really? Well, I wouldn't take it personally. She seems like a very difficult woman to please."

They sat quietly for a few minutes.

"Why did you leave your home in the south?" asked Triti.

Her own childhood seemed a universe away.

Jitter's expression darkened, but cleared as soon as he spoke.

"The day I told my mom I was leaving was...hell. It might matter to know that my Dad had died the year before. Tragic, really. Added twenty years to my mom's face. Overnight she went from looking like my gorgeous older sister to my great grandma. Anyway, Dad had left one of his favorite fishing rods down by the river and he went back to fetch it one beast of a summer evening. Still remember watching him walk down our driveway—plowman's muscles bulging under his white t-shirt. Thankfully, I got his back. And my mother's eyes. Anyway, comin' home later, Dad cut 'cross the farm fields of my mom's second cousin, Jacob; a habit we'd all come to over the years, taking a sure twenty minutes off the trek. Plain bad luck for my father that Jacob had spent most of that Saturday with Jack Daniels. Stone cold sober Jacob had never won a can shoot. But that night when he heard the rustling in his rutabaga rows, Jacob heaved his twelve gauge to his shoulder and let fly. Dad lasted less than a week at St. Michael's Hospital in Charleston."

"He died?"

"He did, indeed. And Jacob drank himself to death. Never got over it."

"I'm so sorry," said Triti.

"Yes, Ma'am. Me, too."

Triti didn't know what to say. Jitter interlaced his fingers and made a triangle with his two index fingers.

"Open the doors, see all the people," he whispered.

"I don't understand."

"Not important. Now, my mother, well, there's a special woman," said Jitter.

Triti squeezed her eyes shut and tried to replace Guru Mari's face in her mind with the image of her mother. But she could not remember what her mother looked like. When she opened her eyes, the guru disappeared.

"Yes, indeed," he said. "My mom realized years before I did that I wasn't destined to marry a letter-sweater girl and give her an armful of grandbabies. When I fell in love with my first boyfriend in high school, she knew I wouldn't find much acceptance in my hometown."

Triti realized what he was saying. She had known two boys in her neighborhood who ran away because they were in love with each other. Their families spread the rumor that they died of malaria, but she never believed that story.

"Did your mother disapprove?" she asked.

"Not hardly. Mom's a mostly generous soul. She wanted me to live and love, and she told me so. Still, the day I left her to go to college in New York City, the woman welled up in billows so dark she looked to rain all over me."

"Do you get to see her?"

"Only if I go home. She's not much for driving at her age, and she doesn't believe in flying on airplanes. No, Lord! And I quote Emma Rae Brown. 'If'n humans were meant to travel up in the air, the Lord would have given us wings.' I'll see her this Thanksgiving. Looking forward to her hugs, and her sweet potato pie."

As the charter bus entered upper Manhattan, Triti marveled at the ordered civility of the city. Taxis signaled and maneuvered for turning lane clearance, and bicyclists cruised two abreast down ribbons of asphalt. Well-dressed couples strolled behind sturdy baby prams as city buses lowered their bumpers to accommodate elderly riders.

There were no gangs of orphans running the streets, no herds of pigs snuffling through mountains of refuse. She saw not a single cow.

This is no Delhi.

When she stepped off the bus in front of the ashram center on Broadway, a resurgence of panic gripped Triti's chest. The buildings of glass and steel that seemed so tall as to scrape the sky seemed to close in around her. With no idea where she was going, or what she was going to do, she moved away from the other devotees and tried to calm her racing heart.

"Ahh, I love Sundays in the city," said Jitter to no one as he descended the bus's steps with his overnight bag in hand. He joined Triti near the curb.

"Such delicious Sunday quietude," he commented. "Usually, I get fresh bagels and the Times from the deli and spend the day lounging on my couch. Damn, it's nearly noon. Looks like I'll be getting a late start today."

Triti looked uptown and downtown trying to get her bearings.

"Want to share a cab?" asked Jitter.

He put two fingers in his mouth and whistled loudly. An on-duty yellow cab heading east on 81st Street pulled over in front of the ashram bus.

"Excellent!" said Jitter. Before he could reach the car, the farting man from the bus lunged in front of him, opened the rear passenger door, and squeezed his girth into the back seat.

"Well, I guess not that one," said Jitter, with a sigh. "Come. We'll have better luck if we walk up a block. Where are you heading?"

The first image that came to her was from a postcard she had sold at Ajit Singh's bookstore in Delhi—a high, arched ceiling above a sweeping, marble staircase.

"I'm going to meet…my cousin, at the Central Grand," she said, feigning confidence.

"I think you mean Grand Central Station," said Jitter.

"Yes, that sounds right," said Triti, embarrassed.

Her left hand ached from gripping the handle of her suitcase, but she held onto it with all her strength.

"I'm heading to the Lower East Side. I can drop you first."

"I…no, thank you," said Triti. "I can walk. Would you just tell me the way?"

"It's over three miles!" said Jitter with a laugh. "You could take a train, though. There's a downtown Number 1 stop up at 86th Street. You'll need to get off at Times Square and switch to the Shuttle. But the trains run infrequently on the weekends. Might wait a long time."

"How much do I have to pay?" she asked, hoping she would remember how to differentiate the denominations of American dollars she had tucked inside her blouse.

"Only two bucks," said Jitter, as he whistled down another yellow cab.

Triti slipped her cloth purse from its place beneath her sari and took out several American bills.

"That one," said Jitter, pointing to a one-dollar bill in her hand. "You need two of those."

He opened the taxi's passenger door and stepped down off the curb. Then he turned to Triti once more.

She stared into his face. The gentleness she saw made her eyes well up with tears.

"Oh, honey, I understand," said Jitter. "It's a big city. Climb in and we'll get you to your cousin."

Triti handed Jitter her suitcase and got into the cab beside him. He struck up a friendly conversation with the cabbie, but Triti barely heard a word the two men said. Her thoughts seemed hopelessly tangled in her head and no matter which string she pulled, the knot of confusion kept tightening. She wished that she hadn't lied to Jitter about where she was going. She had a million questions to ask him about New York, about America. He seemed like a very nice man, but after Ajit, Samir, and Guru Mari, she could no longer trust her impressions of people. Jitter was a stranger, and she should be afraid of him. It was better, she thought, to be afraid. Fear was something she knew how to use. It kept her alert. As she watched countless gray buildings stream by, she hoped there was somewhere to sit in the Grand Central place. If only she could be still for a while and think, she could come up with a plan.

Ten minutes later, the cab slowed to a stop at the curb in front of the train terminal's 42nd Street entrance.

"Here we are," said Jitter.

Triti looked out at a row of dark wood and glass doors that swung opened and closed as people entered and exited the massive building. What would happen to her once she went through those doors? She unzipped her moneybag and tried to hand Jitter a ten-dollar bill.

"No, this was on my way anyhow," said Jitter. "You know, I never asked your name," he said, handing her suitcase to her.

"I'm Minu."

"Well, here, Minu…before you leave."

Jitter scribbled on the back of the ashram's glossy brochure he had in his backpack.

"This is my number. You know, just in case your cousin doesn't show. Still have the 212 area code. And *that's* my address below. Can you make out my hieroglyphics?"

She took the brochure and read out loud.

"156 26th Street, #5J. Thank you, Mr. Brown."

"Jitter, just Jitter. Everything will be ok," he said, smiling at her. "I can feel it."

Triti turned away and did not watch the taxi pull back out into traffic. Instead, she wheeled her suitcase to the nearest terminal door and pushed it open. Without hesitating she made her way down the steep, marble entrance ramp that led into the cavernous main concourse. She felt a sense of lightness coming over her. Her thoughts began to slow down. Her chest relaxed. She took notice of the people moving around her—parents with toddlers, young couples, lone travelers. White people, black people, brown and yellow, too. Old and young, small and large. They were beautiful to her. They moved with purpose; all of them—on their way to somewhere special.

Like me.

For the next few hours, Triti explored the dozens of retail storefronts on the busy main concourse level. The new sights, sounds, and smells drew her into pastry shops and cafes, music stores and jewelry boutiques. She sipped Jamaican Blue Mountain coffee and ate powdered sugar donuts. She tried on green denim jackets, and sampled cubes of smoked salmon. After an hour of flipping through international fashion magazines at the central newsstand, it occurred to her to ask one of the clerks if the store had maps of New York City for sale. She chose a thick foldout map of Manhattan and happily paid three American dollars for it. She wanted a place to study the map, but her feet hurt and she knew that they needed tending. She noticed a busy pharmacy where she purchased gauze, tape, and two bottles of water. Out on the concourse again, Triti leaned against a wall and drank some of the water. It was ice cold, and within moments a searing headache unsteadied her. The rush of people around her suddenly felt overwhelming. All she wanted was a place to clean and rewrap her feet, and to rest for a bit.

"Miss, you gotta a dollar I can borrow?"

Triti lifted her chin off her chest and blinked her eyes at the shabby, young man standing before her.

"Hey, Alex! Leave that nice lady alone."

A uniformed police officer sidled over to the boy; his voice shaded with patience.

"Only Amtrak ticket holders are allowed to be in here. You know the drill. Let's go, buddy. Move it on out."

The teenage beggar hiked up his dirty cargo pants above his plaid underwear and shuffled out of the waiting room.

"Sorry about that, Ma'am."

The officer focused his gaze on Triti who sat primly on the long, wooden bench, her bag on her lap and her suitcase pulled tightly against her legs.

"Catching the late one to Montreal?"

Before she could respond, the officer's radio squawked on his belt. He pulled it from its leather holster and turned toward the double glass exit doors to answer it.

"Yes, Lieutenant?"

Triti flinched as the radio's sharp crackles ricocheted off the waiting room walls.

"Again?" complained the officer. "Second time tonight that alarm's gone off. I'm one minute ETA."

Triti blinked and he was gone.

Worried that the officer might return and demand to see her non-existent ticket, Triti took the nearest escalator down to the food concourse and made her way to the ladies' bathroom. It was nearly midnight. She rolled her suitcase straight past the sink where she had cleaned her feet earlier and found an empty corner stall. Exhausted, she slid the metal bolt on the door and slumped onto the hard toilet seat. She slid her leather shoes from her swollen feet. Then she unfolded the city map and tried her best to understand up from down. There was N for north, and most of the streets were numbered consecutively. She started to read down a list of New York hotels printed on the back of the map, but she never made it past The Grand Hyatt listing. Despite the racket of toilets flushing and hand dryers blowing, she managed to fall asleep.

No time

So jaa…

"I'm afraid, my brother."

Sister! Where have you gone? Do you not hear me calling?

"Dilip, can you feel me?"

Everything is wrong, dearest Triti.

"I'm alive! You must make Papa-ji and Ma believe this."

Our parents have abandoned sleep. They refuse to eat. I'm left to scream at the wind.

"I'm alone."

Where are you?

"I'm frightened…can you come, Dilip, as you always have?"

Wherever you are, darling sister, remember, YOU are the strong one.

TWELVE

A booming voice on a loud speaker rousted Triti in her stall at 1:15 a.m.

"Grand Central Terminal will close in fifteen minutes. Please make your way to the exit doors immediately. The station will reopen at 5:30 a.m."

Triti rubbed her eyes and forced her shoes back on her tender feet. She hurried from the bathroom with her suitcase in tow. The escalators had been turned off, so she climbed them to reach the main Terminal level. As she stepped off the final step, she was nearly mowed down by two red-faced businessmen who raced across the concourse toward a distant track, their suit jackets flapping over their arms. The entire station bustled with activity as patrolmen in blue herded confused people toward the doors on 42nd Street. Most were angry commuters who had narrowly missed Metro North's last trains to Poughkeepsie and New Haven.

"You ladies should have said no to that last round of Mojitos!"

A policeman chided a trio of co-eds who teetered precariously in high heels and too-tight party dresses.

"Taxis are waiting for you upstairs," he said, laughing. "Hope you Cinderellas got enough cash!"

Another officer motioned Triti toward the exit. She followed two women in tight pencil skirts and sneakers as they shuffled up the steep ramp, past the shuttered pharmacy and the darkened bookstore. Once she reached the exit doors, she clenched her jaw and stepped out into the metropolis.

By the time Triti hobbled into the Bowerfield Hotel's empty lobby at three a.m. she had already met with failure at seven other reception desks. She crossed her fingers and approached a man with a red tie behind the computer console.

"Hello, how may I help you?"

The concierge pulled his eyes from the bright screen to address her.

She explained, yet again, that she needed a room for a few nights—a small room—just until she could find a place to stay.

Don't let it be more than $32.

"Our standard room is 200."

The man spoke the number almost apologetically, then leaned over the counter and whispered to her.

"But, if you need a bargain, try the Silvio on 10th. You'll pay around $130, but hey, you didn't hear it from me."

Hungry and discouraged, she walked for several more blocks until she found a 24-hour pizza shop. Out front was a rusted metal bench where she rested her aching feet while she gobbled a fresh, hot slice. The spicy, cheesy taste was delicious; so different from the flavors she had grown up with in Rajasthan. Around her, people were everywhere: walking, running, talking, smoking. Not a single person seemed to notice her. She felt invisible, just as she had at the ashram.

Maybe it is better this way.

Olive oil ran down her chin and she felt around in her satchel for a tissue. Instead, she pulled out the ashram brochure with Jitter Brown's name on it.

156 26th Street.

No. She would do this on her own. She remembered two construction men in Grand Central discussing how Penn Station was a good spot if one needed to rest for the night. Maybe it wouldn't cost her too much to stay there. Perhaps the pizza man knew of it. She would ask him.

Triti walked back into the pizza store and waited while a man in tight shorts paid for his slice and left.

"Excuse me," she said to the baker. "How do I get to Penn Station?"

The man was swirling a ladle of tomato sauce on a flat round of dough behind the counter. He looked past her to something outside on the street.

"Did you leave a black bag out front?"

Triti gasped and realized that she hadn't brought her suitcase inside with her. She ran out of the store in time to see a man sprinting down the avenue with her case under his arm. She started to chase him, but her sore feet wouldn't let her.

Gone.

All of her clothes, the neem paste from Mala, her water bottles, the bandages, and the poetry book had been in that bag. Thankfully, she still had her satchel. Her gold bangles were on her wrists, and her money and passport were safe beneath her sari blouse.

She looked up at the nearest street sign.

53rd Street.

She walked a block.

54th Street.

She turned around, retraced her steps, and kept walking.

Only 28 more blocks to go.

THIRTEEN

When Jitter rounded the corner of Lexington Avenue at seven a.m., he was still sweating from his early morning workout at the Y. He reached the front of his apartment building and stopped, folding his arms on his chest. Sitting scrunched at the top of the concrete steps was the girl from the ashram bus.

"Minu!" he called, delighted to see her again.

He bounded up the steps as Triti bolted awake.

"An early riser, like me, eh? Why didn't you call?"

"Jitter," she said, trying to make her mouth work. "It was too late. Or too early…"

"You ok? Wait, don't answer that. Let's get you some eats."

"As you can see, my kitchen is painfully underutilized," said Jitter as Triti followed him into the gangway alcove.

163

"I'm not much of a cook. Usually grab meals on the run."

Over a breakfast of toast with peach jam and apple slices, Triti told Jitter all that had happened to her since she left him in the taxicab. It felt good to talk to him. His gentle manner made her feel comfortable, just as it had during the bus trip. He listened well, and he seemed to appreciate her difficult predicament.

Triti fell quiet as a sleek, orange tabby cat appeared in the kitchen. It stretched and proceeded to rub against her legs.

"Zen's good company," said Jitter. "Thanks to him, I've never seen a rat here."

Jitter showed Triti his living room and laughed at the sight of his National Geographic and Scientific American magazines strewn across the length of his coffee table.

"Having a moment, were you, Zenny?"

He picked up the cat and nuzzled him.

Jitter led Triti to a large bedroom and motioned for her to enter. Triti walked across the room and leaned into the corner. The shifting clouds beyond the apartment windows dispersed long enough for sunlight to splash across the hardwood floor.

"Southern exposure. I was lucky," said Jitter. "A few years ago, I found this place. Bought it for a country song with the money from Dad's insurance—needed quite a bit of TLC. I tried a couple different roommates, but they just didn't work out."

Triti noticed the immaculate state of the room. As with the rest of the apartment, every surface glistened. She gazed at a sepia lithograph hanging above the sheetless queen bed.

"The Brooklyn Bridge," said Jitter, answering her question before she could ask it.

"Is it a *real* place?"

"Indeed. I can take you there, if you'd like."

Triti tried to cover a yawn with her hand.

"So, you'll be needing a place," said Jitter.

"Yes, but I don't know where to look."

"Well, *this* room's been vacant for over three months now."

"It's just that…"

"You do like it, don't you?" he asked, trying to read her face.

"Of course," said Triti, "but I could never afford it."

"Well, you would sure help me out if you rented it. That way, I wouldn't have to put a roommate ad in the Voice again and deal with all of the crazies who reply. If you can pay, say…$300 per month, it's yours. Stay tonight, and let me know what you think tomorrow."

Half an hour later, Jitter rushed about his apartment.

"Sorry I can't spend the day with you, Minu," he said, grabbing his wallet and backpack off the credenza in the front hallway. "The Dean counts on me to have the Admissions office under control when she arrives. And she's an early bird!"

"I understand," said Triti as she stood near the apartment door. Her back ached and her feet throbbed, but she felt steadier than she had in months.

Jitter showed her how to work the apartment locks and handed her his extra set of keys. "Just make sure you turn all three each time you leave," he said, and stepped out of the door.

"You *trust* me?" she asked, thinking of Ajit.

"Why wouldn't I?" he asked. "Listen, I've spent more time with you in the past two days than I ever did with any other potential roommate. Frankly, the mere fact that the guru dismissed us both is a good enough recommendation for me. Sounds weird, maybe, but that's just how I feel."

"Thank you, Jitter."

"Hi, Mrs. Wasiliwitz," said Jitter to an elderly woman shuffling past them in hall. Her short, gray hair was matted on one side and she wore a ragged cardigan sweater.

"Good morning, Mr. Brown," she cackled brightly.

Jitter turned back to Triti.

"She's a dear," he said. "Lives at the end of the hall. Lost her husband of 61 years last spring. I pick up milk and eggs for her when her bursitis acts up. Oh! That reminds me. Check the blue tin in the freezer. Should be a few bucks there for groceries. The food mart on 3rd has decent produce. I'll be home around six, and you can always reach me at school. My work number's on the fridge. Make yourself comfortable, Minu," he said with a wink, and headed for the elevator.

Triti closed and locked the door and padded back into her bedroom. Her head swam as she tried to prioritize her needs. Her wounds required tending, but she would have to shower first. She was exhausted, but the bed had to be made. Conflicted, she wandered into the living room. The black leather couch tempted her and she surrendered to its thick cushions. A moment later, Zen crawled out from under the television console and jumped up beside her.

"You are a friendly one, aren't you?" she said as she stroked his soft fur. The cat settled himself against her hip, closed his eyes, and began to purr loudly.

Fighting the temptation to sleep, she listened to the hum of the city beyond the apartment windows. All she could think was that she needed to find a job. She must take her time and ready herself properly. Careful not to disturb Zen, she rose and began her preparations. She rinsed clean her only sari in the tub and pressed it dry atop the kitchen table with a hand iron she found in the hall closet. Then she showered and rubbed her scars with olive oil from the kitchen. With her kohl pencil she drew a single black line just above her lashes. Then she smeared a dab of petroleum jelly across her lips. Finally, she combed her hair into a low bun and studied her look in the mirror.

Something's not right.

She pulled her blouse sleeves down to her fingertips and slid off all but a single gold bangle from her wrist.

"Simple is good."

Remembering what Jitter had taught her, she locked all three locks on the apartment door, put the keys in her satchel, and took the elevator one flight down to the lobby. Out on the street, she paused to relish the cool air on her face. Two yellow cabs drove by with their red off-duty signs lit. The second car slowed, reversed, and pulled up to the curb in front of her.

"You heading uptown?" asked the driver as he tossed his half-smoked cigarette out of the car window.

"I'm not sure. Where is the best book store in New York?"

"Dunno, lady. There's a big one near Lincoln Center…"

"How much will it cost to get there?" she asked.

"Jeez, depends on cross-town traffic. Probably be twelve dollars on the meter."

"Twelve dollars…"

Triti didn't need to open her purse. She had counted and recounted her remaining American dollars hundreds of times the night before.

I'll just have to take a bus back.

"Yes, I want to go there, please."

Fifteen minutes later, Triti stood before the Regency Bookstore on Columbus Avenue. She stared at the revolving door that spun continuously as patrons came and went. With all the confidence she could summon, Triti strode into the store.

Instantly, a feeling of peace settled over her—the same kind she had experienced in her school library in Jaipur, and in Ajit's store. Once again in the company of books, her nervousness evaporated. The store was pure magic to her: books of every variety, smart displays of the newest releases, and deep racks of magazines. She wandered the aisles, stopping to page through cookbooks from Tuscany and the best-selling fiction titles. Baroque music played in the background. Though a new sound, it was pleasing to her ears. She rode the escalator to the second floor and explored the tables of discounted books that lined the central aisle. She began to notice a definite order to the place. Someone very clever had placed certain books at the end of aisles or on individual stands to draw shoppers' attention to an entire section. "Everybody Gets Blue" sent her eyes to the ocean-colored jacket of "Weird Waters": a thick paperback about Postpartum Depression in the Psychology section.

What could that be?

In the comedy aisle she picked up a Larson cartoon calendar and shared a laugh with a woman who had stopped to read the captions over her shoulder. The human contact brought her suddenly back into the purpose of her visit. She followed the pink wall signs that led to the ladies' room, and after checking her hair and straightening her sari, decided it was time. She rode the escalator to the first floor and wound her way past the standup cardboard advertisements for Frieda Cahlo coffee table books toward the Help Desk.

"Excuse me," Triti addressed the large man behind the desk. She read his blue and gold nametag silently. Bob T. Manager Regency Books. "Is this where I may apply for employment?"

Bob nodded at her.

"You're in the right place, but I'm afraid we have nothing available full-time right now. None of our stores do. If you want to fill out an application, we can keep it on file."

He handed her a brown clipboard with a form and a pen. "Or try back before Thanksgiving when we hire for the holidays." His tone was matter-of-fact.

Crestfallen, Triti took the clipboard and moved to end of the desk as another customer stepped forward to ask for assistance in finding a book. She scanned the application and filled in as many blanks as she could. She used Jitter's address and telephone number. At the bottom she printed her new name, neatly. She was about to hand in the form when she saw a box in upper right corner with two possible options to check. FULL-TIME/ PART-TIME. The manager had said there were no full-time positions, but what about part-time?

Once Bob T. was alone again at the desk, Triti stepped back before him.

"Oh, I see you finished," he said, reaching for her clipboard.

"Yes, Sir. And I was wondering if you have a part-time position open?"

He read her application.

"You have bookstore experience. That's good."

"I also worked in a library. And an office."

"Well, I have one shift open," he said. "But it's only 25 hours per week."

Triti calculated quickly in her mind. If she stayed with Jitter, her rent would be $300. There would be the cost of food and clothing, of course. She could not very well wear the same sari every day.

"I need $500 dollars every month, Sir. Will I be able to earn that much here?"

"You'd start at ten dollars an hour," said Bob as he read over her form. "So, after taxes I guess you can plan on taking home 800 a month…there abouts."

"800 US dollars?"

Triti gasped at the number. That was more than 36,000 rupees. She had never seen that much money in her life, and she simply couldn't imagine it.

"Oh, here," said Bob, pointing to the bottom of her application. "You forgot to fill in your Social."

Triti looked down at where his finger landed on the form.

"I… don't have one of those…yet. But here is my visa."

She croaked out the answer, her pulse speeding as she pulled her passport from her bag.

Bob glanced at the document stamps, took another long look at her, and puffed up his cheeks like a blowfish.

"Can you work late shifts, six p.m. till midnight?" he asked.

"Of course."

"Well, in that case, you can start next Monday. The first two weeks you'll be on probation though, so don't be late."

"No, I won't be. Thank you, Sir, thank you! So much."

Carl, the cafe supervisor, appeared at the desk complaining about a defective register code. Triti waved to Bob as he and Carl sauntered off. Then she turned to gaze at the store.

Her store.

Ecstatic, she floated down the aisles. She tarried, straightening a book here, a magazine there. She picked up a gum wrapper from the carpet and dropped it in a waste bin. She noticed two women with employee tags chatting in the CD section. *Soon, I'll have my own nametag.*

MINU V. Regency Books.

Oh, great Krishna! She wanted to dance and clap and sing. *Jitter!*

She had to tell him her wonderful, wonderful news. Suddenly she realized that she felt very hungry. Her mouth watered at the thought of saag paneer and hot naan bread. She would take a bus back to the apartment and find a store that sold spinach and coriander and green chilies.

As she headed down the self-help aisle toward the front exit, Triti saw a young girl tugging on a woman's pant leg.

"Mommy! I need to go..." whined the girl. She tucked her other pudgy hand between her legs and hopped in place.

The woman closed a copy of "No Sweat Happiness" and rolled her eyes.

"I have no idea where the shi-shi is," said the woman, sternly. "Can't you wait until we get home?"

The girl shook her head frantically, her brown pigtails flying.

Triti stepped toward the pair and pointed to the store's upper mezzanine.

"Ma'am, the rest room is just to the left at the top."

"Wow, thanks," said the woman who headed off in the direction of the escalator with her daughter in tow.

That evening Triti recounted the story of her job coup to a jubilant Jitter as they finished Triti's delicious Indian meal.

"Brilliant, my dear! Let's celebrate. My treat!"

He insisted that they mark the occasion with a trip to his favorite ice cream shop, which was just a block away.

Minutes later, Triti swiveled on a stool at Delish's busy counter and dipped a blue plastic spoon into her pistachio fudge sundae. Despite her day's sweet success, she felt sad that she could not share her news with her mother. She had confided everything to her, whether it was the triumph of a successful exam or a problem with a girlfriend. Her mother had always been there for her.

Not anymore.

Outside the window, a couple held hands and kissed on the brightly lit avenue. People walked and shopped. There were no burned, teenage girls running for their lives. She was in New York: in civilization. Not like her desert homeland, where the archaic laws of her culture betrayed her. She knew in that moment that she could never return to Rajasthan. Somehow, she would have to find a way to accept her life as it was now. Her new normal.

Jitter took a long sip of his chocolate milkshake and stared at her reflection in the mirrored wall across from them. When he saw her shoulders slump, he waved to the man behind the counter for the check.

"You must be tired, Minu," he said softly to her. "Let's get you back."

Later that night, Triti begged Krishna to watch over her loved ones.

Ma, Papa-ji, Dilip…

Some things were better left to the gods.

FOURTEEN

"Minu, you're next on break."

Triti had nearly finished shelving a full cart of returned books in Regency's popular graphic novel aisle when Jean, the floor supervisor and new employee trainer, came up beside her. It was her first night on the job, and even though there was a great deal to learn, she was thrilled to be working at the store. She thought of how much easier it was to concentrate since the dinner crowds had thinned.

"It's ok, Jean. I can wait until nine to eat."

"Fine, I'll let Thea break now. Her knees have been bothering her. She'll appreciate the chance to sit."

Triti slid the last of the books into its spot on the lowest shelf.

"I guess that's all of them."

"Wow, that was fast!" said Jean, with an approving smile. "Come try the register with me."

Triti followed Jean to the row of checkout stations at the front of the store. Jean unlocked a vacant register and began teaching Triti the intricacies of the computer. Even though it was a vastly more modern machine than the one she had used in Ajit's shop, Triti recognized the basic key commands. Within twenty minutes, she had mastered the system.

"You're really making my job easy, Minu," said Jean. "I'll let you try a few purchases after break."

Twenty minutes later, as she unpacked a box of bridal magazines, Triti looked at the pale brides on the covers and wondered why American women didn't wear red on their special day. White, after all, was for widows. Suddenly, she felt flushed. Her stomach tightened. She was about to dash to the bathroom when she felt a tap on her shoulder.

"Minu, I'm Thea. I just wanted to say thank you for switching your break time. It was sweet of you."

"Oh, I didn't mind."

She looked at the petite woman in a silver blouse standing before her.

No woman should wear gray. It makes us look old.

"I'm the welcoming committee, a little late," said Thea. "Let me show you around."

Thea moved slowly but with confidence up and down the aisles of the store, pointing out different authors and displays that she particularly liked. Some of the names were familiar: Hemingway; Rushdie; Poe, Walker. Others, like Vonnegut and Hitchens, were new. Then Thea took her into the 'employees only' hallway where the time clock and lockers were. There she introduced her to Kirby, Regency's muscular maintenance man. He tipped the brim of his Mets baseball cap and hefted an enormous bag of rubbish with the other hand.

"He doubles as an extra security guard at night," said Thea. "The perfect undercover disguise, don't you think?"

"It's nine o'clock, Thea," said Kirby as he headed toward the store's rear door.

"My, this night is simply racing by," said Thea. "Minu, you know we're not allowed to eat in the Café. Company policy. And you don't want to be out in the courtyard with all the smokers from the pub next-door…goodness no. Come upstairs with me to the break room. You'll get to meet the rest of the night crew."

Triti collected her container of home cooked rice and vegetables from her locker and rode the elevator with Thea to the building's top floor. They opened the Employees Lounge door just as an explosion of female laughter shook the walls. Inside, clustered about a large, folding table, sat a group of women. A radio played rock-and-roll music. Thea was quick to make introductions.

"Everyone, this is Minu," she said. A chorus of hellos rang out.

Triti felt self-conscious and tugged at her sleeves, but managed a smile.

"That's Jean, who you already know," said Thea. "Mare is in the tan jacket. And that's Glory, underneath the choking sign."

"She always sits there," piped Mare. "Makes her feel safer. Isn't that right, Glo?"

The group laughed en masse again. Thea pulled a red plastic chair from against the wall for Triti.

"My, what a pretty outfit you have," said Mare as she wiped sandwich crumbs from her mouth. "Now what's that style called? Oh, I know this. It's...um..."

"A sari," said Glory in a smoky voice. Her black turtleneck set off her short, wheat blond hair and crystal blue eyes.

Mare thumped herself on the forehead.

"Sari, yes! Thanks, Glo. Hey, didn't you have to wear one of those in a play last year?"

Thea half whispered in Triti's ear.

"Glory is our resident thespian."

"Talking about me again, Thea?" asked Glory.

"You don't mind if I toot your horn?"

Glory took a bite of her lettuce salad and shrugged her shoulders. "Have I ever tried to stop you?"

"She's been in Broadway shows," Thea told Triti. "As talented as she is beautiful."

Triti could only nibble at her food for it took all of her focus to understand what the women were saying. Their conversation moved at lightning speed around the table, and there were many strange, new words. From what she could glean, the four women were longtime friends and native New Yorkers. They dispensed tidbits of city savvy whether wanted or not, dishing advice on topics from the best stores to buy makeup to how to spot a shoplifter. They seemed as comfortable as sisters, finishing each other's sentences and laughing at the same place in stories. Triti listened intently, and wondered how she would ever fit in with the group.

"So, where are you from, Minu?" asked Glory, unwrapping a piece of gum. She held the package up in the air. "Anyone else want? It's peppermint."

There were no's all around the table.

"New Delhi," said Triti. "I'll try some."

"India," said Glory. "I'd never go there."

"Why not?" asked Mare. "You've been everywhere else."

"Too dirty."

Triti could not argue with Glory on that point. Still, the comment bothered her and she put her uneaten food back in her bag.

"Does it take forever to blow dry your hair, Minu?" asked Mare. "It's so long."

Triti put a stick of gum in her mouth. Her tongue watered at the minty rush.

"No, I just let it air-dry."

"Ever thought of cutting it?" asked Glory as she took her compact mirror from her purse and fussed with the wisps of hair that framed her handsome face. "With the right coif and some fashion forward clothes, you would look like a whole new person."

"And she could give her hair to 'Locks of Love'," suggested Jean.

Opinions about Triti's hair and style flew about the table. The consensus was unanimous: it was time for a makeover. Her current look, 'though lovely', had to go.

Triti was touched that the women were taking such an interest in her, but she was beginning to feel overwhelmed. To her relief, a knock came on the door and Kirby stepped into the room.

"Hey, ladies, I don't mean to break up the party, but if you're all up here, who's minding the store? Hmmm?"

"Kirby Killjoy!" hollered Mare. The three other women giggled. Triti laughed with them because it seemed like the thing to do.

Kirby walked to the table, picked up the gum, and took a stick.

"Thanks!" He dropped the package and walked back out the door.

"Mooch!" yelled Jean.

"Welcome to the team, Minu," said Thea, as she and Triti headed to the elevator. "Pay no attention to us old hens. You just keep on being who you are."

The next morning after Jitter left early for work, Triti went into the bathroom to begin her daily bathing ritual. Before turning on the shower, she noticed a stack of Jitter's fashion magazines on the floor beside the hamper. She opened the top one and began flipping through the pages, amazed at the variety of women modeling handbags and furry vests and jeans. One image made her stop and stare. A dark-haired woman appeared to be sashaying down a city street, seemingly without a care in the world. The model had a short, bobbed hairstyle, and wore a turtleneck sweater and tailored pants. Triti looked up from the page at her reflection in the mirror.

With the right coif, I could look like a whole new person…

She pulled her long locks out of their braid and combed them down the front of her chest to her waist. She glanced at the magazine photo once again. Then she opened the medicine cabinet door, and looked until she found a pair of shears.

"Ma, forgive me."

An hour later, Triti emerged from the apartment, her smooth, black hair now grazing the top of her collarbone. The cool, autumn air on her neck made her feel light and clean. As she walked, she caught her new reflection in the store windows. The dark slash of her new bangs made her golden eyes even more startling. She crossed the avenue with the light, and headed north to a bargain-clothing store on 3rd Avenue that Glory had insisted she try. With a fifty-dollar loan from Jitter tucked in her bag, she soon became the proud owner of a pair of tweed slacks and a cream-colored turtleneck sweater.

FIFTEEN

By the time January's bitter chill had taken hold of New York, Triti and Jitter realized that they made ideal roommates. When Jitter's yearlong romance fizzled, Triti consoled him with her cooking. On her nights off, she surprised him with authentic Rajasthani cuisine spiced with the turmeric and hot chilies she found in the Indian gourmet stores of the East Village. In appreciation, he bought her gifts from the South Asian curio shops they passed on their weekly walking tours of different city neighborhoods. Sculptures and paintings of Hindu gods and literary icons invariably caught his eye. At his urging, Triti taught him about Shiva, Arjuna, and Krishna.

One chilly night just after New Year's Eve, as they walked up Lexington Avenue toward the apartment, their conversation moved beyond goddesses and the day's news.

"You seem sad today," she commented, gently.

"Oh, just the boyfriend blues. They come and go. Today, they're here. And wearing Betsy Johnson."

"Jitter, you're such a kind person. Certainly, some smart man will see your fine qualities."

"You know, I actually came close one time. About ten years ago. Thought I'd landed myself a Yale guy. Man, we had us a romp! I took Amtrak up to Brookline to meet his parents. What a spread! Wide, green lawns, and a duck pond. After that visit, though, I didn't hear from him for weeks. Finally, late one night, I reached him on his phone. And with just two sentences, my world fell apart. He said he thought I was a very nice person, but he wouldn't be able to see me anymore. His parents wouldn't allow him to get involved with someone who didn't have an Ivy League degree. Got a feather? You could've knocked me over."

"What is this 'Ivy League'?"

"I suppose it's a private club for super-special people. I'm *not* a member."

"What did you say to him?"

"I wanted to plead my case. To tell him I loved him, that I felt happy and free when we were together, and empty and aching when we were apart."

"So, *did* you?"

"Nope. I said, 'Joseph, you're a true bitch,' and hung up."

They laughed the rest of the way home.

Later as she brushed her teeth, Triti noticed that her hands were shaking. Dark circles were forming beneath her eyes. The uncertainty of her future had begun to keep her up nights. Her six-month visa was soon to expire. She wanted to confide her dilemma to Jitter, but she wasn't sure how to tell him. Before turning in that night, Triti paused outside his bedroom door. He was propped up in bed reading The New York Times.

"I hope I wasn't too forward earlier," said Triti, peaking in from the hallway. "It's an old habit that seems to be returning—asking too many questions."

"Not at all. For me, the subject of romance has always been fraught. Ah, well… Besides, I don't really have the time for dating, what with work, and the gym. On my weekends I take courses at school. Next week I'm going to take the Bartending for Beginners seminar. Hey, what's your favorite drink? I'll get the booze and make it for you!"

"I don't care much for alcohol."

"Come to think of it, I don't much either." He lied.

How can I tell him about my visa?

She decided to sleep with her secret one more night.

"Yes, it's been a long day…"

"Well, goodnight then, Minu," he said, yawning in spite of himself. Jitter folded his paper and set it beside him on his nightstand. "By the way, I really like your haircut."

Triti instantly put her hand to her head, and smiled.

"Thank you, Jitter. So do I."

"Something's wrong, Minu. You haven't eaten a thing."

Triti pushed her plate of garlic noodles to the center of Jitter's kitchen table. He was right. Her appetite had disappeared, and she had not slept through the night in nearly a week.

"Tell me. I might be able to help."

Triti took a deep breath.

"I'm in trouble."

She told him that her temporary Religious Worker Visa was about to expire. And there was no way she could return to the ashram to apply for an extension.

"So, does that mean you have to go back to India?"

She shook her head. "I cannot go back."

"Why not, Minu?"

Triti put her hands over her face.

"I…just can't."

"What happened there?" he asked, concern in his voice.

"So much I don't remember…"

"What about your family? Can't *they* help?"

She took her hands from her face.

"They're gone," she said, holding back her tears.

Jitter went to Triti's side and put an arm around her.

"It's ok…don't worry. It'll be alright, I promise."

He gently patted her shoulder.

Perhaps it was Jitter's open, tender manner that steadied her. Or perhaps it was the blue, limitless Manhattan sky she saw beyond the apartment window. In that moment, she sensed a distancing take place, almost as if she were an observer.

Almost.

There was something more—something she could sense, but could not see. Her darkest memory lay hidden within the recessed switchbacks of her mind. There, it festered and grew, like mold. She had no idea that one day it would have the power to tear her panicked from sleep, rattle her when passersby yelled for cabs, and chill her even in the sanctuary of a warm shower.

Let it stay in the darkness. Forgotten.

For now, she had Jitter, and the sky, and the sun, and her job.

Jitter brought her a glass of water and joined her at the table again.

"And what of Samir?"

Triti was quiet for a long while. Among the mysteries she was trying to parse, Samir's betrayal was the second hardest to comprehend. There seemed no use in denying the bruise he had left on her heart. She looked out of the window, and then let her attention drift back into the room to the seam in the center of the tablecloth.

"When I got the message from the guru that I was to leave the ashram, I thought it was a joke. It had to be. Samir could not have brought me all the way to America to just abandon me..."

"I'm not surprised," said Jitter. "It's your beauty, my dear. A light in a meadow on a summer night, you'll have every manner of low-flying insect buzzing your way."

Her spontaneous laugh was a salve on the moment.

As she cleared the dishes, she felt her sari skim the floor as she moved from sink to table to refrigerator. She wore it now as a rare exception to her work pant suits and jeans. Her secret revealed, she felt herself swaying to a voiceless song of relief.

That night Triti dreamed she was a young girl dancing at the edge of a glimmering sea. A rainbow appeared and summoned her to walk upon its wide, colorful bands. She awoke humming the high notes of a scale.

The next evening, they met as usual at one of their favorite Indian restaurants, which was a few blocks from the apartment. Even though she was still deeply anxious, Triti felt less alone with her burdens. In contrast, the man with nerves of steel arrived ten minutes late and quite clearly on edge. Before he even opened his menu, Jitter made his case.

"You have to marry me," he said firmly. "There is just no other way. Before you say no, let's look at the facts."

Triti sat, stunned by Jitter's declaration.

How could he consider such a brazen remedy?

As she listened, he laid out the realities of her situation. In less than a month, her temporary V2 visa would expire. If she stayed beyond the deadline, she could be deported to India. She didn't have enough time or money to apply to college and secure a student visa, and she was clearly unwelcomed back at the ashram. Marriage to a United States citizen was her only expedient, legal option.

"Minu, how could I ever let you get on a plane back to India? I know you can't remember everything that happened, and God knows I wouldn't want to, either. But India's not an option, sweetie. Not as long as this Southern boy is breathing."

"But Jitter…"

"Let's face it. You need a green card…in a hurry!"

He believed that together they could pull off the charade of being a loving, newly-wed couple for any INS agent. Lesser mortals had succeeded, he told her. He would ask a woman friend who had married a young silversmith from Brazil to prevent him from having to return to the slums of Rio. She could help coach them.

"Besides, it would only be for two years," he said. "After that, we can get a divorce and go our merry ways."

"But Jitter, *how* could you do this for me?"

"This really isn't a hard call."

"I get a new life. What do *you* get?"

He bowed his head.

"I couldn't save my dad…"

Triti reached across the table and took his hands in hers. She waited for him to compose himself.

"No one must ever know," she said.

"They won't hear it from me."

She squeezed his hands.

For the first time since her big reveal, Jitter dropped his shoulders. He wiped his eyes, put on his reading glasses, and cracked opened his menu.

"Now then, my dear… You love cauliflower. Shall we share some aloo gobi?"

Triti thought of nothing else that night. Three days later—in a windowless room at City Hall, wearing a plain, white dress—she became Mrs. Jeremy Thomas Brown.

SIXTEEN

Cambridge, Massachusetts
February 2007

"Goddamn it!"

Jaq sprinted. Puffs of hot breath exploded through the wool scarf covering her mouth as she flew past John Harvard's statue. She crossed the Yard's frigid, snowy expanse in seconds, her overstuffed backpack shucking heavily on her shoulders. She was late, no matter how many times she rechecked the time on her digital watch.

Teaching the eight a.m. Spring semester section of Introduction to Eastern Religions was turning out to be a challenging assignment for her, but with just fifteen undergraduates registered, she figured at least the grading load would be light. Her students waited for her, sipping their steaming cups of designer java while rehashing the latest intrigues of previous night's CSI episode. Several itched for a chance to impress their graduate student instructor; the rest just hoped to be ignored.

Taking the steps of Lowell two at a time, Jaq dashed into the building's warm entryway and stopped to fill her lungs. She slid off her furry hat, allowing all three feet of her black hair to cascade down in a single, glossy wave. With practiced fingers, she wove her locks into her signature heavy plait which hung straight down her equally straight back. Just six years older than her charges, in her skinny jeans and teal velvet poet's shirt, she could be any co-ed on campus. Or maybe not.

Jaq stood apart from all other women wherever she went. With exceedingly rare beauty by any standard, her satin-smooth face was a mesmerizing tableau of high cheekbones, arched brows, and pillow lips. Her pale, golden eyes pulled the stunned admirer deep into their luminous centers. Men responded to her in only two ways: either they resorted to shameless flirting, or they beat an awkward retreat and pretended not to notice her. Most women declined her friendship outright—too jealous of the beauty vortex she created simply by entering a room. Some even found themselves wondering, secretly, what it would be like to press their lips against her succulent mouth.

Throughout the past few years, she found it unsettling to look in the mirror, for the face she saw reflecting back was quite different from the one she had worn as a gawky teenager. She had yet to make peace with what a late adolescent bloom had bestowed upon her. In her mind she was just Jaq—a driven graduate student with a monster paper to write, and bills to pay. Sometimes she wondered how different her life would be if everyone she met was blind. Even on the days she left her apartment in sweat pants and a ponytail, passersby gawked. Storekeepers winked. Deliverymen whistled. She continually reminded herself that her acceptance to the university's coveted doctoral program had come because of her intellectual gifts. She set her focus on performing at the highest academic level. And all too soon she realized that achieving success in modern day Athens was complicated. There were strategies at play, and important people to appease, her looks be damned.

On campus, in spite of her best efforts at being friendly and sociable, it quickly became clear to Jaq that her looks put her at a stark disadvantage. From the first day of orientation, her plainer female colleagues avoided her. She somehow never received the memos about weekend study groups, and she wasn't on anyone's short list for campus walks or movie nights after the Dean's tea. Both of the fulltime female faculty members in her department virtually ignored her at university functions. As the months went by and opportunities for collegial dialogue dried up, she became more and more isolated. She tried everything she knew to remedy the situation: volunteering at various graduate school functions and dropping in on weekly library meetings. She even dressed modestly and shunned all makeup and jewelry. Still, the personal rejection persisted. It seemed that in the ugly world of Ivy doctoral politics, beauty could be an unfortunate burden to bear.

Halfway through Jaq's lecture that morning on the differences between Mahayana and Hinyana Buddhism, Ina Young, the Religion Department's secretary, shuffled down the hall's center aisle. Zipped up to her chin in a down jacket, she handed Jaq a folded note, then left without saying a word. Jaq could have sworn she saw an uncommon look of glee on Ina's wind-chapped face.

This cannot be good.

Jaq reread the crumpled note as she hurried out of class. Being summoned to the Dean's office in such dramatic fashion had shaken her so that at precisely 9:15 a.m. she adjourned the class, stuffed her lecture cards into her backpack, and darted out of the building, leaving a short queue of tittering students behind. She barely felt the sting of the blustery morning as she made her way across the campus to the Graduate School of Arts offices.

Christ, all this drama for a few late starts?

Jaq hated to be late to anything—a failing of her mother she had long ago rejected—but tardiness to her early classes was becoming her norm rather than the exception. Like many other doctoral students, she supplemented the pittance she earned student teaching with a second job: a bi-weekly stint as the evening hostess at the popular Sumati's Palace in downtown Boston. Working the restaurant's late shift made for very late nights, but the pay was decent and the hours dependable. The essential perk, the one that made her perpetual exhaustion worth it, was eating as much chicken tikkas and dal as she could put away on her ten-minute rest between seatings. Somewhere close to midnight, she caught the late T to Somerville, trudged the seven long blocks from the station along Somerville Avenue, and then hiked up the steep hill to her one-bedroom apartment near Harvard Divinity School. Once inside her refuge, Jaq relaxed. She thrived amidst order, so her home was spare and tidy. Pillows on her couch were tilted at the same angles; bath towels were triple-folded and stacked neatly in the hall closet. Routines kept her sane. Every night after the restaurant, she scrubbed the curry smell from her body with lemon soap, double checked the next morning's class notes, glanced at her email, and fell asleep with any one of a dozen Hindu temple books tumbled open across her chest.

"Report to Dean Kraik's office immediately," Jaq muttered as she hurried past groups of students heading to their morning classes.

The single sentence command set her teeth on edge. Eldred C. Kraik. The esteemed Allenberg Professor of South Asian Civilization and Dean of Religious studies, Kraik was her thesis advisor and, as she had discovered, a lecherous dinosaur. Her doctoral topic, Erotic Feminine Representations in Hindu Temple Sculpture, thrilled him from the moment he read the heading on her initial research outline. She would never forget the uneasy feeling she'd had two years prior when she met him for the first time.

Looking back, Kraik had exhibited a near-prurient interest in her work from the start. He often scheduled late afternoon meetings with her, ostensibly to review her research progress. But over the months their sessions devolved into his questioning her about her boyfriends, (she had none), and what type of lingerie she preferred (she wore none and it was none of his business). She repeatedly refused to answer him, and spent most of their meeting times attempting to steer him back to a discussion of the thesis process. At the beginning of her second semester, he insisted that she attend private slide shows. They featured images of ancient façade carvings depicting orgiastic couplings — common at many Hindu temples throughout India. Kraik delighted in running the projector, stopping frequently to assess the sexual practices depicted on the screen. He commented on positions that he personally enjoyed or had not yet tried. Throughout each session, Jaq sat mortified, speechless, until finally she blurted out any excuse to leave: she had papers to grade, or a quiz to prepare. It was all she could do not to run out of his office.

Jaq never told anyone about Kraik's menacing.

Who would believe me?

She rationalized her silence.

He was a preeminent scholar with an endowed chair, and the author of five seminal textbooks. Kraik quite literally held her degree and her career in his hands. She hated that. Behind every lascivious comment and lingering touch on her shoulder, she felt his silent but perceptible threat. As the weeks and months went on, she faced the pervasiveness of his power play with increasing grimness. After more than a year of Kraik's ceaseless pressure, she felt herself cracking. Gone was her trademark New York City girl confidence, her carpe diem attitude. She had become tentative, and self-doubting. She felt very much alone.

Nothing she tried seemed to stem Kraik's pursuit. She dressed in baggy pants and flannel shirts. Some days she did not even comb her hair. Still the comments, the touches, the cornerings continued. Kraik was clever. His efforts were always clandestine. Never when other students were about, and certainly never when Ina was in her office down the hall. At first, Jaq wondered if she was imagining it all. But not anymore. His offensive was clearly taking its toll. She went to sleep and awoke exhausted. Dark bags appeared beneath her eyes. She lost her appetite. She was uncharacteristically irritable and jumpy. Then, her period stopped coming. And for the second time in her life, Jaq was truly afraid.

In her dwindling lucid moments, she reconsidered confiding her dilemma to someone else. *But who?* Her mother was far too unpredictable of late to be good counsel—not that she had ever really been. The female colleagues she had met in her graduate classes were consumed with their own life dramas and the demands of the rigorous doctoral program. Having devoted all of her time and energy in the past six years to making her Harvard acceptance a reality, she had neglected to nurture her New York friendships.

Jessica, the one friend she had known since high school, had recently stopped emailing her.

It's all on me.

She could not imagine dealing with Kraik for the five more years it would take her to finish her Ph.D.

Kraik met Jaq at his office door.

He motioned for her to sit, not in her usual place on a stool beside him at his desk (the position in which he preferred her, forcing a deep arch in her back and the ideal, eye-level view of her breasts). Instead, he directed her to a wooden chair opposite him. Her head pounded. She strained to refresh the calendar in her mind of her writing deadlines and teaching chores.

Kraik could not hold back his smirk.

"You have something to be worried about, Jacqueline."

He used her given name to annoy her, knowing full well that she answered only to Jaq. Tense with excitement, he held back the ace card a little longer, toying with her.

Jaq silently reviewed a jumble of recent gaffes that could be coming back to haunt her. When nothing stood out as egregious, she spoke.

"I've been pushing it a bit too hard, I suppose."

"You're not complaining about your workload, are you, Jacqueline?"

"No, Dean. I'm not."

"Something you feel you need to tell me?"

A million thoughts.

"Nothing springs to mind."

Kraik's upper lip curled back ever so slightly.

"Well, it seems that a student has lodged a complaint against you."

"For what?"

Incredulous, Jaq confessed, her voice trembling. "If this is because of lateness, really… I mean, I was never more than five minutes…"

Kraik leveled his gaze at her. Poor little gazelle.

"Tardiness *is* a problem, but it won't necessarily cost you your candidacy."

Jaq felt her chest constrict.

"No, I fear a young man in your Fall Semester class claims that you sexually harassed him."

Kraik waited, watching her exquisite face as the news sunk in.

"What!" Jaq reeled. "That's impossible! He must have me confused with someone…"

Then, she remembered.

No fucking way.

In September, as the new instructor on the Quad, Jaq had made a special effort to get to know the twenty sophomores in her Buddhism section. Her classroom approach was personable, and she often stayed late after lecture fielding questions and discussing basic religious topics with stragglers. She arranged for a special on-campus study session for the mid-term, bringing juice and popcorn for a three-hour cram-athon. As she left the building for her fifteen-minute walk home, Trey Russell said he had one more question. The conversation had been all 'Middle Path,' but she felt increasingly uncomfortable that the brooding, intense young man kept finding yet another point to make. He ended up walking with her across campus and through the back streets to Somerville Avenue, where finally she shook free of him. Reaching her apartment up the hill, she was startled to see Trey still lingering beneath the street lamp on the avenue below. A red flag waved off to the right of her peripheral inner vision, but it quickly disappeared in the haze of exhaustion from her sixteen-hour workdays.

The encounter slipped her mind until she saw Trey after the next Buddhism class. He asked questions she had already answered in lecture, seemingly just to interact with her. Unlike the other students' obvious attempts at sucking up, Trey seemed intent on creating the opportunity for something more than a student-teacher relationship.

Who could she talk to? Kraik? Certainly not. And not the two female professors in the department who continued to ignore her. She knew she would have to deal with this problem by herself.

Not wanting to embarrass Trey in front his classmates, she had agreed to meet him on the steps of Widener Library later at noon that day. Best place to deliver potentially ego-crushing news, she thought: a public space, mobbed with people, lots of escape routes. She promised herself to be pleasant and professional.

Trey met her halfway up Widener's marble steps.

"Here's something for you," he said. He held out a note to her, preempting the start of her carefully rehearsed speech.

Jaq took the folded paper and held it unopened in her hand. She looked across the Yard at the ivy-covered buildings. She took a deep breath and channeled her rusty, Manhattan-raised edge.

"Mr. Russell, I'm happy to help you with anything pertaining to your Buddhism studies. I do appreciate your enthusiasm, but it would be unfair to your classmates if I spent extra time outside of class with you."

"Have lunch with me, Jaq."

Jaq?

She flushed. An attractive, young man was making it very plain he desired her. The familiar vibrations in her pelvis felt simultaneously wonderful and completely inappropriate.

She re-gathered herself.

"Mr. Russell, thank you for the invitation. But I cannot see you outside of class. I'm going to go now."

She turned and walked briskly toward the Coop. She felt his eyes on her back as she slid the note, still unopened, into her jacket pocket. She had waited until she reached the steps to her apartment to unfold the note. She could only bear to read the first line of his note to her, a poem, that began with: "My hands belong nowhere else but on your body, my mouth…" and she ran to her kitchen to burn it to ash in the blue flames of her gas stove.

Jaq had not been surprised that Trey missed the last five class sessions. She was admittedly relieved not to have to face him again. His take-home essay final came back with all the others; a passable job, though clearly not the work of which she knew he was capable. She had given him a B for the course—a fair grade in her mind, considering his no-shows. His "complaint" was the stuff of poorly-written B movies: the unrequited love, sick puppy-love gone bad.

I can't handle this.

Jaq wanted to stand and run out of Kraik's office, but her legs were leaden. Kraik rose up from behind his desk. Then he was beside her, his bulk blocking the dim morning light outside the arched window.

"The young man claims that you lured him off-campus to your apartment and that when he refused your sexual overtures, you retaliated by giving him a low semester grade."

Kraik held up several official looking documents in front of her face.

"Harvard takes a charge like this quite seriously," he hissed. "Especially from the son of a prominent alumnus."

"But I didn't..."

"These are the papers recommending your immediate suspension from the doctoral program until the Student/ Faculty Ethics Committee can meet to hear this complaint. All they require is my signature. Another graduate student will take over your teaching duties until a hearing has been convened."

He placed the papers on her lap.

She stared up at him, paralyzed. She couldn't breathe.

"I must say, this all comes as quite a disappointment to me, Jacqueline. You have such promise."

He put his hand on her left shoulder, sending icy spasms down her arm. She winced as his fingers caressed the wisps of hair at the nape of her neck. He leaned in closely to the side of her face, his hip next to her shoulder.

"I'm prepared to tear these papers up and tell the committee they've made a serious error."

Jaq's mind raced. Her hands cramped as she gripped the edge of the chair.

"You will meet me at the Boxer Hotel downtown tonight at 10:00 p.m. Promptly. You know how I hate to be kept waiting."

As he spoke, he pressed his hard stiffness into her shoulder.

There it was. His endgame.

Sixteen months: the whispers, the touching. It all led to this moment. His coup d'état.

Jaq's cheeks burned. She trembled with rage and fear.

"And for our *first* time, wear something white."

A victorious smile crawled across Kraik's face.

Jaq blinked, repulsed by the images that thrashed before her eyes.

"No."

"Think carefully, Jacqueline."

"Go to hell."

Jaq lurched to her feet, spilling the papers onto the office floor. As she hurtled out the door and down the hall, she could hear Kraik's laughter echoing after her.

Jaq could not remember where she was supposed to be.

She had just started walking and ended up back at her apartment. Nothing seemed to matter. She found half a bottle of vodka in her pantry and promptly drained it. Then she curled up on her stuffed armchair where she remained for two days, rising only to pee and mouth water from beneath the bathroom faucet. On Monday morning, an official letter from the university was slipped beneath her apartment door. Her case would be heard in committee in early March. Until then, her academic privileges were suspended. Any academic appeal could not be considered until the summer.

Two weeks later, with her few belongings and furniture in a local storage unit and her overstuffed suitcase in the foyer, Jaq looked out of her front apartment window at the snow melting on the sidewalk below. It would ice over by nightfall, but she wouldn't be there to slip on it.

She hated to leave her apartment. Despite its wafer-thin walls and drafty corners, it had been her one place of sanctuary for nearly two years. Financially, she had always managed to squeak by, but without the money from her student teaching, she could no longer afford the place. Academic suspension meant she could not apply for any loans to cover her living expenses, either. Even if she could wrangle more nights at Sumati's, she still wouldn't make enough to pay the rent.

Numbers don't lie.

She had faced the hard reality of her predicament. The committee would never find in her favor; Kraik would see to that. Even if by some miracle she was reinstated, the process could take months. That morning, she had used her last reserve of energy to fill out the forms for an official leave of absence. She would have until the end of December to figure out her life.

As she prepared to close and lock her apartment door for the last time, the landline telephone rang—its loud ringtones bouncing off the barren living room walls. She hesitated before picking up the receiver.

"Yeah?"

"Jacqueline Morel, this is Martin Freer, staff assistant at the office of the Student/Faculty Disciplinary Committee at GSAS."

Jaq remained silent, waiting until Mr. Freer, who was unknown to her, worked a little harder to determine her identity.

"Hello... Is this Miss Morel?

"I'm listening," said Jaq, dully.

"Oh, ok. On behalf of my supervisor, Mr. Park, I am calling to inform you that Mr. Trey Russell has withdrawn his complaint against you and refused to cooperate in any further investigation of the incident. Therefore, all charges against you have been dropped and your university privileges have been fully reinstated without prejudice. You may return to your Spring semester class schedule on Monday. You'll receive a letter within the week from the Committee confirming the disposition of your case."

Numb, Jaq could just stare at the receiver.

"Your advisor, Dr. Kraik, wants to meet with you tomorrow to discuss this development. His secretary, Miss Young, will contact you to set up an appointment with him. Do you have any questions?"

Silence.

"Well, should you have questions, contact the Committee office at the number listed on the letter. Hello? Are you still there, Miss Morel?"

A beat.

"No, I'm not."

Jaq hung up the phone, locked the bottom lock for the last time, and pushed her keys back under the door. She lugged her backpack, briefcase, and suitcase down the stairs to the waiting taxi. Settling into the back seat, she pulled up her sweater cuff and checked her watch. If the traffic on Mass. Ave was light, she would make it to the train station in time for her one-way trip home to New York City.

SEVENTEEN

March 2007
East Village
New York City

Crossing 8th street against the light, Triti was just about to run when the cab coming up on her slowed to a crawl to let her pass. The driver tossed his dreadlocks off his face and leaned out of his window.

"Mahhrree me, Gorgeous!"

She acknowledged his compliment with a wave and stepped up onto the curb.

"He certainly has good taste."

Triti turned to the voice she knew so well. Standing behind her was Jitter.

"How have you been, sweetie?" Jitter hugged her warmly.

"Mr. Brown, it's been entirely too long. Wouldn't you agree?"

It had been ages since their divorce party, she thought. *Could five years have gone by, already?* The very weekend after an INS agent visited Jitter's apartment and adjudged them a legitimate international couple, they celebrated together for the last time. Seeing Jitter brought her back to the summer of 2002 when she had moved out on her own and rented her small one bedroom in the East Village—all she could afford on her Regency management salary. It seemed like the right thing to do, as she found herself craving privacy—especially on the nights when Jitter brought dates home for overnight visits. For the first couple of years, she called him when she came upon something that reminded her of him—a cookbook on Southern fare, subway ads for The New School. But he rarely returned her messages. To her sadness, their contact devolved into the mutual exchange of birthday and holiday cards. Standing before him on the street, she was overcome with emotions.

He looks older, she thought. *And far too thin.* She reached for his hand and felt his bones protruding through the skin on his wrist.

"Your hair is beautiful that length again, Minu. I'm glad you let it all grow back."

He dropped his eyes away from hers when he realized that she was staring at him.

"Jitter, can I treat you to lunch? Knowing you, you're probably in a hurry," she said. "I should just give a call, you know, call ahead sometime…"

"I *could* go for some Dojo's, actually," said Jitter. "Remember the Hijiki tofu burgers? Let's hit the one on St. Mark's. It's *so* close."

They had barely tasted their food when Jitter fell into a violent coughing jag. After several minutes, Triti paid the restaurant tab and helped him walk out to the street. His face was painted with sweat.

"Jitter, what's wrong?"

He held his hand up, and she waited another few moments as he methodically wiped his forehead and mouth with a handkerchief.

"Let's just walk," he said, with a tone of embarrassment.

She slipped her arm around his and they gingerly made their way toward Broadway. She was surprised at how much she had to steady him.

"Are you ok? That cough..."

"I'm actually having a fairly good day."

Triti suddenly realized why her friend was so ill.

"This is from the Pile, isn't it?"

On September 11th—New York's darkest day—Jitter had run south when it seemed the world was running north. Feeling the need to help, he had been one of the emergency volunteers helping to recover victims from the Trade Center rubble. For 58 days he had worked at Ground Zero: knee-deep in dust and wreckage, filling buckets, shoveling debris shoulder to shoulder with hundreds of other Samaritans. Every few days he would come home, shower, eat one of Triti's meals, and head back downtown. She had hidden in their apartment after the Towers fell — paralyzed with fear. Then one day, several weeks after the attacks, she awoke determined to keep her life exactly the same way it had been: rising early to bathe, a bagel with scallion cream cheese and coffee for breakfast, reading the New York Times, doing her laundry, shopping for food, dressing for work, riding the subway. The city was not what it had been. She had to make adjustments, like every other New Yorker. She felt the comradery on the streets like so many others; they were all in it together. The eyes and prayers of the world seemed to make a difference. Nothing was the same. Even five years on, things in NY were still tender. Jitter had eventually returned to his job at the college, but he was clearly a different man. He had grown timid. His sense of humor had faded, replaced by a moribund weariness that he could not find the will to shake. She remembered wondering if he would ever be himself again.

"Right around Christmas, '02, I began to feel sick."

Jitter leaned up against a bus stop sign to catch his breath.

"At first it felt like a bad cold that wouldn't go away, bronchitis maybe. I checked my HIV status repeatedly; relieved each time I find out I was clear. But the sickness hung on. My doctors scratched their heads. Antibiotics didn't touch it. I got too weak to exercise and cancelled my gym membership. Within two years, my lungs rattled day and night. Breathing became painful. My head pounded from migraines. Of course, I started missing work at the college, and soon ran out of sick days…"

He stopped walking and began hacking again. This time the cough ended in a shrill whistle. Triti held him the elbow as he tried to clear his lungs again and again in vain. Eventually the cough subsided, and he shuffled forward into a slow walk.

"I arranged to work part time, but even that became too much. In 2005, I made the decision to resign. Broke my heart. A year later my medical coverage expired. My savings is 'bout gone. The apartment's all I've got left. And I'm not only one, you know. Thousands of other volunteers and city workers are sick like me."

"How are you getting by?" Her voice cracked with sympathy.

"Since February, I've been living on credit cards. They're just about maxed out." He modulated his tone trying to appear nonchalant.

Triti knew from experience that his placid demeanor was just a cover.

"How much do you owe?"

"Today? Oh, about $ 5,000, give or take. But I just started tending bar in Chelsea. Should be getting a full schedule of shifts next month. I'll be flush soon; don't you worry. When I have to, I'll put the apartment up for sale."

"And Teddy? Are you two still…?"

"Theodore? Oh, goodness, no. Once I got sick, Mr. Selfish had other places to be. Just like Maya Angelou said. 'People will show you who they are. Believe them.'"

"Do you have a roommate?"

"Nope. After he left, I tried a few different tenants, but they all made me crazy. Or maybe it was me driving them nuts… Anyway, I'm there alone now. Probably better that way. I'm up a lot at night, what with my coughing."

Triti suggested that they walk toward Second Avenue together. She asked him to wait outside her bank, that she would only be a minute. When she emerged, she found him leaning up against a mailbox, wheezing. She put her hand on his back and felt the bony outline of his ribs through his windbreaker.

"Jitter…?"

He looked at her and smoothed the worry lines between her eyebrows with his index finger—an old habit of his that she missed.

Triti handed him a stuffed bank envelope.

"I know how much you hate presents. Call it a loan. Pay me back whenever. And keep in touch, please. Don't let so much time go by before I hear from you, Jitter Brown."

He shook his head, but she pushed the envelope into his hand. Resigned to her kindness, he put the money inside his jacket pocket and zipped it up to his neck.

"Just a few weeks, that's all," he said, apologetically. "I'll call you soon and we'll get together again."

"Promise?" Triti hugged him tightly, not wanting to let him go.

"Bye, my Beauty."

Jitter shuffled into the rushing masses on lower Broadway. Triti stood, reeling, thinking of what she had just done. All of her savings—$4,000—were in that envelope. Six years of scrimping, but she had not hesitated. It was time to put her foot on Karma's scale.

EIGHTEEN

Lower East Side
New York City

"You let him smoke in the apartment?!"

Jaq whispered loudly in her mother's direction, the volume of her disdain rising above the morning television talk show that blasted from the living room. She trained her eyes through the half-open kitchen door on the large man beached in the center of the couch, his sweat-shiny baldness barely visible within a menthol haze.

"Sshh! He'll hear you."

"It's only 9:00 a.m. and Evan's already down half a pack."

Banni stirred a double batch of pancake mix in a carnival glass bowl. A yeasty splatter on her wrinkled, denim shirt reminded Jaq of a constellation.

Orion, maybe.

"And what's with the volume? Is the man hearing-impaired?"

"Your father smoked. Never seemed to bother you."

"Ma!" Jaq took pleasure in calling her mother that, as it invariably incited paroxysms of disgust in Banni. That she elicited no such reaction from her mother that day puzzled her. "Ma, you know that Poppi only smoked a pipe…and only when he struggled with palette selections at the start of a new painting. Besides, I liked the smell of his tobacco. It was sweet…"

"Yes, yes. And I suppose the man was perfect?"

Jaq thought of snapping back at her mother, to say that yes, he had indeed been perfect…to her, anyway; but she would not be sucked into such drama. Jaq shifted her stare from Evan's head to the gas flames beneath the griddle. They were too high. She watched as a pat of butter sizzled past brown to black.

Twelve years.

A split second, an eternity, had passed since her father's heart attack; since he abruptly left the two of them—a beautiful, bereaved widow and a precocious, teenage daughter—in a shabby, two-bedroom walkup on the Lower East Side, with only a miniscule life insurance policy and two hundred paintings of various, arguable values to sustain them.

Twelve years, and still her mother's anger smoldered beneath her delicate, almond-colored face. She wondered if Banni would ever forgive Guy for dying before her, for making her a widow.

Jaq wanted to take her mother by her slender shoulders and shake the present day into her, but it was too late. Something dark seemed to be working on Banni. Jaq looked closely at her mother's face, surprised to see that for the first time since Guy's funeral she wore no kohl or lip stain. Her hair, normally lustrous and flowing over her shoulders, was stuffed rudely into a terrycloth twist.

Banni would burn the pancakes.

Two weeks of mornings passed with Jaq awakening in cold sweats on the mallard duck sheets of the daybed in her father's art studio. As each sun rose over the city, the gross magnitude of her Boston debacle roared into the room on tsunami-sized waves. She agonized that she could have been so naïve.

How? I'm from fucking New York!

Unable to slip an arm around her floundering self-esteem and make for clarity's shore, she gulped air and dove, hoping that if she waited long enough, her life's storms' fury would pass. It seemed logical to her in the moment.

How long could she hold her breath? She wasn't sure.

'Voluntary Leave of Absence' from Harvard. Whatever the hell that was supposed to mean.

She was growing tired of lying to herself, but the truth was damnably painful. Mired in total defeat, she had slunk, tail tucked, back to the city. Completely broke, she was forced to move back in with her mother—back into the apartment and, to a greater extent than she could have imagined, into the turbulent life of her childhood. Familiar howls of racing fire trucks and screeching car alarms awakened her to the nauseating smells of yawning garbage trucks and human urea—all of which reassured her that she had yet another day to make sense of her life's big mess.

Jaq opened her eyes and looked around. Surrounded by the tools of her father's joy and genius, she became aware of an odd but growing sense of comfort. The room, his domain still, drew her in with its orderliness. It reminded her of her apartment in Boston—everything precisely placed, just so.

"This nut didn't fall far from your tree, Poppi."

The room and its contents appeared untouched. She knew full well that Banni rarely summoned the will to enter, and only then to quickly dust and vacuum. Her mother had been unable to touch anything of Guy's since the afternoon she found him slumped cold over his easel—lost to her forever. Jaq wished she had been the one to find him that bleak, winter day. She had long known that her mother's frail psyche would not cope with the haunting memory of seeing her only true love stiff and gray.

Spared such visceral horror, Guy's space was full of dear memories for Jaq. She had grown from toddler to teen there beside him. Whenever she knocked on his studio door for a visit, he paused his brush strokes to scoop her up, kiss her cheeks, and pet her silky hair. She always felt welcomed and would daily contrive ways to sneak away from Banni to go to him. He never failed to make their time special for her, setting a place for her on the floor near him where she delighted in mixing up swirls of tempuras in complete freedom. Standing there in his space again, Jaq felt the same sense of wonder she had as a child. For her, it was all about the marvel of his neatly-arranged oil boxes, silver cans of paint thinner, red-rimmed buckets of natural hair brushes, half-moon wooden palettes dashed with his signature green mixes, and clear bins of folded rags. Her father, her saint, was alive to her in that room.

Lining the room's north-facing brick wall were the last of Guy Morel's canvasses. The pieces stood on end, ceiling high, rolled tight, wrapped in muslin; mysterious sentries guarding her memories. Though hidden from view, the paintings captivated her imagination. They were the last remaining evidence of Guy's love affair with life, of his penchant for working 'big,' of his deft ability to integrate color and shapes. It had been years since Jaq had unfurled the massive cloths and been astonished anew by the moody swaths of bruising indigo and audacious triangles of cantaloupe orange. Maybe tomorrow, she thought. Yes, she would open all of the canvasses.

A faint, lingering whiff of Guy's fragrant tobacco made her glance over her shoulder.

"Poppi?"

She smiled imagining him, arms akimbo, head tilted, chewing on a wooden pipe stem, working a painting with his eyes. How she missed his kind, hazel eyes.

Jaq considered the four walls. Within them, there were no judgments, no standards to meet. The room did not care that she had failed epically in the face of her demons. It did not care that after two weeks of utter despair she had yet to begin to pull herself back from the brink. But in the room, she felt safe enough to come up for air. She became aware of a regenerative heat radiating from within her head, as if a long-dormant seed of reason pulsed warm and fertile once again.

Jaq took great consolation in knowing that she was her father's daughter. Whenever the pushing came to shoving, she could, like Guy, access a survivor's pragmatism. She had learned how to navigate life's frequent bumps by watching him. When one of his wealthy patrons died just after commissioning an ambitious mural, Guy took his easel and colors to Central Park and set up outside the Metropolitan Museum. After four days of sunrise to sunset painting, he attracted the attention of a tourist couple from Spain who bought two of his works on the spot and asked for a third for their Swiss country house. When the electric company threatened to turn off the power in their apartment during one particularly lean patch, Guy went down to the Con Ed office and sketched such a keen likeness of the Customer Service manager while waiting on the queue that she stamped his account paid and told him to go home.

"Where ingenuity meets grit, you have success," Guy used to tell his daughter.

With no money for a new school bag one fall, Jaq commandeered one of Guy's zippered sweatshirt jackets, sewed the bottom closed, knotted the sleeves tightly, filled it with her schoolbooks and slung it over her shoulder, starting an unlikely fashion trend among her classmates at P.S. 41. When she needed an extra six credits for early high school graduation, she convinced the principal and her teachers to let her take two independent study courses over the summer and completed book reports for every required novel on the senior English syllabus in less than two weeks.

Like father, like daughter.

The next day when a letter arrived confirming the grant for her long-planned research trip to India, Jaq realized that her moping must stop. Decisions had to be made.

'Straighten up and fly right!' She could almost hear her father's thick Marseille accent as he uttered a quintessential appeal to his girl to reach past the trivial concerns of mortals and attend to goddess matters. Lest she veer too far off the 'Exceptional' path.

"Okay, Poppi."

But there was Banni to worry about.

Jaq had underestimated the changes in her mother. To her eyes, virtually everything about Banni seemed diluted since she her departure for Boston a year and half ago. Her movements were dramatically slower; her voice, her reactions dull. She was thinner than Jaq had ever seen her; the weight loss made her arms and once-glamorous face look underfed. Knots of arthritis in her hands and feet appeared to rob her of her usual energy, and she had difficulty walking. She complained of lightheadedness and frequent headaches, but as usual she refused to see a doctor. Most of the day she sat on the couch with Evan, watching television and leafing through DesiTalk magazines, rising only to attend to his frequent food and beverage requests. Jaq could not help but notice Banni's lack of concern about her sloppy appearance. In the past, her mother had complained without pause about her poor fashion sense. Now there were none of Banni's typical zingers about her baggy pants and bare face. Her mother rarely even acknowledged her presence.

Then, there were the mirrors—or rather, their conspicuous absence. Banni's precious mirror collection had disappeared. Since grade school, everywhere Jaq sat or stood in the apartment, she had been able to see her own reflection staring back from one of Banni's treasured looking glasses. Each mirror was unique in size and shape from the others. A stranger might have viewed them as tools of her mother's vanity, but that would have been only a small part of the equation. The day Guy died, Banni cut up her black chiffon dupattas and covered every mirror in the apartment. Months passed. Then one day the shrouds came down, and life continued on. But when Jaq returned from Boston this time, the mirrors were mysteriously gone.

One night as they sat together at the dining room table, Jaq had to ask.

"Mom, where are all the mirrors?"

Banni stared quizzically at Jaq for a moment and then looked around the room.

"I don't know. I thought you moved them."

Banni went back to picking the mushrooms off her cold slice of pizza.

The next afternoon, while her mother napped on the sofa, Jaq searched the apartment. She found the mirrors face down in piles under her parents' bed. The smallest and most precious ones were boxed and stacked beneath the right side of the mattress, where her father had slept.

Jaq did not know what to make of Evan. To her knowledge, in all the years since Guy died, her mother had never so much as talked to another man. She was too painfully shy even to ask male store clerks for help, and would go without items instead. There had been no Evan last summer. Before she left for Boston, Jaq remembered that the apartment phone rang often with Banni's girlfriends catching up on daily gossip and arranging visits and outings. Now the house phone never rang, and Banni rarely left the apartment. When Jaq asked her about Jeri, Banni's close friend of nearly fifteen years, her mother drifted into one of her ever-more-common fogs. She would amble about the apartment from room to room in her powder blue scuffs, compulsively turning off lights and unplugging appliances. Jaq saw a withdrawn, distant stranger who bore scant resemblance to the feisty, energetic woman who had raised her. She wondered if somehow Evan was to blame.

One evening, Jaq passed Banni in the hall before bed.

"Evan doesn't like Jeri," said Banni, frowning. She shrugged resignedly and closed her bedroom door.

NINETEEN

April 13, 2007

Surely someone in New York City needed Hindi lessons. With only two days left on her free Craig's List ad and still no calls of inquiry, Triti considered whether or not to renew her notice. Toward the end of her work shift, she noticed she had a message on her cell phone. She listened to the voicemail and her spirits lifted. A young woman was interested in learning conversational Hindi. The caller said she lived only a few blocks away and could stop by the next day, if it was convenient.

If she wants to meet me at midnight, in the pouring rain, without an umbrella, it will be convenient.

Once back in her apartment, Triti flipped through her checkbook memo sheets and circled the outstanding check numbers.

"Can pay, can't pay, hopefully can pay…"

May 1st was coming soon. She scribbled a new total in the margin. She would make it this month, but finances were tight—very tight. Two weeks earlier, her supervisor Kit delivered the news that her 45-hour weekly management schedule was being trimmed to 35 hours. Overnight she saw her salary decrease. Coming on the heels of her gift to Jitter, she had begun to literally count her pennies. She would agree to pretty much any arrangement her potential student suggested.

Triti looked around at her apartment's Big Box décor in dismay. The plaid seat covers, beige throw pillows, and generic framed prints on the walls did not convey the home of an authentic Hindi teacher.

"I know."

She hurried to her bedroom closet and crawled past a knee-high tower of paperback 'For Dummies' and a box of summer blouses to find the cache she sought. Secreted away in two oversized shopping bags were the long-abandoned accouterments of her Indian identity. She sat on her bed like a curious child and slowly picked through the items. There was a lone set of earrings and bangles from Vrindavan that she put on immediately. Her pierced ear holes stung as she poked the shiny silver hoops through them. Then she unwrapped four deity statues from her first New York puja. Krishna, Durga, Ganesh, and Lakshmi would be perfect on the table beneath the living room's bay window. She could complete her proper altar with a pewter ghi bowl and some offering sweets.

Other treasures—hand-painted images of Vishnu, and Krishna—were gifts from Jitter during her first year in New York. They would be perfect replacements for the Klee posters in the living room. She would hang the red wall tapestry of Durga as the ferocious Kali with wild, white eyes and a bloody mouth next to the front door.

She went to the corner Korean deli and bought a spray of orange lilies and arranged them in a turquoise vase. *Something with a scent.* She poured Champa oil in a tiny, ceramic bowl and set it on her bathroom counter. Then she spread a block print scarf from a street sale across the top of her sofa.

There must be more.

Crawling to the very back of her bedroom closet to the spot where the lightbulb light could not reach, she felt around the assorted dry-cleaning bags stuffed full with her winter coat and bulky, knit sweaters.

"I know they're here."

Her hands found a canvas bag and she dragged it into the light. She unzipped the top of the bag and slid her hand inside, touching something very soft and smooth. How many years had passed since she had seen it? *Five now?* Triti brought the bag out of the closet, sat on the end of her bed, and let out a long breath. Slowly, she pulled out a sparkling sari—a pale crème confection that Jitter had surprised her with for their first anniversary.

Trembling, she stood and swept up the nine yards of fabric and turned to face her full-length mirror. Then, in a swirl of movement, she arranged the folds of filmy beaded chiffon in its familiar wrap about her body, finishing, as always, over her right shoulder. She stood motionless, staring at her image, aware of the rise and fall of her chest.

"I know you."

She stepped closer to the mirror. Deep within her eyes, she saw something: shadows of unwelcomed memories.

NO. Leave me alone.

She turned and checked the sari's draping from the back.

"That's quite good."

Still, something was missing.

Oh, yes.

The other bag.

The next morning when Triti opened her apartment door to Jaq, both women were rendered speechless.

With their matching caramel-gold eyes, dimples, cleft chins, and long, black manes, the two were near duplicates of each other. Both slim and of average height, the only noticeable difference was their manner of dress—Triti in her crème-colored sari and gold bangles, and Jaq in her faded blue jeans and black tee shirt.

Triti found her voice first.

"I'm Minu. Please come in…"

She stared at Jaq as she led her into the small living room.

"Thank you for seeing me on such short notice," said Jaq. She walked directly to the elaborate altar and pointed to the nearest female statue. "Lakshmi."

Triti nodded, impressed.

Jaq studied the display, entranced by the bronze divinities and the lacquer plate brimming with white rosebuds and fresh mango cubes.

"Have a seat if you'd like. I'll bring the chai," said Triti. She went to the kitchen and brought out a tray with cups and a steaming teapot.

"So, where are you from?" asked Jaq as she took a seat on the couch.

"Have you heard of Rajasthan?"

"The north Indian state of the Rajs. Old India. I've dreamt of it. Tough to be bordering Pakistan, what with Musharaff…"

Triti could not help but to gaze into Jag's eyes. She wondered if people felt that way when they looked at her.

"Forgive me, this is awkward," said Triti. "But it's as if I'm sitting before a mirror."

"Were we separated at birth?" asked Jaq, unable to suppress a giggle.

"My grandmother was convinced that every person had an identical twin somewhere in the world," said Triti.

"One of my aunts told me the same thing, but I never believed her."

"I'll be twenty-five in July," said Triti. "How old are you?"

"Twenty-five. December."

"Seems I'm always the elder," murmured Triti.

She offered Jaq a cup of chai.

"So, how did you come to own such a fine Indian face?"

"My mother. Her family is from Delhi…"

Jaq's voice trailed off as she looked about the room at the many wall hangings and paintings. She took a bite of a sugar cookie and found her eyes drifting back to the altar.

"Is that why you want to learn Hindi?" Triti pressed.

"No. I'm doing my doctoral dissertation on Hindu temple sculptures, and I'll be spending two months in northern India starting this fall. I've studied Sanskrit for several years, but that won't be much help when I need water. That's pani, right?"

"Yes, very good. For most westerners, Hindi is quite difficult. The aspirations, the dental sounds, the rhythms… One really needs to hear it to learn it. Doesn't your mother speak Hindi at home?"

Jaq was embarrassed by the truth: despite Banni's upbringing in an Indian household in New York City, she resisted speaking Hindi once she learned English in school. When Guy came along, she studied French to please him. In spite of Jaq's pleadings, Banni refused to teach her daughter her mother tongue. Jaq was convinced that speaking Hindi would help her stand out among her talented classmates, but her mother was adamant. English, French, even Mandarin was acceptable; but not Hindi.

"No, she doesn't speak it much anymore. But I'm a quick study."

Jaq pulled several texts from her backpack.

"I have a few books here…"

Triti stopped her with a shake of head.

"You want to be conversational?"

"Yes."

"Then just keep a Hindi-English dictionary with you. Start collecting a list of words and phrases you wish to know. Then look them up and write them phonetically. During class I'll incorporate your list into our discussions."

"When can we start? My schedule is fairly flexible right now. Can we meet twice a week?"

"Well, that might be alright at the beginning, but you'll need more lessons if you expect to speak by October."

"You're probably right, but I'm on a serious budget. What's your fee?"

"For a sister?" Triti's divine face came alive. "My usual rates won't apply. Let me say $25 per class."

"Really? In that case, I'll take three classes a week."

"Very good," said Triti. "Let's meet here Mondays, Wednesdays, and Fridays at 2 p.m. We'll go to Indian restaurants so you can learn the different foods and dining customs. If you'd like, we can rent some Hindi films. And we'll take the train to Jackson Heights. It's an excellent place to try out your Hindi."

"Sounds great! I look forward to it."

Jaq slid her backpack on her shoulder.

"So, we shall see each other on Wednesday?"

"Yes, Wednesday," said Jaq, standing. "Sorry I have to leave so soon. Gotta pick up a research book they're holding for me at the library on 42nd. I'm heading to the 6."

"I'll walk with you," said Triti, gathering up her keys and purse. Having not worn a sari in years, Triti felt a strange nervousness when she stepped out on the street. As she and Jaq headed west toward 2nd Avenue, she noticed several other women wearing saris and felt instantly less conspicuous.

"How old were you when you left India?" asked Jaq.

Triti slid on a pair of sunglasses and looked up at the morning sky. She flashed back to the plane as it took off from Delhi, when her life was filled with fear and confusion. She forced the memories back down into the dark pit of her past, just as she had done for last seven years.

"I was eighteen."

"Not too long ago."

"An eternity," said Triti.

"Have you been back?"

Triti pulled the long sleeves of her cotton blouse down over her knuckles.

"No. I can't …"

"Understandable. I mean, how many desert summers can a girl take?"

Jaq laughed heartily at herself.

"See you on Wednesday, then," said Triti as they arrived at the subway entrance.

"Looking forward, Minu. I'll start my list of words today."

"Bahut acha."

"What does that mean?"

"Look it up!" said Triti, wryly.

"Namaste!"

And as the women went their separate ways, neither could resist looking back at the other. They waved one last time and hurried off, each certain that something remarkable had just occurred.

T W E N T Y

June 5, 2007

"Jaq, you've reread the same phrase *three* times."

Triti leaned forward on her elbows to make eye contact with her pupil, who was physically in her living room and mentally on some distant shore.

"What…? It's what?"

Jaq stared at the white three by five flash card in her hand. "Oh, sorry."

"We can stop if you'd like…it's almost three anyway," said Triti. "If you're hungry, I've got some leftovers for lunch."

Jaq shook her head.

"As tasty as your cooking is Minu, I wouldn't be able to get it down."

"No appetite? That doesn't sound like you."

Jaq's blank expression worried Triti. She had never seen her new friend so dull.

"Yeah, well, there's a lot you don't know about me."

Triti moved to sit on the coffee table, directly in Jaq's line of vision.

"Do you want to talk?"

"No," said Jaq. She squeezed her eyes shut and slumped deep into the sofa. "I just want to run away."

"And where would you go?" Triti asked gently.

"Somewhere obscure. Tonga. Greenland, maybe."

"Jaq, you can talk to me."

"Oh, it's so fucking complicated…"

Jaq rose and walked to the puja altar. She picked up the Lakshmi figurine and turned it over in her hands.

"She can help, you know," said Triti, rising to join her.

Jaq set the statue back in its place and sighed.

"I don't know… I'm a real mess."

"Perhaps," said Triti as she scooped up a handful of offering sweets from a bowl behind the altar and poured them into Jaq's hands. "But I can tell you, she likes a challenge."

"…So, as of today, the committee has denied my written request for a new advisor."

Triti had listened carefully as Jaq recounted her two-year saga of university power politics. She remembered Samir and Jitter's stories about life in academia, but the world of higher education was still a mystery to her. She could not understand how her new friend had been treated so unjustly.

"Reading that letter on official university stationery felt literally like a kick in the stomach. I never told the committee the real reason why I wanted a new advisor, but...it wouldn't have mattered anyway."

"Can't you go above him?" asked Triti.

"He's the chairperson. He's got the final say. And the Administrative Board will back him up. That's what they do."

"What will *you* do?"

"I don't know," said Jaq. "Seems like I've been up against this thing forever."

"This 'thing'?"

"You know. The V problem—owning a vagina."

Triti reddened. "I'm not sure I understand..."

"Until I was thirteen, I thought of myself as a person—not a female of the species. My lens was intellect, not gender. I remember filling out my high school application and being offended by the SEX - M or F section. Why did it matter what I had between my legs? I scratched out both boxes and wrote 'Yes'."

Triti chuckled shyly.

"Shit! I didn't judge others based on the shape and function of their reproductive organs. Come to find out, the rest of the world does! From our first breath, we're either pink or blue blankets...and *woe* to us pink ones. Darwinistically brutal, but true."

"What happened when you were thirteen?" asked Triti.

Jaq grew quiet. She blinked, but the memory of her day of shame would not fast forward nicely, regardless of how rapidly she fluttered her eyes. She would have to see and feel each agonizing second of her prepubescent humiliation again. She had a talent for hiding the psychological damage that memory had inflicted upon her. Her outward mask of good humor and brightness had fooled everyone for twelve years—including herself. Lately she had begun to notice cracks in her well-polished façade. Maybe it was time for her to tell. Not since that day, when her father held her and listened and petted her hair, the wisps of his pipe smoke encircling them, his cognac-smooth voice assuring her that he would make sure the creep who did it would never hurt her again.

Jaq settled her eyes on the painting of Krishna above the altar and the brilliant blue of his hands as he beckoned to his minions. *So blue.*

"Thirteen. I was free…"

"You were thirteen…"

"Working my first job—behind the register at Sal's grocery store down the street from our apartment. Just before opening on my first day. I remember breaking open the paper on a nickel pack into the change drawer…when the assistant manager, Larry, came around the cashier counter…and pressed his bulk against me from behind. He slid his sweaty hand under my skirt and beneath my panties, grabbing at my crotch. I tried to scream STOP! But no sound would come out. Nothing. I couldn't move. I couldn't scream! I just…stood there, shaking, while he rubbed and grunted…like a pig. Then, just when I wished I would die, he walked out the front door and smoked a cigarette."

Triti sat in silence, her shoulders trembling imperceptibly.

Jaq continued in a monotone.

"The sun was shining. I tried *so* hard not to cry as I ran back to our apartment. I crawled behind my father's easels."

"God, Jaq…"

"Took him an hour to coax me out."

Whoop, whoop, whir. A police siren trailed up the street.

"That's weird," said Jaq.

"What is?" asked Triti, her heart thudding in her chest.

"I *never* made the connection until now…"

Jaq looked at Triti and slowly nodded.

"The reason behind my shadow life in high school…"

"What do you mean?"

"Less than a year after my father died, I started staying out all night—anything to avoid my mother's incessant mourning. I couldn't *stand* to be near her. Christ, she turned the whole apartment into a shrine."

"You missed him," said Triti, thinking of her own father.

"Guess I craved paternal comfort. For two years I tried to find it as Ginger, Tess, Loni… I had so many fakes names I can't remember them all. The men all knew my real name. Schoolmates' fathers, guidance counselors, even one of my Social Studies teachers. I'd meet them in cheap, short-stays in Chelsea, near the West Side Highway. The fucking pervs. I just went numb."

Triti reached out and touched Jaq's hand.

"You're a good friend, Minu."

"I'm *so* sorry, Jaq. I can't imagine…"

"Guess it all goes back to fat Larry."

"Whatever happened to him?"

"He begged my father for his life then fled. Hasn't been seen in New York since."

TWENTY-ONE

Jackson Heights
New York City
June 15, 2007

Triti savored the last sip of her beverage, sorry to see the bottom of the heavy white cup.

"How can restaurants in Manhattan believe they serve a proper Masala tea with cold milk on the side? For the cardamom and pepper to take effect, both the tea and milk must be piping hot. We had to come to Queens to have it made right!"

"Yes, but it was *so* worth it!" said Jaq, slumping sated in her seat. She rubbed her full belly and moaned. "We haven't even made a dent in the pakoras or tandoori chicken."

Triti waved their young waitress to the table.

"I'll let you ask for the check, Jaq."

"Pop quiz? Cool."

Jaq cleared her throat and looked up at the waitress.

"Bil le āiye."

"Bahut acha!" said Triti. "Very good."

"Thanks, Teach! Uh, oh," said Jaq, pointing toward the street. "Where did our sun go?"

Beyond Samosa Heaven's front windows, the sky above 74th street darkened.

A light rain moistened the women's faces as they stepped out the restaurant door. Across the street, waves of disgruntled transit riders thundered down the local train trestle's steep stairs. Some popped open their umbrellas, while others sought shelter beneath their New York Posts and queued at the bus stop. Others jostled at the curb to hail taxis.

A tan sedan pulled up to the curb before Triti and Jaq. The weather-worn sign on the side of the car read Emmitt's Car Service. The Indian driver leaned toward the open passenger side window and called out to them in English but with a heavy accent.

"Where are you two ladies heading?"

"Do you know what's going on?" Jaq asked him, pointing to the subway exodus.

"The scanner is saying no inbound number 7 train. Police activity in Flushing."

Jaq was already moving toward the car. She gestured to Triti to follow suit.

"Two stops…East Side," said Jaq.

The driver nodded and sprang from his seat. He held open the rear passenger door for Triti and Jaq, closing it just as the rain became a downpour.

Back in his seat, the driver angled the rearview mirror for a brief view of his face to smooth back his wet, black curls. Triti watched him discretely, struck by his luminous green eyes. Their glances met and she looked away, shyly.

"Aap ka-haā se haī?" Jaq asked the driver as she settled into her seat. "Was that right, Minu?"

"Well done Hindi, Miss," said the driver, nodding enthusiastically. "Where am I from?"

Triti sensed that the man's praise was heartfelt, and not a compliment intended to extract a larger tip. She wondered if he knew how handsome he was.

"Minu is teaching me," said Jaq, gesturing at Triti.

"How fortunate for you."

The warmth in the man's voice made Triti flush.

"You haven't answered her question, Sir," said Triti.

"Please, call me Anand," he said as he pulled the taxi out into the flow of traffic. "I'm from Delhi."

He looked into the rearview mirror again to see Triti. This time she did not look away.

"My mother's family came from there forty years ago," said Jaq.

"Is that so?" Anand asked.

"I plan to go in the fall."

"Ah, very good." He looked over his shoulder at Triti. "And you, Ma'am?"

"Maī Rajasthan se huū. Jaipur."

Anand bobbled his head.

"Of course, you're from Rajasthan. I recognized the lovely accent."

With that, Triti and Anand fell into a discussion in Hindi of all things Desi. For her, the twenty-minute drive flew by. He made her laugh with his newbie-resident observations of life in New York; she amused him with her penetrating critiques of Bollywood films. Together they bemoaned the dearth of competent wait service in New York's Indian eateries. Their banter flowed effortlessly, as comfortable and familiar as everyday talk between two lifelong neighbors. At first, they made efforts to include Jaq in their conversation, explaining to her in tandem the woeful lack of government regulation of productive agricultural land in Rajasthan, and the myriad, practical difficulties of sustaining a working electrical grid capable of handling the energy demands of over 14 million Delhi residents. In their shared excitement to connect with someone from home, they translated less and less.

"So, Anand, what do you do when you're not driving people around?" asked Jaq, steering the conversation back to English.

"Actually, I've just finished a novel. I hope to sell it soon."

"You're a writer? Wow!" said Jaq.

Triti leaned forward in her seat, ever more intrigued.

"What is the title of your book?"

Anand's face lit up.

"I call it, 'Ani's World.' I named the main character after my great grandmother."

"What's the story about?" asked Jaq.

"The misadventures of an Indian girl, Ani, who can read minds and fly. She's reluctantly magical."

"I would read that," said Jaq.

"Me, too," said Triti, smiling.

"Oh, thank you both for saying so. Hopefully, one day you will."

Triti admired the casual, confident way Anand responded to their questions. His aura was entirely calming to her. Each time he spoke, she felt her pulse drop ten beats.

When at last Anand turned the car south on Second Avenue for the final leg of the ride, Jaq was glad to be dropped off first. She tossed Triti a mischievous wink as she climbed out of the cab in front of Banni's apartment.

"See you on Monday, sister!" Jaq called from the top of her stoop.

From Triti, a blush and a wave.

Triti's left leg had lost all sensation crooked beneath her as she sat in the cab's front seat but she didn't care. Talking with Anand felt as natural as breathing to her — and as necessary. When at last she checked her watch, she could scarcely believe that three hours had passed. To her it seemed that he had turned off the meter and parked in front of her apartment only minutes ago. She reached into her wallet to pay the fare, but he declined the money.

"I insist," said Triti, placing the bills on the seat next to him. He scowled at her playfully.

Anand escorted Triti into the foyer of her building and waited while she checked her mailbox. As she turned the key in the box, she found herself wishing that their time together could continue. *How can this be?* She had only just met him; yet parting from Anand seemed wrong somehow. She had never experienced such a feeling of attraction before. The intensity of the pull surprised her.

Won't he ask me out for tea? Or to join him for a walk in the park?

She could hardly believe the audacity of her thoughts. Anand held open the front door for her. As she walked past him, he smiled and said not a word.

When she reached the elevator, she turned to see him waving to her from behind the front door glass. She nodded in acknowledgment. He continued to smile and wave. She pressed the fifth-floor button and watched his face disappear as the elevator door slid closed.

"Namaste, Anand."

Before going to bed, Triti turned on the lights of the puja and sprinkled a pinch of sweets on Krishna's feet.

"Lord, am I a silly girl thinking I'll ever see him again?"

As she licked her fingers clean, she wondered what Anand was doing.

She went to sleep that night with him in her thoughts. The intelligence in his eyes and the music of his laughter were unforgettable to her. But it was his innate ability to put her at ease that amazed her most. The feeling of calm she experienced with him was unlike anything she had ever known. It was that very feeling she craved. No other man had ever made her feel so quietly confident, so completely secure. Not Samir, not even her father.

Admittedly, she had not really given other men the chance to get close to her. Since her divorce from Jitter, many men had asked her out, but she turned them all down. She found different excuses to avoid dating. She had convinced herself that she needed to concentrate on her job, or she wasn't ready to get involved yet. More often she used the pretext that casual dating was frowned on in her culture. While her justifications were partly true, she knew she spent her weekend evenings alone because of the residual pain from Samir's betrayal. She had long since shut her feelings away, determined to make herself impervious to romance; yet somehow, in the course of a single afternoon, Anand Behar had caused a fissure in the sturdy wall around her heart.

When Triti arrived home from work the next night, she found a pink long-stemmed rose wrapped in cellophane propped against the vestibule wall beneath her mailbox. The attached card read: 'For Minu, the lovely lady from Jaipur. Your friend, Anand.' Elated, she danced to the elevator. She sniffed the flower for hours until its scent was gone.

She found a pink rose with a similar handwritten note every night for the next week. Coming and going from the apartment, she scanned the parked and passing cars, hoping to see Anand in his taxi, but she kept missing his visits. She even contemplated staying home from work to wait for him on her front steps. Instead, she placed each new blossom in the vase on the altar beside Krishna. And waited.

On the eighth night, Anand's card held a different message.

"Would you care to join me at Sukhadia's for dessert tomorrow evening? I'll be there at 7 p.m. Your friend, Anand."

"Yes, Anand! Of course, I'll come!"

TWENTY-TW0

July 1, 2007

"Minu, you're not going to believe this."

"Let me guess…you're calling because you can't make it for your lesson?"

"Nope. Do you have electricity right now?"

"Yes, my fans are working, all praise to Krishna."

"Well, 'Blue-boy' is slacking off big time on my block. The power is out, and the cute Con Ed repair guy on our corner just told me, confidentially, not to expect service until tomorrow afternoon at the earliest."

"Oh, a day is nothing. We were sometimes without power for a week in our neighborhood in Jaipur. One just gets used to it."

"No way! I'll melt in this apartment… Good God! Evan just showed up with a six-pack and a fresh carton of menthols. The cherry on the top of my day."

"Oh dear…"

"Would you mind a roomie for a night? Please, Minu? It's Friday. You're off work. Tomorrow we can sleep late…"

"I don't know, Jaq."

"Come on, it'll be fun! I'll bring food…I'll even do the dishes! Please? PLEASE?"

"Alright, alright, come. The couch should be comfortable enough for you."

"Unless you have other, ahem, plans. Anand? You've seen him every day since you met, haven't you?"

"Nonsense! Only three times this week… And are you counting?"

"A habit. Just wondering."

"It's 5:30. Give me an hour," said Triti. "Don't bring food. I'm already cooking."

"I'll get a movie! Any requests?"

"Surprise me."

Jaq slipped her sandals off at Triti's door and padded behind her into the kitchen. She set two shopping bags on the counter.

"Wow! Smells good in here! What are you making?"

"Just a few of my favorites…paneer, aloo, tofu curry."

"What, no homemade rotis? You're slipping, sister."

Triti held one of the pots threateningly over the garbage can.

"You would prefer Chinese take-out?"

Jaq laughed and opened the lids to the other dishes on the stove. She dipped her finger into a small pot of savory sauce. Triti slapped her hand playfully.

"Mind your manners."

"Oh! Quick, put this in the freezer."

Jaq lifted a bottle of tequila from a yellow box.

"I got these as well."

She pulled a lemon and lime out of a paper bag, along with two shot glasses.

"The good stuff isn't a depressant. It's a hallucinogen. Big difference. I take mine neat, but I thought maybe you needed a garnish. Do you like fruit with your shot?"

"I...don't know. I've never tried it," said Triti.

"Oh, no? Well, we're going to have *some* fun tonight!"

"Let's eat first. And go over your new vocabulary."

"Hanji!"

Jaq scraped the last bite of spiced potatoes from her plate.

"It's a shame you didn't like it," said Triti.

Jaq laughed.

"So, I would say, 'Bah hoot a chah' for this amazing meal?"

"No, like this… Boat-aht-cha. Remember the woman from Jammu who sold us the samosas in Queens? Typical pronunciation in northern India."

"Boat-aht-cha."

"Right. You're improving."

"Thanks to you. It is frustrating, though. The words on the page sound so different when you speak them."

"Keep making your list of phrases."

"Hanji! And now!" said Jaq, heading to the freezer. "Reward time!"

She returned to the table carrying the icy liquor bottle and two frosty shot glasses. Like a surgeon, she sliced open and removed the plastic wrapping from the hand-blown glass topper, then eased the fat, round cork from the bottle's mouth. She filled both glasses and presented Triti her shimmering golden beverage.

"Here's to summer in the city," said Jaq.

"Am I'm supposed to…?" Triti tossed her head back, imitating the motion of shooting a drink she had seen in the movies.

"No, no. Consider this as you would a fine cognac. Sip it, roll it on your tongue, breathe it in…"

The women clinked glasses and drank.

"Yessss," said Jaq, licking her lips.

Triti squinted her eyes tight shut and stomped her right foot.

"Ah! It burns!"

"Perfection in a glass," said Jaq, smiling.

Beads of sweat dotted Triti's face.

"Miss Minu, aren't you dying in those long sleeves and pants? Even with the fans it must be 85 degrees in this room."

Triti tugged at her salwar cuffs so that just her fingertips showed.

"No, I'm fine."

"What am I saying? You grew up in Rajasthan."

"That was a *dry* heat."

"Of course."

Triti took a bigger sip of her tequila and swallowed hard.

"Do you miss your family? You never talk about your them," asked Jaq.

Silence.

"I was just wondering, is all…"

"You're starting to behave like a real Indian, Jaq. Questions and more questions…I didn't really expect an inquisition."

"No one expects the South Asian Inquisition!"

Jaq choked with laughter.

"Sorry, sorry, no, really…Python, I couldn't resist."

Triti left the table and sank into her sofa's plush cushions.

Jaq managed to suppress her giggles.

"Ready yet for round two?"

"I'm still drinking this one," said Triti, becoming aware of a warm sensation radiating throughout her chest. Jaq carried the bottle to the couch and topped off Triti's near-empty glass. She returned the bottle to the freezer and wandered over to examine the puja altar.

"So, we're thinking safety here?" Jaq asked, pointing to the electric candles.

"What do you mean?"

"I thought only Catholics did the fake lights on the altar thing." She touched the tip of Ganesh's trunk. "You can leave these on all night. Cool!"

Jaq looked around the room at the colorful wall hangings and prints of Hindu pantheon royalty.

"Shiva, Krishna, Parvati..." Jaq stepped from frame to frame examining the artwork. "Do you have any pictures of your family? I'm a sucker for photo albums."

Silence again. This time Triti stood and headed into the kitchen.

"What did I say?"

Triti ignored Jaq's questions, determined to steer her mind away from the door her student was trying to force open.

From the living room, Jaq heard the microwave start. Soon the smell of fresh popcorn filled the apartment. She pulled a DVD out of her backpack and pushed the disc into the player beneath the television. Her second shot of tequila was beginning to make an impression.

"Need any help in there, Teach?"

"No," Triti called out as she rummaged in a cupboard for a bowl. "Can you set up the DVD? The remote should be on the ..."

"Got it," said Jaq. She curled up on the sofa and played with the buttons on the clicker.

"So, what movie did you bring?" called Triti.

"Oh, no! You told me to surprise you!" said Jaq, raising her voice above the shrill of a car alarm on the street below.

A minute later, Triti returned to the couch and placed a container of buttered popcorn between them on a bath towel, just as the car alarm died.

"It's all ready." Jaq tucked her feet beneath her and grabbed a handful of popcorn.

As the film's opening music swelled, Triti bolted upright in her seat.

"Lagaan? You got Lagaan? I *love* this movie!"

Halfway through the raucous Bollywood classic, Triti ached for home. She was back in the land of her past: walking across red desert sands, hearing familiar singsong dialects, seeing the colors and sights of her youth.

"Where ya goin'?" asked Jaq.

Triti made her way into the kitchen for another shot of tequila. She was amazed that the third round didn't burn quite so much. Returning to the living room, her homesickness nearly unbearable, she stood next to the couch, unsure if she could watch another minute of the movie. But her body, with its own memories, started swaying as another of the elaborate musical numbers began. She closed her eyes and began to move her arms to the music.

"Can you dance like that?" asked Jaq, pointing to the performers on the screen.

"Of course."

"No way."

"All self-respecting Jaipur girls can!" Triti pushed the coffee table and ficus tree to the side of the room and turned up the film's volume. "But I won't do it alone," she said as she pulled Jaq up off her seat.

"No, no, sister. This girl doesn't dance!" said Jaq, attempting to sit back down.

"Nonsense!" said Triti, as she demonstrated a series of simple arm moves and hip thrusts. Jaq tried lamely to imitate Triti's graceful style.

"You've got it!"

The two pranced and mugged about, posing for each other.

Triti caught hold of Jaq's heavy, lank braid.

"This will *never* do."

She removed the rubber band and worked her fingers like busy worms through Jaq's black waves.

"*Now* you can truly dance!"

Together they spun about the room, hair flying, laughing hysterically, each trying to out-vamp the other.

"Those women," shouted Jaq, pointing to the screen, "They're incredible looking. Like you, Minu. You could be a Bollywood star!"

"And you as well!"

"Yeah, right," said Jaq, rolling her eyes.

Triti stopped in mid-swirl to assess Jaq's appearance.

"Wait," she said, and disappeared into her bedroom. A moment later she returned with two diaphanous scarves; one lime green, the other neon purple. She draped the purple chiffon on Jaq's neck and they both whirled about again.

Triti was unsatisfied.

"Those jeans are just wrong. Come."

In her bedroom, Triti tossed several salwar suits and dupattas on her bed, all the while the movie roared on in the living room.

"Try this!" Triti thrust a sea blue outfit into Jaq's arms. Without hesitating, Jaq changed into the suit.

"I'm not loving it."

Triti was back in her closet again.

"*This* one."

She handed Jaq a salmon ensemble with a pink-and-gold dupatta. Jaq changed quickly and turned around to show Triti.

"That is your color. I *should* have known. It works for me too."

Jaq looked in the full-length mirror and smiled.

"But you're still not quite right."

Triti took Jaq by the hand and danced her down the hall into the bathroom. She pulled a plastic container from the top of the cabinet.

"Sit," said Triti, indicating the commode. Jaq sat obediently. With a large tortoiseshell barrette, Triti pulled Jaq's thick mane away from her face. Before her beamed an eerily familiar canvas. With a sure hand, she wielded pencils, powders, and gloss in a flurry of artistic fervor.

"You really like Anand, don't you, Minu?"

Triti smiled as she pictured his face. She brushed peach blush along Jaq's cheekbones.

"Yes, I enjoy our times together. We laugh a great deal."

"He seems very romantic," said Jaq, closing her eyes for Triti to apply black liner. "Your table has roses on it every time I've come for class."

"He's certainly different from other men I've met."

"In what way?"

Triti thought for a moment.

"He's gentle with himself."

"Is he a good listener?"

"Yes! And he *actually* remembers what I've said!"

"What do you do together?"

"The usual things, I suppose. We go out for dessert. Or for walks in Central Park. We've been to South Street Seaport. And we rode the Staten Island Ferry. Twice. I love watching the seabirds fly in circles above the boat."

"You see each other often?"

"Since we both work nights, we try to meet for lunch. He's partial to Chinese food. Wontons, especially."

Jaq opened her eyes and looked up at Triti.

"The most important question of all...is he a good kisser?"

Triti felt herself flush.

"I...have no idea."

"Really? I, just expected..."

"Anand is old fashioned, you could say. And that suits me well."

Jaq burped and rolled her eyes. Triti smelled the tequila on her breath.

"Well, Minu, take it from me...that makes him *very* different."

"What about you, Jaq? Was there ever anyone special?"

Naveen. Jaq instantly saw him in her mind and felt the same, heated rush come over her she always had when remembering him. Then, as always, right behind it came the sting.

"Yes," she said, resignedly. "There was *one.* Unfortunately, I wasn't special enough for his world."

"I'm sorry, Jaq…"

"No, don't be. He's so ancient history."

Triti worked scented patchouli oil into Jaq's hair and arranged it in long tendrils down her shoulders and back. Then she applied red polish to Jaq's fingernails and toes. The cumulative effect of her soft touch was so relaxing that Jaq nearly drifted off. In the background, the movie's rambunctious musical score ramped up for the big finish. Crescendo stacked upon crescendo as the good guys triumphed, lovers reunited, and justice won the day.

"Stay there and don't look yet," said Triti.

She returned to her bedroom and retrieved her red velvet bag from the back of her bureau's top drawer. Its familiar, hand-sewn mirrors sparkled beneath the fluorescent overhead light. She knew what was inside, even though she had not touched them or even looked at them for nearly five years. Carefully, she pulled open the drawstring and removed six gold bracelets—Mala's gifts to her—in another life.

Mala. Could she let herself remember the young woman who had saved her? Triti perched on the edge of the bed; the bracelets heavy in her lap. Mala had given her so much: healing, food, shelter, clothing. *Life.*

Dowry.

Suddenly she could not help but remember the tenderness of Mala's touch and her kind eyes. Guilt raked Triti's heart. In her flight for safety, survival had been her sole concern. What had happened to her angel of mercy? She thought of Mala's marginal existence. *Was she safe?* Had she found happiness, in spite of the constant knocks on her door?

Triti doubted she would ever know.

With a sigh, she returned to the bathroom and slid the bracelets onto Jaq's arms—three and three. From a jewelry box on a shelf above her rattan hamper, she selected costume earrings, a necklace, anklets, and several rings. In moments Jaq sat, bejeweled.

"And *now*, let's see you."

Jaq jingled from head to toe as she stood up and stepped in front of the bathroom mirror.

"Is it…*me*?"

Triti could only nod and admire her handiwork.

"I…can't believe it."

Jaq ran her hands lightly over her face and hair. She lifted a chandelier earring for a closer view.

"It's all so…feminine. But I *like* it. I do. Thank you, Minu."

"You're welcome."

Triti joined Jaq in the mirror's frame. Side by side, they were virtually identical.

"We could be twins," said Jaq.

As Triti looked on, Jaq's features began to shift and change until she saw her brother Dilip standing next to her. She rubbed her eyes until they hurt, and when she reopened them, Jaq was smiling back at her.

Shaken, Triti turned away sharply and began collecting her cosmetics.

"It's late, Jaq. I need to clean up in here."

Half past midnight, Manhattan sweltered in a summer fever. Triti had disappeared into her bedroom, so Jaq found a spare sheet in the hall closet and draped it over the couch. Sluggish from the heat and alcohol, she moved slowly. The jewelry on her ears, arms, and ankles jangled with each step. The silky swish-swish of the kameez against her thighs and buttocks stirred sensual memories.

"I suppose one just gets used to it."

Carefully, she slipped off Triti's clothes and folded them neatly. Then, piece-by-piece, she removed all of Triti's jewelry. She considered arranging the gold on the puja.

Would Krishna appreciate the ornaments?

Unsure, she decided she would put the jewelry away for her friend.

But where?

Jaq cracked open the top drawer of Triti's desk. Batteries, a manual for the DVD player, two packs of sugarless gum… Not in there, she decided. There was too much jewelry to fit such a shallow bin. She tugged at the larger drawer below it. It stuck at first, but with a little muscle, she managed to slide it open. Jaq blinked at what she saw. Wrapped in tight bundles of twenty or more, secured neatly with twine were hundreds of letters—stamped, sealed, and addressed. She picked up the top bundle and flipped through the stack. Every letter was identical with the same address hand-printed on the envelopes:

M. Sharma, J – 1,

Sawai Jai Singh Highway

Bani Park, T0141 2204638.

Each had colorful, international postage stamps precisely affixed. Even the pen ink appeared to be the same.

Who is M. Sharma? Where is Bani Park?

"Why haven't you sent these, Minu?"

Mystified, Jaq put back the stack of letters just as she had found it and closed the drawer tightly. Then she took off her damp bra, pulled on her white tee shirt, and planted herself directly in front of the floor fan. Even on high speed, the artificial breeze brought her little relief. Hearing Triti moving about in her bedroom, Jaq trundled to her door to say goodnight. She pushed it open slightly and saw Triti hunched naked on the bed, her hands glistening with oil as she vigorously massaged her naked feet.

Triti's swollen eyes met hers.

"SHUT THE DOOR!"

The force of Triti's words sent Jaq stumbling backward down the hall. She flinched as Triti slammed her door. The click of a lock. A moment later, the strip of light beneath Triti's door vanished.

"Jesus! *What* just happened?" said Jaq, stunned.

She retreated to the living room just as a spinning cloud of rubbish and city dirt lashed the apartment's front windows. A flash of lightning lit the street as bright as midday. With a roar, torrents of grape-sized raindrops plummeted earthbound and sizzled into an ashen miasma that hovered, ghostlike, above the scorched pavement. Jaq went to the closest window, pushed open the fire-escape gate, and crawled out onto the black, iron platform. Sitting cross-legged on the warm, wet slats, she lifted her face to the deluge as her makeup ran down her body in streams—off her cheeks, over her chin, down her neck, between her breasts and beyond.

In less than a New York minute, Jaq's face was her own again.

TWENTY–THREE

Triti strolled, unsettled, beside Anand along the busy footpath that wound through northern Central Park's forests and fields.

The park was crowded with couples and families sprawled on blankets sunbathing and picnicking on the warm Sunday afternoon. Anand was telling her his ideas for the cover of his book, but she was too distracted to pay attention. Her evening with Jaq was haunting her. Two weeks had passed, yet she was still shaken up. That night had stirred so many memories: Dilip, her parents, Mala. She could not keep her mind from drifting to images of the older girl grinding spices at her rustic table, or preparing rotis. She was alternately wracked with guilt and sorrow. What of the vision of Dilip? Why had she seen him in her bathroom? Just when she thought she had found a way to push away all of her past thoughts, another fear crept in. Her secret was out.

Jaq had seen her feet. What would she do if her friend began to ask questions? Although their Hindi sessions continued as before, Jaq now seemed somewhat aloof, even suspicious.

Across from a children's playground, Anand spied a rare empty bench.

"Thank you for the meal," said Triti as they sat and opened their Curry in A Hurry pint boxes from the crowded nearby food truck. The aromas of turmeric and cardamom made her mouth water.

"I'm only sorry I have to leave so soon, Minu. My shift starts at four today."

"It's fine, really," said Triti. "I agreed to cover for the other night manager this evening. I so rarely get a chance for overtime these days. I said 'yes' right away."

Anand scooped potatoes and spinach onto his plate and took a taste.

"What do you think?" she asked.

"Well…it's certainly no competition for my mother's cooking. I fear she's truly spoiled me."

Triti had loved helping her mother prepare the spicy, lentil soup of daal-baati. She remembered cutting the vegetables for pakodi and the tantalizing smells in the kitchen as they sizzled in the frying oil. Those memories felt safe to her, though now tinged with melancholy. She didn't want to feel sad at that moment.

"Tell me more about your progress with 'Ani'. It must be difficult work to write a book."

Anand shrugged and swallowed a bite of potato.

"Work and patience… It's been nearly seven years since I wrote the first paragraph. Yesterday two literary agents asked for the first chapter of my manuscript. *Finally!*"

"You must be excited!"

"This morning I ran to the printing shop and made two copies. First thing tomorrow I'm going to hand-deliver the packages."

Triti picked up her water bottle. "Here's to Ani's success!"

They touched their bottles together and sipped.

"Your parents must be so proud of you, Anand."

He wiped his forehead with a napkin.

"Minu, there's something I need to tell you."

At the seriousness of his tone, Triti put the paratha she was about to eat back in its box.

"What *is* it, Anand?"

He ran his hands through his black curls.

"About my parents…they don't know I've submitted my book to agents."

"Why not?"

"I haven't told them, yet. They think I'm working in a novelties store, learning the business from the bottom up…"

"I don't understand."

"…from my future, rather ex-future father-in-law."

"Anand, you're confusing me."

"You see, I came to New York from Delhi four months ago on a marriage visa."

Triti's eyes narrowed.

"But…but the marriage wasn't meant to be. When I met my bride for the first time, she was a different girl than I'd spent a year communicating with. Her family here in NY had put an ad online and used her younger sister's photo. Naina was fully three times the size of the woman I thought I was going to marry. And seven years older. I'd only been here a few hours when I found out I'd been tricked."

"What happened?" Triti asked as her mouth went dry.

"Straight off the plane from Delhi, I was taken to a restaurant in Astoria where two dozen of her family members were waiting to welcome me. I never got to speak to my 'bride', but judging by her forlorn expression she'd been through the sad charade before. Me, I was exhausted from the flight, and completely panicked. I didn't know what to do. Several of the cousins had been drinking and a row flared. I used the fight as cover and managed to slip out the restaurant's side door. It was *all* a mess: a big, embarrassing, impossible mess."

"Why are you telling me this?"

Anand look at her, his green eyes shining.

"Because…I like you, Minu. You're a very sweet person. Even though we've only known each other six weeks, I've grown quite fond of you…"

Triti could not help but feel as though she was about to have the rug pulled out from under her feet again.

"It's just that…my visa expires in September," he said with a sigh. "I'll have to go back to Delhi. I needed you to know."

Triti sat quietly for a few minutes. She picked at her food with her fork, unable to formulate a sentence. All she knew was that the thought of him leaving made her heart hurt.

"I'm not sure what you want me to say, Anand."

"Just say that you like me, too."

"Don't you know that already?"

"Yes, I do. That's why telling you the truth was so difficult."

Now it made sense to her why Anand had never spoken of his parents. She thought of their many dates and how relieved she felt that the subject of family had never come up. Now with *his* revelation, she feared for her own secrets. It would not be long until he would begin asking about her past.

"Anand, what kind of tree are we under?"

"I'm not positive, but judging by its size, and the shape of the leaves, it must be an oak. "

"Do oaks grow in India?" she asked.

"We have the Silver Oak. I believe the wood is used for cricket bats."

"I wonder if a seed from an Indian Silver Oak…"

"They're called acorns, I think."

"…could grow in America?"

"I don't know. In order to survive, it would have to change a great deal."

Anand tossed his roti crusts on the ground, which immediately caught the attention of a drove of speckled sparrows. The birds flitted about their feet tussling over the hard, dried pieces—thoroughly unfazed by the onslaught of pedestrians, bicyclists, and runners passing within inches of them.

Thirty feet up the path, Triti caught sight of an elderly woman attempting to rise from a stone bench. Her cane shook noticeably in her blue-veined hand. A female attendant in a pink cotton uniform lay sound asleep on the adjacent bench; a cell phone nestled between her enormous breasts. The old woman strained and managed to get upright and take a few faltering steps. A pack of skateboarders whizzed by her prompting her to stop.

"That was entirely too close," Triti said to Anand while pointing at the woman.

The immediate danger past, the woman began moving again, gaining momentum as she shuffled down the slope.

"The old people *here* look like *our* old people," said Anand.

The woman, undeterred by the joggers and baby strollers, seemed completely determined to get somewhere. As she passed by Triti and Anand, a sparrow landed at her feet, snatched up a remaining roti crumb, and flew off. The woman turned to look at the two of them.

"A brave act," said Anand.

The old woman sighed as her faded eyes met his.

"I'm envious of the little fellow," she said, her voice creaking with the start of each word. "Every night I say a special prayer for wings, but in the morning, I awake with these damned-near useless things." She pointed at her legs.

"I've always wanted to fly," said Anand. "And this year, for the first time, I did."

He leaned closer to the woman and rocked his head from side to side.

"To tell you the truth, I'm quite relieved to be back on earth."

The woman attempted another step, but her orthopedic heel jammed in a crack in the sidewalk and she toppled forward with a yelp. Anand lunged from his seat to catch her featherweight frame just before she hit the pavement. He placed her down gently beside Triti on their bench.

The attendant never stirred from her nap.

"Where did that divot come from?" she said, concern gripping her face. "I didn't hurt the little fellow, did I?"

"No, Ma'am. The bird is fine," said Triti. She couldn't help wondering where was the woman's family.

Anand stood beside the woman.

"Are *you* alright, Ma'am?"

The woman caressed the top of her bronze-handled cane, and then shifted in her seat so that she could look up at Anand.

"Tell me. Am I invisible?"

"No, Ma'am. I see you as plainly as my hand."

The woman nodded, satisfied with his answer.

"You have a lovely way about you, young man."

"Well, thank you, Ma'am."

"I would like to go home now," she said.

Triti and Anand glanced at each other and then at the nurse, whose open-mouthed snores were now audible over the traffic on Central Park West.

"Let her sleep, poor creature," said the woman. "She works two other jobs and attends night school in the Bronx. She's going to be a dental hygienist."

The woman slipped a frail arm around Anand's elbow, and as he helped her to her feet, Triti rousted the nurse.

TWENTY–FOUR

July 22, 2007

J aq scanned the glossy Asia Society brochure while Triti stood on a short line for two tickets to the newest exhibit featuring female Hindu deities. She handed Jaq a round black pin for her collar.

"Now we're official," said Jaq, as she slid the museum button into the front pocket of her faded jeans. "I've always enjoyed this place. Haven't been here since I went to Hunter."

"From what I've read, this show is in line with your thesis topic, and will give us a chance to play with language."

"Good plan," said Jaq.

Triti was relieved that Jaq had agreed to meet at the museum for their class. Since their sleepover, her student had probed her with questions about her childhood in India. Although she had managed to change the subject each time, she was tiring of having to concoct yet another clever dodge. Making matters worse, she was exhausted from three sleepless nights in a row. Today she had to keep things simple: art and Hindi.

As the women strolled down the exhibit's halls, they chatted about the bronze sculptures and miniature paintings of Indic goddesses.

"Whoa!" said Jaq, pointing to a ten-foot-high oil mural of a goddess in her warrior fierceness. The blood dripping from her lips and fingertips looked dark and wet enough to be real.

"I've seen many depictions of Durga/Kali before, but yikes! How do you say 'scary' in Hindi?"

"Daravna," said Triti, as they moved on to the next set of paintings.

Near the exhibit's central Shiva fountain, a middle-aged Japanese tour guide announced to the large group behind him that they were late for the daily tea ceremony taking place two flights below on the atrium level. People began shuffling quickly toward the elevator bank, and in the fracas, Jaq lost sight of Triti. She rounded the nearest corner and made her way into the next exhibition room to wait. There she found herself before James Peggs's 1832 etching of a young Indian woman sitting on a funeral pyre with her dead husband's head in her lap as enormous flames engulfed them both. The woman's face was serene, and she had her arms up in the air.

"Oh, my God," she said. "That poor thing."

At that moment, Triti came up beside Jaq and stared at the scene on the canvas. Suddenly she was *there*—the searing flames, deafening shouts, choking smoke. Triti's face drained white. Her mouth filled with warm water as bile surged up her throat. Moaning, she bolted from the room.

Startled, Jaq hesitated before chasing after her. On Park Avenue, she found Triti dry heaving over a fire hydrant. Jaq hailed a cab with her trusty, two-fingered whistle, and within moments the women were riding downtown. Triti's tears ran hot over her cheeks. Even with the cab's air conditioning on high, her body felt as if it were burning. Jaq put a hand on her shoulder to calm her, but she couldn't stop shaking. She looked out the car window. Second Avenue...bridge traffic...delivery trucks...dog walkers...cross walks...suitcases swinging.

The city didn't care.

It had begun.

Huddled in the corner of her couch, Triti clutched her white floor-length skirt tightly to her legs and pressed her head against her knees. She dared not speak. Maybe if she stayed quiet, the Memory would retreat.

Hours passed.

A narrow swath of afternoon sun receded along the wall.

Shadows consumed the light.

Jaq waited quietly beside her friend, relieved to see that she had finally stopped trembling. She kept playing the morning over in her mind, trying to understand what had happened to cause Minu such distress. She was stumped. Jaq reviewed the catalogue of her teacher's eccentricities she had observed since their first meeting: her incapacitating fear of fire, and how even a stranger lighting a cigarette on the street made her flinch; her staunch refusals to speak about her family, or reveal any substantive details of her life in India; her obsession with covering up her hands and feet, and the absence of any family memorabilia in her apartment, but for a bizarre collection of stamped, unmailed letters. Then there was her outburst the night of the sleepover, and her frantic rubbing of her feet. It was clear to her that a critical piece of her friend's personal story was still missing.

"Are you ok, Minu?"

Triti opened her eyes to Jaq.

"That's not my real name." Her voice was emotionless.

"What do you *mean*?"

"My name is Triti."

"Wow. Ok."

Triti searched Jaq's eyes for safety, and found it. She sat up and pulled her sleeves down over her fingers.

"Triti… What happened to you back there?"

Triti spoke the words for the first time.

"*I* was that widow."

Over the course of the next several hours, in fits and starts, Triti revealed to Jaq what she could remember of the terrible time. Many of the details still would not come, while other images rushed back in, newly painful. She began with flashes from the day Rakesh died.

She had risen early the morning of his death and written a letter to her parents in which she pleaded with them to let her do the unthinkable—return home to Jaipur. She knew that her culture demanded that she live in her husband's family home, but she was desperately sad and didn't know what else to do. She told them of the pressures of her new life spent in strict purdah, with the mandate that her head and face be covered completely by her sari drape at all times, and how she was not permitted to leave the confines of the women's zanana, nor use any telephone. She lamented to them that she was forced to spend all day cleaning floors and fetching firewood, and that her mother-in-law and sister-in-law openly shunned her, speaking to her only when they had another chore for her. She was too ashamed to share with her parents that her young husband had abandoned their marital bed after their first night together when his impotence made their coupling a dismal failure. She couldn't admit that even though just three weeks had passed since her marriage, she had cried herself to sleep every night. At the end of the letter, she begged her father to come get her. But she had not been able to send her letter. That evening her new husband's lifeless body was brought to her—laid at her feet by his brothers, like a Rajput warrior slaughtered in battle.

"At first, I thought he was asleep," she told Jaq, tucking her feet under the sofa cushion. "But he was *so* pale. And there was all the wailing—the men screaming to the heavens, the women beating their chests. Was I supposed to beat mine too? I didn't even *know* Rakesh. How could I cry for him?"

Jaq shook her head and said nothing.

"*That* night, the weeping turned into whispers. Something had changed. People rushed in and out of our bedroom. Sounds made no sense. False smiles came toward me."

"What else can you remember?" asked Jaq, moving closer to her on the couch.

Triti's eyes grew wide with the task.

"Anything else? What did you see? A smell? Or a taste, maybe?"

Triti strained, but there was nothing. And then…

"Yes," she nodded slowly. "My mother-in-law. She gave me tea early the next morning. I remember not liking it, but she insisted that I finish it, so I did. I know it was morning because the light made me squint. I remember thinking that Rakesh would never see the sun again."

"The *tea*?"

"It was…strange. It tasted like bitter almonds."

"You *hate* almonds," said Jaq.

"Actually, I used to love them. Until *that* day."

"What happened after the tea?" Jaq pushed.

No. Don't show me.

"I…can't."

"Someone hurt you."

Triti was in the Void. Her eyes were open, but there was nothing in her vision. Suddenly, a strange weight pressed in on her, as if she was being compressed between enormous pillows. She couldn't move, or even breathe. Just as she began to choke, she felt a great shove, and she tumbled into dense blackness that surrounded her and then abruptly parted, and a grainy film began playing indecipherable images in her mind. She saw *herself*—a blur—moving at astonishing speed.

"I ran! Yes! All the rain! But I ran!"

The women hunched elbow-to-elbow at Triti's kitchen table. The day's revelation sat beside them—an entity demanding further investigation. Jaq's mind itched with more questions, but all she could do was to sit with her friend and try to imagine Mala, Rattan and Samir, the train, the monkeys, and the guru's kiss.

Triti was shaken and exhausted. She had recalled far more of her story than when she confided in Jitter seven years earlier. The Memory seemed to be literally coming alive: its sounds and odors were now detectable, its colors and sensations startlingly vivid. When she noticed Jaq looking at her hands, she tugged at her sleeves.

"You're safe," said Jaq. "Really."

Jaq reached out and took Triti's right hand in hers. Triti tried to pull away, but Jaq held her firmly. She looked into Jaq's eyes to challenge her, but the tenderness she saw made her relent. Gently, Jaq slid her sleeve up past her wrist. Triti saw what she always did: red, mangled evidence of the terrible time. But the scars were barely visible—faded and smooth. Jaq took her left hand and examined it as well, and then motioned to Triti's feet. Triti shook her head without conviction. Her tears began to fall. Slowly, she extended her legs and closed her eyes as Jaq pulled her white knee socks off one at a time. Seeing Triti's scarred toes and heels, Jaq's stomach wretched, but her face remained placid.

"Who did this to you?"

Triti pulled her feet beneath her again and tugged at her sleeves.

"I…don't remember."

"Your family! Do your parents even know you're *alive*?"

"No! And they can never know. They'd be in danger."

"Someone tried to kill you!"

"They *did* kill me."

The bleak truth.

"But Triti, you've *got* to call your parents. Your mother must be…"

"Triti is dead. As long as she stays that way, my family is safe."

"But you're *not* dead!"

"You don't understand…"

"I *want* to understand. Please let me help. I can try to find out…"

"No, Jaq! This secret dies here, now, for once and for all. You *must* promise me. Promise me!"

"But Triti…"

"I'm *Minu*! *This* is my life. It is what it is."

Jaq ground her teeth in frustration. Before her sat her friend—murdered yet alive— scarred within and without. There had to be some way to find the perpetrators and bring them to justice. Her head swam with scenarios.

"I'm sorry to upset you. Not my intention."

The two women sat in strained silence for several minutes.

"Triti is a lovely name. What does it mean in Hindi?"

Triti closed her eyes and tried in vain to picture her mother's face. All that came was a blurry image of a thin woman dressed in a sari.

So jaa…

"One translation is 'a moment in time'. Ma named me. She said my birth was a moment she would never forget. Six minutes later, my brother arrived."

"You have a *brother*?"

"Dilip. He was supposed to be my protector…"

Well after three a.m., Jaq stretched out on the sofa with Triti sitting beside her.

"Are you tired? I can go."

Triti shook her head.

There was more.

"The hardest part for me was leaving."

"India?"

"Rajasthan. We Rajput have old ways. If you're a girl and your parents choose well, you marry and move west. I just never thought it would be *this* far west."

"Were you afraid?"

"Yes, I was petrified! Amreeka! It was *so* unknown. But compared to what my family and I would have faced had I been discovered alive... As children we heard the tales of widows who had tried to run from their fates, only to be caught and dragged back to the flames..."

Jaq stood and walked to the altar. She felt a flutter of guilty relief. *But, for the grace of God...*

"And you *can't* remember what happened?"

"I've tried. Good God, I've tried. A week of my life... vanished. Every night at the ashram I prayed for my memory to return. Nothing. Then the night walks with Samir, and Guru Mari..."

Triti's legs twitched and she felt the unmistakable urge to rise and run.

"You came here with so little," said Jaq.

"It sounds ridiculous now, but when I stepped on the ashram bus to leave, all I could think was that I hadn't emptied out my library desk. I left behind the necklace, a key chain with a picture of Guru Mari, and two ballpoint pens."

"And the red sari?"

Triti raised her eyebrows.

"It's in a bag, under my bed."

No Time

Smoke
Cries
Flames…
"Noooo! Ma!!!"
So jaa raajkumari so jaa…
"Ma, where *are* you? I'm frightened…"
I'm here, main bali haari, my precious one…
"I can't see you! Help me, Ma!"
Triti wrenched herself from the nightmare, soaked in sweat. Wrapping her arms around her knees, she rocked in place, shivering on her bed until dawn.

TWENTY-FIVE

August 15, 2007
New York City

S ATI. DEATH BY FIRE.
Could there be a more hideous way to die?

At her desk in Guy's studio, Jaq's fingers flew across her laptop. Google Search—SHARMA, TRITI. No search results. SHARMA, TRITI 2000. No search results. RAJASTHAN SHARMA, TRITI.

She waited. Rajasthan travel sites loaded automatically on the screen.

"No, no. Another way..."

BRIDE BURNING INDIA.

The very act of typing the words made her nauseous. She pressed Return and waited.

Jaq recoiled as dozens of matches lit up her screen. She clicked open the first article.

Journal India, 2005. "Today, women and young girls are dying all over our country from the vile crime of 'bride-burning' or 'kitchen fires'. These unfortunate newly-weds are suffering the most horrific death at the hands of their husbands' families and often the husbands themselves. Set on fire alive, they are modern day satis, dying not to follow their dead husbands in devotional sacrifice but because their families failed to meet staggering dowry demands of their new in-laws."

Next article. Click.

Hindustan Times, 2004. "Dowry deaths by fire have become all too common tragedies across India. Each year tens of thousands of young brides suffer in 'kitchen fires' set by unscrupulous men intent on profiting from multiple dowries by way of serial marriages."

Click.

Commission Report on the Status of Women, Madra, India, 2002. "The fortunate victims of the pernicious and disturbingly prevalent practice of 'bride-burning' die in the flames. Throughout the Indian rural country side and the pulsing metropolitan meg-cities, for those women and girls unlucky enough to survive, a wretched life of agony awaits. Their bodies and minds forever scarred, they live in unimaginable pain, unable to remarry or return to their parents, they are left to the mercy of under-funded local agencies or the poverty of the streets."

"How can this be?"

Jaq felt a stab of shame that she knew so little about the problem.

WIDOW BURNING INDIA

Click.

Jaq's screen filled with articles, reports, and treatises in a list that went on for a dozen pages. She felt overwhelmed.

Where do I begin?

Jaq scanned the titles. One name appeared in reference after reference—Roop Kanwar.

Click.

Roop Kanwar—Died in 1987 in Deorala, Rajasthan. Her sati death, celebrated by the fundamentalist Hindu community and denounced as murder by secular feminist factions, caused nationwide attention to be paid to the plight of widows in Indian culture.

"Rajasthan…"

Sati. Alibris Book Search—7 publications; Harvard on-line library—21 matches, New York Public Library—43 hits. Jaq's hands cramped from typing. She hit Print and watched as page after page of references piled up in her printer's tray.

Where is the law in all of this?

Jaq scrolled through dozens of accounts of rural satis reported in the last two centuries. The 1829 proclamation by Lord William Bentinck officially banning sati in India appeared to have done little to stem the horrific practice. Even Gandhi's assertion that widows deserve and must be afforded the same chance to experience love and remarriage as male Indian citizens did not seem to ease the cultural pressures on widows to "die" with their husbands. Millions of widows were forced to flee their villages for the cities where they begged on the streets and in Hindu temples, just barely surviving on the fringes of Indian society. Jaq learned that whether on their husbands' funeral pyres or in their home kitchens, women throughout the subcontinent were still being burned alive.

It's too quiet.

It seemed as though only minutes had passed since she had heard the routine sounds of the Evan's eleven p.m. departure with his lumbering to the foyer, Banni's whispered goodnight, bolts and tumbles of the front door locks, water running in the bathroom sink, slow footsteps down the hall, and the creaking of Banni's bed springs.

She stifled a yawn and checked the time on her laptop's screen.

3:45 a.m.

Her thoughts ran back to Triti. Their Hindi class two days earlier had started out normally: chatter about the day, the red color of Triti's nails, and of course, Anand, who was taking her that night to Saravanaas for properly-puffed pooris. Then she pushed Triti too hard, trying to force some clue from her mind. The tipping point came when she suggested that she call Triti's family for her.

Eruption. Class over.

Too much, too fast, Jaq concluded. She would be smarter next time.

Bleary-eyed, she typed until dawn.

"Yes, I'm still on hold…it's been over 20 minutes. What? Yes…CAN YOU HEAR ME?"

Jaq shouted into the receiver of her cell phone, relieved to at least hear a human voice on the other end of the line. The snapping and crackling of the connection made a complete sentence out of the question. *Perhaps more volume…*

"YES! I'M IN THE U.S. AND I'M LOOKING FOR INFORMATION ON THE DEATH OF TRITI SHARMA… SHE WAS FROM JAIPUR… NO, SHE DIDN'T DIE THERE… NO, NO! Please, don't transfer me again… SHE'S… WHEN? SHE DIED IN 2000… Hello? HELLOOOO?"

On the seventh attempt, Jaq managed to reach a desk clerk in the Sikar District Office of Shekwarti.

"Morel. I'll spell it. M O R E L. CAN YOU HEAR ME?"

"I can hear you, Mrs. Morel, you need not shout. How may I help?"

From his tone, the man clearly had better things to do.

"Oh…thank you. I'm calling from Harvard University. I'm doing research on Triti Sharma's death in 2000. From what I've learned so far, there may have been criminal activity involved. Could you check the records for a cause of death?"

CRACKLE…hiss…

"…makes it quite impossible for me to comply with your request. Documents are sealed by law. A court order is required…"

"Yes, I understand. But perhaps her name is on a list with a cause of death? Any mention of next of kin? I'm hoping to find out where her family lives."

"What is your office, this 'Harper'?"

"HARVARD…University…Boston. AMERICA."

"You're calling from America?"

"Yes!"

A point of understanding.

Crackle…

"Are you a relative of the deceased?"

"Well, no, just a friend."

"Only relatives…HISS…request court orders."

"And how long would that take?"

"Processing typically…CRACKLE…one year…but you see, the office is severely backlogged at this time…HISS."

"Dilip Sharma. Can you at least tell me his phone number or address in Jaipur?"

"You…try…CRACKLE…general…directory."

Beep…beeeeep.

"Information, Jaipur…"

"The number for Dilip Sharma. S H A R M A."

STATIC…Waiting…

"What street?"

"I have *no* idea…Dilip Sharma, Jaipur. That's all I know."

How many could there be?

"Ma'am, I'll need a street name."

Jaq strained to remember the address on Triti's mystery letters. A highway? Singh something?

"Just give me the numbers and I'll call them."

"There are over 300 listings for D. Sharma in the Sikar District. Without an address…"

Click. HISS.

"Mother of God."

TWENTY-SIX

By late August, Triti struggled through her workdays in an ever-deepening malaise.

She regretted taking a promotion to assistant day manager. The daytime crowds were far more numerous and demanding. There were additional deliveries to sign for and boxes to route, more young children racing underfoot, longer lines at the registers, and increased noise. She sulked about, miserable that she no longer had her night shift friends to eat with and talk to. Of the original Biddies, only Jean made the switch to days, but her new position as general manager meant that Triti rarely saw her outside of staff meetings or high-profile in-store promotions.

Alone and unfocused, her minor work gaffes mounted. She neglected supply orders, and misdirected customers. She ordered two stock boys to unload an entire delivery palette of historical fiction novels in the cookbook aisle, and could not remember why. She began to forget important things: signing in for work, locking her apartment door, picking up her mail, and even eating. She spent her lunch and break time talking to Anand on her cell phone. He alone could steady her, albeit temporarily. Agitated most of the time, she found herself glaring at the store clock all day, impatient to punch out and rush to his waiting arms. She took to writing his name on scraps of paper, curling the small, cursive d into concentric circles that eventually filled entire pages with ink blotches.

By Labor Day, the Memory was demanding her full attention. It assaulted her senses—cruel in its unpredictability and effect. It came in the screech of car tires, a smoldering rubbish pile, even a steaming cup of tea. Its triggers were legion. The slamming of a door, the act of bathing, even sitting to empty her bowels could jar her. And after each episode, the fear that gripped her made it impossible to eat or sleep. Unlike her rare flashes of recollection over the past few years, each new incident now seemed to leave behind a malevolent residue that was growing inside her brain.

As upsetting as her daily episodes were becoming, the nightly visitations were far worse. When she could actually fall asleep, she dreamed exclusively of death. It chased her up mountains, and down thorny paths. It forced her into oceans of blood and out of rivers of ash. Slumber, her once precious respite, now loomed ominously at each day's end. Dreading sleep, she fought it. Double espressos at 10 p.m. No Doz at midnight. Infomercials at 3:30 a.m.

Anand held his finger on Triti's doorbell too long to just be in the neighborhood. His news would not wait.

She heard his hello as he barked it into the intercom.

"Are you there, Minu?"

"Anand? Is that you?"

"Yes, it's me!"

"We're in the middle of a lesson…"

He mulled his response for several moments.

"Thīk hai," he said, dejectedly. "It's ok. I'll call you later."

As he stepped out of the vestibule, the sound of her voice overrode his disappointment.

"Anand, come in… Are you still there?"

He flew up the stairs to her door.

"We were actually just finishing," said Triti from her doorway as he charged down the hall to her. Before she knew what was happening, it spilled out of him.

"I've sold my book! They want to buy it!"

"Wow, Anand! How great!" Jaq chimed in, joining Triti at the door.

"Who's buying it?" asked Triti.

Joy pulsed from his entire being.

"Belk Publishing! Can you believe it? I can't believe it! I ran to tell you!"

"All the way from Queens, my God!" said Triti. "Come in, come."

She opened the door wide. For the first time, he walked into her apartment. Two steps in, but *in*, nonetheless.

"This is huge!" said Jaq, shaking Anand's hand.

"Belk… Are they in California?" said Triti. "I can't place the name."

"Hey, are you a rich man now, Anand? Is dinner on you tonight?" Jaq laughed.

"Delhi," Anand said to Triti, deflating some. "Belk is in Delhi."

Triti took an unconscious step backward and folded her arms against her chest.

"Delhi?" Jaq stammered. "As in India?"

"Yes," he said, clearing his throat. "India."

"Anand, how strange is that?" said Jaq. "You've come half way around the world to sell your book and luck takes you straight home again!"

"It's more than luck," said Triti, measuring her words. "Whether he publishes in India or the U.S. makes no difference, really. Anand has a gift for telling *stories*. People will read ANI and they will love it."

"Thank you, Minu."

"Your parents must be thrilled," said Triti.

"Well…they don't know yet. It's only three a.m. in Delhi, after all. No, you're the first to hear. I wanted you to be the first."

"So, when do you leave?" asked Jaq. "You have to go back to work with editors and artists, right? Isn't that what happens?"

"Yes, I'll have to get a ticket…"

"How soon?" Triti's voice grew weak with despair.

"Three weeks."

Her face fell. And she made no effort to hide it.

"Well, congrats, Anand! Big news!" said Jaq, awkwardly.

Sensing Triti's distress, she moved for the door.

"I'll go and let you two talk."

"Oh, no need, please," insisted Anand. "I've interrupted you ladies. Besides, I'm double-parked on the corner. I'll call you later, Minu."

He gave her a peck on the cheek and left.

"Yes, that will be fine."

Triti waited until he had descended a full flight before closing her door.

"He called you 'Minu'."

"That's my name."

"Haven't you told him the truth yet?"

"How can I? He's already got enough on his mind."

TWENTY-SEVEN

September 14, 2007
6:45 p.m.

Jaq hunkered on the brick steps of Triti's apartment building feeling stiffer and more perturbed by the minute. Her tutor was late for class. Although it had only been forty-five minutes, not a lot of time considering how unpredictable city traffic could be, Triti was never late. *The British could set Big Ben by the girl.* Anand would have picked her up at work as usual, spot on 5:30, and driven her straight home.

Jaq scanned the street east and west and saw no sign of them. She stood up slowly, aware of the blood circulating once more in her legs and hips. She dialed Triti's cell number for the fourth time and groaned upon hearing the automatic answering message yet again.

"646.456.6046. Please leave a message. Beep."

"Hey, Miss. It's me, one more time. Where you be, girlfriend? You've got me waiting on you. I'm not sure I'm gonna survive in Khajuraho with the paltry Hindi I have. When you get this, call me. Guess I'm gonna cruise… No, wait, here you come, I see Anand."

Jaq ended the call as the ragged sedan pulled up in front of Triti's stoop. Anand was at the wheel, his expression frantic.

"Tough coming cross-town?" asked Jaq, approaching his window.

"Minu's not *here*?!" he asked, panic rising in his voice as he looked about.

"No. Isn't she with *you*?" Jaq glanced at the empty passenger seat.

"I waited on Broadway in my regular place, but she never came out of the store. After twenty minutes I went in, and they said she hadn't shown up for work today."

"Has she called you?"

"Normally we talk half a dozen times a day, but not today. I haven't heard her voice since last night, before she turned in."

"Were you two supposed to go out tonight after my class?"

"Yes, to a movie. Do you think she's forgotten?"

"Well, I…"

"Lately she seems…far away. Have you noticed?"

"Yes, I have," said Jaq.

"She's so distracted. And now, with my leaving…"

Jaq read the anguish on his face.

"Anand, take my cell number. And give me yours. Call me when you hear from her and vice-versa. She'll be fine," she said, hoping to reassure him and herself.

Sister, where are you?

It was eleven p.m., and Jaq still had no word from Triti. Or Anand. From the window of Guy's studio, she watched the activity on Avenue A on the late summer night as an eclectic mix of barhopping Bohemians, Gen X-ers, and Yuppies shared the sidewalks and outdoor cafes. She thought of going out, but she knew that the crowds would distract her from figuring out reasons for her friend's disappearance. *Was Triti overwhelmed at work?* She had been looking tired since her recent promotion. Of course, Anand's pending departure had been a big blow. Perhaps she just needed to be alone to sort through her feelings for him. If only she would confide in Anand. From what Jaq could see, the man clearly loved her. And yet Triti refused to tell him what had happened in Rajasthan. She had not even told him her real name. Logical excuses seemed inadequate to explain her friend's increasingly aberrant behavior. Jaq thought of how odd Triti seemed all summer—haunted, and skittish. When she closed her eyes, Jaq could visualize the scars on Triti's feet and hands. What were her friend's memories doing to her? Jaq stood before the wall-sized map of Northern India taped above her desk and put her right index finger on Jaipur.

"And it all began there."

Her attention shifted to the titles on the spines of the books she had stacked along the back edge of her desk. SATI: Widow Burning in India; Death by Fire: Sati, Dowry Death and Female Infanticide in Modern India; SATI, the Blessing and the Curse, The Burning of Wives in India.

She pulled a volume off the top of a pile and flipped to the Introduction.

"All the actions of a woman should be the same as that of her husband. If her husband is happy, she should be happy, if he is sad, she should be sad, and if he is dead, she should also die. Such a woman is called pativrata - perfect wife."

- Shuddhitattva -

God! People really believe this?

12:45 a.m. Jaq opened another book to a flagged page. A Rajasthani woman described the hellish life of a Rajput widow.

"They cannot remarry, wear jewelry or good clothes or eat good food. Locked indoors for the rest of their lives they cannot even go to the well to draw water. Banned from all happy occasions, ceremonies and family rituals, they are inauspicious and treated with contempt."

No wonder some of them choose death. The idea revolted her the instant it crossed her mind.

"Then there are those who are chosen for the flames…"

The face of her cell phone flashed brightly beside her elbow. ANAND. She snatched up the phone.

"Tell me," she said.

"Jaq, she's home…I see her lights on now."

"You've waited there all this time?"

"Yes, I left only once to find a restroom. Damn it. She must have come back then. I rang her doorbell, but she wouldn't answer. But she did take my call, finally."

"What did she say?"

"Her voice…it was so small. She said she was tired and couldn't talk. Jaq, I'm worried."

"Me, too."

Jaq spent the rest of the night wracking her brain. She wanted to help her friend, but she was not sure how. Triti could not—or would not—remember the circumstances surrounding her sati, so Jaq decided to discover the truth for her. Her efforts to investigate via telephone and the Internet had failed so far. She needed someone with official clout; someone who had access to government channels who could make meaningful inquiries in Rajasthan on her behalf. It would have to be someone she could confide in—someone who would be willing to pry for her.

It would have to be someone good at keeping secrets.

TWENTY-EIGHT

September 15
United Nations Plaza
New York City

"Impressive."

Jaq looked out at the cityscape view from the 30th floor office and wondered how she was going to get that for which she had come. The sapphire sky was stretched out before her, marred by a solitary cloud hovering above mid-town Manhattan.

"You *think* so?" said Naveen Tikaram from behind his broad desk. "That means something, coming from you, Jaq."

She drew a slow breath, careful to not let him see her do so.

"And to what do I owe this very pleasant surprise? It's been a while."

Jaq resisted looking at him. Instead, she focused her gaze on the lines of tiny humans trailing across the plaza's block-wide concrete mall far below.

"If I said I've just dropped by for a hello, would you believe me?"

"Now, Jaq, our respective hours in the day are far too valuable for such an obvious charade, no?"

Jaq pulled back her shoulders and turned to face him. Her smile felt pasted on, but it was the best she could do under the circumstances. Asking for help from anyone made her uncomfortable; but asking him? *Now?*

There would be strings.

Naveen gestured to the chair opposite him as she opened the buttons on her black suit jacket.

"Are you in trouble?" he asked.

Ever the subtle prince.

He rolled a new number two pencil back and forth beneath his palm on his green desk blotter.

"Me? Oh, no… Just struggling with a bit of research, when it occurred to me that you might have an idea as to how to approach a delicate situation."

There, she'd said it.

"A political issue?"

"Probably not. I was hoping…"

"You're as lovely as ever, Jaq. Something new with your hair?"

The energy between them caught her off-guard. He was even more handsome than she remembered. *Damn him.* Wisps of premature gray salted his sideburns giving him a roguish look—far more mature than his puppy-like appeal when they met in her first year of college. She flushed, in spite of the room's Arctic air-conditioning. A low squawk from the desk intercom relieved the moment.

"Yes, Miss Nuñez? He's early, but I'll see him right away, of course. Thank you."

Naveen stood abruptly, adjusting his silk monochrome tie. He seemed taller to her.

"Forgive me, but I *must* take this meeting. It shouldn't last too long. Let's continue our talk over dinner. Shall we say 7:30? May I have my driver pick you up?"

"Better if I meet you," said Jaq. "Josephine's?"

"Marvelous choice."

Naveen monopolized the conversation, and Jaq let him prattle.

"You can understand. A chance to get in on the ground floor of a steel company destined to rival Mittal's? And what with Mumbai and Delhi exploding, not to mention Bangalore and Kerala? Pankaj is a true visionary. All of India's major cities are expanding, but even beyond South Asia, he's already setting up contracts in China and the Middle East. I should tell you—their offer was far beyond my expectations, really. A car, a penthouse apartment in D.C. The sign-on bonus alone was more than I make in a year at the Council. Plus, a gym membership, tennis, sauna…"

Naveen talked as he ate—the one grotesque habit she remembered him having. She tried to focus on his eyes, but it was impossible to avoid seeing his carrots and spinach mashed into an orange-green paste that coated his teeth and tongue.

Drink, for God's sake. Stop and swallow.

"Sounds as if things are lining up just the way you've always hoped, Naveen."

"So, you see, I had *no* choice. I gave my notice here last week."

He took a few more bites of food. An alert busboy picked up Jaq's untouched plate. The volume in the restaurant ebbed as patrons began to leave. Jaq ran the tips of her fingers down the stem of her half-empty wine glass.

"I know you, Jaq. That look in your eyes. Something's under your skin."

She took a long sip of her Cabernet.

"Well, I've been trying, unsuccessfully, to find information about a young woman who died in Rajasthan in 2000."

"Natural causes?"

"Doubtful, but that's what I need to find out. It's been so difficult to get the basic facts. I've called the police stations and government offices in Jaipur and Ajmer, but I keep getting the runaround. I can't even confirm the location of her family. It's as if they've all just... disappeared."

"Ah, well, that's Rajasthan. It's the Wild West there, you know. And like the rest of India, it has a chaotic government. I can make a few calls, if you'd like. You're sleuthing. Part of your dissertation?"

"It may be, if I can crack the code. You know how I hate mysteries. I've called every bureau, bank, and city agency. Nothing. The official walls I keep hitting have me scratching my head."

"And a very pretty head it is."

Jaq finished her wine in one quick gulp.

"I've another month in the office before I leave for London. Why don't you call me next week and I'll let you know what I find?"

"Thanks, Naveen. Here are the names: the girl who died; her parents and brother, the in-laws, and the town where she died."

She slid a three-by-five-card across the table to him.

Naveen looked closely at the card.

"Sharma… It's a terribly common name, I'm afraid."

"Yes, I've been told. Hopefully you'll have better luck with the Jaipur bureaucracy."

He folded the card and put it in his wallet. "There's someone I can call."

"Can we keep this just between us, for now?"

"Why?"

"Well, I'm trying to help a friend of a friend, but she's not too keen on dredging up the past."

"So, we'll add it to our collection of secrets?"

There it was; the assured tone he used whenever he knew she was about to give in to him. Four years had passed and yet she felt just as she always had with him: vulnerable.

Why did she think it would be any different now? Yes, they had secrets between them: the night on the golf course near his family's Hampton's summer home; losing and then finding his wallet in Atlantic City, and the time he snuck her into his parents' Manhattan apartment for sex only hours before his mother-in-law-to-be arrived from India for her first visit. The truth remained that she had been the biggest secret between them—and one with which she finally realized she could not live. It had been too easy for him—indulging his passions with her in New York while his young fiancée, a proper, untouched girl, with little curiosity about the universe beyond Connaught Place, waited faithfully for him in Delhi.

Surely, he was married by now. But in the intensity of Naveen's stare, Jaq recognized his unremitting expression of entitlement. He would take considerable convincing that her intentions were purely professional. Sitting only inches away from him, she wasn't sure that she could pull it off.

"Share a dessert?" he said, reaching for her hand. "The banana mousse is to die."

She picked her napkin up from her lap, avoiding his touch.

"No, I should get home. I still have work to do tonight."

"Of course. Do you mind a taxi? I've let my driver go for the evening."

When the Yellow Cab came to a stop in front of Turtle Bay Towers, Naveen pulled Jaq close to him.

"I've thought of you, Jaq, but you probably know that."

She managed to turn her face just in time. His wet kiss met her cheek, where he let his soft, full lips linger on her skin. Everything slowed down as the scent of his sandalwood cologne enveloped her. If she didn't move right then, it would be decided for her.

She leaned away from his embrace.

"Thank you again, Naveen. I'll call you next week," she said, reaching her hand out to him.

He took her hand and pressed a kiss into her palm—his signature exit.

"Take her to 5th and A, please," he said to the driver as he opened his door to leave.

"Good memory," said Jaq.

"I remember everything," he said.

As did she.

TWENTY–NINE

September 17, 2007

"I'm on hold for Mr. Sharma."

"And your name, please?"

Jaq's twenty-eighth attempt to locate Triti's brother looked promising. The only real clue she had from Triti was that Dilip, in a concession to their parents' wishes, had agreed to attend architecture school in Delhi after high school. She made the leap in logic and began calling the top architecture firms within India's Golden Triangle: the area between Delhi, Jaipur, and Agra. Having met with defeat thus far, she was prepared for yet another negative response to her telephone query. "No, you've reached the office of Deepak Sharma…I'm sorry, Dasiya Sharma is no longer with our firm…Are you looking for Dev Sharma? He retired last year."

The receptionist on the other end of the line spoke English in a thick, North Indian accent on a telephone connection so oddly crystalline she might have been in the very next room.

"This is…Ms. Morel."

"Is he expecting your call, Ma'am?"

Not in a million years.

"I'm calling from the U.S."

"One moment."

Hold. Indian music. Bollywood soundtracks on acid. Hindi lyrics. Jaq understood one phrase, and part of another. Something like, "Love her forever and don't let her go".

"Hello, Ma'am? Mr. Sharma's on a conference call and cannot be interrupted. But I will make sure he gets your message. May I take your number and your firm's name?"

"When will he be done?"

"I don't know, Ma'am. I have someone on another line. Will you please hold?"

"No, no… I'll call back."

How best to kill time? Or at the very least, hurry it along?

Jaq straggled into the kitchen and opened the refrigerator. She was not in the least bit hungry, but as it had been two days since her last meal, she figured it might be wise to consume a few calories. Pesto pasta…how old was that container? No way. Rice? Left uncovered, it was dry—like a thousand little bones. A salad would work, but no. The red leaf was black.

Jaq looked around at the cluttered kitchen. Pots with burned food were stacked three high on the stove. The counters were strewn with open metal cans and empty fast-food containers. From the living room, she heard Banni and Evan talking. Something about him wanting to attend the New York auditions for Jeopardy.

Hey Evan, try this one. He'll take Manners for $1,000, Alex. Answer: Rolls up his sleeves, turns on the hot water, and washes the fucking dishes! Question: What any decent houseguest does for his hostess?

Jaq directed her search to the freezer where she found a frozen macaroni and cheese entrée under a pair of empty ice cube trays. She placed the icy rock on the microwave's crusty turntable and set the timer. Then she watched through the glass window as the lump of food revolved and thawed past warm to steamy beneath its clear, plastic cover. At the sound of buzzer, Jaq gripped the container with the tips of her fingers and slid it onto a plate.

"Fuck, that's hot!"

She padded down the hall back to her room blowing on a forkful of scalding, yellow noodles.

"Hello, this is Dilip Sharma."

The man's deep bass voice reminded Jaq of Guy's favorite New York disc jockey, Frankie Crocker. WBLS.

Back in the day.

Keep it together, Jaq—and talk fast.

"Mr. Sharma, *so* glad to finally reach you. I'm calling from the U.S. My name is Jacqueline Morel. I'm doing research at Harvard and was hoping to talk with you. Do you, rather did you, have a sister...named Triti?"

Silence.

Then the storm.

"WHO IS THIS?" His voice boomed into her ear.

"I'm Jacqueline Mor..."

"WHAT do you know of my sister?"

"I, well..."

"Which swami put you up to this?"

"Mr. Sharma, please let me explain..."

"Don't you EVER call me again! Or...I'll report you to the authorities!"

"Wait! Please, I've been trying to reach you..."

Dead line.

"Damn."

DSharma@panag.consort

September 17, 2007

Dear Mr. Sharma,

I'm sending this email to your office Internet address hoping to convince you that I am who I say I am. Please note my Harvard email address. I'm currently on leave of absence from my Ph.D. program at Harvard University.

Please call the below listed number to verify my academic standing, if you wish. I look forward to hearing from you soon, either by email or telephone.

Jacqueline Morel

JMorel@harvard.edu

JMorel@harvard.edu

September 18, 2007

Ms. Morel,

I've contacted the Administrative Office at Harvard's GSAS.

I apologize for my abruptness yesterday, but you must understand that your call came out of the blue.

Please contact my office tomorrow at 10 p.m. New York time.

Dilip Sharma, Architect, Panag Consortium - Delhi Mumbai Bangalore London.

THIRTY

September 19, 2007

The early morning customers at Regency Books were few but finicky.

With only one cashier working the first-floor register, several impatient shoppers deposited their books and magazines on random shelves and huffed out the revolving doors. Triti stood and reread the author's name on the cover of the book in her hand. Zinn. Howard Zinn. She could not remember why she was holding it.

"Wait…"

Trench coat. Man standing. Customer Service desk.

"Right."

He wanted Volume 1—A People's History of the U.S.

Her cell phone vibrated in the deep pocket of her slacks.

"Jaq, I'm working. I can't talk now," she whispered.

She had agreed to resume Hindi lessons after Jaq's persistent requests, but was having second thoughts.

"I'm sorry to bother you, but I won't be able to make it to class tonight. And I'll have to skip the movie after."

"Oh, ok." Triti felt relieved.

"Yeah, just handling some stuff here…we're still on for Wednesday evening?"

"I don't know. Anand leaves that morning."

"Oh, come on. We'll have a 'cheer up Triti' evening after my lesson."

"I've got to go…"

"Sure, ciao, uh…Namaste."

Jaq's nervous childhood habit of counting everything was working overtime. She combed out her hair twice. She refolded all thirteen towels in the linen closet. Eleven steps to the kitchen. Seven steps to the bathroom. Surprised that her mother had retired early, she checked on Banni four times. As the evening settled in quietly around her, she could not help but wonder if the man who would soon be on the long-distance line was in fact Triti's brother. What was she going to say to him? The seconds clicked by—60 to the minute, 360 minutes to the hour. She counted them to be sure. *Why was time moving so damned slowly?* So, it was true what her father had said about 'watched pots.'

10:02 p.m.

"Mrs. Morel, I've only a few minutes."

"Mr. Sharma, thank you for taking my call. I'm sorry to have caused you distress with my inquiry. It was certainly not my intention."

"Yes, well…*why* have you contacted me?"

Jaq took a running start, speaking quickly.

"Well, you see, I'm writing a book on the family members of burned brides and the impact the events had on their lives."

"Burned brides??"

"Yes, and it's been difficult to locate extended families, and harder still to find anyone willing to talk about their experiences. I was hoping that when I'm in Delhi in late October I might be able to interview you. I completely understand the need for discretion, and will make every effort to shield your identity."

"I don't know what happened to my sister, really. The authorities in Rajasthan were of no help to us."

"I understand your frustration, I do. So far, I've found no public records about her disappearance, and the accounts in the local press were confusing. One indicated that a sati had taken place…"

"Oh, my god!"

"Another rumor is that your sister ran away."

"She would *never* leave and not let us know. Never!"

"I'm coming to India to research in person. Your memories of that time would be very helpful."

"I don't know…this has all come so suddenly, I'm just not sure. I'll have to think about it."

"Of course."

"Ms. Morel, I need to ask. *Why* are you writing this book?"

"It's … part of my dissertation project."

Jaq realized that the concept was becoming less of a lie every day.

"So, this is just an academic exercise for you?"

"Well, it began that way…"

"And now?"

Jaq wasn't sure how to answer him.

"Things are…changing all the time."

"Not quickly enough."

The vinegar in his voice mellowed.

"Have you ever been to India?"

"No, this will be my first time. But my mother was raised in Delhi."

"Is that so?"

His words came out more as a statement than a question. She waited for him to continue.

"Very well. I'll email you regarding my decision."

"Thank you, Mr. Sharma. I look forward to hearing from you soon."

Hours later, Jaq was still awake at her desk.

She could think of nothing else except telling Triti and Dilip about each other. She wanted to. But the timing just wasn't right yet. She would need to replay her conversation with Dilip Sharma and plan her strategy carefully. *Very carefully.* She opened one of the studio windows wide, allowing both the streetlight and the mugginess to filter through the aqua drapes. Sleep finally called her, and knowing better than to resist, she collapsed face down on the brown duck sheets. Her body relaxed. With one last yawn, she was fast asleep.

September 30, 2007

Ms. Morel,

I can meet with you the morning of October 27th.

For the purposes of discretion, I shall come to your hotel.

Please confirm the location and time as soon as possible.

Dilip Sharma

P.S. She was my twin.

THIRTY-ONE

"Reading my mind, Jaq? Witchy as ever. I was just about to ring you."

Calling Naveen only three days after their dinner, Jaq half expected one of his lectures on what he referred to as her 'American' tendency to force situations. Her confidence, bolstered by her breakthrough with Dilip Sharma, made her anxious to know if he had been able to wield his considerable charm with any Jaipur officials. The tone of his greeting made the hair on her arms stand up. Something in him had shifted.

"Naveen, I know you said to call you in a week, but I think I have…"

"I must see you tonight."

His demand threw her. She knew what he wanted, what he always wanted from her: uninhibited Kama Sutra sex, on the order of fantasmagorical; precisely the kind he would never have with his proper, Indian mother-selected, Indian mother-approved wife. With all of her psychic muscle, Jaq pushed memories of their past, sweaty tangles back into the "can't/won't/shouldn't go there again" vault and leaned her hard-won, self-protective wisdom against its door.

Now, how to secure the deadbolt?

"Tonight? It's tough. I'm on a deadline. Just curious if you'd had any luck with the names?"

He tried another tack.

"Yes, in a manner of speaking, I have. But it would be better to discuss this in person. Come to my place, say…8:00. I'll fill you in."

Vintage Naveen, she thought. Clever as a stone.

"I'm thinking for time's sake it would probably be best to do this on the phone. You did find out something, didn't you?"

"Jaq, Jaq… So, it's going to be *all* business, is it?"

Resignation in his voice, then again something more ominous.

"Listen carefully. I can't speak for long. I'm expecting an appointment soon. What I have to say won't please you, but I'm thinking of your safety…"

Jaq recoiled.

My safety?

"Why the preamble, Naveen?"

"Listen. I made a few calls. This…enterprise of yours, investigating a woman's disappearance…"

"She was murdered, Naveen."

"Good God, listen to yourself! Spreading rumors of things you know *nothing* about. I'm telling you. Let this alone. What happened seven years ago is not important today. People have moved on. Besides, the authorities consider this a closed case."

Jaq's back stiffened.

"To whom did you speak?"

"The specifics are irrelevant."

"A girl, barely 18 years old, was set on fire, Naveen. Alive!"

"HOW do you know that? If you know so much, why did you need me? To whom are YOU speaking?"

"I...read several accounts in the local press, and I... talked to one of the girl's friends. I promised I'd look into it. Damn it! Women and girls are being burned alive..."

"Sati is a Hindu woman's God-given right. Read the Laws. Perfected women choose to follow their husbands onto the pyre. They are truly goddesses."

"Their right? Their choice? What laws are you talking about? Sati is a crime. It was outlawed almost 200 years ago!"

"An illegal mandate imposed by a terroristic, former occupier. The British had no authority to abridge Hindus' religious freedom."

"Women are DYING!"

"This is not your culture, Jaq. You're American. These are things you cannot understand. India's old ways, ancient ways...they've worked for centuries."

Jaq stared at the phone in her hand.

"My God, who's been feeding you this crap?"

"My mother knows a great deal about sati. She's part of the leadership of Dharam Raksha Samiti."

"Samiti? India's pro-sati movement? You've *got* to be kidding me."

"What about Samiti?"

"I've been studying them. They organize mass demonstrations supporting the legalization of sati. In Jhunjhunu, Deorala, and Umaria—all over Rajasthan. And Madhya Pradesh. Even in Delhi… and the south. These people are just like the fringe Christian Right in the U.S. They twist the scriptures to suit their misogynistic agenda."

"There you go again, making wild accusations. This is a local issue. An Indian matter. People there don't take kindly to ferenghis snooping into their affairs. I'm telling you, Jaq. Let it go."

Jaq felt sick to her stomach. How had she ever kissed him? Contemplated having a child with him? Once she had held out hope that his time in New York would dilute his mother's rabid influence. Clearly, it had not done so.

"Be the smart girl you are. Don't take on an ancient culture and hope to change it. You're an outsider. You're a woman."

Then, his coup de grace.

"Believe me. I care about you, Jaq."

He modulated his voice seductively.

"Meet me tonight. I want you."

"For what, Naveen? You're bored? Wifey back at home in Chanakyapuri? Mrs. Tikaram? The ideal woman, pick of the litter for the fine, respectable son? The good son? Who mouths all the right words for his family back home in India while indulging his grand appetites in America?

How modern of you, you fucking hypocrite! Spewing your mother's fundamentalist crap and in the very next breath inviting me for an evening bang? Fuck you."

"Vulgarity. Always your fallback tactic…"

"You've no right to lecture anyone on what's vulgar."

"Perhaps not. But I really do care about you, Jaq."

"Oh, please. You live in a Naveen-centered universe and you know it. We're done."

Silence.

"Over the phone? Really? That's it? Let's meet at least. I know you want to."

"Gotta go."

"Fine."

"It's not fine, Naveen. Nothing's fine. But, whatever."

"Be careful, Jaq."

"Don't you worry about me. Remember, I'm from New York."

THIRTY–TWO

October 7, 2007

T riti elbowed her way past the suited, somber commuters pouring out of Penn Station. She felt as if she were trying to swim in mud. She was late on the one day she could not be late. The cheerless day—the one perpetually in the offing. Anand was leaving America, and leaving her.

8:50 a.m. In six hundred seconds, he would go, and it would tear her apart. No matter how acute his wordsmith cleverness, he could not craft a commentary to assuage her sadness. She knew that the waves of ache in her heart would drown her once he stepped through the air train's doors. They would rage over her, holding her under, choking her as he dragged his suitcase past the hovering red caps outside the airport entrance, checked in for his flight, and hiked to the gate.

8:55. She broke into a run and dashed across the terminal.

She reached the ticket room for the New Jersey Transit and moved along the periphery of the milling crowd, searching the montage of faces for the only one that mattered.

"ANAND! Thank God!"

She ran to him, too slender in her orange sari, and sank into his arms.

"Minu!"

"The trains are so slow today…I thought I'd missed you."

"So, it is set."

He held her close as he spoke, a calm authority in his words.

"Once I've finished Ani's final revisions, you will come. My mother will be ecstatic. It shall all be arranged."

Triti hid her tears in his shoulder. She closed her eyes and the pictures flashed: the rainy day they met; the night drives through Central Park, the meals they had shared, the walks, their laughter. She inhaled the smell of his clean madras shirt and felt the strength of his embrace. She already knew these sensations as they were part of her. He was part of her. This was the man to whom she could one day reveal all of herself—her fears, her past, her name. In him, she had found comfort, yet the thought of returning to India—even for him—made her wither.

Anand lifted her face with his hand.

"Say you'll come to me, Minu. Just say it, and I'll be able to leave."

Her tears brought his. He stroked her hair, helpless as the droplets ran down his cheeks.

"Anand, there are things…I need to tell you."

Anand pulled his stuffed canvas bag toward the ticket counter as his turn came.

"Newark Airport, please."

"Round trip?" asked the middle-aged, Hispanic booth attendant, who lifted her heavy, black lashes to see him standing before her.

"No," said Anand, sadly. "Just the one way."

An announcement thundered from the loud speakers.

"ATTENTION, NEW JERSEY TRANSIT PASSENGERS. The 9:01 to Newark International Airport will depart from Track 18."

"Minu," he said, pulling his bag with one hand and her hand with the other as he headed toward his track. "I want to hear everything. Come to India. Promise me you'll come…"

"I'm… not…"

"Promise."

"ALL ABOARD ON TRACK 18."

People rushed past them down the ramp.

"Anand, your train!"

"Please, Minu?"

"I will come."

Anand's smile broke, wide and wet. She hugged him tightly one last time, then once again. He whispered in her ear.

"I'll write you every day, my sweet Minu."

Then he kissed her lightly on the lips and ran with the crowd.

Strangers' stares shamed Triti from her crying spot near Track 18. She was soon navigating a set of congested subway stairs. An uptown #1 arrived just as she reached the bottom step. She strained to make the usual mental calculation: wait for the next one, or squeeze on? She was already late for work. *Would another ten minutes really matter?*

In her split-second hesitation, she had not performed the necessary sidestep and was pushed onto the last car by a posse of raucous teens. The car doors slid closed behind them and the train moved in the direction of Times Square. Squished from all sides, Triti fought to grab hold of a center pole. People pressed against her body. Her pulse quickened.

The crowd will get off at 42nd Street.

They would get off, and she would move to the emergency door. The metal surface would be cool against her skin. She licked her lips and began to sweat.

The lights in the car flickered as the train picked up speed.

He was gone.

In two weeks, Jaq would leave her also. Self-pity welled up in her. She wanted to brush her tears from her face, but the crush of bodies kept her arms pinned to her sides. Outside the train car's windows, sparks shot like fireworks, lighting up the tunnel walls. There came a deafening clang, and the car rocked violently. People screamed. The train screeched down the tracks to a halt.

There were shouts and low murmurs. Some people laughed. Then, the lights died.

Groans erupted throughout the car. People began yelling and cursing. Others shushed them, imploring calm.

"I can't do this."

Triti's hands slipped off the pole and she lost her balance, but the pressure of all the bodies against her kept her upright. She hyperventilated. Her body temperature climbed. A blue light flashed off to the right side of her brain. There was more shouting, but now it came at her in Hindi. It was louder, closer. More blue flashes lit up angry faces. Wide eyes loomed as hands pushed at her. Then came the flames…

Clang, jerk. Light filled the car again. Weak applause erupted as the train limped into the station. The doors opened and passengers rushed out onto the platform.

"THIS TRAIN IS TEMPORARILY OUT OF SERVICE," blared a female voice over the station's loudspeakers.

Triti stumbled out of the car and made her way to the nearest stairway. She was shaking, her sari drenched and sticking to her skin.

She had to get above ground, up to fresh air.

On the street, she opened her cell phone. There were five messages from Jaq. She deleted them without listening. Then she dialed a number.

"Jean, I'm not coming into work today. Sorry. Feel sick. Don't know about tomorrow…

Seven p.m.

Jaq turned the keys in her apartment locks as quietly as she could.

"She's probably asleep, but I should check. This last month she's not been…herself. This weird Indian summer heat doesn't help. And now, since the idiot's gone, I have to…"

"Jacqueline…is that you?"

Banni's words floated out from the living room. There was no energy in her voice.

"Answers that question. Sorry, Minu. I'll be back in a minute."

Jaq left Triti in the foyer and disappeared.

Triti leaned against the front door and tried to settle her breathing. Ten hours since her subway scare, and her heart was still thumping too fast. Jaq's fourth-floor walkup was not the culprit. There were other triggers. The stale odors of burnt brownies and Evan's cigarettes still lingered weeks after Jaq had caught him filching cash from her desk. Triti was grateful not to have witnessed the flying ashtrays. *Bye, Evan.*

She stared down at her open-toed sandals. She had bought them to appease Jaq, and while she could admit that her feet felt cooler, she chafed against the impulse to cover them. Noticing the colorful Afghan rug, she was reminded of the carpet runners her mother chose for their home in Jaipur. She wondered if the wool had come from Bikaner—

maybe even Rattan's company. Perhaps she could get lost in the lavender and fern paisley.

Two minutes passed; then five more. She had not wanted to go to dinner. She struggled trying to picture herself sitting in a restaurant, listening to her friend's humorous stories. She doubted that anything would seem funny to her, now that Anand was gone. The dinner's sole merit was that she would not have to be alone. With the Memory becoming bolder, keeping company might forestall the next visitation.

"Sooorrry…she's unsettled," said Jaq as she strode into the breezeway. "Too many meds, I think. She's in the bathroom now. I'm going to help her into bed. This might take a while. Do you want to go ahead and get us a table?"

"No, really. I can wait."

"Sit in the living room if you'd like."

"Mai thik huu."

"I know you're fine, Triti."

Jaq gave her a weary smile and walked back down the hall. Triti watched as she guided her mother into a doorway. She heard them talking—no words, just sounds; Banni's voice, teary and plaintive; Jaq's, steady and reassuring. A door closed. The voices became barely audible. More minutes passed.

Nature's call soon made her shift back and forth in place. Her face felt hot. The humidity in the apartment was stifling. She needed a bathroom. She made her way down the hall and peeked into the first door. Just a linen closet. The next was Banni's bedroom. She continued a few more steps and she reached another door that was slightly ajar. Different smells there. Lacquer? Glue? She leaned her head into the room. Twilight illuminated canvasses and easels. A map of Northern India papered the wall above a desk next to a small day bed.

"Jaq's space," she whispered as she stepped inside and inched closer to the map. She could see that New Delhi was circled in red marker, as were several other cities. On the desk she saw several stacks of books. She read their titles one after another: Death by Fire - Sati; Dowry Death in Modern India; Widow Burning in India; Sati, The Blessing and the Curse, Religion and Rajput Women…

Triti began to tremble. She turned on the desk lamp and scanned the desk. Beside an open Day-Timer lay a printed travel itinerary. Trembling, she picked up the sheet. Her panic mounted as she read aloud the list of destinations.

"Vrindavan, Jaipur, Snake Mountain…"

They were *not* Jaq's dissertation sites.

They were the footprints of her terrible time.

Triti dropped the paper, ran down the hall, threw the door wide and fled.

Her India itinerary on the floor and the open apartment door told Jaq exactly what had happened.

Her first instinct was to chase after Triti—to find her, and to apologize. Yet right behind her genuine remorse came the realization that at least now Triti might see how committed she was to helping her unravel her mystery.

Maybe now, with the investigation secret revealed, they could work together to achieve some justice for her.

Banni's sleeping pill did its job quickly. With her mother resting comfortably at last, Jaq slipped out of the apartment. She walked to the restaurant, but Triti wasn't there. She continued walking. North, west, south—the act of moving made her feel less impotent. Three blocks, seven, twelve. She resisted touching the bump in her back jeans pocket, but with each step the pressure of her cell phone against her right buttock made it harder to ignore.

Twenty blocks, and the urge won. She dialed Triti's number.

Rings—message—beep.

"Hey...I've been wanting to tell you for a while now."

Pause.

"Can you call me? Please?"

Please.

THIRTY-THREE

Jaq did not hear from Triti the next day. Or the next.

With only two weeks before her trip, she had hoped to focus on packing, practicing Hindi, and delving deeper into sati research. She was concerned about Triti, but her mother's bizarre behavior was consuming the bulk of her worry quotient. Banni had taken to lying on the couch and moaning about a headache that would not go away. She was fixated on the Weather Channel, surrounded by empty candy wrappers and crumpled chip bags.

Finally, the ripe odor of the matted-hair stranger in the living room got to Jaq.

Clearly an intervention was required.

She ran a hot tub and drizzled Banni's favorite lemongrass oil under the tap. Then she lit a fat white candle and watched as the inviting glow transformed their tenement bathroom into a spa.

Her efforts met with Banni's predictable resistance, but Jaq was undeterred.

"Really, Mom…you'll be amazed at how good this is going to feel."

"I don't want to, Jacqueline. Just leave me be."

"Mai esa nahi soch ti hu," said Jaq as she took Banni's hands and pulled her up to standing.

Banni turned to her daughter in surprise.

"What do you mean you 'don't think so'?"

"It's okay, Mom. Acha."

Jaq put her arm around her mother's waist and guided her slowly down the hall toward the bath.

Banni lifted her nose.

"Jasmine rice? You're cooking?"

"Anyone can boil water, Ma. It won't be as good as yours, but it'll be ready when you're finished."

While Banni soaked, Jaq stirred fresh spinach with minced garlic in a cast iron skillet. A few flecks of grated ginger would be plenty, she decided, sprinkling the amount that Triti typically used. She turned the flame low and covered the dish.

She fished her cell phone out of her backpack and dialed Triti's number again. She had already left her friend half a dozen messages, but this call was different. An inspiration had come in powerfully. There was something she had to tell her friend.

Rings—message—beep.

"It's me again. I hope you're getting these… Anyway, I've been thinking… Come with me to India! Come! Let's go together! At least let's talk about it."

Pause.

"I miss you… Call me?"

She hung up, looked around at the filthy apartment, and launched into a cleaning frenzy. In half an hour, the space felt livable again. Then she helped her mother out of the tub, and gently combed her hair.

"Dhanyavad," said Banni, staring sheepishly at her own reflection in the bathroom mirror.

"You don't have to thank me, Ma. I'm sorry I've been so distracted lately."

Jaq looked over her handiwork with a child's swelling pride.

"So, what do you think?"

Banni ran her hands down her graying lengths. She looked at her daughter's lovely face, her approval-seeking eyes.

"It's fine. Yes, good."

Jaq smiled.

"Thanks, Ma. And now, dinner?"

That night, the rice was perfect.

When Jaq unlocked Banni's mailbox the next morning and pulled out the fistful of bills, one last piece of mail remained wedged against the back of the box. Jaq thrust her hand back in and tugged hard. She extricated the envelope, neatly slicing her thumb on the edge of the casing in the process.

"Shit!" She sucked on her bleeding appendage.

The letter, addressed to her, had no return address, which struck her as strange. She tucked the rest of the mail into her backpack and tore open the envelope. Inside were two sheets of stationery.

October 10, 2007

Jaq,

My hands, which did not suffer the worst of it, eventually healed. They are not horrors for the accidental gaze of strangers. Young children on the bus no longer point at them and stare. Bank tellers take money from my palm without flinching. These many years later, my hands appear as slightly leathered mitts of a farmer. All ten fingers work. And I suppose I could one day wear a ring, if I cared to. I consider this minor fortune daily. Still, I'm compelled to shelter them beneath the generous sleeves of my cholis.

As you know.

But my feet… How I wish I could remember them. What I would give to smooth warm sesame oil on my teenage feet once again. Below me, finishing my legs, are their melted remains.

As you know.

Every day my feet make my contact with the earth, but I still mourn them.

What you ask of me is impossible.

For seven merciful years, I've wrapped myself daily in the not remembering. There is solace in amnesia. But I'm tired. This secret wearies me. I'm not naïve. I know the Memory is lurking. It was less patient today than yesterday.

It bides its time, no doubt waiting for my most unprotected moment. I don't know what I'll do when it finally arrives.

Justice compels you, so you say. But at what cost?

What are you willing to risk, Jaq?

My family? My life?

Your own?

Don't do this.

Triti

THIRTY–FOUR

Triti read Anand's fifth postcard in as many days as she climbed the stairs to her apartment door and a rare smile softened her expression.

He had kept his promise. That day, he wanted her to be the first person to know that he had just returned from his initial meeting with his editor. ANI was in the best of hands! Of course, he was missing her terribly. All would not be right in his corner of the world until she arrived in India. The photo of Buddha Jayanti Park's lush papal-treed enclave held her rapt. She transported herself there and walked with him down the winding, garden paths. Could their destiny be as serene as the park's reflecting pond? Once in her apartment, she affixed the postcard to her refrigerator door with a silver dragonfly magnet alongside the four others.

She headed to her bathroom and was about to loosen the waistband of her pants, when the door buzzer sounded.

She ignored it at first, but the visitor rang again with a long, deliberate buzz. She poked her head between the sheer curtains of the left front window and saw a mustard-colored delivery truck idling in front of the building.

"What now?" she moaned as she went to the intercom. "Yes?"

A man's voice barked from the box on the wall. "DHL. Delivery for Minu Vanik."

Triti slipped on her shoes, met the driver in the vestibule, signed for the small package, and trudged back up to her apartment.

With a sigh, she closed and locked her door. As she tore open the package, she noticed the purple postmark stamp.

"South Carolina? Who do I know there?"

One look at the handwriting on the envelope and she immediately knew the sender.

Dearest Minu,

My wonderful friend…

First, I miss you. I can't deny it—the sight of you on the street last spring set this 'ole swamp cat's heart a thumpin'!

Second, I'm on the mend; just moving a bit slower. Things happen at a more civilized pace here in the land of Spanish moss, which is right fine by me. Could be the heat, but likely it's been the extra helpings of cheese grits and butter biscuits my mother sees fit to feed me daily. I know you're the worrying kind, so please take my name off your list. Jitter Brown's gonna be fine.

And third, well… Your kindness with the loan made all the difference in my life. There I was at my lowest ebb, and you didn't hesitate to help me. I'm still shaking my head about it. Enclosed is a check to repay your loan, plus interest. Got to say, it feels so good to be able to send this to you.

My apartment sold in August for a silly amount of cash. Lawyers, agents, realtors, and Uncle Sam all had at it, but I still came away with a bundle. Not sure what'll be next for me. For now, I'm really okay with settin' on the old front porch, watching the fireflies wing by.

If you ever get a hankering for some true southern comfort, come on down for a visit. We'll have the black-eyed peas and fat-back ready.

You're in my heart, Beauty. Always will be.

Jitter

She opened a small envelope and unfolded a blue bank check.

Pay to the order of $ 20,000.00. MINU VANIK.

Written in the memo line: My Angel.

THIRTY–FIVE

October 21, 2007

Five days before her flight to India, Jaq was running on adrenaline and caffeine.

Her dog-eared to-do list taunted her, but that day she was able to cross off her most important chore. Just after seven a.m., with ticket number 414 clenched in her hand, she waited on a block-long cue outside the Indian Embassy on the Upper East Side with hundreds of other travel visa hopefuls. It took most of morning for her to inch down the concrete steps past the Indian security detail in their smart uniforms, into a stifling waiting room, and then up to one of the four service windows where a harried, female clerk behind a thick, glass partition took her passport and forms and told her to return after 3 p.m.

With four hours to fill, she rode the number 7 train to Jackson Heights where she purchased two cotton salwar suits and ate a thali lunch. As she nibbled on naan and yellow dal, she reviewed the final details of her trip. The only piece that was not fitting into place was Triti. She was worried to not have seen or spoken with her friend in over two weeks. She had lost track of how many voicemails and texts she had left for her. When she had gone to the Regency hoping to see her, a new day manager informed her that Ms. Vanik was unavailable. Would she care to leave a message?

Undaunted, Jaq resolved to go to Triti's apartment that night and ring the buzzer until she answered her door. She would tell her about Dilip, face to face. She had no idea how her friend would react, but she knew that this was not news Triti should hear on the telephone. *Maybe they should each have a shot of tequila first.*

When Jaq emerged from the embassy at 3:45 p.m. she had her six-month Indian travel visa in her hand. Tired but jubilant, she crossed Fifth Avenue at 64th street and walked south along Central Park. The autumn afternoon had turned decidedly crisp and she felt underdressed in her long-sleeved tee shirt and jeans, but she needed to see the fall colors one last time and the park's trees did not disappoint. The brilliant orange and red canopy reminded her as always of a stained-glass ceiling in a grand cathedral.

"If there is a god, she must be an artist," said Jaq as she walked through windswept piles of dried leaves, relishing the crunching sounds beneath her feet. At Columbus Circle, she took a long, final look at the park before making her way east to the Lexington line.

Jaq reached home just past dusk. Her legs throbbed, and she couldn't wait to sit down. Despite her exhaustion, she knew she had to rally long enough to model her new outfits for Banni as the dress-up ritual from her childhood always gave her mother pleasure. She hung her keys on the metal hook above the umbrella stand in the front hallway, and felt her cell phone vibrating in her pocket. She checked her voice mail.

"Hi, Jaq, it's Jeri. I just wanted to say it's no problem for me to stop by once a day while you're in India. Been a while since I've seen your mom. I probably won't be able to come by too early. My bridge games run late in the evenings. Call me and confirm the dates again? Ok, then. Safe travels."

Jaq sighed in relief. Another key item checked off her to-do list. Jeri had come through for her mother. Banni was lucky there.

It's so quiet.

No TV blaring, no talk radio chirping. The silence unnerved her.

"Ma?"

A chill prickled her scalp.

Jaq rushed down the hallway to her mother's room. The door was ajar. She found Banni gasping for air on the floor at the foot of her bed. Foamy strings of saliva hung from her teeth. She reached toward Jaq, but only her left arm lifted into the air.

"MOM! It's me! Oh, Mommy!"

Jaq grabbed the phone off the sideboard and dialed 911.

"Don't 'reve me," Banni pleaded, her eyes wild with terror.

"It's okay, Mom…I'm here!"

She cradled Banni's head in her lap.

"I won't leave you."

In the dimly-lit ICU cubicle, the respirator that breathed for Banni sucked and whirred. Nurses in mint-colored shirts padded in to check her vital signs every fifteen minutes. Powerless to help, Jaq watched the dizzying medical production from a stiff plastic chair in the corner of the room. The nursing team ripped open syringe packets, drew her mother's blood, and noted statistics on official-looking clipboards. An orderly and a nursing assistant had just begun the process of changing Banni's soiled bedding when a new intern waved Jaq out into the hallway.

"She's holding on," he said, obliquely. "Now, we wait."

Half an hour later, the head nurse was kind enough to provide a translation of the doctor's statement. "If" her mother came out of the crisis alive, she would not be the woman Jaq had known and loved before her stroke.

For Jaq, the next two days in the hospital felt like a month. Except to hustle to the bathroom or raid the vending machines, she did not leave Banni's side. Staff members brought her bottles of water which she more often than not waved away. Near the end of the second afternoon, a hospital administrator asked if there were any relatives she might contact—someone who could bring her a change of clothes, and some real food?

"Surely there must be someone. A friend? Co-worker?"

Jaq shook her head.

"No. It's just us...my mother and me."

Jaq bought her second pack of M&M's from the vending machine on the mezzanine level and tore open a corner with her teeth. She dumped half of the chocolates into her mouth and chewed and swallowed without tasting them. Then she poured the rest of the pieces into her hand. This time she counted them: five brown, two greens, and a blue.

Blue?

Two young women walked past her toward the elevator, holding each other as they cried. Jaq considered turning away so as not to intrude on their private moment, but the women's intimacy held her attention and she watched them until the elevator doors closed and the hallway was suddenly quiet once more. On her cell phone, she pressed #3 autodial and left a final voice message for Triti.

"Banni stroked. We're at Beth Israel."

"Miss, I'm afraid you can't bring those in here."

The night shift nurse at the ICU front desk confiscated the bouquet of daisies in Triti's hand.

"How about I put them in water for you?"

"Sorry," said Triti. "I... didn't know."

She scanned the patient list scribbled on a chalkboard at the desk.

"Banni Morel?"

"Family? Friend?" asked the nurse.

"Yes."

The nurse raised one eyebrow and handed the guest sign-in pad to Triti.

"I'll go check to see if her daughter's awake. Wait here."

Jaq shuffled through the sliding glass doors of the ICU's entrance and rubbed her eyes twice at the sight of her friend. Triti handed her a bag of Italian takeout and wrapped her in her arms and the whole nightmare became somehow bearable. Later, after the onion rings and spinach lasagna had grown cold in their containers, the two women sat quietly side-by-side, holding hands.

THIRTY–SIX

The next evening, Jaq rang Triti's doorbell, and for the first time in nearly a month, Triti buzzed her in. When she reached the third-floor landing, Triti was waiting at her apartment door.

"How is she?"

"Touch and go."

"Come in?" asked Triti.

"No."

Hollow-eyed and desperate for sleep, Jaq handed Triti a large manila envelope.

"What is it?"

Jaq just nodded.

Triti opened the envelope and pulled out Jaq's passport stuffed with her boarding passes.

"Jaq, what…?"

Jaq turned and walked back down the stairs.

Midnight found Triti alone in her living room trembling as she turned the envelope over and over in her hands.

For two hours she had paced, all the while fingering the metal clasp, unable to put down the package. Finally, she shook the contents out onto her coffee table. She flipped open the passport again and looked closely at Jaq's photo. There was her friend, with her Cheshire cat smile and dark hair pulled back off her unadorned, perfect face. On another passport page she saw a purple and orange Indian visa. Looking back on the table, she noticed a piece of paper beside the plane tickets. She unfolded it and read the first few lines.

INDIA ITINERARY
Depart: Newark International, 10/26 7:00 p.m. (EDT)
Arrive: Indira Gandhi International, 10/27 10:00 p.m. (IST)
Meeting: The Park Hotel, Delhi 10/28 9:00 a.m.
Dilip Sharma.

"DILIP! Oh, my God!"
Stunned, she read the itinerary words again. And then, once more.
Brother? Did Jaq find you?
She went to the freezer, put the frosty tequila bottle to her lips and took a long, cold slug, grimacing as the icy liquid seared her esophagus. She poured a second shot in a juice glass.

"Dilip..."

She scanned the living room for something that could ground her. Her eyes found the painting of the Three Gopis with their Lord Krishna resting beside the Yamuna River sheathed in golden moonlight.

"Merciful Krishna, I *need* you tonight."

Triti drained her glass and took Jaq's passport into the bathroom. She propped it against the medicine shelf and stood before the mirror. Carefully, she brushed her hair and pulled it back with a wide, silver clip. Piece by piece, she removed all of her jewelry, growing calmer and clearer with every passing minute.

Then she washed her face.

THIRTY–SEVEN

October 25, 2007
Beth Israel Hospital
New York City
7:45 P.M.

J aq sat on the floor outside Banni's hospital room and screwed up her mouth at the cherry soda's sharp bite. She burped into her nose and winced as the carbonation sting ripped through her sinuses. Instantly she remembered why she never drank the stuff.

She waited as the shift nurse finished checking the webbed network of tubes and vents that kept her mother alive. The long-term ICU staff smiled sympathetically at her as they rustled past her on their rounds. Jaq closed her eyes to their looks of pity. There were some things she could not bear to see.

At the far end of the corridor, an elevator door opened. No one seemed to notice the young woman walking down the hall. She passed through the sliding glass doors by the busy nurses' station and made her way to Jaq.

Immersed in her thoughts, Jaq sensed the air shift around her. She opened her eyes and looked up, shocked to see Triti standing before her. *Triti?* Her friend wore a simple white top and blue jeans. Without makeup or jewelry, Triti beamed with natural beauty.

"I'm stuck," said Jaq, shrugging her shoulders at her friend.

Triti put out her hands.

"Let me help," she said, pulling Jaq to her feet.

Jaq held her friend at arm's length, assessing her transformation.

"Your bangles?" she asked, looking at Triti's naked ears, nose, and wrists.

Triti handed her the red velvet satchel with the embroidered mirrors.

"I was hoping you could look after these. Seems I won't be needing them for a while."

Jaq nodded, understanding, as she wiped at the tears pooling in the corners of her eyes.

"I'll miss you, Triti."

"Me, too. So much. But we both know I have to go. Dilip, Anand…"

"They're waiting for you."

Triti nodded, her words catching in her throat.

"Savdhani se jaiye. *Promise* me you'll be careful."

"Of course, dear sister."

Banni's night nurse leaned out of her room and signaled to Jaq the all clear. Triti followed Jaq inside and hovered near the radiator where a lone spray of violet silk carnations provided the only color in the drab, sterile room. Sliding off her shoes, Jaq crawled into Banni's bed and gently spooned her mother, careful not to disturb the snare of wires and IV's. Banni did not stir.

Once the nurse had left, Triti began to sing softly.

"So jaa…"

THIRTY–EIGHT

October 27, 2007
Delhi, India

T riti awoke just after dawn to the racket of Parliament Street outside her fourth-floor hotel window, as vehicle horns sounded out drivers' impatience in the crowded Connaught Place shopping district for the well-heeled Dilliwalas.

Much to her surprise, she had slept soundly. The sumptuous room, with its elegant bed, provided true comfort after her daylong trip from America. She would enjoy only one more night there, as Jaq's original itinerary had her moving to a humble homestay just south of Delhi in Gurgaon. But she could not think past that morning. In her mind, there was only Dilip.

Squatting in the bathroom's spotless white tub, she washed in haste. She longed to soak in a hot bath, but even a shower was out of the question, for she would not risk wetting her hair with so little time to dry it. As she rubbed her body with oil, she noticed her scars glistening in the morning light. She hoped that he would not notice them. She selected her turquoise sari from her suitcase and dressed quickly.

"Your favorite color, my brother."

She adjusted the swag of her sari and took care to pull down the long sleeves of her black choli. As she slipped her watch on her wrist, she saw the time.

"Ten minutes!"

She searched her reflection in the mirror and sighed.

"Krishna, guide me. *Please.*"

Her hands trembled slightly as she drew the slimmest of kohl lines above her lids and brushed clear gloss on her lips.

She fretted that she might have made the wrong decision.

What if it isn't really him?

Or far worse, what if it *was* her brother—and he didn't want to see her? Could he accept her after all this time? She tried to imagine what he might look like now: seven years older, and a grown man.

Will I even know him?

At precisely nine a.m., the phone rang on the nightstand.

"Good morning, Ms. Morel. Mr. Sharma has arrived for your appointment. He is waiting just now for you in the lobby."

"Bahut dhanyavad."

Triti sat on her unmade bed in a final effort to slow her racing heart. No trick of breath or positive affirmation would calm her. There was no mother's lullaby to soothe her, and no gentle melody in her ears.

In less than a minute—the time it took for the elevator car to descend to the hotel's concierge level—her questions would be answered. She cleared her throat and stepped out into the hall.

When Triti reached the front desk, a clerk pointed across the open-air atrium.

A tall man, impeccably dressed in a gray Western business suit, was standing with his back to her between a matching pair of giant ferns, talking on a cell phone. He ended his call and turned toward the sound of her footsteps clicking across the lobby's marble floor. Confused, he tried to process the familiarity of the stranger approaching him.

Triti recognized his handsome face at once.

"DILIP!"

Her voice made her real.

"SISTER!"

Triti shouted again as they rushed to embrace, their cries dissolving into laughter and then back into tears as they kissed and touched each other's faces. Triti looked over his shoulder, searching.

"Ma? Pitaji?"

Dilip inclined his head and pursed his lips, just as he had as a boy when he could not bring himself to upset her. Triti read her twin instantly.

They were gone.

She pressed her forehead against his broad chest and wept.

"Triti, meree bahan…my sister, I always knew!" he exclaimed, stroking her hair. "Somehow I *knew* you were alive. I don't know how… Dear God, you're here!!"

She tried to speak, but he quieted her with a tight hug as she quaked in his arms.

"Shhhh…there'll be time to talk," he said, his voice breaking. "My dear, sweet sister. You're safe now. At last, *everything* is alright."

THIRTY-NINE

An hour later, Triti followed Dilip into his Preet Vihar flat and paused just inside the white-trimmed door. There was her brother, walking across his living room floor. She could barely believe that she was with him again. She felt a swell of sisterly pride that his teenage cuteness had matured into the perfect combination of their mother's elegance and their father's smolder. With his strong shoulders and deep voice, it was clear that her twin had grown up. He clapped his hands and spun on his heels—his old tactic for amusing her—and she laughed at how perfectly normal she felt in that moment.

Her mind raced with questions and observations.

"You'll stay in my bedroom," said Dilip, as he led her past the galley kitchen into his room and set her luggage on the painted green floor beside a rattan bureau.

"You have a small attached bath, just there. The water pressure is best in the early morning."

Triti was not surprised to see Dilip's spartan quarters. Even as a young boy, he had favored a frugal environment. The walls were unadorned but for a rambling mosaic of spidery cracks that had over time intruded from beneath the layers of faded, red plaster. A cotton pajama lay folded in the center of the tidy, double bed. Under a wooden chair, a pair of leather sandals waited.

"I've displaced you. Where will you sleep?" Triti asked with concern.

"In my home office," he said, directing her down the hall. When he opened the door, a blast of air-conditioned cool hit their faces. They sighed simultaneously and then laughed at each other. The room was an efficient workspace, complete with two laptop computers, a fax machine, an industrial copier, and a wide-screen monitor. A spotless modern desk stood in one corner, while in the opposite corner a thin rolled mattress stood beside a plastic-sealed window.

"It's the only room with AC. My electronics have to live here otherwise they would die in the summer. I crash here on the beastly nights and during monsoon. Not to worry. You know I can sleep just about anywhere."

Triti nodded, remembering Dilip as a youngster slumbering blissfully on their father's shoulder amidst the rowdy throngs of camel traders at the Pushkar festival. It was always he who could drift off to sleep across their mother's lap on the balcony of their family home in Jaipur while the fireworks of the Dushara street celebrations thundered below.

"You have so much space," she said. "More than twice that of my apartment in New York. It must cost plenty."

"No, not really. The monthly tariff is actually quite average for two bedrooms and two baths on C block. I took over the lease from my co-worker when he transferred to our Mumbai office. But what really sold me is directly above us."

Triti followed him out into the fifth-floor hallway and up a set of narrow stairs at the end of the hall. At the top of the steps, Dilip spun the tumbler on a combination lock and pushed open a heavy metal door. Together they stepped out onto the roof. To the west, beyond the Yamuna River, Triti could see the golden minarets of Delhi's temples and mosques.

"The lease says I may do what I want up here, so I installed that wooden decking."

He pointed to a large, rectangle-shaped platform.

"I suppose I should buy some furniture. Maybe a few plants…"

Triti looked out over hundreds of surrounding roofs. Each building-top tableau buzzed with its own dramas and cast of players. Directly next door, two soapy toddlers fussed knee-deep in tin buckets as their patient mother scrubbed a day's worth of city grime from their wriggling bodies. On one roof across the street, bare-chested men pinched half-smoked bidis between their lips and knelt beside used bicycle wheels, patching tire holes and repairing broken spokes. Two roofs down, a spectacled boy tossed a dragon-shaped kite into the air and watched as the breeze lifted the rainbow bright creature high above his concrete and brick world. Everywhere Triti looked she saw families gathered by steaming pots of dal and scooping up savory mouthfuls with fresh-made chipatis.

"I don't come up often," said Dilip, fumbling for a justification. "By the time I get home from work…Well, you know."

Indeed, as his twin, she knew the reason he avoided the roof deck. There was too much life up there. Too many memories stirred, too many points of pain. Without his saying a word, she understood how for the last seven years the sound of babies burbling had filled him with sorrow, how teenagers dancing to the latest radio hits had torn at his heart. She knew his pain, because it mirrored hers. Every day for seven years they had suffered the same losses—father, mother, twin—each in their own way.

"Dilip, tomorrow let's buy a proper pair of lounge chairs."

He looked down at the empty wooden deck. "Yes. We'll go to Chandni Chowk. Perhaps we'll find a potted tuberose."

"Or two."

The next morning, Dilip arranged his schedule to work from home.

Although Triti insisted that he go about his usual routine, she was relieved to have him with her all day.

By habit, she rose at dawn to bathe and dress. Once she had boiled the water for tea and set up a bowl of flour dough, she went down to the corner newsstand to fetch the morning news editions. By the time Dilip shuffled squint-eyed into the kitchen, her head was spinning with reports of lurid urban crimes and gossipy updates on Bollywood's recent stars.

"Be careful, or you're apt to spoil me," he chided her as he took his seat at the table. She set a plate of sliced guava and buttery parathas before him, and filled his cup with steaming fresh coffee.

"Nonsense," she scoffed, trying her best not to laugh. "You think I've done this for you? I've already eaten. But I'm happy to share the leftovers."

For the next few days, they embraced a simple, predictable timetable. Dilip spent mornings in his home office hunched over his computers, manipulating CAD images and recalculating engineers' specifications. His afternoons consisted of lengthy conference calls that often lasted until supper. But every thirty minutes, he found some excuse to look in on Triti. It was not enough for him to know that she was in the next room or down the hall; he had to see for himself that she was safe. As the effects of her jet lag abated, Triti looked for things to occupy her time. In addition to cooking, she busied herself with cleaning the apartment. Dilip argued that he should keep his weekly house service, but she would not have it. The act of scrubbing had always had a soothing effect on her, with its repetition and immediate results. She took her time mopping the burgundy floor tile that ran throughout the kitchen and living room, pleased to see the shine come up. When she dusted around the lone bookshelf in the living room, she wondered why it is was empty—and what was in the mound of taped boxes beside it.

She queried him over dinner that evening.

"Have you plans to move soon? I saw the stack of boxes."

Dilip shook his head.

"Naheen. Not for at least two more years. What you see is a workaholic's procrastination. I'm embarrassed to say that most of them are textbooks from university. Can you imagine?"

"You'll need more shelves! All those books…"

"And some other things. From home."

She listened, hearing his heart in his voice.

"Perhaps you'll go through them," he said. "When you're ready."

On Friday morning, Triti agreed to join Dilip for an excursion into New Delhi. She looked forward to being out in the city with him, and to have time to talk. There was so much that she needed to say, and even more that she wanted to understand. She was still overwhelmed by their reunion, but her many questions could wait no longer. She hoped that he was ready to give her answers.

"You should have been the one in college," he confessed to her as they strolled through the gates of Lodi Gardens

Park. "I went because it was expected of me. Quite frankly, I didn't know what else to do. But you! You were always the one with your nose in a book. You were the student. I was just a pretender."

"I wanted to go, but..."

"Yes, I remember."

He measured his words.

"There were circumstances..."

They walked beneath the broad fern canopy of a jacaranda tree. The sunlight shining through its leaves onto the pavement made the cement appear as lace.

Triti slowed her pace to a full stop.

"Dilip...I *want* to know."

He shook his head.

Suddenly, she was unsure whether she could bear to hear the story for which she had waited so long.

"Oh, sister, there is too much..."

"Tu manne pyaar kare hai?" She slipped effortlessly into Rajasthani slang.

"Yes, Triti. I love you."

Looking at him, the courage returned to her heart.

"Then please, tell me everything."

He moved closer to her, and slowly they began walking again.

"Papa-ji took it hardest. I would have thought Ma, but no. He started crying as soon as the Verma's car pulled away from our door with you after the wedding. He refused to eat or sleep—just inconsolable. Wept every night. He ranted that you were too young, that he should have never agreed to your marriage. He fumed about an old debt. He and Ma argued constantly. Many mornings I found him asleep on the sofa."

"And you, my poor Dilip? Tu kaain karyo?" she asked, her voice full of tenderness.

"What did I *do*? I wept when I knew no one would see. I felt hollow. Groundless. When we hadn't heard from you in several weeks, Pa turned wild with worry. He phoned the farm repeatedly, but no one answered his calls. Finally, he took one of his work trucks and drove out to get you. I begged him to let me go along, but he refused. When he returned that night, I was still awake in my bed. Ma's screams woke up the neighbors. It was the worst night of my life…of all our lives."

Triti startled as a young couple and their pre-school aged daughter hurried past, toting a pair of tiffin towers and a picnic blanket. The little girl's laughter joined the choruses of songbirds that fluttered among the canna lilies and palm trees. Grateful for the interruption, Dilip waited until the family was out of sight before continuing.

"At first, Rakesh's family insisted that you'd gone to the pyre voluntarily, joyfully. But I didn't believe them! And neither did our parents. After three weeks, the coroner admitted to Papaji that only Rakesh's skeleton had been found in the ashes. Overnight, the Vermas changed their story. They called you a runaway bride. The local police captain, one of the Verma's cousins, claimed that without your bones, there was no reason to investigate a sati. He refused Pa's requests to file a missing person's report.

No one from the village was willing to talk to our father. It seemed that he alone wanted to find you. We heard rumors that once the sati case was officially closed, all of the worshippers left the site. The public drama was over. But our parents' hell had just begun."

Triti listened in grief and disbelief as Dilip recounted their father's desperate efforts to find her. How he hired local townspeople to search nearby villages for her, and fought with the Vermas to recover her wedding jewelry and dowry money. For weeks, he traveled from town to town, showing her photo to everyone he met. Dilip told her that their mother had fasted for days at a time, becoming so weak that it made it difficult for her to stand for her daily pujas to Krishna. At first, she went several times a day to pray at the Govind Dev Temple, and beseeched the flower wallahs en route for their most beautiful garlands. But her health deteriorated and toward the end, she spent most of her days in bed.

"She kept your room *just* as you'd left it," said Dilip.

By then, Triti could scarcely lift her gaze from the ground.

"I broke their hearts, didn't I?"

With as much tenderness as she had ever felt from him, Dilip confessed that, in a manner of speaking, she *had* done just that. Two months after her disappearance, severe chest pains put their father in hospital. Two weeks later, Ajay Sharma died, his body burned in a solemn ceremony on the ghats of Lake Pushkar. Consumed by her grief, Chandi Sharma joined her husband soon after his death—swallowing a jar of sleeping pills the very morning Dilip departed Jaipur for the University of Delhi. At nineteen, orphaned and alone, he was left to settle the sale of the family apartment and his parents' financial affairs. He had not set foot in Rajasthan since the gloomy day a bank lawyer handed him the cashier's check that permanently closed the family's modest account.

"I've kept your portion in a CD," he said, brightening. "I suppose I was waiting… It's not a fortune, but it's yours. For now, or for the future."

The future. Triti repeated the word silently. Just then, a male tailorbird flew into a nearby ashoka tree. He carried a long, gold ribbon that he wove artfully into the top of his egg-shaped nest. As she looked on, a familiar face came into her mind.

"Dilip, there's someone I need to see."

"Anand! Phone!"

His mother called out from her dining room in Old Delhi.

Anand pressed the light button on his digital watch. 8:15 a.m. Who would be calling him on a Saturday morning? With the deadline for his revised manuscript fast approaching, he had written well past two a.m. and was desperate for another hour of sleep.

"Anand…You have a phone call!"

In his stupor, he guessed that it was probably his coworker, Ray, wanting him to cover an extra shift at the newspaper. He hated hawking subscriptions almost as much as waking up early on the weekends. He groaned and pulled his bedclothes up over his head.

A moment later, his bedroom door creaked open.

"Anand, did you *hear* me calling you?"

"Mother, please, I'm still asleep. Can't you just take a message?"

He rubbed the thick stubble on his chin and turned over.

"Fine, fine. As you wish, your Highness. I'll let her know you're not available."

"Her?" He sat up instantly in his bed.

"She says her name is Minu."

Anand raced across the city by cab to East Delhi. The drive seemed to take forever, but he was grateful not to be the one behind the wheel in the city's dense traffic. He had long dreamed of this day and he wanted it to be perfect. Following his mother's wisdom to bring a gift, he stopped twice along the way: once to buy a bouquet of pink roses, and again at the street cart of a kabulli wallah for a small bag of dates and a tin of cashews.

With Dilip still asleep upstairs, Triti waited nervously on the street outside his apartment building. They had talked nearly until dawn, and although she was physically exhausted, her spirit was energized. She had told him as much of her story as she knew, and they had cried together. When she admitted her feelings for Anand, he encouraged her to follow her heart.

His brotherly advice? "Don't keep the poor chap on tender hooks!"

She wondered how it would be to see Anand again. The three long weeks since last she saw him vanished from her thoughts when a car pulled up to the curb.

"Anand!"

The moment he wrapped his arms around her, she felt silly for having doubts. She was *home*, once again. So when he told her where he wanted to take her, she instantly agreed.

The woman attendant at the entrance to the Lakshmi Narayan Temple took three rupees from Anand and placed his shoes side-by-side with Triti's on the crowded shoe rack behind her. Thousands of people from all castes and religions had made the pilgrimage to the heart of New Delhi that day to ascend the massive flight of steps leading to the temple gardens.

"Follow me," said Anand, as he led her through the swarms of worshippers past two life-sized elephant sculptures on the central path of the waterfall gardens.

They found a small, stone bench beside a peacock fountain where they sat, just looking at each other, smiling. Triti had waited a long time to share her story with Anand. When she saw that his smile did not waver despite the dire truths she spoke, her heart overflowed with love for him. When she finished speaking, she pulled up her long sleeves and put her scarred hands in his.

"They are…as beautiful as the rest of you, *Triti*."

When he said her real name for the first time, she looked away, modestly.

"Triti. It suits you."

She leaned forward to remove her socks, but he shook his head and held tighter to her hands.

"Naheen. If one day I am to be the luckiest man in the world, I shall gaze upon your entire, glorious splendor. Until then…"

He kissed her hands and returned them to her lap.

"Nand, I'm suddenly feeling very grateful to your ex-fiancé."

"Why is that?"

"Well, had it not been for her, you wouldn't have gone to America."

"Surely, we would have met somehow. Some things are meant to be."

"So, you believe in fate?"

"You're here with me now, Triti. *Now*. And that is *all* that matters."

Triti's days in Delhi were a blend of light and reality. For three weeks, she reveled in the company of the two most important men in her life. Together they explored the bazaars of Old Delhi, shopping for exotic spices in Khari Baoli market and glass garlands in Churiwali Gali. Dilip showed her the architecture of the Red Fort and the historical Indian treasures in The National Museum. Anand took her to Khan Market where they spent hours perusing the bookshelves of Bahri & Sons and Faqir Chand's. With each excursion in the city, Triti's confidence grew. When Diwali arrived, she scrubbed and polished Dilip's flat as was custom, and he surprised her with a gift of a beautiful salwar suit. That evening, the three of them exchanged candies and carried sparklers down to the Yamuna where they witnessed the traditional lighting of the river lamps.

It pleased her that the men got on well and had quite a bit in common, from their love of soccer to liberal politics. They enjoyed her home-cooked dinners, often eating and laughing until midnight. No matter how late the evenings ran, or how chilly the northern winds that swept across the river, she and Anand adjourned to Dilip's roof for a brief, good night kiss.

Triti felt happier and stronger than ever before. There were no bad dreams claiming her sleep, and no dark visions disturbing her days. She wondered if the Memory was hibernating, or if it was gone for good? She could not be certain. The only thing she was sure of was that with Dilip and Anand by her side, she was *safe*. The time had come at last.

She would go to Rajasthan.

FORTY

November 23, 2007
Cambridge, MA
4:15 P.M.

H ere goes…
As she waited in the outer office of Harvard's Dean of Art History, Jaq straightened the folds of her rose gold sari just as Triti had taught her. Her daylong odyssey had begun after breakfast in Manhattan when she applied lipstick and mascara carefully and donned every piece of jewelry in Triti's velvet bag. On the early Amtrak train to Boston and then the T into Cambridge, she drew more than the usual admiring glances. The difference this day was that her outward appearance was not the only part of her renaissance. She felt completely invincible, for only two days earlier, the brain specialist on rotation from NYU had uttered the most wonderful four words she had ever heard: 'Your mother is stable.'

"Stable!"

For Jaq, the news had been like a hundred Christmas mornings in one. Banni had regained consciousness, and was finally, mercifully, off the ventilator. Her doctors agreed that with therapy and time, she could regain considerable movement and speech. A rehabilitation facility in Boston had an opening for her after the holidays. When she received a letter that her academic scholarships had been reinstated, Jaq breathed another sigh of relief; she could be near her mother while she completed her Ph.D. She was unsure what would happen once she stepped back into her graduate school life, but she finally felt ready to rejoin the fray.

The new dean, a sharp woman scholar from Chicago, had generously agreed to meet with her on the Friday before Thanksgiving break. She listened to Jaq's impassioned account of how Triti's story had inspired her to change her thesis topic.

"I'd like to concentrate my studies on representations of brides and widows in Southeast Asian art."

The dean nodded and wrote a few notes in Jaq's academic case file.

"This will mean extra hours in the library. I assume you already know that, Ms. Morel."

"Yes, Dean, I do."

"And you'll be resuming your teaching duties."

Jaq nodded. "I'm looking forward to it."

"Do you have any questions for *me*?"

Only one.

She hoped that the new dean would not notice the tremolo in her voice when she uttered his name. She knew there was nothing she could do to change history. There remained just one final accounting—but it was not to be done in this office, and not with this new ally.

"Professor Kraik?"

"Early retirement," said the dean, dryly. "You'll hear rumors. Believe what you will. You'll need a new advisor, Ms. Morel…"

"Jaq."

"Great—Jaq. I spent a year in Amristar as a grad student. I'll sign on. Come back to me with a tight research plan the first week of January."

Jaq exhaled in relief. "Thank you for your time. I'll have the proposal ready right after New Year's."

Jaq hurried across the Yard.

An exorcism was in order. An earthquake. And she *had* to witness the rubble with her own eyes. Six p.m. on the Friday evening before Thanksgiving. *Lowell should be a virtually empty building.* Hopefully, her timing would be right.

She imagined Kraik as he had always been: alone, immersed in some new research project, smoking Pall Mall's to the nub. Half way down the second-floor hall, Jaq could see that his office door was open. As she walked, she thought of Triti, and Banni, and Jitter. She saw her father in her mind, smiling and nodding encouragement. And her nervous stomach settled out.

Twenty-seven more steps.

"Twenty-six, twenty-five…"

She finished the rest of the count silently.

The tiny bells on Triti's bracelets jingled on her wrists as she stepped into the frame of Kraik's doorway. The scene she saw shocked her. His office was empty. His desk was utterly bare, but for his ragged, brown briefcase. A wastebasket overflowed in the corner. Barren walls revealed a mosaic of sun-bleached rectangles where Kraik's framed academic accolades and celebrity photos no longer hung to impress or intimidate.

Kraik himself, in his yellowed oxford shirt and navy-blue tie, was bent, elbow deep in the bottommost drawer of his desk. Hearing a trespasser, he bolted upright. Surprise, then menace flashed across his black eyes from behind his dark-rimmed glasses.

"You're *too* late, Jacqueline."

His eyes traveled up and down the length of her.

"Or should I say *Sita*?"

Careful. They're unpredictable when cornered.

Jaq quickly assessed the emptiness of the room with her peripheral vision. In the days and nights when he had tormented her, his office had been a treacherous labyrinth of stacked articles and crates of art journals. Against this newly-naked backdrop, he appeared much smaller to her. She gestured at the bare walls.

"Guess I missed a lot last semester, Professor. Redecorating?"

Kraik seethed. The sarcastic grin that had once anchored his sagging face was now a malefic scowl.

"Took two first year cunts to force me out. The lawyers are on a romp. Whores, all of them."

He seemed desperate for a fight.

"*You* didn't have the guts, Jaq."

The remark stung because it was true. She had not had the courage to tell. She had not fought. She had run, mute with humiliation—just as she had once run from Larry and Naveen. Standing against Kraik had been impossible for her nine months ago. But now that her mother depended on her, and her brave twin had gone halfway around the world to face her terrifying past, Jaq realized that she was through with silent running. Her transformation had been a slow turning, from the inside out. The blush rising on her cheeks was not shame, but the flush of pride that she would never again be anyone's victim.

Pulling herself up to her tallest height, Jaq looked down on her impotent nemesis. She spoke softly, forcing him to lean toward her to hear.

"You have no power over me anymore. I'm much stronger now. For a man with such a large intellect, you are really *very* small. And pitiful."

Before he could speak, Jaq swirled out the door, her beaded sari swinging behind her. She accelerated her pace, descended Lowell's central staircase, and strode out into the brisk New England night.

FORTY-ONE

November 26, 2007

Rajasthan

Triti rode alone in the back seat of the rented car, becoming more anxious with every passing mile. The NH8 from Jaipur to Ajmer was congested with overloaded commercial trucks that swayed precariously as their drivers weaved in and out of the traffic streams. She took little notice of the countless trailers crammed with boxes of face soaps and crates of live chickens. Instead, she fixated on the endless miles of parched, barren land where yellow and green buds should have been preparing to flower.

"Where are the mustard fields?" she sighed, for once glad for the veil that covered her head and shoulders. It kept secret both her identity and her homesick tears.

"Monsoon has abandoned Rajasthan," said Dilip, slowing the car to pull around a stalled tractor-trailer stacked high with dusty cars. The angry driver kicked a flat front tire and fumbled to replace his cell phone's SIM card.

"Such devastation," said Anand, who sat beside Dilip as they drove past dozens of abandoned farms. The three travelers gawked at tumbleweed-choked foot trails that had once connected bustling villages to verdant fields. Ragged twists of sun-bleached stalks dotted the desolate fields—stark evidence of a decade-long drought. Only the rugged babul and kjeri trees kept their shady, roadside posts.

"And the people?" Triti asked aloud, reeling from the sight of her home land so devoid of life.

"Gone. To the cities, mostly" said Dilip. "I've heard that thousands, tens of thousands and more families packed what they could carry and headed to the urban centers—Delhi, Mumbai, Goa, even as far as Bangalore—hoping to find jobs as brick makers or steel workers or servants. They're willing to do anything to feed their families—scavenging garbage, even killing rats for pay!"

Just then a rickety flatbed mounded with cases of Bisleri water sped up alongside their car. Without warning, the driver accelerated and swerved in front of them, his truck spewing a black cloud of diesel exhaust in its wake. Dilip slammed his foot against the brake just in time.

"Bevakūf!"

The smoke cleared, revealing a common Indian proverb printed in English on the truck's tailgate in bold, orange letters.

GOD SEES THE TRUTH BUT WAITS.

Farmers from a tiny, hillside village walked in pairs along the highway, visibly fatigued from yet another day in the parched fields. One man straddled a load of broken rocks and tried to wrangle a pair of gray burros that refused to pull his cart. Dilip steered around the road's deepest ruts and finally stopped beside an old man who yanked his camel's red tassel reins in vain.

"Hello," said Dilip. "Can you tell me where I may find the Verma farm? It's supposed to be near by."

Before the old man could answer, an overcrowded public bus with half a dozen riders clinging to its metal roof cheated a curve in the road and thundered past them, kicking up towers of dust. The driver honked at the old man, who raised a withered hand in acknowledgement.

Bemused, the old man turned his attention back to Dilip. "Verma, you say?"

"Hanji."

The man's mustache was covered with silt. Twisted and curled down at the ends, it frowned with him. As he spoke, his crooked mouth revealed three remaining teeth, stained brown from a half century of puffing bidis.

"Tu kathi se aayo?" The man directed his question to Dilip, all the while eyeing the two other strangers in the car.

"We come from Delhi," said Dilip, casting a cautionary glance to Anand.

"Delhi! Yes, so. All the way in the big city," he replied

in simple English. "I knew Verma. He's long dead. Drank the pesticide."

"What?" Anand whispered to Dilip.

"Suicide," said Dilip. "There are stories in the papers *all* the time now. Farmers across India are killing themselves. Literally. One every thirty minutes. It's a vicious cycle. The drought or locusts make them desperate for any advantage. Corporate seed merchants have become the new moneylenders. When the crops fail from thirst, the farmers have no way to repay their exorbitant debts. They lose their land and their pride. And make widows of their wives."

The old man gestured with his walking stick toward the right side of the road where a weedy, gravel drive wound a half-kilometer through patchy fields toward a sparse forest at the base of the Aravalli foothills.

"Killed himself?" Anand shook his head, still puzzled.

The camel owner adjusted his tight, beige turban.

"What *choice* did he have?" The man spat on the ground and yanked his camel into a steady cadence west.

"There," said Triti. She pointed to a distant cluster of structures centered in the midst of the vast dry fields.

Dilip turned down the rough road and drove on slowly, taking the divots and rocks as carefully as he could. A young village woman appeared on the trail that cut across the road. She balanced a great faggot of sticks on top of her head, her lime-green sari a tart burst of color against the dreary vista. As their vehicle drew nearer to her, she pulled the edge of her veil down over her face and stepped off the path into the brambles. Dilip continued driving to the end of the rugged road and stopped within ten meters of a group of ramshackle buildings.

Triti's stomach turned to concrete as she stepped out of the car. She recognized the remains of some of the equipment shacks. Beyond them she spied the walls and roof of the main haveli. Dilip and Anand joined her as she surveyed the deserted ruins. Their looks of sympathy helped to steady her.

"I'm so grateful that you're here," she said.

"Of course," said Dilip. "Where else would I be?"

Anand put his hand on her shoulder.

"Are you alright?"

"I don't know," she said. "I just have to see…"

She took a deep breath and walked with deliberateness toward the furthest building. Wordlessly, the two men fell into step behind her.

When she reached the entrance of the converted barn, Triti saw a familiar door panel, wind battered and hanging awkwardly from its corroded hinges. The cords in her neck tightened as she shoved open the door with her shoulder.

She was back in her bridal chamber.

Stepping across the splintered, wooden threshold, she saw that the windows and walls were nearly all broken out. Fingers of blown sand stretched across the broken floor tiles. In the far corner of the room were the remnants of a shrine. She moved to get a closer look. Stapled to the remaining bits of plaster walls were long-faded photographs, but she could still make out the ghostly-pale images of Rakesh and her on their wedding day, their stoic, young faces staring toward the camera. The muscles in her neck became leaden ropes. She looked about the room and saw their marital bed had been stripped all the way down to its metal frame. The crumbling remnants of dried flower garlands hung over the bed's end posts, and on the floor below the bed was a musty, flattened ring of melted candles.

As she stood amidst the decay, a high-pitched screech shattered Triti's ears. Like the static of a microphone with its phantom speaker's lips too close to the mouthpiece, the sound sliced through her consciousness. She winced and dug her fingers hard into her ears. The squeal quickly resolved into a confluence of human whispers, faint at first, and then stronger, quickly becoming a rising chorus of recognizable voices. Sinister voices.

Them!

Triti glanced at Dilip and Anand who waited, watching her protectively from the doorway. They had not heard a thing.

She stepped toward the bed and stood at the foot of its rusted frame. Before her eyes, a mattress appeared: new and whole. Live candles flickered with light along the bedroom floor. Strings of fresh ginger blossoms draped the bedposts, filling the room with their spicy perfume. Women in dark lehengas swarmed the bed, blocking her vision of a lone, reclining figure. She shuffled forward to get a better view.

She froze at the sight of herself propped up in the bed. Her hand flew to her mouth.

"My God!" she cried.

The voices in the room became clearer. She could make out the words.

"She's still conscious…what do we do?"

"Make her drink again."

No, no more tea!

"You've suffered a shock, girl. Drink."

Mother-in-law, please, no more!

The women shifted in their tight circle. Sisters-in-law hovered near the headboard.

"The dress. She must wear the dress."

"And the mehndi. Do this *right*!"

Other women came into view as new voices echoed about the room.

"Nonsense! We've *no* time for mehndi! Get her dressed! They are waiting…"

"I feel sick…please. I need to sleep…PLEASE!" Triti heard her own voice as the vision faded.

"Sister, what *is* it?" asked Dilip stepping a foot into the room.

"They want me to drink!"

Triti turned and lunged past Anand and Dilip out the door. Stupefied, the men followed after her. Moments later they found her behind a roofless storage hut, staring up at the mountains. Dilip approached her cautiously.

"Do you want to leave?"

Triti shook her head and slid off her veil. She turned from the men and walked along the edge of the forest, searching. Dilip and Anand paced behind her, keeping their distance. Soon she came to a circular scattering of ruined timber. Triti stopped and stared at the ground. Sun-bleached for seven years and overgrown with weeds, the scorched remains of a wooden sthall were visible to her.

Wavering before the site, Triti began to moan.

"They're *pulling* me," she cried fearfully, as the Memory roared fully to the surface of her consciousness.

"WHO is it? *Who's* pulling you?" asked Dilip.

Triti could hear Dilip talking, but other sounds soon drowned out his voice.

Stop pulling me! No, I can't go on… I'm tired. I feel sick.

Anand stepped forward and reached for Triti, but Dilip held him back.

"Who is there, Sister?"

"*Can't* you see them? Mother-in-law, sister-in-law…the brothers, and now, the others…"

Dilip and Anand scanned the desolate countryside. The only creature in sight was a palm squirrel scurrying for seeds.

"What do you see, Triti?" Dilip kept his voice low.

They were there. Some of them she knew, though most were strangers, all howling, to the left and the right of her.

Them. Big faces. Cruel eyes.

"So many…they're pointing at me, clapping. Chanting! Can't you *hear* them?"

"What do they say?" Dilip asked as he came closer to be by her side.

She clamped her hands over her ears, but the shouting blended into one continuous chant, again and again, shriller and shriller, the piercing sound vibrating up through her legs and into her chest. At last she had to scream out loud.

"SATI MATA KI JAI!"

"God, no," Anand rasped.

"SATI MATA KI JAI!!"

"Victory to the Sati Goddess," Dilip translated, his eyes fixed on Triti.

Triti watched helplessly as a group of men hoisted a body wrapped in cloth onto a bare plywood platform two meters above the ground. Below it was a great stack of logs and dry kindling. Other men milled about the sthall wielding long, pointed spears. Veiled women gathered a short distance away, wailing and rocking in place. She could barely see them in the shadows. Their heavy bracelets jangled as they clapped in growing fervor.

"What's *happening?*" Dilip asked Triti, fear in his voice.

"The fog... It's so dense, like a wall. I can smell rain coming. Someone is tossing purple gulal. The powder is everywhere!"

She twisted her hands frantically beneath her chin.

Dilip walked around Triti to stand between her and Snake Mountain. Anand joined him, hanging back behind Dilip. They saw that her eyes were wide open but it was if she looked right through them.

"I feel *sick*. Thirsty. Don't! They're shoving me...toward the platform. Shoving me up!" Now she was shrieking. "DON'T push me! DON'T!!"

She sniffed the air.

"Something is burning! That smell. *Burning!* It's so much stronger *now*."

Helpless, Anand's eyes widened with dread at Triti's words. Above them, the desert sky was turning scarlet.

"STOP pushing me! I don't want to sit! What's *this*? This on my lap? It's heavy. Can't see...."

Dilip leaned in closer to look at Triti's face. Her eyes were focused on something very far away. Suddenly, she screamed toward the mountain.

"MY God, NO!! Rakesh! His HEAD! GOD! Get it OFF of me!"

"I *can't* take this," choked Anand, backing away.

Dilip grabbed his arm.

"She needs us *both*, Anand!"

"I CAN'T SEE! The air, it's SO thick... Oh, God, smoke. I smell smoke! It's near. Beneath me! It's BENEATH me! FIRE! NO! NO! NOOOO!!!"

Triti twisted and shuddered in place, her arms thrashing wildly in the air.

"I'M BURNING! HELP MEEE! Can't move my legs! It's shaking! Everything's SHAKING! I can't *see*... AAHH! I'M FALLING! HELP ME!! Someone HELP ME!!!"

Anand bit his fist.

Just then Triti dropped to a crouch at the edge of the sthall. She slashed her hands about the earth near her feet, then leaped up to standing again.

"The GROUND! I'm on the *ground!* RAIN! YES! RAIN! MUST GET AWAY! GOD, WHERE DO I GO? MUST RUN!

NOW! TO THE FOREST! YES, THE FOREST! GO! RUN! RUN! NOW!! GOOOO!!!"

A slight breeze lifted Triti's hair from her shoulders. She opened her eyes. Snake Mountain appeared gold before her—tinder-dry in the setting sun. The smoke and the flames and the rains were gone.

Beneath her feet, the ground was nothing more than a thirsty patch of earth.

Sati Triti was no more. The Memory—gone. Swept up and away on the barest of desert winds.

I am free.

Slowly, she became aware of a kind of tranquility flowing through her body. Triti looked at the scars on her hands and let out a long sigh.

Dilip and Anand crept forward, their expectant faces taut with worry.

"Sister, I'm *so* sorry…"

"You have *nothing* to apologize for, Dilip," she said, tenderly.

"Yes, *yes* I do. I was supposed to protect you…I should have been there."

"But my brother, you're here now."

"And you, my darling, Nand."

She turned to Anand, who was still crying. She reached up and wiped the tears from his cheeks with her fingers. His smile returned at her touch.

The three of them turned to look up at Snake Mountain one more time; its rocky face still awash in bright amber.

My mountain.

"What now, my sister?" asked Dilip.

Triti clasped each of the men's hands in hers. Together they turned to walk back to the car. She thought for less than a second and answered him.

"Now, I am going to be happy."

FORTY-TWO

"Good thing you didn't arrive two nights ago. Just like the rest of Pushkar, we were completely sold out."

The cheery Sufi manager of the Heritage hotel retrieved two sets of room keys from the wall of keys behind him and handed them to Dilip.

"I've given you adjoining suites on the third floor. Not a problem, since the American tour groups departed early this morning for Ranthambore. They've gone on safari every year for a decade and have yet to see one tiger. Perhaps this year they will have luck."

Triti, Dilip, and Anand sat to eat a late meal in the near-empty, hotel dining room, but soon abandoned their plates and headed to their rooms. Triti said good night to Dilip and Anand in the hallway outside her room.

"We're right there should you need us," said Anand, pointing to the door next to hers.

"Yes, please. For any reason at all," said Dilip.

"I'll be fine, really. I'm just tired. You two get some rest."

Dilip kissed her on the top of her head and disappeared inside his suite's door.

"Are you sure you're ok?" asked Anand, searching her eyes.

"Yes, 'Nand. Thank you for being here, and for caring about me."

He kissed her gently on the lips, and held her door open for her.

"I'll always be here for you, Triti."

Snuggled peacefully beneath her blankets, Triti dreamed that she stood on top of a great wall looking toward a horizon of shimmering sand. Thousands of silver sea birds called out her name as they swooped past her shoulders. She leaped from the wall and became one of them, the fastest of the flock, soaring ahead of the formation. Higher and higher she ascended until she was floating above the clouds. When she awoke just after dawn, she felt deeply rested—as if she had slept for years.

She slipped out of the covers and pushed open a set of ornate doors that opened onto a small balcony overlooking the hotel's grand swimming pool. Its placid, blue expanse reflected the brilliance of the morning sky.

"Durga Maa! How shall I thank you for this day?"

Beyond the hotel confines, the adjacent hillside echoed with the sounds of village life. Triti listened to the school children jabbering in loose cliques as they ambled down the dirt lanes. Wandering cows lowed as they chewed on discarded newspapers. She could hear women scraping the bottoms of cooking pots and sweeping front stoops. Some men squatted in groups and hammered granite chunks into gravel, while others honked their bicycle and car horns at the parade of hotel buses chugging around the hairpin turns of the main access road. She laughed thinking that with the exception of the cows, how strangely similar were the sounds of morning in New York City.

When she arrived famished in the hotel's crowded dining room, Triti spotted Dilip and Anand at a table near the sumptuous buffet spread. The men had already started their breakfasts, but both rose simultaneously to greet her. As she made her way across the room, conversations in Italian, German, and English halted as tourists' heads turned to her—a vision in her magenta sari.

"Good morning," she said, beaming at Dilip and Anand. "I hope you two had a good rest. I certainly did."

"Indeed," said Dilip, as he pulled out the chair beside him for her.

"Such a gentleman," she teased.

Anand was overjoyed to see her so bright.

"And you, Nand?"

"Once my head hit the pillow, I was out."

"He was an ideal roommate," said Dilip. "Didn't snore once, that I can recall."

"Triti, how are you feeling, really?" asked Anand.

"You know, it's strange, but when I woke up this morning, all I could feel was relief. It's amazing… I mean, I'm sitting here, unveiled, and I'm not afraid. People are eating their meal and the wait staff is busing tables…it's just a normal day."

A waiter brought a fresh pot of chai to the table, and as Triti stirred hot milk into her cup she thought of Jaq. How her friend would love to be sitting there now. She would call Jaq as soon as they returned to Delhi. There was so much she needed to tell her. She reached for a cube of sugar and noticed the pink carnations in the table's centerpiece. They reminded her of her mother's daily ritual of placing a fresh flower beside her father's morning teacup. She broke off two of the blossoms and put one beside each of the men's plates. Anand picked his up and sniffed in the light fragrance.

"Dilip, do we have time before we have to leave to visit the ghat where you blessed Ma and Papaji? It would mean so much to me to go there and say some prayers."

"I was going to suggest it," he said. "Afterward, if you would like, we can check out one of the bazaars. We should make it home by midnight, so long as we're on the road by five p.m."

"Is that all right with you, Nand?"

"Of course," said Anand. "I'm honored that you would include me."

Mid-morning sunrays pierced the film of fog above Lake Pushkar, scattering random patches of light across its dark green surface. From the main road above the lake, the trio watched spellbound as the mist lifted — revealing its legendary shoreline of dazzling, whitewashed buildings, each one mirrored in the sparkling, holy waters. Rising from the edge of the lake's shallows, Mukti Ghat's broad, steep flight of stone slabs teemed with activity as religious pilgrims from all over India honored their dead in mukhagni cremation rituals and waded hip deep beside local residents to bathe away their sins.

Triti and Anand followed Dilip down a succession of crowded lanes to arrive at top of the ghat. On their way, they stopped at a street vendor's stand where Triti selected a round aluminum platter, a white votive candle, a small bottle of ghee, and two strands of yellow orchids for an aarti. At the top of the ghat, they removed their shoes and descended the wide stone steps. They passed ashen-faced sadhus who held knotty postures on worn, bamboo mats amidst flocks of cooing pigeons, and pink-horned cattle that shared precious space with hollow-bellied dogs and grieving families.

As she approached the lake, Triti's buoyancy flagged. She thought of the last time she had seen her parents — weeping, side by side, on the street outside of their apartment in Jaipur after her wedding. There had been too little time then to say goodbye.

This day, she decided, she would offer a daughter's loving farewell.

She joined Dilip at the water's verge and held the tray as he lit the candle and incense. Anand remained behind, his head bowed in a private prayer. Triti nodded to her brother and began to make slow, counterclockwise circles in the air with the tray.

"Would you chant?" she asked him.

"God, I'm blanking...I can't remember *any* song."

"Something joyful," she said. "Ma would like that. What about Gayatri Mantra? You *know* that one."

"I'll try. Help me out if I get stuck."

He cleared his throat and began to sing, shakily at first.

"Om kaatyayanaya vidmahei..."

While Dilip sang the song, Triti whispered her personal prayers to Krishna and Durga, thanking them for watching over their parents. She gave a handful of orchids to Dilip and together they tossed the flowers into the lake. Their colorful blossoms merged with the countless other offering flowers, confetti for the gods' pleasure.

Dilip finished the song and they stood together looking out over the lake.

"They're at peace now," said Triti. "I feel their serenity. Can you?"

Dilip pushed his hands into his pants pockets and shook his head.

"It must have been so hard for you," said Triti, leaning close enough to him for their shoulders to touch.

"I did as I was supposed to as the oldest son. Shaved my head, wore white, sat by their pyres all day waiting for dusk, for the release. But I don't remember much else; my heart was too broken. First you, then Father, then Ma…"

"My poor brother…"

"No! Not poor Dilip! I thought it was all my fault. For years I believed I'd killed you! *And* mother and father."

"Dilip, why? What are you saying?"

"The raakhi…I broke the string! Right after our last Raksha Bandhan the summer before you married…I couldn't bear to tell you. The bracelet you chose for me was so beautiful, with the turquoise silk and cowry shells. Everything had gone perfectly for once; I remembered the prayers and you tied the knots so well. Ma was proud of us. You managed to center the tilak exactly in the middle of my forehead. And you even let me put the sweets in your mouth without squirming. Remember?"

"Yes, vaguely… But what has this to do with anything?"

"I made the Promise…to take responsibility for you, for your safety, to stand by you in all circumstances. But the very next day I damn well lost the raakhi. I searched everywhere, but never found it. I must have gone to ten bangle shops before I found one to replace it. The string I wore for three months was not yours."

His face was a grimace of regret.

"My brother…"

"If I hadn't lost the raakhi you wouldn't have…"

"Dilip…"

"All of this sorrow. If only I'd…"

"Dilip, listen to me. You and I have never needed a thread to prove our devotion to each other. The love that binds us is unbreakable."

Her words seemed to help him. In that moment, she felt closer to him than she ever had.

"Besides, what more proof do you need? I'm *here*, and we're together again," she said. "Thanks be to Krishna."

"And to Jaq," said Dilip. "Had it not been for her…" he said, looking into his sister's eyes. "I'd like to thank her, face to face. One day."

Suddenly, Triti thought of Mala.

She handed the aarti tray to Dilip and walked out into the cool, lake water and slipped beneath the surface for her blessing.

On their way to the Sarafa Bazaar, Triti, Dilip, and Anand moved among hundreds of camel herders, horse wranglers, cattle ranchers, and merchants—the last stragglers of a mass exodus—departing Pushkar with their families and animals in tow.

Triti watched a young boy, barely ten years old, shuffle along the littered ground, dragging his legless half body on a ragged lunch tray, plastic flip flops on his dirty hands, while an Italian tourist bent low to take a photo of him. With her short shorts and low-cut tank top, the woman drew disapproving stares from a pair of Rajasthani sisters shopping at the fruit stand next door. Triti opened the car door and went to the boy, who peered up at her with dull sadness. She crouched and put 100 rupees in his soiled shirt pocket.

When they reached the bazaar's front gates, she and Anand waited for Dilip to park the rental car on an adjacent block. While he was gone, Triti asked Anand to keep her brother occupied for a while.

"I'd like to find a gift for him, but I want it to be a surprise."

Anand grinned, delighted to play his part in her scheme.

"No problem. I'll tell him you were looking to buy a present for me. We can meet back here. Will thirty minutes be enough solo time?"

"Should be. I know exactly what I'm looking for."

Triti set out down the market path, searching stall after stall, intent upon her goal. With the official end of the mela two days past, the tourist crowds had thinned considerably, and she easily navigated the lanes. Even though she had visited Pushkar often as a child, it was her first time at Sarafa, and she saw immediately why the market was renowned for its highly coveted textiles, embroidered fabrics, and camel covers. Tempting though they all were, she had one prize in her mind—a Bikaner wool rug. She knew that the carpets made there ranked among the finest in India, and she was determined to find the perfect, colorful piece for Dilip's apartment.

At every flooring shop she flipped through piles of rugs, checking the colors and quality of the pieces. Some vendors offered patterns that she liked but not in the size she wanted. She checked her watch and, seeing that she had barely ten minutes left, decided to try only two more vendors. If she didn't find her ideal carpet—navy and teal with long fringe—she would be more than content with the exquisite, blue oval rug she had admired at the very first stall near the bazaar's entrance. Surely it would enliven Dilip's living room.

Ahead of her, the path opened into a much wider street that was hectic with local foot traffic, motor scooters, and oxen. The shops there were considerably larger and jammed with customers haggling for the best price on sari fabrics and popular music CD's. The sun cast near-blinding light on one side of the street, and most vendors had unfurled shade curtains at the front of their stands. A bangle wallah's eye-catching wares twinkled in the glare. Triti was tempted to stop and try on the shiny trinkets, but she was on a mission, and walked past them. Just as she reached her turnaround point, she spotted another upscale rug stall.

"Mewar's."

She wondered if she had ever been there before.

"But I couldn't have, could I?"

She quickly assessed the neat stacks of round rugs at the front of the shop, admiring their superior colors and fine workmanship.

This is promising.

She ducked beneath the canvas awning and walked up two steps that led into the shop's cool interior. Cedar wood incense filled the shop. Flute ragas played from a cassette deck in the corner. A female shopkeeper was busy attending a middle-aged couple as they attempted to find a rug to match a paint chip from their dining room wall at their home in Switzerland. As she waited, Triti perused mounds of rugs, selecting two of them from near the top of the pile for further inspection. With a strong tug, she pulled both rugs out onto the floor. In the fluorescent lights of the showroom, the sea blue and navy designs impressed her. Either one would be ideal for Dilip's gift. She found no price tag on the pieces, and after a few minutes of calculations decided to make an offer. She checked her watch again. Less than ten minutes remained before she had to meet Anand and Dilip. To her relief, the couple before her settled their bill and left the shop.

"Welcome to Mewar's," said the well-dressed clerk as Triti approached the register. The woman wore an elegant lemon-yellow sari that sparkled with delicate crystal beading. Her graceful arms jingled with gold bracelets as she reached below the counter and produced a plate of sugar-dusted malapuas.

"Would you care for some?"

Triti cocked her head at the familiar voice. She looked closely at the clerk's swanlike neck and distinctive hairline. When she caught a whiff of the woman's lotus perfume, she slid her veil off her head and gave her answer.

"Mujhe peaas loghi hai."

She hoped the woman would remember the first words she had said to her when they met seven years ago.

The clerk's ebony eyes gleamed as shocked recognition swept over her.

"Is it *really* you?" the woman exclaimed, reaching across the counter to clasp Triti's hands in hers.

"Yes, Mala. It's me."

Mala rushed from behind the counter and threw her arms around Triti in a tight embrace. Triti hugged her back and for a long moment they simply held each other. Triti shook with emotion. Her heart flooded with joy as she rested her head on Mala's shoulder. Minutes passed until finally Mala loosened her grip and held Triti at arm's length. She cupped Triti's face in her hands. Feeling her familiar, gentle touch, Triti burst into tears.

"Aap kai se hai?" Mala asked.

Triti croaked through her tears. "I'm fine. Very good."

Mala took Triti's hands in hers and turned them over. Seeing Triti's faded scars, Mala smiled broadly.

"Dhanyavaad, Mala," said Triti.

Mala beamed and shook her head.

"I'm just so glad you're alright."

As Triti leaned forward to embrace her again, a three-year-old boy scampered out from beneath the counter skirt and wrapped his arms around Mala's legs.

"Ma, I'm tired," he whined, burying his plump cheeks between her knees.

"Rattan?" asked Triti, grinning at the sleepy cherub.

Mala nodded cheerfully and rested a bejeweled hand on the boy's head.

"He left for Jodhpur this morning. You've only just missed him."

Mala settled her son down for a nap at the back of the shop, retreating once more to soothe him with kisses. Then, she prepared Triti's carpet, rolling it tightly and securing it in several places with thick, jute twine. As she worked, Triti watched her closely, taking in every detail of the woman she had so longed to see again. Radiant in her fine clothing and jewelry, Mala exuded an undeniable happiness. They shared briefly about their new lives: Mala revealed that she lived in Pushkar in an apartment that Rattan had purchased for her and their son. Triti confided that she had finally made it to America. They laughed easily together, and it was clear to Triti that their shared, secret past no longer weighed down either of their spirits. When she put a pile of rupees on the counter and tucked her purchase beneath her arm, both women grew wistful.

"May I come see you again?" asked Triti, hesitating at the top of the steps.

Mala placed one of the shop's business cards in Triti's palm.

"You will always be welcomed, Triti. Always."

Three English backpackers stumbled up the shop steps, laughing uproariously. Mala hurried back to the counter to collect Triti's rupees. She placed them uncounted into the register drawer, and waved once more to Triti.

Triti returned Mala's enthusiastic farewell and walked out into the bazaar's busy thoroughfare. She would be a few minutes late to meet her men, but they would forgive her. Suddenly, she realized she had not sampled any of Mala's sweets. No matter, she thought. She would make sure to enjoy some on her next visit.

FORTY-THREE

8:25 a.m.
January 15, 2008
Vrindavan

Triti ducked into the empty communications kiosk of the Hotel Ashok's lobby and stood before one of the telephones on the international desk. She checked her watch and quickly calculated the time difference. It would be nearly ten p.m. in Boston—an hour earlier than her weekly call. After a series of clicks and beeps, she heard the ring tones of Jaq's cell phone.

"Hello, this is Jaq Morel…"

"Namaste!"

"Hey, Sister! Was hoping it was you! I didn't recognize the state code. You're not at Dilip's?"

"No, I'm in Vrindavan. I arrived late yesterday."

"Whoa, *that's* intense. Krishna called you back to His city, eh?"

"In a way, yes. How've you been? Your mom?"

"Me? I'm fine. Banni? She must be feeling better. She corrected my Hindi the other day."

Triti laughed. "Well, someone has to!"

"Hey, before I forget, thanks for sending back my passport. Looks like I'm going to need it this year after all. My research project was approved. I should be in Delhi mid-August, just in time for the Krishna Janmaashtami celebrations."

"I can't wait to see you!" said Triti.

"Me too! Maybe I'll finally get to meet your bro."

"Dilip will make sure of it."

"Loved that snapshot of you and Anand. Quite the handsome couple. Is he there with you now?"

"No, but he'll visit in a few weeks."

Triti opened her wallet and pulled out a miniature-sized copy of his picture she had sent to Jaq. At the sight of Anand's face, she grinned with delight.

"Everything's ok with you kids?"

"Yes, very. His book comes out at the end of the year. We've talked of getting married…"

"Wait, what? Congratulations! Where? When?"

"Thank you, but we've decided not to make any plans yet. Not until I know how long I'm going to be here."

"A secret project?" Jaq said, half-joking. "You're starting to sound like me."

"Not exactly. I'm here to volunteer with Mata Madad, an agency that provides shelter, food, and medical assistance to the widows of Vrindavan. I met with the executive director in Delhi two weeks ago, and she said that they needed teachers for their literacy program. I'm heading to the MM Living Center in town this morning."

"That's brilliant, Triti. Really. Do you know what your duties will be?"

"I'm not exactly sure. There are over 20,000 widows in this city, and most live on the streets. The luckiest ones find Mata Madad. Right now, the Center is housing several hundred "mothers" as they're called here. Less than two percent of the women can read or even write their names, so I expect to be teaching. I'll find out more today."

"How does it feel…to be there again?" asked Jaq.

Triti already knew the answer to that question. It was all she could wonder about on the car trip south from Delhi. To her astonishment, the moment her Sikh driver left the mayhem of Highway 2 for the relative peace of the Bhaktivedanta Swami Marg east to Vrindavan, she felt a serene sense of purpose that seemed to grow deeper with each passing hour.

"I'm here this time by choice," she said, assuredly. "It's where I want to be now, where I need to be."

"I think I understand," said Jaq. "Hey, if you're still in Krishna-land when I arrive, you can show me around the temples. I'd love a private, guided tour!

"It would be my pleasure."

"Let me know how it goes this week. I'll be thinking of you," said Jaq.

"And I you, sister."

Triti paid the tuktuk driver and walked up a neat, brick foot path toward a set of green double-doors at the front of a crumbling, two-story haveli. As she lifted her hand to knock, the left door swung open and a youthful, middle-aged man appeared. "Namaste!" she said. "Is this the Mata Madad Center?"

"Hanji," he said, pulling a striped kerchief from the back pocket of his trousers and sopped up the sweat on his face and neck. "Are you here to visit one of our mothers?"

Behind him, Triti could see several dozen veiled women walking slowly in twos and threes across a courtyard made of concrete slabs.

"All of them, actually. Mrs. Chaturvedi sent me."

"You must be Miss Vanik! Oh, welcome! Please, come, come."

The man closed the thick, wooden door behind them and secured it with a heavy slide bolt. Triti followed him beneath a carved portico splattered with monkey droppings across a red sandstone foyer toward a modest, well-lit office. A petite woman in a rainbow-colored lehenga stood talking with a lively teenage girl who pranced and spun in modern jeans and a bedazzled tee shirt. They both turned to look at Triti as the man ran ahead to introduce her.

"Miss Vanik, this is my wife, Aditya, and our daughter, Mona. Please let me know should you need any help during your stay. I'm heading out to our new facility on the edge of the city. They're pouring the foundation of the main kitchen today, and I must oversee the construction."

Mona kissed her mother on the cheek and disappeared up a winding stairwell.

"She's obsessed, that one," said Aditya. "Her favorite dance show starts now. Thank God the grid came back on this morning. We're so glad you're here. Come, I'll show you."

Triti trailed behind Aditya as she made her way down a narrow corridor. On either side of the hallway were tiny windowless rooms, each with a single wooden door. Most of the doors were open. Triti glanced into the darkened spaces to see dozens of older women sitting on spare cots. All were dressed in faded saris. The decaying walls of their rooms were plastered over with paper posters of Krishna and Durga, as well as Hindu holiday calendars and photos of well-known swamis in prayer. Seeing her, the women began to come out of their rooms. They moved slowly, many burdened by infirmity and age. Two teenage widows scurried from room to room, calling out to their older companions, asking if they needed assistance. One elderly mother, her left eye missing, waited on the stone path outside of her room, a bony finger raised to get Aditya's attention.

"And what may I do for you this fine morning, Devyani?" said Aditya, her voice caramel sweet.

The woman pointed up to the impressive, bronze bell hanging high above the patio doorway, its heavy rope-pull black and smooth from the years. She clasped her hands together beneath her chin and nodded expectantly.

"You'd like to ring the bell today? Haan bilkul. Yes, of course. We have a guest today. Let's show her how we do things here."

Triti followed Aditya through the low, curved entryway that opened onto a spacious, enclosed verandah lined with small terracotta pots of bright green tulsi. The pungent scents of cardamom and anise greeted them, rising on the steam from a large aluminum pot that sat, importantly, in the center of the space. Behind her, Triti heard the great clang of the ashram bell as it sounded out three times, its tones blending in with the hundreds of other ashram tea bells ringing throughout the city. Before the echoes could fade away, the widows formed a long queue at the patio entrance. They pointed to Triti and chattered amongst themselves.

Aditya took Triti's elbow and led her toward the urn. Triti whispered a request in her ear, which made her smile. The women all fell silent as Aditya offered a brief prayer of thanks to Krishna. Triti gazed into the wizened eyes of the mothers who inched their way toward her, their clay mugs clutched in their wrinkled hands.

"Everyone, let's welcome Miss Vanik," announced Aditya, as she handed Triti the serving ladle. "She's arrived just in time for chai."

AUTHOR'S NOTE

The cover blurb for *Inauspicious* ends with the phrase "transcendent brilliance of synchronicity" and so it has been that the synchronous events of the past thirty years of my life made it possible for me to write *Inauspicious*. This novel is an homage to Roop Kanwar, a teenage bride from Rajasthan, India, who died in a sati in 1987. Her brutal death sparked a religious and socio-political uproar throughout the sub-continent regarding the mistreatment of women and girls and was the inspiration for *Inauspicious*. The writing and research for the novel took me to Rajasthan, Vrindavan, Delhi, and northern India in pursuit of stories of women's lives in the shadows of religious and cultural oppression, and the ongoing problem of violence against women.

In 1992, as a Master's student in World Religions, Ethics, and Gender at Harvard, I was researching Hindu temple sculpture for a term paper when I stumbled upon the topic of sati. Deep in the stacks of Andover-Harvard Theological and Widener libraries, I emersed myself in ancient Hindu texts, religious art, and historical literature, committing myself to learn all I could about this horrific, ancient ritual. It became an obsession of a sort, and I knew, even then, that one day I would write about sati.

In 2003, I began considering themes for a novel. The subject of sati kept resurfacing in my mind, so I reviewed my earlier Harvard research and launched a preliminary internet search. When I learned of Roop's sati death in Rajasthan in 1987, I was profoundly shaken. I'll never forget the feeling of dread I experienced reading the online accounts of her sati. It was literally in *that* moment when Triti's incredible story rushed in: ghastly and important. Her voice soon became a constant plea, imploring me to save her life on the page. Whereas countless women in our human history have perished in satis, at witches' stakes, in "kitchen fires" and myriad forms of abuse around the world, Triti would be the rare survivor.

I should have been terrified at the task. To do this right would take all that I knew how to do and far more. But my muse refused to let me sleep. At first, I felt like a simple scribe, taking down Triti's words as fast as my fingers could fly. Over the next few years, I continued writing Triti's tale while studying in earnest all that I could find on sati, Roop's death, Rajasthan, northern India, and the plight of widows in India. It became clear that in order to bring authenticity to Triti's story, I would have to travel to the place where Roop died. I meticulously planned a trip to Rajasthan, not knowing how it would come to pass. In 2004, the tragic death of my baby sister, Michelle, broke my heart. A gifted writer and beloved teacher, she knew of my determination to bring Triti's story to life. I will forever be grateful to Shelly for her infectious smile, her loving heart, and her generous bequest that made possible my trip to India.

In early 2006, I spent a month in India, traveling by car and train across the vast state of Rajasthan. I explored Jaipur,

Pushkar, and Ajmer. I went to Jhunjhunu to visit the famed Rani Sati Temple. The day finally came when, accompanied by an American colleague, I traveled by car from Jaipur to the tiny, rustic village of Deorala. Upon arriving, my driver introduced us to some villagers explaining that we were there to see Roop Kanwar's sati shrine. We were taken on foot 100 meters down the village's main walking path, little more than a rutted, dirt road bordered by a muddy trough of open sewage where scavenger birds and goats gorged. We were led to a wide-open field of rocks and earth. Several emaciated cattle roamed untended, nibbling at random patches of wild grass. By that time, we were accompanied by several of the town elders along with dozens of curious local boys (the little girls were hiding). At the center of the field was a circular cement and iron platform. Weathered kurtas lay upon the sati spot, left by recent religious pilgrims. It was the eeriest moment of my trip, standing before the sthal site, knowing what had happened there only nineteen years earlier. An elderly man asked us in English if we wanted to see where Roop and her husband Maal had lived before their deaths. We agreed and were taken through the pitted back streets to the most elegant of all the older dwellings. The haveli was a wash of pink paint with a bright blue contrasting filigree. We spied several women behind the heavy iron gates who watched us from beneath their colorful veils. He told us that Maal's father was around, but he never did not materialize. We did not go in, but were invited to stand on the front veranda where we talked with another older man. Our driver helped translate as we asked him about the local children, their schooling, and what the town was like before and after September 4, 1987. He explained that no worshipping could be done at Roop's site, and that the government police were very watchful. Although Maal's family and friends insisted that Roop went willingly into the flames, the man took me aside to say that she had to be pushed onto the pyre repeatedly, and that someone in the village saw that and called the police.

As we headed back to our car, we were told that one of the townspeople had just been to the US and spoke English. We were introduced to an affable young man, who invited us into his huge, modern home, which seemed distinctly out of place in the rural village. He and his wife served us delicious chai and *dilkushar*, a sweet dessert cake. The young man spent a great deal of time showing me features of his house, which was far more opulent than any of the other homes in Deorala. According to him, on the day of his death, Roop's husband, Maal Singh, had been playing soccer with him and "many of their boys" when he complained of pain in his chest and stomach. Maal suddenly collapsed, and by the time the doctor came and Maal was finally taken to the appropriate medical facility, he was dead of an apparent heart attack. This came as a terrible shock to his family and friends. He was very young - only 24 years old. Our host went on to say that Maal's body was brought back to the village and presented to Roop in the middle of the night. Although she was only 18 and was married only six months in a matched marriage, our host told us that Roop insisted to everyone that she wanted to sati, even though her in-laws urged her not to. He went on to say that the whole town gathered in the central field for the burning of Maal's body and that Roop voluntarily climbed on the funeral pyre and that she sat cross-legged and held her dead husband's head in her lap. Our host told us that "others" claimed the flames ignited spontaneously, but that it was not so. He said that from his vantage point, it was Maal's brothers who set the flames and within ten minutes all that was left were ashes. I asked him if anyone tried to convince Roop to leave the pyre before the flames began. His response was, "No, no one said anything at all." He added that a villager contacted the police during the sati and "within half an hour the place was filled with cops. Within a few hours, the national press descended, along with worshippers and government officials plus protest groups on both sides of the sati issue, and the town was full to bursting." As we left his home, our host remarked that my colleague and I were the first people from the West to come to Deorala in twenty years.

In Delhi, I had the great good fortune to meet with Meera Khanna of The Guild for Service, a national voluntary developmental organization dedicated towards the empowerment of marginalized women (widows) and children. She helped arrange my visit to Aamar Bari, a home for widows (mothers) in Vrindavan and I am so grateful for her kindness to me. Also, many thanks to Gita, the wonderful caretaker at Aamar Bari, who made my three days in Vrindavan with the mothers so memorable. My gratitude to some of the mothers who spent time with me during my stay in Vrindavan. They include: Anjali, Amita, Anguri, Bishaka, Lalita, Kamla, Premdasi, Kalyani, Menka, Lokhi, Gopika, Kaushalya, and Maya.

I offer my endless thanks to the people of India who welcomed me and took such good care of me during my journeys there. Every day I was humbled by the kindliness of the train conductors, the cheerfulness of the hotel front desk personnel, and the friendliness of the street merchants and chai-wallahs. To the widows who sat with me to share their life stories; the traveling musicians who serenaded me; the wonderful management of MVT in Vrindavan; the excellent drivers and coordinators, Mr. Arya and Mr. Gulati, who got me safely to and from my many stops across India; the charming owners of Bajaj Homestay, the helpful staff of the Jamuna Resort, and my gracious hosts at Jas Vilas Resort, Wongden House, and Chonor House in McLeod Ganj; to the new friends I met along the way including Neelakshi Jamwal, Roberta Wall, Rebecca Phyland and her adorable twins, Zali and Anise, Dalpat Singh, Tseyang of Volunteer Tibet, Aditya Sircar – Jagat Palace, Glenn Fawcett – Lotus Outreach.org, and the hundreds of citizen-ambassadors who showed me compassion at every turn. I miss India dearly, and I hope to return soon.

My list of personal US thank-yous must begin with appreciation for my father, Richard B. Henderson. I discovered my passion for words and stories very early in my childhood because of him. Books became like food for me. They were my safe havens then, and still are. I asked my father to be my "first reader" for *Inauspicious*, which was a brave act on my part given his poet/English teacher facility with language and his infamous predilection for wielding his red pen. I knew that I had to "bring it" to gain his praise. To my surprise (and relief), his patience and good counsel made it possible for me to find my writerly "legs". *Inauspicious* is a better novel because of him. Thank you, Dad.

I owe a great debt of thanks to my literary agent, Joy Tutela. She won me over with her email love-note revealing that she sat under a tree in Central Park and read my entire manuscript in one sitting. Joy truly met my vision for the book. For several years, Joy worked with me to hone the arc of the story and bring to life *Inauspicious'* lengthy cast of characters. Thank you, Joy, for your guidance and care.

My family's support throughout the writing and research phases for *Inauspicious* was key to the completion of the project. They gave me the time and space to write and edit and literally kept the home-fires burning while I traveled to India. Like so many women authors, I have had to juggle writing, researching and editing, with working (teaching college philosophy and composition courses) and being a mother. I will always be thankful for my family's assistance in *Inauspicious'* birth.

Susan Szabo, *Inauspicious'* amazing cover artist and my dear friend of 24 years, perfectly captured the essence of the novel in her stunning painting. I can never repay her for her incredible gifts of talent, time, and heart. I'm so grateful that she was an essential partner in bringing *Inauspicious'* vision to life. Thank you, Susie. And special thanks to her wonderful fella, Steve Szabo, who lent his tech wizardry to the project. Much aloha to you both and to your ohana.

I've been lucky in my life to have had long and precious friendships. One special man in my closest circle, Douglas Hatschek, has given me much in the thirty-five years I've known him. Douglas has been a touchstone, a confidant, and a tireless cheerleader. His wit and intellect bring me humor and relief, while his generosity of spirit and radical goodness remind me of what is most important: Love. Douglas, you will always have my heart and my gratitude. Thank you.

I am very thankful to author Mira Kamdar for reading *Inauspicious* early on for me. Mira gave me excellent critical feedback on my manuscript which definitely helped me improve the novel. I am so grateful for her support and her lovely blurb for *Inauspicious*.

Finally, to my new readers, and all of my friends, colleagues, students, gym buddies, and neighbors who have cheered me on all these years, thank you. You mean the world to me. The wait is over. I hope you like *Inauspicious*.

BIBLIOGRAPHY

Adiga, Aravind. *The White Tiger*. New York, Free Press, 2008.

Blaise, Clark and Bharati Mukherjee. *Days and Nights in Calcutta*. Minnesota: Hungry Mind Press, 1995.

Chandler, Clay and Adil Zainulbhai. *Reimagining INDIA: Unlocking the Potential of Asia's Next Superpower*. New York, Simon and Schuster, 2013.

Danielou, Alain. *The Hindu Temple: Deification of Eroticism*. Vermont, Inner Traditions, 1994.

Desai, Kiran. *The Inheritance of Loss*. New York, Atlantic Monthly Press, 2006.

Fouchet, Max-Pol. *The Erotic Sculpture of India*. New York, Criterion Books, 1957.

Giri, V. Mohini. Editor. *Living Death: Trauma of Widowhood in India*. New Delhi, Gyan Publishing House, 2002.

Grewal, Royina. *In Rajasthan*. Lonely Planet Publications, 1997.

Harlan, Lindsey. *Religion and Rajput Women: The Ethic of Protection in Contemporary Narratives*. Berkeley, University of California Press, 1992.

Hawley, John Stratton. *Krishna's Playground: Vrindavan in the 21st Century*. New Delhi, India, Oxford Press, 2020.

Hawley, John Stratton. *Sati - The Blessing and the Curse: The Burning of Wives in India*. New York, Oxford, 1994.

Hossain, Rokeya Sakhawat. *Sultana's Dream: A Feminist Utopia and Selections from The Secluded Ones*. New York, The Feminist Press of The City University of New York, 1988.

Jain, M.S. *Concise History of Modern Rajasthan*. New Delhi, Wishwa Prakashan, 1993.

Jogendra, Saksena. *Art of Rajasthan*. Delhi, Sundeep Prakashan, 1979.

Kamdar, Mira. *Motiba's Tattoos: A granddaughter's journey into her Indian family's past*. New York, Public Affairs, 2000.

Kamdar, Mira. *Planet India*. New York, Scribner, 2007.

Leeson, Francis. *Kama Shilpa*. Bombay, Taraporevala Sons & Co. Private Limited, 1962.

Markandaya, Kamala. *Nectar in a Sieve*. New York, John Day Company, 1954.

Meredith, Robyn. *The Elephant and The Dragon: The Rise of India and China and what it means for all of us*. New York, Norton, 2007.

Minturn, Leigh. *Sita's Daughters: Coming Out of Purdah*. New York, Oxford University Press, 1993.

Moore, Erin P. *Gender, Law, and Resistance in India*. Tucson, The University of Arizona Press, 1998.

Naidu, Sarojini. *The Broken Wing: Songs of Love, Death, and Destiny*. John Lane Company, J.J. Little & Ives Company, 1917. Public Domain – The United States of America.

Narasimhan, Sakuntala. *Sati: Widow Burning in India*. New York, Anchor Books/Doubleday, 1990.

Roberts, Gregory David. *Shantaram*. New York, St. Martin's Press, 2003.

Rushdie, Salman. *Midnight's Children*. New York, Random House, 1981.

Sen, Mala. *Death by Fire: Sati, Dowry Death and Female Infanticide in Modern India*. London, Phoenix, 2002.

Sidhwha, Bapsi. *Water*. Milkweed Editions, 2006.

Tharu, Susie and K. Lalita, Eds. *Women Writing in India - 600 B.C. to the Present. Volume ll: The Twentieth Century*. New York, The Feminist Press, 1993.

Toomey, Christine. *The Saffron Road*. London, Portobello Books, 2015.

Van Lynden, Pauline. *Rajasthan*. New York, Assouline Publishing, 2003.

Webster's New Universal Unabridged Dictionary. Barnes and Noble Publishing, Inc. 1996.

FILMS

A Suitable Boy. Mira Nair. BBC Studios, 2020. DVD.

Born Into Brothels. Zana Briski and Ross Kauffman. THINKFilm HBO, 2004. DVD.

Children of the Desired Sex. Mira Nair. T.V. Movie-documentary, 1987.

Dor. Nadesh Kukunoor. Sahara One Motion Pictures Percept Picture Company, 2006, DVD.

Earth. Deepa Mehta. Cracking the Earth Films, Inc. 1998. DVD.

Fire. Deepa Mehta. Trial By Fire Films, Inc., 1996. DVD.

Kama Sutra: A Tale of Love. Mira Nair. Trimark Pictures, 1996. DVD.

Khoon Bhari Maang. Rakesh Roshan. Filmkraft Productions, 1988. Streaming.

Lagaan, Once Upon a Time in India. Ashutosh Gowariker. Sony Pictures, 2001, DVD.

Matrubhoomi: A Nation Without Women. Manish Jha. 2003.

Mississippi Masala. Mira Nair. Cinecom Productions, 1991. DVD.

Salaam Bombay. Mira Nair. Cinecom Pictures, 1988. DVD.

Slumdog Millionaire. Danny Boyle. Fox Searchlight Pictures, 2008, DVD.

The Bandit Queen. Shekhar Kapur. Koch Vision, 1994, DVD.

The Forgotten Woman. Dilip Mehta. Mongrel Media, 2007. DVD.

The Namesake. Mira Nair. Fox Searchlight, 2006. DVD.

Water. Deepa Mehta. Mongrel Media, 2005. DVD.

Widow of Silence. Praveen Morchhale. Oration Films, 2020, Streaming IMDb.

A NOTE

This is not an exhaustive list of the authors and works I consulted for *Inauspicious*. My sincere apologies if I have omitted any source materials. Omissions will be cured in all future editions.